The Cutest Little Demon in Town

William Leigh

Published by Bruce W. Leigh, 2024.

This is a work of fiction. Similarities to real people, places, or events are entirely coincidental.

THE CUTEST LITTLE DEMON IN TOWN

First edition. April 9, 2024.

ISBN: 979-8224639755

Written by William Leigh.

One

The unlucky dead guy, Caucasian, mid-thirties, had turned up in a Chinatown alleyway with his head ninety-five percent severed from his body. Right away, this was an annoying incongruity. If you're insane enough to go to all the trouble of cutting off someone's head, why not finish the job? Instead, it had been left hanging by a thin layer of mottled tissue, tilted back at an obscene angle, as if the victim were about to perform some complicated acrobatic maneuver. The poor bastard's face hadn't fared much better; both eyes gouged out, most of the nose missing and several deep lacerations running from forehead to chin. As bad as all this was, the man's upper torso, split open and pried apart from sternum to navel, took the carnage to a whole new and difficult to process level. Whoever this killer was, no one was ever going to accuse him of lacking a sense of the dramatic.

Stone rubbed his desperately-in-need-of-a-shave face, looked up from the crime scene photos splayed across his desk and saw Lisa. She was attempting to navigate her way through a group of cops doing a very believable impersonation of a pack of sexually agitated hyenas; so much for the gender sensitivity classes everyone in the Department had been required to take. Not that Lisa appeared to be in any distress. She obviously knew how to work a crowd of admirers, even a crowd of dangerous carnivores impersonating police officers.

Newest addition to the Department, Detective Lisa Malone, former small town beauty queen from somewhere inside the Bible Belt turned big city cop. Plenty of speculation, but nobody knew for sure the details of that improbable transformation. Stone figured it was none of anyone's business; every cop in the place had some kind of weird narrative trailing behind them, some private and peculiar event that had somehow shifted their trajectories into the dark, chaotic world of the homicide detective. As far as he was concerned, the past was more or less irrelevant. There was only the present, the next crime to solve, the next twisted perp to put behind bars until he was too old to pee standing up. No doubt that Malone had her lurking demons to contend with, or more likely try to escape from, but then who didn't? Demons, in one form or another, pretty much came with the territory. Maybe someday she'd feel the need to tell him the whole story, and he would do his best to pretend that it actually mattered. In the meantime, she was smart and eager to learn, not to mention out of this world gorgeous. She had the kind of looks that could bring most men to their knees, no questions asked. Factoring in the 9mm Beretta holstered on her adorable left hip gave her the potential to single-handedly cut the city crime rate in half. He imagined dangerous felons lining up in an orderly fashion, waiting patiently for their turn to be busted by the hottest detective in the N.Y.P.D.

They had been partners for a little over a month. He'd been a little nervous about it at first, spending so much time with this beautiful, young woman, coping with the need to keep the line between professional and personal clear and uncomplicated. But he had handled it as a dedicated cop with his priorities intact. A good cop knew where to draw the line, and Stone was, if nothing else, a good cop. Still, the sudden surge of overwhelming temptation could, under the right circumstances, get the better of anyone. Situations occasionally arose within which principles and sound judgment just didn't stand a chance. Stone understood this all too well. His resolve had faded and resistance surrendered two days previous, after an ugly, late-night excavation of a triple homicide in an upper west side tenement – two young women and a guy, all shot in the face with something large caliber, most likely drug related. After several hours rummaging through bits of skull and brain tissue, he and Lisa had ended up back at his apartment, exhausted but agitated, like a couple of all-night speed freaks on the verge of the inevitable crash. Half a bottle of vodka later, they were in the shower together.

Maybe it was just the easiest way of dealing with the emotional overload of violent death on a daily basis. Homicide cops tended to exist inside their own private trauma wards. The pressure constantly built up and it sometimes took an act of reckless stupidity to relieve it. He knew it should never have happened. He was pretty sure that a voice somewhere inside his head had told him as much, something about it being a disaster in the making, at the very least a very bad career move. First rule of the job, don't fool around with your partner, even if she is a beautiful, sexy woman; especially if she's a beautiful, sexy women. Don't even allow yourself the luxury of fantasizing about it. The best advice, unfortunately, is often the hardest to take, particularly when it involved a great-looking, naked redhead in a shower

"Do you have a license to carry this thing?" Lisa had laughed, her soapy fingers working his penis with the agility of a blind masseuse. "It's so formidable, like some extremely well-fed serpent."

The snake imagery had gone straight to the still active remnants of his reptilian brain. He pulled her towards him, her ruby-tinged nipples grazing his chest. Loved the feeling of a woman's nipples rubbing against him. In the murky scheme of modern existence, they were the moral equivalent of a Sunday sermon, reason enough not to totally discount the possibility of God. He kissed and nibbled her neck, pushed his fingers through her thick hair, licked her forehead, her eyebrows, her nose and finally her delectable lips. Lisa moaned, tightening her grip on his erection. He moved his hand down her back, slipping between the halves of her small, taut backside, until the tips of his fingers were touching the soft creases of her sex.

"I really want to perform fellatio now," she had whispered.

On the formal side, he had thought at the time, more clinical than sexy, but he was also a firm believer in action taking precedence over mere words. People were always going to talk, say things they didn't really mean. It was an unfortunate but inevitable consequence of an overly evolved brain. The real heroes were the people who knew when to just shut up and get down to business. With a renewed appreciation for all of life's little mysteries, he watched as the top of his partner's head vanished into the shower mist. And then the rational mind had succumbed, pleasure ascended and the reptiles once again ruled the planet.

Lisa entered Stone's office and shut the door behind her. In her snug tee shirt and form-fitting jeans, the sparkle in her green eyes and her shoulder-length red hair looking both wild, yet somehow under control, she was the perfect antidote to all of life's annoying abstractions; so physically present, so palpable and precise in her movements, that it actually hurt a little bit watching her.

"Impressive how you handled that hormonally charged male gauntlet," he told her.

"Not my first male gauntlet," she smiled. "So how long have you been staring at those photos?"

"Just hoping to catch an insight."

"And have you?"

"Only that torn-apart bodies are not very attractive."

Lisa moved around the desk and stood next to Stone, ostensibly to get a better look at the evidence, but really because she wanted to nudge her body up against his. "Not exactly like looking at pictures from your last fun-filled vacation, is it?"

"Unless you happen to be a seriously deranged psychopath. Notice anything odd?"

"I'm struggling to find anything that isn't."

"Try getting past your emotions," Stone suggested, resting his hand on Lisa's arm. "See it with the eyes of a Detective."

Was he kidding, she wondered? His expression suggested that he wasn't. Okay, the emotionless eyes of a Detective. She could handle that, right? "Well, I guess I'm wondering why all the damage was inflicted above the victim's waist."

"Exactly!" Stone said. "And why are the guys pants pulled down around his ankles?"

"The attack was sexually motivated?"

"Pretty rough sex, wouldn't you say?"

"Some like it rough," Lisa said, the hint of a smile on her lips.

Stone took note of the smile, briefly speculated on its possible implications "And then there's the... uh ..."

"Penis?" Lisa asked, thinking how cute it was that Stone was shy about using the word, particularly after her recent run in with his.

"You see it, too?

How could she not? Show a girl photos of a naked guy and what else is she supposed to focus on? Okay, it was a dead, very messed up naked guy, but still ... "Yes, I do," she confirmed.

"It looks swollen and slightly bruised, right?"

"Clearly."

"The question is why?"

"I suppose we should ask Doctor Hammer about it," Lisa suggested.

"That will be interesting," Stone laughed. "Getting Hammer's opinion on a swollen penis."

Lisa didn't know if it was the dead guy's dick - although she really hoped it wasn't - or the proximity of her body to Stone's, or the still vivid recollection of their shower together, but she was suddenly caring a lot less about crime detection, more about having sex with her close-to-irresistible partner. Not that it mattered. Whatever the source of the urge, she was determined to resist it. She was, after all, a Police Detective, not some sex-crazed slut with nothing to lose; unless, of course, she was a hopeless, sex-crazed slut who also happened to be a Police Detective. Her sense was that the distinction was probably important, although Stone apparently didn't see it that way. He moved his hand to the small of Lisa's back, applying light pressure. From there it slid down to her left buttock. It wasn't as if he had much choice. She had one of those tightly-packaged, boyish backsides, the kind you noticed on young Asian women vacationing in the city wearing next to nothing, but still able to project the shy, innocent persona. As ass, in other words, that virtually cried out to be caressed.

"What exactly are you doing, Detective?" she asked him.

"I'm not exactly sure."

"This could easily be construed as sexual harassment in the work place."

"I apologize," he told her, unable to prevent the movement of his hand downward towards the crotch of Lisa's jeans, which felt hot enough to spontaneously combust. "Is this any better?"

Lisa shivered, biting her lower lip to ward off what would have otherwise been an inappropriate yelp.

"You are aware that we're in your office, right?" she asked.

"I am."

"And you know that we're supposed to be investigating a murder."

"I do."

"Then you no doubt recall our agreement."

"Our agreement?"

"No fooling around on the job."

"Did I actually agree to that?"

"Would it stir your memory if I drew my weapon and placed the muzzle against your groin?"

"Safety off?"

"Count on it."

"It would probably only get me more worked up."

"Stone, please. I'm about two seconds away from a noisy orgasm."

Is this woman incredible or what? "Would that be such a bad thing?"

"Let's take a moment and consider."

"Okay, I see your point."

"Not to mention that we have work to do," Lisa added.

"You're right," he said, removing the hand from between his partner's legs and standing up. "We need to stay focused on gruesome, unnatural death. Forensics?"

"Actually," Lisa told him, moving towards the door. "I should probably go alone."

"May I ask why?"

"Do you really want to confront the M.E. with that?" Lisa asked, nodding at the glaring physiological event underway inside his trousers. "Besides, the Captain wants to see you, I'm guessing without the hard on."

"Fine," Stone said. "You go to forensics. I'll get this under control then go see the Captain. Just don't forget to ask Hammer about the, you know, penis thing."

Lisa left Stone's office, wondering if it was obvious to everyone that she was in a state of total sexual arousal. Okay, maybe not total. Total sexual arousal probably equaled death, or at the very least some sort of permanent brain damage; potentially worth the risks, but not now, not with a job to do and an insane killer on the loose. Don't forget about the penis. As if she even could. She loved the whole getting-the-guy-turned-on thing, toying with her prey, dangling the tantalizing bait just out of reach of the hungry, male penis fish. Seduction, unlike homicide detection, was something in which she already had a certain expertise.

So, in other words, you are a sex-crazed slut.

Sorry, not even close.

How about one-dimensional whore? Does that work any better for you?

How about just shutting up!

The other night had been like a dream, the kind in which you get to do all sorts of 'stuff' with total impunity and you don't wake up screaming, or feeling guilty to the point of wanting to die. One minute she and Stone had been going over the details of three teenagers with most of their faces missing, the next they were out of their clothes, washing each other's bodies. Strange perhaps, possibly even self-destructive, but then wasn't it the seemingly dangerous contradictions in life that made things fun and interesting? Besides, avoiding the occasional bout of naughtiness was just not in her nature. If growing up with a mother and father who spent every waking minute espousing the imperative of correct moral behavior at all times had taught her anything, it was never to miss an opportunity to be bad. Not that she was defying God or anything, only that her version of Him (or possibly Her) was far more tolerant and open-minded than her parent's. As far as she was concerned, Stone, with his luscious kisses and skillful fingers, was practically doing God's work. She was also pretty sure he had appreciated her spiritual take on the situation. After doing his 'Oh Sweet Jesus!' thing in her mouth, he had apologized, explaining that holding back was just not a realistic option. No need to be sorry for that, Detective. She knew that some women did it only out of a sense of obligation, others who wouldn't do it even with a gun pressed to their heads. Needless to say, she belonged to neither of these subsets, although she was not averse to role playing games in the bedroom that might involve the use of firearms.

But getting back to the point, she, Lisa Malone, also had her job to think about. She was one of only four female Detectives in the Department. She had worked very hard to get where she was and wasn't about to blow it, no pun intended; hence the absolute necessity of not only having an agreement, but sticking to it. Of course she liked Stone putting his hands on her in his office, wouldn't have minded dissolving into his arms, forgetting everything else and having crazy sex right there on his desk. But there was a time and a place, right? "Right!" she said out loud, although somewhat less enthusiastically than she might have hoped for.

The elevator opened on the basement floor, last stop forensics, a collection of labs, autopsy room and, of course, the morgue, all of it permeated with the same chilled, medicinal-smelling air of death. Doctor Beverly Hammer, who ran the department, was standing over the remains of last-night's victim, her green smock smeared in blood and other stuff Lisa really didn't care to know about. Hammer, an attractive blonde in her early forties, with a hard edge, a natural flair for sarcasm and a reputation as a brilliant, if highly eccentric, Medical Examiner was the closest thing Lisa had to a friend in the Department. Her first homicide case had been a young prostitute badly carved up by some impotent asshole with a hunting knife; her first trip to forensics, seeing the girl stretched naked on the table, had not been easy. Hammer, sensing her distress, had helped her through it. It wasn't exactly big sister tenderness in play, but Hammer was someone Lisa felt she could trust, or possibly even confide in, if the need ever arose.

"Ah, Detective Malone," Hammer said. "Right on time. I've just finished up with this one and, sorry to say, I don't think he's going to make it."

"That's too bad," Lisa said, positioning herself so that the Doctor was blocking her view of the mess on the stainless steel table. The photos of the crime had been more than enough. She wasn't sure if her emotionally neutral Detective's eyes could handle the real thing. "I was hoping to question him about last night's attack."

Hammer smiled. "I'm afraid anything he told you about it would fall into the category of the hard to believe."

"How so?" Lisa asked.

"The major wounds, severing of the head, bifurcation of the torso, appear to have been made by some sort of claws."

"As in animal claws?"

"Possibly."

"What kind of animal?"

"Not sure. A very powerful, pissed off animal would be my best guess. But then the particulars of the attack lessen the credibility of this scenario."

"Meaning?"

"The killer knew what he was doing, where to cut and tear, finding the lines of least resistance. Not especially neat, but fairly precise. Further complicating things, some of the internal organs were removed."

"That sounds like something an enraged animal might do."

"Except that the removal was accomplished with a certain finesse, almost surgical in nature. Paradoxically, no traces of these organs were found at the scene, forcing us to conclude that they were either carried off, or consumed."

"Yuck!"

"Yes, but then even a monster has to eat."

"Uh, what about the lower body?"

"Not a whole lot going on down there."

"In particular, the, uh, genital area?"

"Average, I would say. No pencil dick, by any means, but nothing to get all hot and bothered over either."

"Doctor Hammer?"

"Sorry. I'm actually glad you asked about it. There were traces of semen and some other substance, possibly saliva, on the penis. The semen is definitely his, the saliva, if it is saliva, is more problematic. I'll have to run a few more tests on it before I can say anything definitive. There is also some bruising, quite likely caused by teeth."

"So from this you would surmise ..?"

"The victim had oral sex performed on him prior to the attack."

"How prior?"

"Very prior. I'm almost inclined to say during."

"Is that even possible?"

"Men have been known to ejaculate while in the process of being hanged. When it comes to the male member, anything is possible."

Lisa briefly contemplated the possibilities of the male member. Surely, there had to be things it could not do. Operate a motor vehicle, for example, or learn a foreign language. Or was there actually some scientific basis for its reputation as the organ of miracles?

"Detective?" Hammer asked. "Are you still with me?"

"Absolutely," Lisa said. And I'd like a copy of your report?"

"I'll send it up as soon as I've finished. Oh, by the way, we got a hit off the fingerprints in the National Data Base. Your mutilated friend here is, was, Clifford Goth, a mid-level functionary with the I.R.S. Could be a possible motive."

"Kill the tax man?"

"Who hasn't fantasized about it?"

"Why not just shoot him?"

"Too mundane. This is a political statement that resonates."

"I'll certainly mention the possibility to Stone."

"Speaking of which, how are things going with you and your new partner?"

"Things are going fine, I guess."

"Just fine?" Hammer asked, moving closer to Lisa, her large, blue eyes probing, looking for the easiest route into Lisa's head. "Are you sure?"

"I, uh, don't know what you mean."

"A beautiful woman like you, a steamy, conflicted hunk like Stone, it's hard to imagine there isn't a little spark happening there."

"Sorry," Lisa told her. "No spark. I prefer to keep my professional relationships strictly professional."

"You're especially lovely when you lie," Hammer said, lightly stroking Lisa's cheek. "Just a word of caution. All the gore and guts can, over time, become a catalyst, a kind of perverse sexual turn on. Not your fault, but it happens. Don't try to fight it, but try not to lose yourself entirely in it either. In any case, it will be the best sex you've ever had. Until it isn't. So enjoy it while you can. Plenty of time to hate yourself for it later on."

Lisa expelled a nervous laugh. "I don't really see that happening, but thanks for the advice, Doctor."

"That's what I'm here for," Hammer winked. "Well, that's not exactly what I'm here for, but I'm always here for you, Lisa.

Captain Frank Burke was a large, impatient man, who ran Homicide South like a despot with a chronic stomach ulcer. He liked to huff and puff, rant and rave, scowl and grimace. He especially liked results, really didn't like not getting them. But he was also a wise, veteran cop who preferred giving his Detectives the leeway they needed to get the job done. Up to a point, anyway. Screw up too often and Burke would have your head, or other parts of your anatomy, depending on how foul a mood he was in.

First thing Stone noticed was the Captain's .38 service revolver lying on his desk.

"You wanted to see me, Captain?" Stone asked.

"A half hour ago I wanted to see you, Detective."

"Is that why your gun is out?"

"You think I'm going to shoot you for being late? This is for the next one of you pussies who comes in here and tells me he's got no leads. Now, what's happening with this Chinatown de-cap job?"

"Well, we've got no witnesses, no physical evidence at the scene and, as yet, no identification on the victim."

"So what are you telling me?"

"Uh, we've got no leads."

"Are you deliberately trying to antagonize me, Stone?"

"Not at all, Sir."

"What about forensics?"

"As we speak."

"This is exactly the kind of fucked-up, psycho-homicide bullshit that I hate. You have to kill somebody, do it in a fucking reasonable way. Is that asking too much?"

"I don't think so, Captain."

"You let me know as soon as you've got something on this. Understood?"

"Loud and clear."

"Now on to other matters," Burke said, going to the small refrigerator in his office and taking out a diet coke. "This god damn heat doesn't help much either. You want something?"

"No thank you, Sir."

Sufficient fluid intake is critical, Stone. Particularly in this kind of weather."

"I'm fine, Captain."

"Well you don't look fine," the Captain said, taking several loud gulps of soda. "More to the point, you look like crap. Do you even own a razor, Stone?"

"I, uh ..."

The Captain waved one of his arms through the humid air, indicating that an answer was neither required nor desired. "So tell me, how's Malone doing? I don't particularly like the virgins having to deal with the really bad stuff so soon, you know?"

"I seriously doubt Malone is a virgin, Captain."

"Spare me your attempts at witty double entendre, Stone. I'm not talking about her sexual bio, as you damn well know."

"Sorry, Captain," Stone said, wondering if his partner's sexual bio actually existed and, more importantly, could he get a copy of it? "Malone is smart and a lot tougher than she appears. So far, I'm completely satisfied with her performance."

"Really? You've never said that before about any of your new partners. As I recall, you wanted to shoot the previous two and, to quote you, 'ditch their useless bodies in the river.'"

"What can I say, Sir? Third time's a charm."

"Malone is a very attractive, young woman."

"Is she? I hadn't really noticed."

"You know how upset I'll be if I find out there's anything going on between you two."

"Trust me, Captain, furthest thing from my mind."

"Cause it will be your sorry ass getting thrown in the river."

"Understood."

"Meanwhile, you keep an eye on her. In this city, in this weather, there's no telling what abomination is coming our way."

"Yes sir, I will. Is that all?"

"No, that is not all, Detective. I'll let you know when that is all. Now sit down. We've got a police Lieutenant flying in tomorrow from the Tokyo Metropolitan Police Department, something about a case they're working on that may involve us here. I don't have the details, but the Chief and the Mayor want us to extend all the usual courtesies."

"What are the usual courtesies in this situation, Captain?"

"I have no idea, but you'll figure it out and let me know."

"I'll figure it out?"

"I'm assigning you and Malone as official liaisons for this guy. You'll meet him at the airport, show him around, take him wherever he wants to go, basically, be helpful. His name is Ishikawa, supposedly speaks English and arrives at 7:30 tomorrow morning. Any questions?"

"Captain, considering the case Malone and I have just started working on ..."

"I have considered it. Look, the guy will be here two days, three tops. You don't have to be his babysitter, just keep tabs on him. I don't want him getting swallowed up by this city and then having to explain to the Chief how we lost him. If something urgent comes up on your case, Malone can take care of Lieutenant Ishikawa."

"But Captain ..."

"Non-negotiable, Detective. Keep me informed."

Two

"Let's go over it again," Stone said. "We've got a dead I.R.S. agent killed under circumstances that apparently make no sense."

He and Lisa were sitting in her apartment, sipping vodka with ice. It was late, but no less hot. Fortunately, Lisa's air conditioner was humming away and, unlike the one in Stone's place, actually cooling the room.

"Could be an animal," Lisa said. "A big cat, or maybe a bear."

"Yeah, and we know how many of those are walking around loose in the city," Stone laughed.

Lisa Frowned. "It was only a suggestion."

"Besides, how do we mix wild animal attack with sexual activity immediately prior to death?"

"Okay," Lisa said, getting up to refill the glasses. "How about this? It's an insane woman with a trained tiger, possibly a disgruntled circus employee looking to get even."

"Get even for ..?"

"I don't know. Maybe she's dedicated her entire life to the circus, patiently waiting for her big break, but meanwhile the ravages of time have taken their toll. She's finally in line for the high profile trapeze job, but gets passed over by the beautiful, young bimbo who can not only pull off the triple flip, but is willing to perform it topless."

"So she goes on a killing rampage with her trained tiger."

"Why not?"

"Hey, anything's possible," Stone smiled.

"Okay, so you don't like the circus idea," Lisa said, handing Stone his drink and sitting down.

"Actually, I do like it," he told her. "I'm just thinking that a simpler solution might make more sense."

"For example?"

"Okay, let's say it's two people, a man and a woman, possibly they're married. He's the sexually repressed sadist who only gets off by inflicting pain. He very likely has some sort of medical training. She, on the other hand, is the sexually insatiable masochist, who sees every man, i.e. victim, as the father she wants to both make love to and brutally murder. She seduces the victim, brings him to climax, then Doctor Death swoops in to inflict the required punishment."

"You're right," Lisa smirked. "That's much simpler."

"Okay, your turn," Stone said, finishing his drink.

"All right, you want simple? It's a sexually ambivalent guy with a full-blown psychosis wearing some kind of fake claws."

"He'd have to be unnaturally strong."

"What's stronger than a sexually ambivalent, enraged psychotic?"

"Are you suggesting the Captain might be involved?"

Lisa sat on the opposite end of the couch, sipping her drink, watching Stone. His black hair was getting long and he needed a shave. If she didn't know anything about him, her first guess would have been tough guy, probably something criminal, but smart; a smart, tough, bad guy. She though about his chest minus the black tee shirt he was wearing, solid, muscular, covered in just the right amount of curly, black hair. Was he thinking about her, or only about the case? Since their brief interaction in his office this morning, he hadn't touched her, not even a friendly kiss. Maybe he was worried about coming on too strong, or even worse, he was having second thoughts. Or was he simply less sensitive than she had originally thought? How could he not be aware of just how hot she was feeling at this moment? She thought about what Doctor Hammer had said, that the blood and the violence could become a sexual turn on. Was that a factor in her attraction to Stone? And, if so, why wasn't he feeling it, too?

"No, it definitely can't be an animal," Stone sighed, closing his eyes.

No, Lisa thought, you're the animal. In fact, we're both animals.

"Has to be a big, scary lunatic with some kind of tool. Maybe a claw hammer."

It's your tool I'm thinking about, Lisa said to herself. Hammer me with it, why don't you?

"What?" Stone muttered.

He heard that? At least his hearing isn't impaired.

She decided to try mental telepathy, something she'd fooled around with in college. Her psychology professor had told her that her psychic ability was well above average. Focus the mind, project a mental image at another person and, in theory, get the intended reaction. She conjured up the image of Stone lying naked on her bed, beckoning her seductively with his strong hands. Take off your clothes and come here to me now, he was saying.

Stone snorted, or possibly snored. Oh well, parapsychology never claimed to be an exact science.

He suddenly opened his eyes and looked directly at Lisa, soft and dreamy eyes, the trace of a question mark on his lips.

On the other hand ...

"I'm sick of thinking about this case," he told her.

"We could think about something else," Lisa said.

"Maybe we should take a break from thinking."

"Or that."

Lisa didn't exactly float out of her seat, but it felt that way. She moved from one end of the couch to the other, making a perfect landing on Stone's lap. She was facing him, her knees on either side of his thighs, her lips as close to his as they could be without actually touching.

"This is probably not the best idea," Stone said, placing a hand on her back and pulling her towards him.

"I was thinking the exact same thing," Lisa told him.

As they kissed, Stone slipped his hands under her tee shirt and unhooked her bra. He pulled the shirt and bra off in one smooth motion. Not wanting to be outdone in this race that would end, hopefully, with both of them finishing together, Lisa returned the favor. Once Stone's shirt was off and her breasts were rubbing against his chest, things got warm, wet and fuzzy. After several hungry kisses that seemed to stop time altogether, Lisa stood up and pulled off her jeans and panties. She undid Stone's belt and slid his jeans off. He wasn't wearing underwear. His cock was already fully erect. Was it always hard, she wondered? She had never actually seen it when it wasn't. Maybe he had a condition, perpetual erectile something-or-other. She could only hope.

"Is this thing always ready to batter down doors?" she asked, stroking the object in question with her fingers.

"Yeah," he said. "For you."

Have to love a guy who can come up with the right answers under pressure, even if he's most likely lying.

"The question, I suppose, is what to do with it?" Lisa said, straddling Stone again, rubbing the head of his cock against her pussy.

"It's your call, Detective," Stone said, gently agitating her nipples with his fingers. "I'm entirely in your hands."

"I do like you in my hands," she told him. "But perhaps there's a better place for you to be right now.

Lisa shifted her body forward and guided Stone into her. She moved slowly, raising and lowering herself on him, allowing the ripples of pleasure to meander up her spine, radiating outwards to several million hungry nerve endings. This was just how she liked it, the languid, dreamy fuck that subtly builds like an invisible tidal wave, eventually hitting without warning. Low-lying coastal areas beware. She opened her eyes and looked at the man she was having sex with. She hardly knew him, this strong, soft-spoken cop with the near-perfect penis. Too soon to assign perfect status. What she did know was that, as a homicide cop, he almost certainly had issues; some weird shit that would sooner or later come roaring up at her. But then she had no long term expectations. The occasional fuck, no strings, was pretty much her only objective. She could handle the non-committal approach; question was, could he? Stone opened his mouth and growled softly. Lisa put her hands on either side of his face and moved her lips to his for a deep, slow motion kiss.

After fucking for what felt like hours, but was probably more like fifteen minutes, they both fell asleep on the couch. One unbelievable orgasm – well, two, actually, his and hers, as in sync as orgasms are likely to get – was all they apparently needed to depart the world of the conscious, cognizant biped. Not the most comfortable sleeping arrangement, but they were both too exhausted to move. Lisa started dreaming almost immediately about sex, with Stone no less. He was lying flat on his back, his hands secured to something above his head. She was on top of him, vigorously moving her body up and down on his cock, which felt even bigger than his awake cock. The fact that they were having unprotected sex didn't particularly worry her because, after all, it was a dream. Can't fault a sleeping girl for not insisting on a condom, can you? Sensing orgasms on the horizon, she opened her eyes and looked at Stone. She wanted to see his expression when all the fireworks started.

Odd thing was, Stone did not look happy, not even close. More like terrified, the way a guy might look just before you shoot him in the head, or accuse him of cheating on you with your best friend. A caring, sensitive girl might have taken a moment at this point to inquire about it, but Lisa, the dream Lisa, started laughing, a creepy, guttural laugh, like some twisted sex offender with a sore throat. She felt her arms move, saw her hands sliding up his belly to his chest, only they definitely did not look like her hands. It wasn't so much the longer fingers, as the sharp, black claws on the ends of them. She wanted to stop, but couldn't. Her new hands, complete with Velociraptor fingernails, apparently had a mind of their own. Stone made faint, groaning sounds as her claws began slicing into his flesh. The amount of blood was a big surprise, but not quite as surprising as feeling Stone begin to ejaculate powerfully inside her. Call it an odd time to come, just as your new girlfriend is flaying the flesh from your body. Her own orgasm erupted from some unknowable depth and burst like a super volcano on one of Jupiter's moons. Someone screamed, but the absence of a sustainable atmosphere rendered it soundless.

And then a telephone started ringing.

"Shit!" she heard Stone say.

Lisa opened her eyes and saw Stone, half-asleep, trying to locate the source of the ringing.

It's only a dream, she wanted to say, but was unable to speak. Then she realized that she was awake and that a phone was indeed ringing.

"It's my fucking cell," Stone said, looking around the room for his pants.

Who would be calling so late? Lisa wondered.

Oh, right. We're cops. People call the cops whenever they feel like it, the later the better. And, as cops, we can't complain. No such thing as off duty. Please, call me, day or night. It doesn't matter if I'm in the middle of a seriously kinky, not to mention terrifying sex dream.

"What the hell time is it, anyway?" Stone asked, pulling the phone from the pocket of his jeans.

"Night time, I think," Lisa said, picking up her watch from the end table and trying to read it."

"Where?" Stone said to the mysterious caller. "Okay, I'll be there as soon as I can."

"It's 4:47," Lisa said. "And who was that?"

"We've got another victim," he told her. "Looks like a replay of last night."

"Velociraptors," Lisa murmured.

"What?"

"I didn't say anything."

"Hey, are you all right?" he asked. Your face is flushed and you're perspiring. And you're naked."

"So are you, naked, I mean, and I'm fine. Just a nightmare."

"Do you usually have nightmares after sex? Or only after sex with me?"

"Ask me again after we've had sex a few more times."

"Will we have sex a few more times?"

"I don't know. Will we?"

"Anyway," Stone said, realizing that wherever this conversation was headed was probably not a place he wanted to go right now. "We should get to the crime scene."

"Right," Lisa said, reaching for her underwear. "No, wait a minute, what about Ishikawa?"

"Who?"

"The Japanese cop?"

"Shit!" Stone said, pulling on his pants. "Forgot about him. So, I'll go to the scene, you go to the airport."

"How will I know who he is?"

"Just look for an Asian guy who resembles a cop."

"You make it sound so easy."

"Okay, let's see, maybe you can make an 'Ishikawa' sign, hold it up at the arrivals gate."

"Hey, that's something I've always wanted to do," Lisa said, making no effort to conceal the sarcasm.

"Well there you go," said Stone. "Your lucky day."

"Assuming I locate him, what should I do with him?"

"Just check him into his hotel and then bring him to the station. I'll meet you there later."

Middle of the goddam night, but it still took Stone thirty minutes to drive from Lisa's downtown apartment to the Upper East Side. There was a lot more traffic than there should have been. Stone wondered if it had something to do with the ongoing heat wave. Maybe people had started living in their cars, driving around all night in the desperate hope of ending up somewhere cooler. Sleep deprived, strung out on caffeine and over the counter stimulants, they didn't realize that they were merely driving in crazy circles around the city.

The crime scene was a run down park on 110th Street, adjacent to the river, used primarily as a battleground for the neighborhood's rival gangs. The sun was just coming up, bathing the park and surrounding streets in an eerie orange glow. Several squad cars and an ambulance were already on scene, as was Chet Hogan; old school, no nonsense Detective from Midtown Homicide, who should have retired years ago, but, like so many old timers, couldn't imagine a viable alternative. Spend long enough in Homicide and the boundaries of reality start to get fuzzy. Murder works away at the spirit, turning cops into sharp-eyed ghouls who can solve almost any crazy crime you throw at them, but are fairly useless in all other areas of life. Stone, with a mere ten years under his belt, still had options, but he knew the clock was definitely ticking.

"Stone," Hogan spat, digging a cigarette out of his pocket and lighting it. He did not look happy.

"How's it going, Hogan?" Stone asked.

"Well, let's see. I'm here on the fucking edge of the civilized world at 5:30 in the fucking morning, looking at something that really pushes the limits of my tolerance as a human being."

"That bad?"

"Hey, don't take my word for it."

Stone walked over to where the body was lying, two guys from forensics working the site. It was a male, best guess, early 40's, probably nicely dressed before his clothes had been shredded and soaked in blood. The body was in two pieces, cut in half just below the navel, deep lacerations on the chest and face, eyes gone, throat torn open, but at least the head was still connected to the body. Everything from the waist down untouched. Trousers tugged down below the knees.

"Body parts accounted for?" Stone asked.

"We found an eyeball," one of the forensics guys told him. "The other eye and three fingers on the right hand still missing. Hard to say on the internal organs."

"Nice, huh?" Hogan sighed, taking a deep drag. "I figured it matched up with the M.O. on that Chinatown deal the other night, which is why I had them call you."

"Unfortunately, it does look familiar," Stone said.

"What kind of sick fuck pulls a guys pants down, then cuts his body in half and rips out his eyes?" Hogan asked to no one in particular, possibly God. "What do you think, some weird S&M thing that got way out of hand?"

"Who knows?" Stone shrugged, checking the hand with the missing fingers. "Any I.D. on the body?"

"Yeah, it was still in his pocket. John Burnett, the Third, no less. The guy was a fucking stockbroker. What the hell was he doing up here in the middle of the night?"

"Trying to live on the wild side," Stone mused. "No witnesses, I'm guessing."

"None that have come forward, but then people in this part of town are not known for their willingness to cooperate with law enforcement."

"Still, it might not be a bad idea to have a team push some of the local gang bangers on this," Stone said. "It's definitely not their work, and they might be pissed off with some outsider mutilating a guy in their territory. Maybe somebody saw something."

"Counting on the credibility of a bunch of moronic crack addicts, but okay, Stone. I'll do that for you."

"Thanks, Hogan. And could you have all of this, the body and whatever evidence there is, sent to South?"

"Sure," Hogan said. "The further this shit is from me, the better."

"Getting soft in your old age, Hogan?"

"Maybe I am. Thirty years I've been dealing with the worst the human species can dish out. You get used to it. But this is something else, this I'm having a hard time getting up against. You know what I mean, Stone?"

"Yeah, I think I do."

"This feels different. It smells different."

"And it just keeps getting hotter."

Lisa had been standing at the Arrivals Gate holding her Ishikawa sign for an hour, feeling like a complete idiot. Something close to a million Asians had walked past her in that time, not one of them even bothering to glance at her sign. Maybe she had spelled the name wrong. Only thing to do was to start asking people.

"Ishikawa? Ishikawa? Has anyone seen Ishikawa? Does anyone know Ishikawa?

No response. Not even a glimmer of recognition. She concluded that Asians were either very shy, or extremely rude.

"Can anyone see me?" she shouted. "I need Ishikawa and I need him now!"

"Excuse me," someone right behind her said, tapping her lightly on the shoulder.

Lisa jumped, spinning around to face the source of the voice. The man standing very close to her was tall, well dressed in a three-piece suit, an impeccably arranged tie and definitely of Asian origin.

"Jesus," Lisa said. "You scared me."

"I am very apologetic for it," the man said. "Do you seek Ishikawa?"

"Yes, do you know him?"

"In point of fact, I am."

"You are? You're Ishikawa?"

"Regretting my off-putting appearance, but yes. Are you Detective Stone?"

"No, I'm Malone. Stone couldn't make it."

"You are Malone, not Stone."

"Right," Lisa said. "He sent me. Sorry."

"No obligation to be so," Ishikawa said. "I am very pleased to be met in such fashion."

"Well, great!" Lisa laughed. "Shall we go?"

Outside in the parking lot the air felt like it was on the verge of boiling. Could air boil? Lisa doubted it, but a feeling was a feeling, valid despite the so-called scientific evidence to the contrary.

"Hope you don't mind the heat," Lisa said. "We're having kind of a wave, of heat."

"Summer in the city," Ishikawa said, without even a trace of perspiration.

"How's the weather in Tokyo?"

"Hot as Hell, I believe the expression to be. Tokyo in the summer is very much like Hell, only much more crowded."

"So I guess you're used to it."

"More accurate to think of me as immune."

"You're immune to the weather?"

"To most things, you may think of me so."

"Interesting," Lisa said, not sure whether or not it was. "So, I understand you're here on a case."

"I hope that I am not," Ishikawa said. "But all my professional instincts inform me that I am."

Maybe it's a language thing, Lisa thought to herself. Something lost in translation. Or possibly his English teacher had been a corporate lawyer. Or maybe Ishikawa was simply on the weird side. He was probably thinking the same thing about her, unless, of course, he was immune to weirdness, cultural or otherwise. Not bad looking, though. Sort of sharp-faced and rugged, short black hair, dark eyes that seemed to look right through things to other things most people couldn't see, sensuous lips, although he seemed way too serious to ever kiss on the first date. He was like a samurai, an immunized samurai in a well-tailored suit. She wondered if he was married, but had a feeling that was not something you asked a Japanese ten minutes after meeting him for the first time. Asking his age probably fell into the same category. Lisa spent the next ten minutes or so trying to think of things she could ask Ishikawa. What was his shoe size? How much money did he make as a detective in Japan? Was he circumcised? Whoa! Talk about totally inappropriate.

"Please forgive my obscene behavior," Ishikawa murmured.

Oh my god! Lisa thought. He has the ability to read minds, knows I was thinking about his dick and now he's going to show it to me.

"The enormous flight is catching up to me. I am forced to briefly close my eyes."

"Not a problem," Lisa said, relieved. "We'll just talk later."

Three

Stone stood there watching Beverly Hammer poke and probe the ravaged torso of the former John Burnett. Not necessarily something you wanted to do on an empty stomach, or, to be completely honest, under any circumstances. The bottom half of Mister Burnett waited patiently on another table. Hammer's preliminary investigation merely confirmed what Stone already knew. John Burnett, stockbroker and Clifford Goth, I.R.S. agent were almost certainly murdered by the same killer.

"First the I.R.S., now the stock market," Hammer mused, while rummaging through what was left of Mister Burnett's internal organs. "The motive is obviously money."

"As in money, the motive for 90% of all crimes committed?"

"I'll bet you a hundred bucks that the next victim is a lawyer, or possibly a banker. Although it really should be a lawyer, don't you think?"

"Isn't your ex-husband a lawyer?"

"There's another good reason."

"Besides, there may not be a next victim."

"You know as well as I do that there will be."

Yeah, he knew. This killer was just getting started.

"You'll let me know when you're finished," he said to Hammer.

"Anything for you, Detective." Hammer smiled.

It was the same Hammer smile, a mixture of playful wickedness, a declaration that anything goes as long as you're willing to accept the consequences, and a subtle reminder that almost nothing is what it appears to be. She looked a little bit older, a few more wrinkles around the eyes and mouth, but still beautiful in her pale, ghost-like sort of way. Had it been ten years since the wise Doctor Hammer had initiated the young Detective Stone into the specialized world of sex in the N.Y.P.D. morgue? The perfect intersection of desperation, desire and death was how she'd described it.

He had been standing next to her as she worked on the partially decayed body of a young woman recently fished from the river, when she suddenly said, "So tell me Detective, does this get you excited?"

"If by excited you mean on the verge of puking, then maybe."

"So this isn't giving you an erection."

"What? Of course not!"

"And what if I don't believe you?"

"Well, then, uh ..."

"Never mind," she had said, dropping her scalpel in the tray, pulling off her latex gloves and unzipping his fly. "I'll see for myself."

He had wanted to protest, say something about it being extremely inappropriate, definitely a breech of professional ethics, but once his penis was in her mouth, at the mercy of a tongue that clearly had talents beyond issuing the occasional sarcastic barb, the pretense of having principles didn't seem to matter much. Only afterwards did he realize his ass had been pressed up against one of the dead girl's hands.

"Almost a three-way," Hammer had laughed. "Call it a two and a half and forgive the poor girl for being so passive."

He felt bad about it afterwards, but then how does a healthy, twenty five year old male refuse a beautiful older woman in a white lab coat, a woman with science on her side, no less, even if the circumstances are surreal, possibly bordering on pathological? After that, they met more or less regularly, always in the chilled seclusion of the morgue surrounded by Hammer's playthings, as she liked to call the bodies and body parts she spent her time with. And then one day it was over. Nothing was ever said, it was simply mutually understood, as if desire had been satisfied and death had been restored to its position of prominence.

"Something on your mind, Detective?" Hammer asked, her blue eyes teasing.

"Just momentarily revisiting the distant past," he told her.

"Well don't. The past is as dead as our Mister Burnett here, and in at least as many pieces. Besides, you have more important things to think about."

"Whatever you say, Doctor."

Back upstairs in the land of the living – although considering the state of some of his colleagues, this might have been an over-generous assessment - Stone grabbed a cup of coffee and went directly to his office for what he hoped would be twenty minutes or so of undisturbed meditation, otherwise known as an unauthorized nap. It was not to be. No sooner had he got comfortable, beginning to conjure up images of Lisa in various modes of undress, than the intercom buzzed. Stone rolled his eyes and hit the button.

"Detective Stone? Captain wants to see you."

"Of course he does," Stone said, finishing his coffee and leaving the office.

The Captain, to no one's surprise, was not smiling, not even close. The forensic report on victim number one was open on his desk.

"You wanted to see me, Captain?"

"It's not so much that I want to see you, Stone, as that I am compelled to see you. Tell me something," he said, picking up the report and waving it in the air. "Does this make any sense to you?"

"Which part specifically, Sir?"

"Well, let's see, 'wounds on body most likely inflicted by extremely sharp, powerful claws, or some implement or device, as yet unknown, capable of simulating wounds of this nature'. Or this, 'the victim almost certainly was engaged in sexual activity immediately prior to, or during, the fatal attack'. Or how about this, 'traces of a saliva-like substance were detected on victim's genital area. DNA extracted from this substance does not correlate with any currently known species groups, suggesting unknown variables and/or corruption of the sample's integrity'. Whatever the hell that means?"

"Admittedly, Sir, it is puzzling."

"Puzzling?" Burke shouted. It's ridiculous, preposterous, fucking impossible is what it is."

"Well, yes, that too."

"Do you suppose I can go to the Chief and inform him that this year's summer maniac is a member of a currently unknown species group?"

"Probably wouldn't be your best move at this point in the investigation."

"Damn right it wouldn't be. So, what do you suggest?"

"Well, you could tell him ..."

The Captain cut him off by throwing up an oversized hand, which generally meant stop talking immediately, or suffer the unfortunate repercussions. "I am not actually asking for your advice, Stone. What I'm asking you to do is to work this case, get your head out of your butt and apply that Stone magic of yours. And get me some results that are not completely outside the realm of fucking reality. Soon!"

"I'll do my best, Captain."

"Now, where is Lieutenant Ishikawa?"

"He's with Malone."

"And where is she?"

"Presumably with him."

"In other words, you don't know where either of them are."

"Not exactly, no. But I am confident that Malone will have him here within the hour."

"Do let me know when that occurs."

Stone left the Captain's office thinking about the so-called Stone magic. So far, it had never failed him, maybe because it was so simple. Gather up all the bits and pieces, fit them together at just the right angles and wait for the big picture to emerge. You knew it when it felt right. Catching a killer was a lot like finding salvation. You had to have faith in the process. Believe in your method, trust in the fact that the physical evidence never lies and go with your gut instincts. Only problem this time was that Stone's gut was telling him nothing, except maybe that he hadn't eaten anything in awhile. Then there was his head, which should have been totally focused on the case, but seemed more interested in thinking about his partner; her smell, the taste of her skin, her lips, her wonderful nipples, the patch of dark red hair between her legs; arranging the bits and pieces of Lisa Malone into the perfect shape, the perfect feeling that would somehow compensate for all the darkness and despair, at least for a little while. Was that such a bad thing?

Stone shook his head, walked back into to his office. This is what you get for fooling around with your partner, he told himself. The magic gets compromised and suddenly you're just like every other cop who doesn't have a clue. You start stumbling around in the dark, making mistakes, taking short cuts, and before you know it you're either an alcoholic, sprinkling amphetamine on your breakfast cereal, or thinking about swallowing a bullet courtesy of your own gun. Stone shuddered and dropped into his chair. Instantly, the phone rang.

"Stone."

"Detective Stone? I've got Detective Malone on line one and a Detective Hogan on line two."

"Thanks," Stone said, pressing one. "Lisa?"

"Hi, it's me."

"Where are you?"

"I'm at Ishikawa's hotel."

"And he is?"

"Asleep."

"Asleep?"

"As soon as we got into his room, he lay down on the bed and was gone. I mean totally, like the sleep of the dead."

"Are you sure he isn't?"

"He's definitely breathing, although barely. I tried to wake him, but no response. I've never seen anyone sleep like this."

"He must be tired."

"You think? Question is, what should I do?"

"I don't know. I guess you should just hang out there until he wakes up."

"Boring, but all right."

"I've got another call. Just get back here as soon as you can. The Captain is very anxious to meet the Lieutenant."

"I'm sure they'll get along fabulously. And Stone?"

"Yeah?"

"I miss you."

Okay, Lisa asked herself, why the hell did I say that? I miss you? How girlie- vulnerable-pathetic did that sound? Why not just start weeping over the phone? Where was Malone, the tough, street-smart cop? And what the fuck happened to casual? Sure, she had a heart, but she knew how to keep it under control. When you live and work on the edge, showing a soft side just didn't cut it. All right, she admitted, that person didn't really exist. She was neither tough, nor particularly smart regarding the street. But she was good pretending she was, and that counted for something. At least she had been good at it until Stone strolled into her life.

She walked over to the bed and scrutinized the sleeping Ishikawa. He looked so relaxed, totally calm, the hint of a smile on his lips. Was he dreaming? What was it like to dream in Japanese? Aside from taking off his shoes at the door, he was completely dressed. He hadn't even bothered to remove his suit jacket, or loosen his tie, before slipping into a simulated coma.

"Tell me something, Ishikawa," she said. "You're a guy. A Japanese guy, granted, but a guy's a guy, right? So say you're having sex with a woman you work with. What? That would never happen? Fine, but say it did. Shit happens, you know? Sure, you didn't want it to happen, you understood the obvious dangers and pitfalls, but the woman is irresistible in an edgy, mysterious sort of way. And she's beautiful, and hot. Not to mention that it's the best sex you've ever had. Besides, you're both professionals, quite capable of keeping the realms of business and pleasure separated. Then one day, in the course of a routine, work-related phone call, she tells you that she misses you. It just slips out. She bites her lower lip as soon as the words leave her mouth, but, of course, it's too late. Panic grips her body, because she knows she has violated the unspoken rule against making needy-sounding, emotionally laden comments, particularly to a co-worker she's sleeping with. The question is how do you react? Do you ignore it, pretend it never happened, take it in stride, or silently freak out?"

Ishikawa remained inert, silent as a long dead Buddhist monk.

" Need a few minutes to formulate your answer?" Lisa told him. "No problem."

She went to the small mini-bar, took out a bottle of vodka and made herself a drink. Drinking on duty was, needless to say, frowned upon, but in her new assignment as bored-out-of-her-mind babysitter, it not only seemed acceptable but necessary. She carried her drink back over to the bed and sat down next to Ishikawa.

"I have to be honest with you," she told him. "This is turning out to be the dullest first date ever."

She laughed and stretched out on the bed next to him; nothing else to do but wait for sleeping beauty to come out of it. She wasn't planning on closing her eyes, it just happened, something about being in the same room with a sleeping person. It's like you're breathing the air of the sleeper. The urge to sleep takes possession of you. Lisa told herself she was just resting her eyes for a few minutes. And then the world went black.

It was mid-afternoon by the time Stone made it to the Midtown station house. Traffic had snarled to a halt in the heat, a million or so cars and trucks locked in a slow motion dance of burning steel and rubber. The sidewalks weren't much better, the usual rapid throng of pedestrians having slowed to a crawl; the last remnants of the human element praying for a quick death, or, better still a cold beer and an early sunset. Bring on the night, as unpredictable and dangerous as it was. We'll take our chances. Nothing could be as bad as this.

Stone had to park his car on the sidewalk, almost hitting a large, middle-aged woman, who gave him the finger, shouting something about illegal parking and where the hell was a cop when you needed one? He walked into the station thinking the same thing. Midtown appeared abandoned. The single officer behind the reception desk barely flinched when Stone announced he was there to see Hogan. He took the stairs to the second floor homicide unit. Hogan was sitting at his desk in his undershirt, a cigarette sporting a two-inch ash hanging from his mouth.

"What the hell is going on around here?" Stone asked.

"Air conditioning went down this morning," Hogan growled. "It's been like a ghost town in the Mojave since then. What's happening outside?"

"A midtown meltdown in progress."

"Maybe it's the end of the fucking world."

Stone nodded, not sure if the world ending would be such a bad thing. More likely it wouldn't change anything. It would be all the same shit, just happening elsewhere, possibly in some parallel universe. "So, why am I here?"

"We did a run on the uptown home boys this morning and got lucky. Picked up a seventeen year old kid packing a .9mm and enough crack to put an elephant into cardiac arrest. Turns out he's on parole and would do just about anything to stay out of jail. So I let it slip that we were looking for information on the dead body in the park, and he says, yeah, he was there, saw what went down."

"Probably bullshit."

"That's what I thought, except that when I mentioned it, he looked real scared, which is kind of unusual. These kids will kill their own grandmas for a few bucks, but showing fear is something they generally don't do."

"What's his name?"

"Jesus Sanchez."

"What else would it be?"

"Yeah, talk about taking the Lord's name in vain."

"Well, let's go have a chat with Jesus."

Hogan had Jesus moved from the holding cell to one of the interrogation rooms. Stone went in alone and introduced himself. Jesus, a small, well-built thug with snake tattoos crawling up both arms and a cross carved into the top of his skull, only sneered.

"Hey, man," he said, "I don't give a shit what your name is. All I want is to get out of this place."

"I don't know," Stone said. "It's really hot outside."

"Yeah? It's really fucking hot in here."

"So you tell me what I want to know and maybe you can leave."

"Okay, your mother gives a half-decent blow job."

"I'll tell her you said so."

"Anything else?"

"Last night, the park on 114th Street."

"What about it?"

"Were you there?"

"Yeah, I was there."

"Who with?"

"A couple of my boys. No big deal. Just hanging out."

"Did you see the well-dressed white guy?"

"Yeah, we saw him. Thought it was some kind of fucking ghost. A real pale motherfucker, and way out of his zone."

"Was he alone?"

"No, with some chick."

"Get a good look at her?"

"Hey man, it was dark."

"Was she white?"

"No. Some Chinese bitch, or something."

"So what happened?"

"They start making out. We figure she's a pro because she's got his dick out like real fast. We're trying to decide whether to just watch the show, or go over there and, you know, lay down some law."

"You mean rob and kill them?"

"Hey man, we didn't kill nobody."

"Okay, go on. What happened next?"

" I'm not sure. Something fucking happened."

"Just tell me what you saw."

"It's what I saw that worries me. Like out of nowhere, this wind starts blowing and it gets real cloudy, like some fucking fog or something. Then we hear the guy start moaning, real loud, like it was the first time some bitch was touching his dick. We couldn't see shit, so we like tried to get closer. It just felt weird, like the air was alive or something and it was holding us back. Anyway, we got close enough to see the guy lying on the ground ..."

"What about the girl?"

"No sign of her, just this weird cloud hanging there on top of the guy. There was this crackling noise, like electric short circuits or something. My boys were telling me we should get the fuck out of there, but I couldn't move. I didn't want to be watching this shit, but I couldn't help myself. That's when I saw them."

"Them?"

"Those fucking eyes, big, blood-red, creepy-as-shit eyes, staring right at me, like burning into my brain. Next thing I know my boys are pulling me out of there and we ran, man. We just ran and kept running."

"You were scared."

"Fuck scared. We just didn't want to get dead."

"So tell me, how stoned were you?"

"How stoned? Not stoned enough."

"Anything else you can tell me?" Stone asked Jesus.

"Yeah. God hates all cops."

Four

Two things occurred to Lisa. One, she couldn't move. It was like she was paralyzed from the neck down, like something heavy was sitting on her chest. (*During the Middle Ages, women often complained about this. They claimed that ghosts or devils were visiting them in the middle of the night and sitting on their chests. These women were invariably branded as heretics and eventually burned at the stake.*) And two, someone was sucking on her left nipple. Oh, and three. She was naked. She tried to recall anything previous that might have led to her being in this situation, but nothing came readily to mind. It was like there was a large Mid-western storm cloud blowing through her head, temporarily disabling all critical brain functions. Being from the Mid-west, she knew that this happened much more often than most people were willing to admit.

Meanwhile, whoever had been sucking on her nipple abandoned that pursuit, slithered down her torso, stopping briefly to lick her belly button and was now busy chewing on her pubic hair. What kind of weirdo chews on pubic hair? She wanted to say something about it, but there wasn't any time. She felt her legs being spread apart and a pair of what felt like strong hands sliding under her ass and lifting her. And then four, someone's tongue was licking her pussy; rather skillfully she had to admit. Her abdominal muscles tightened as the tongue found her clitoris, licking, poking and stroking it with the agility of an oral sex magician. Lisa felt the crackle of heat at the base of her spine, the warm pulse of pleasure circling downward from her belly to her vagina and all points east and west. She was going to come. There was really no way to stop it. Someone could have pulled the Beretta from her holster (wherever that was?) and shot her repeatedly; she would still have had to come, one incredible orgasm before the paroxysms of death kicked in.

The thought, as extraneous as it was irritating, couldn't have occurred to her at a worse time. How inconsiderate can your own disabled brain be? Lisa remembered where she was, on the bed of the sleeping Ishikawa, a Japanese cop she was supposed to be keeping an eye on. Only one conclusion was possible, the oral expert between her thighs was Ishikawa. Did this transgress the boundaries of showing him all the usual courtesies? Almost certainly, it did. Not to mention that Ishikawa had undressed her while she was sleeping and was now in the process of having sex with her paralyzed body; kinky for sure, but also a little strange, not to mention borderline criminal. A shudder rippled through her, barely pleasurable. Pleasure, in fact, was receding faster than a typical middle-aged white guy's hairline. She sat up with a gasp and opened her eyes.

First thing she noticed was that she was still completely dressed. Second thing she noticed was that Ishikawa was gone.

Stone hit the terminate button on his cell and threw it on the seat next to him. He leaned forward and rested his head on the steering wheel. No reason to keep his eyes on the road. Traffic was going nowhere. All streets south were impassable, gridlocked for the duration of time. Coming on to five in the afternoon, it was safe to say that the day was not going to turn out well; two over the top, brutal murders, information about which remained both sketchy and hard to believe. No sign of the Chinese woman identified by the crackhead Jesus. No trace of a fog with glowing, red eyes. Oh, and then there was Lisa's call, reporting that she had lost Ishikawa.

"How exactly is that possible?" he had asked her.

"I don't know," she said. "I only turned my back for a second."

"Lisa?"

"Okay, I fell asleep, but only because I was so bored watching him sleep. It was like the power of suggestion."

Stone could see no reason to rush back to the station with nothing but bad news for the Captain, so he took a left on 23rd and parked midway down the street, directly across from a bar, as luck would have it. He needed some cool air, a little down time to clear his head and yes, he really needed a drink. The bar, a low-keyed local establishment so far resisting the urge to turn trendy, or, God forbid, hip, was already crowded; mostly working class guys, a few suits, several women of questionable moral character preparing themselves for another night on the streets. In a word, Stone's kind of place.

He took a seat at the counter and ordered a beer.

"Rough day?" the bartender asked.

"Yeah," Stone said. "The kind of day when all the answers turn out wrong."

"Maybe you're not asking the right questions."

The wisdom of the bartender, as trivial as it was profound.

"Maybe I don't want to ask those questions," Stone told him.

"Maybe that's why you're here," the bartender said, handing him his beer. "On the house."

Stone sipped his beer and thought about Lisa. Was she out on the street looking for Ishikawa, back at the station being flayed alive by Burke, or in a bar somewhere trying to do the same thing he was? Which raised the question why they weren't in the same bar doing it together? What was it about Lisa, anyway? Since the divorce – his wife's idea, based on what she claimed was extreme and unbearable mental cruelty, due to the fact that he was rarely, if ever, home, which Stone had to admit was a more or less accurate assessment, although the 'extreme and unbearable' had always seemed a bit over the top – he had been sexually intimate with a number of women, some in the Department, some he had run into in bars; all of them, with the brief exception of Beverly Hammer, younger than himself. It was just something cops did, a survival tactic based on the time-honored principle of non-commitment. Keep it casual was the rule. The minute a woman started feeling the need to tell you her 'story,' or even worse ask about yours, it was time to get out. The 'cops can't afford to get emotionally involved' routine usually worked. 'Falling in love just wouldn't be fair to you.' He knew the procedure by heart. So why, all of a sudden, was Lisa getting under his skin, making him feel things he didn't need to be feeling, making him ache in that annoying though still slightly pleasurable way?

"Wow! I hope she's worth it."

He hadn't noticed the woman come in and take the stool next to his. He turned and looked into a face that was striking, almost mesmerizing. Not so much beautiful as compellingly cute, with a pair of dark, oval eyes that seemed to see much deeper into him than he was generally comfortable with.

"Who?" Stone asked,

"The woman who occupies your mind," she said.

"How do you know I was thinking about a woman?"

"I didn't, really. Just playing the odds," she said, laughing.

It was a strange laugh, complex, delightful and, at the same time, unnerving. It made the hair on the back of his neck bristle, sending a nervous pulse down his spine.

"I mean," she continued, "you're a guy, and most guys spend most of their time thinking about girls, unless, of course, they're gay. You're not ..?"

"Uh, no."

"I didn't think so. And then there's your expression."

"My expression?"

"Sort of sad puppy dog looking at the moon face."

She laughed again and Stone had the strong desire to kiss her small, full lips. He had to turn away to resist the urge.

"I don't think anyone has ever described my expression quite that way," he said, sipping his beer.

"First time for everything, I guess. I'm Sato Yui, by the way. From Japan."

"Nice to meet you, Sato Yui from Japan. I'm Stone."

"Nice to meet you too, Stone."

"Can I buy you a drink?"

"Thanks," she said, shifting her stool closer to his. "I'll have a Black Russian."

"So, what brings you to New York?" he asked.

"I'm doing research for a book," she told him. "Crime American Style will be the title."

"Small world," Stone said, gesturing to the bartender.

"Don't tell me you're a writer, too!"

"Not exactly. I'm a cop."

"Really? A cop? No kidding?"

"Homicide, actually."

"How great is this?" she cried, bouncing up and down on her barstool. Now I have my own personal connection into the world of the American criminal mind. Can I interview you sometime?"

"Why not?" he said. "Anything for literature."

"I think I love you, David Stone," she whispered, brushing her lips across his cheek.

It certainly didn't even qualify as a kiss, but Stone felt that something intimate had occurred between them. He closed his eyes and immediately began to float up out of his body. The space he found himself in was cool and comfortable, the light softly romantic. He felt aroused, the pulse of blood surging into his groin, but also completely relaxed. Sato Yui appeared in front of him, wearing a crimson silk robe, a dragon embroidered in gold running the length of each sleeve. She smiled, her dark eyes glowing, her small, tapered fingers coaxing him towards her.

"Undress me," she ordered.

Stone reached for her, barely touching the robe's sash. It fell away, followed by the robe, which slowly floated off, rippling the air as it disappeared somewhere beneath them, revealing her naked body. The sight of her punched the air from his lungs. She was perfect: her small, firm breasts, the dark, swollen nipples, her taut belly, the smooth line of her hips, the patch of soft, black hair between her legs. She moved against him, close enough that he could feel the precise points of her nipples through his shirt. He wanted to put his arms around her, touch her back, her ass, kiss the nape of her neck, but Sato Yui's eyes commanded him to remain still.

"Don't worry," she said. "I'll take care of everything. And when I'm through we will be one."

Stone didn't quite understand, but the sound of her voice made him tremble, creating a knot of pain in the center of his chest that he knew would eventually burst and most likely kill him. He didn't mind.

"Yes," he said. "Kill me."

"Kill you?" she laughed. "No, it's much too soon for that. All I'm interested in now is a small sample of your blood."

"Of my ..?"

She cut him off with a finger to his lips, her breath warm and moist against his face. "Relax," she told him, slipping her hands under his shirt and beginning to stroke his chest. He sighed, his body trembling, heart rate accelerating. She slowly moved her hands from his chest down to his stomach, her fingers slipping inside the waistband of his jeans, and then the sound of his belt buckle being undone, zipper unzipped, the sensation of his jeans being eased down over his hips. "Don't be alarmed," she whispered, her fingers grazing the tip of his penis. "But there is something quite large and hard inside your pants."

Stone wanted desperately to suggest that she take a closer look, possibly interact with it in some imaginative way, but the words would not come from his throat.

"You probably want me to suck it, don't you?" Sato Yui asked.

"Yes," he shouted inside his head. "Please!"

"I wish I could say I was the kind of girl who did that sort of thing on the very first date, but alas, I can't. Still, maybe this will make up for it."

He felt something sharp and cold pressed against his abdomen, followed by the very distinct sensation of being cut. Forcing himself to look down, he saw the adorable naked Asian girl slicing open his gut with what appeared to be one of her fingers, which was already covered in blood, as was most of her delicate little arm. He began to scream, either inside his head or out loud, he wasn't sure.

"Oh my God," Sato Yui cried. "Look at the time."

"What?" Stone mumbled, shaking his head and looking around to get his bearings. He was still sitting at the bar, his half finished bottle of beer on the counter.

"The time," she repeated.

Stone tried to focus his eyes on the clock hanging on the wall behind the bar. It seemed to read 8:30. "Is that possible?" he asked.

"Afraid so," she told him. "Sorry about that. I've been chattering away like a monkey. You must think I'm one crazy Japanese chick, huh?"

"Not at all what I was thinking," he said, pretty sure that he hadn't been thinking anything at all.

"That's a relief. Anyway," she said, jumping off the barstool. "Got to go, have a date. But I will call you for that interview."

Stone watched her as she walked towards the door, her small, sleek body, her thick black hair bouncing behind her, the perfect lines of her petite behind nicely contained within the tight, black jeans she was wearing. He briefly considered following her, but realized that might be construed as weird. Instead, he finished his beer, called the bartender over and pointed to the bottle of bourbon sitting on display.

After making a purely perfunctory search for Ishikawa in the immediate vicinity of his hotel, Lisa had given up and returned to the station. The captain, fortunately, was not there. She hung around for a while, trying to think about the case, glancing at the forensics reports again, but her mind kept wandering back to Stone. She tried calling his cell, but there was no answer. Why hadn't he called her? Was he okay? Was he thinking about her?

"Jesus, Lisa, get a grip. You're a cop, right?"

"Right!"

"You're also a grown woman who prides herself on her independence."

"Again, correct!"

"So how about behaving accordingly?"

"I'll try?"

"Not good enough, young lady!"

Rather than get involved in a long drawn out argument with herself, which was, after all, a telltale sign of possible derangement, Lisa decided to go home. She would have taken a cab, but based on the current traffic situation walking was like a million times faster. Once inside her apartment, which felt like it was 100 degrees, she stripped off her clothes, turned on the air conditioning and made herself a drink. She needed to calm down, try to focus. It had not been the best of days. Not only had she fallen asleep on the job and misplaced Ishikawa, she had also had a weird sexual dream about the weird Japanese cop. What was that about? Yes, okay, she was a sexual being, she enjoyed sex, often craved it with addict-like determination, but she also knew how to keep her sexual appetite under control, compartmentalized, safe and secure in its assigned place. Now it seemed that sex was trying to slip past the agreed upon boundaries, storm the barricades she had so meticulously erected and interfere with her job. She had no choice but to blame Stone.

When the apartment had chilled to the point of hardening her nipples into small, blood-colored daggers, Lisa decided to take a bath. She added bath salts and bubbles, refilled her drink and sank into the warm water; the perfect place to clear one's head and take stock of one's situation, in theory, anyway, assuming one could resist the temptation to touch oneself. Think, Lisa, think, she told herself, but her right hand was already exercising its option to behave as it pleased, teasing up her right thigh and beginning to stroke the swollen flesh of her labia. Her clitoris, meanwhile, had become a magnetized, underwater buoy. The first touch sent an electrical jolt through her body. She closed her eyes, gently squeezing the hood, rotating the flesh between her two fingers. Small pleasure bursts began in her anus, spiraling up her spine and into her belly, like a bubble of pure light under intense pressure. Lisa's hips began to move in the water, her ass rising and falling in a gentle, tidal rhythm, her breath coming in short, sharp gasps. She tried to imagine the anonymous cock that was moving inside her, the large, thick cock that belonged to no man in particular, which would bring on a delicious, waterlogged orgasm.

But she couldn't do it. Anonymous cock suddenly had a name, anonymous no-man had a face, Stone's face. How dare he insert himself into her anonymous, fantasy sex life? But then maybe the fault wasn't entirely his. Was it possible she was starting to fall for her partner?

"Not at all good, Lisa," she told herself.

Stone was great, an interesting, lovely guy with a terrific body, and the sex, so far, had been delicious, with every reason to assume it would only get better. Okay, the fact that they were partners was a potential hindrance, but nothing that couldn't be handled. Getting emotionally involved, on the other hand, allowing feelings of love to rise to the surface and gain a foothold in her life, was not part of the program. Lisa's history of love had been the recurring story of various men attempting to push her into a tight-fitting mold of their own design. Love, as far as she could tell, equaled control, the imposition of other people's expectations and the inevitable loss of possibilities. Hadn't it been everyone's expectations of her that had finally convinced her to escape Merlin, Ohio and move to New York? Her parents, needless to say, had had other plans for her. Her father, in particular, had never gotten over what he referred to as her recklessness and utter lack of responsibility. Her deciding to become a cop was simply icing on the cake of familial betrayal, proving that Lisa Malone, who could have had the perfect life – her parents version of it, anyway - was not entirely in possession of her mental faculties.

From Lisa's perspective, on the other hand, a little reckless irresponsibility was just what the doctor ordered. Freedom, after all, always came with a price; in this case love. Men who wanted more than she was willing to give didn't stand a chance. Besides, she was doing something that she actually enjoyed, tracking down the twisted weirdoes that prey on the weak and the innocent. It was a noble cause. Her father, who still believed that a woman's place was in the home, supporting her husband and raising his children, didn't see it that way. Cops were men, women wore pretty dresses, spoke in hushed tones and smiled a lot. They did not carry guns. They most certainly did not indulge repeatedly in casual sex. And that, young lady, was final.

Lisa groaned, closed her eyes and sunk down into the water until her head was submerged. It was quiet and warm, the perfect place to escape her troubles, real or imagined. Except for the not-being-able-to-breathe thing.

Five

L isa was already at her desk, going over the day's briefing sheets, when Stone stumbled into Homicide. He looked disheveled, as if he had slept in his car all night, but also attractive and sexy in a messy, 'I'm a guy, what can I say?' sort of way. He smiled at her, rather lamely, she thought, then went into his office and collapsed in the chair behind his desk. All men, ultimately, are disappointments, she thought to herself, pouring a cup of coffee and taking it into the rumpled mass that was her partner.

"You look like you could use this," she said, placing the cup in front of him.

"Thanks," he groaned, taking several gulps of the hot liquid.

"You also look like shit."

"Nothing compared to how I feel."

"What happened to you last night, anyway?"

"I wish I knew."

"I mean, I thought you might stop by, or at least call."

"Yeah, sorry about that. I'm almost certain I intended to ..."

"But then you ran into a bottle of bourbon?"

"I only stopped off for a couple of drinks. Next thing I knew I was waking up in my car."

Nice detective work, Malone.

"Sounds less comfortable than, I don't know, cuddling up next to me in my bed."

"Much less," he said, placing his hand on hers. "And I am sorry."

"Hey, no big deal," she said, thinking that it actually was a big deal, while at the same time feeling annoyed with herself for thinking so. "As long as you're okay. Besides, we have other things to worry about."

"Any sign of Ishikawa?"

"I called his hotel this morning, but he wasn't there."

"I guess we're just going to have to tell the Captain we lost him."

"I lost him, not we. I fell asleep on duty."

"Yeah, well, maybe we won't mention that part to the Captain. Anyway, perhaps his rage over the loss of Ishikawa will distract him from asking about the progress we've made on the two murders."

"No leads from uptown?"

"Only what Jesus told me."

"Well, he should know, right?"

"You would think, but our only possible suspect at this point is a Chinese female with glowing red eyes, who travels in an unnatural ground fog."

"Another thing we might not want to mention to the Captain," Lisa said, running her fingers lightly over Stone's hand. Despite the fact that he clearly needed a shower, possibly a shot of adrenalin, she wanted nothing more at this moment than for him to take her in his arms and kiss her. *Read the signals, Detective.*

"Lisa," Stone said, taking hold of her arm and gently tugging her towards him. "About that rule ..."

Lisa felt herself go warm and slightly damp. Stone's eyes probed hers for a course of action, but his body had already made the call. There was going to be a kiss, as inappropriate as it would be delicious.

"It is, after all, the exception that proves the rule," he said, his eyes narrowed to insinuating slits focused on Lisa's mouth.

A cliché, she thought, but under the circumstances forgivable.

Lisa closed her eyes, happily resigned to the inevitable. Risky, unprofessional behavior notwithstanding, this kiss felt like perhaps the most necessary kiss in the history of kissing. Two sets of lips moving through time and space, the delectable agony of anticipation. Lisa smiled. She could feel Stone's breath against her face, his lips so close now she could already taste them.

Neither she nor Stone heard the knock. It was the sort of polite tapping that virtually demanded to be ignored, even if the people inside weren't about to have the kiss that would alter the collective course of human destiny. Only when the door burst opened and the face of Ishikawa appeared did the romantic moment crash, like window glass shattering in a tornado. Lisa gasped, grabbing the desk and pushing herself away from the now less than inevitable meeting of hungry lips. Stone's body stiffened, his brown eyes widened to the point of painful, as if his mother had just walked in on him while he was masturbating.

Ishikawa stepped into the room and bowed deeply. "Please forgive this untimely intrusion," he said.

"Who ..?" Stone stammered.

"Lieutenant Ishikawa," Lisa said.

"At your service," Ishikawa said, walking to Stone and extending his hand.

Stone reluctantly offered his hand, noticing that Ishikawa was wearing a long, black trench coat over a suit and tie on what was probably going to be the hottest day of the century. "We're, uh, just relieved that you made it."

"As am I," Ishikawa smiled.

"Which raises the question of where you've been for the past twenty-four hours," Lisa scolded. "We've been worried about you."

"For which my apology has great depth. But I can say with some assurance that my time was not ill spent. By the way, Detective," Ishikawa said to Stone. "We have much in common."

"Do we?" Stone asked, glancing at Lisa, a look of bemused bafflement in his eyes.

"Our names, for example. You are Stone and I am Ishikawa. In Japanese, ishi is a stone, kawa is a river. I am a river stone. You are simply a stone, but stones, in essence, are always and only stones, regardless of where they call home.

"That is interesting," Lisa said, fighting back a laugh.

"Uh, maybe we should take you in to see the Captain now," Stone said.

"Nothing would fill me with greater joy," Ishikawa said, "But perhaps first we should discuss our case."

"Our case?" Stone asked.

"There have been three murders thus far," said Ishikawa, "horrific even by your New York standards."

"Actually," Lisa said, "there have only been two."

"I fear that your information is not entirely current."

"And your connection to these murders would be ..?" Stone asked.

"We seek the same thing, Detective."

"Early retirement and a decent pension?" Stone laughed.

"The same monster," Ishikawa said, his eyes staring intently at some imaginary point just above Stone's head.

"So you're saying," Lisa asked, "that the killer we're looking for has also killed in Japan?"

"Tokyo, Osaka, Hong Kong, Shanghai, Moscow, Budapest, Munich, Paris, London and now here. This beast is international. I have been tracking it for ..." Ishikawa paused, counting off the passage of time on his fingers ... "numerous years."

"Years?" Lisa exclaimed, sounding more surprised than she intended.

Ishikawa sighed. "Suffice it to say that the one we seek has, among other talents, a well-developed ability to avoid capture."

"Apparently," Stone snickered, "Is there a description for this 'one we seek'?"

"Ah," Ishikawa hummed, as if about to break into song. "This is where our path becomes both convoluted and dangerous."

"Our path?"

"The path we are now required to travel."

"Look, Lieutenant Ishikawa," Stone said with a trace of annoyance. "Forgive me, but this is all very vague."

"You are, of course, completely forgiven," Ishikawa bowed.

Lisa watched the two men as they talked. In some way they were just being male, less interested in the facts, more in asserting primal, alpha male status. Who can count up the dead bodies more accurately? Who has the guts to bite the head off a live chicken? Who has the bigger dick? She thought about how the conversation would go if both men were naked. Hard to imagine Ishikawa being able to compete with Stone's body, but then the Japanese were well known for their ability to be both agile and deceptive. Who knew what Ishikawa was concealing under all those layers of clothing? If his technique in the oral sex department was any indication, she wasn't quite ready to rule him out as a serious contender.

Hello? Detective Malone? That was dream oral sex. Let's not give up entirely on reality.

"Right," Lisa said out loud.

"Damn right," Stone added.

"Then we are all in agreement," Ishikawa said.

"Uh, I think what Detective Stone means," Lisa said, "is that we are not entirely sure what it is you're talking about."

"Forgive my unruly English," Ishikawa said, "but we are face to face with concepts that can play havoc with both the mind and the bowels. I will, of course, explicate more fully, but first I would appreciate seeing the scene of the third murder, and also have the opportunity to peruse the physical remains of the first two victims."

"Again," Stone sighed, reaching for the ringing phone, "only two victims. Stone. What? Are you sure? Okay, thanks."

"What is it?" Lisa asked, as he hung up.

"It seems we have a third victim, Battery Park."

"Excellent!" Ishikawa shouted, spinning around and moving to the door. "We should go immediately!"

The Captain was standing, looking out the window when Stone knocked and walked into his office.

"What are you doing here, Stone?" the Captain asked without turning around.

"I just assumed that you'd want an update on the, uh ..."

"You should be on your way to Battery Park, don't you think?"

"Exactly where I'm on my way to, sir."

"And yet you're still here. Where is Malone?"

"She, in fact, is on her way to the scene, with, uh ..."

"Lieutenant Ishikawa?"

"Yes, sir, and I know you're probably wondering why we have not yet brought the Lieutenant in to see you."

"Actually, I was not wondering that."

"You weren't?"

"Why would I? Lieutenant Ishikawa was in here early this morning, before either you or your partner arrived. We had a long and informative chat."

"Really?"

"And it seems fairly clear that his case and ours are somehow connected."

"Doesn't that strike you as slightly odd, Captain?"

"A coincidence, perhaps, but odd? I don't think so."

"Okay, but what about Ishikawa? He is certainly odd."

"Cultural differences, Detective," the Captain said, turning and dropping into his chair. "Try opening your mind a bit. Everywhere else is not exactly like here."

"I suppose that's something to be thankful for," Stone said with a smile.

The Captain either did not get the attempted humor, or chose to ignore it. "Ishikawa may be on the eccentric side, but from what I've learned he's also a damn good cop. One of Japan's elite, in fact."

"I don't know, Captain."

"Fortunately, I do. Look, Stone, I know you like to work out on the edge, on your own, without constraints, which I tolerate because you get results. Until now, that is. No shame in asking for a little help."

"I'm not asking."

"And I'm still running this department. Ishikawa's insight into this killer could be invaluable. I want him included in the investigation, which means your total cooperation. Understood?"

"But Captain, it's a hundred degrees outside and the man is wearing an overcoat."

"If he helps us catch a killer, a killer I will soon have no choice but to begin referring to as a serial to the media vultures, I won't care if he comes in here wearing a pink cocktail dress. Now do me and my blood pressure a favor and go find me a killer."

It was another car ride with Ishikawa, Lisa struggling to come up with something to talk about. What do you talk about with a man who never perspires? Luckily, Ishikawa took the initiative.

"I hope I was not stepping on anyone's nose this morning."

"Nose? Lisa wondered. "Oh, you mean toes."

"Of course, toes," Ishikawa said, pulling a small notebook and pen from his jacket pocket and making a notation. "Idioms are indeed the Devil's details."

"I wouldn't worry about it," Lisa told him, not really sure what it was that shouldn't be worried about, while at the same time feeling slightly worried. "And I should probably apologize for yesterday, you know, falling asleep on your bed."

"Not at all," Ishikawa said. "I am a solid believer in the value of a brief daytime sleeping session."

"Taking a nap, you mean?"

"Precisely! The nap, a beautiful word, don't you think? So perfectly suited to its meaning. It clears the mind, allowing ideas to flow with total freedom. I have solved many difficult cases during nap time."

"Still, it's not something I usually do while I'm supposed to be working."

"You should begin at once."

"Taking naps?"

"If you feel the urge, I'll drive."

"No, that's all right."

"I insist!"

"Actually," Lisa said, pulling into the parking area on the north end of the park, "we're here."

Even before Lisa had stopped the car, Ishikawa was out the door, jogging towards the crime scene at the far end of the park like some pent up Labrador Retriever chasing an imaginary Frisbee. She had no choice but to run after him. By the time she reached the body, she was exhausted, soaked in sweat and thinking how nice a nap would be right about now, possibly a cold shower first. Ishikawa was down on all fours, his face a centimeter or two from what on better days had most likely been an adult male. Two uniformed officers were in the process of trying to pull him to his feet.

"It's okay," Lisa told them, showing her badge. "He's with me."

"If you say so, Detective," one of the cops said, throwing Ishikawa a look of total disdain.

The body, which looked like it had been carved up by some kind of insane, near-sighted butcher, was already beginning to stink. The heat, the foul-smelling breeze off the harbor and the spread of human entrails on the park grass made it impossible not to feel like vomiting. For some reason, it also reminded Lisa of picnics she had been forced to endure as a girl along the banks of the polluted Cayuga River; inexplicable cheerfulness, the aroma of overheated tuna sandwiches and egg salad well past its expiration date, armies of ants, hordes of flies simulating dark storm clouds, all of which again made her feel like vomiting. Ishikawa, on the other hand, seemed almost gleeful, like a kid discovering presents under the Christmas tree.

Immune, Lisa said to herself. "Look familiar?" she asked.

"Like an old friend," Ishikawa smiled. "Or possibly an ex-wife."

Okay, that rules out marriage as a possible topic of conversation.

"Do you smell it?" he asked her.

"I'm smelling so many things right now."

"Come closer."

"Are you sure that's absolutely necessary?"

"The closer we get, the closer we get, if you get my drift?"

Needless to say, she didn't, but with enormous reluctance Lisa squatted down and leaned in for a better look at the latest unlucky victim. She felt slightly dizzy, wondered what the damage to her reputation would be if she threw up on it. She tried to sniff without actually sniffing. "What is it?"

"That," Ishikawa said with a scary gleam in his eyes, "is the distinct aroma of our adversary."

Lisa stood up and tried to find some fresh air to suck into her lungs. "So we're not only after an insane serial killer, we're after an insane serial killer who smells really bad."

Ishikawa looked up at her and smiled broadly. "Exciting, isn't it?"

Stone was about to get into his car when he heard someone calling his name. He looked up and saw a young woman running towards him from across the street, waving frantically. She was Asian, petite, with short, spiky black hair, wearing the smallest pair of shorts he'd ever seen and a cut-off tee shirt that just barely covered her breasts.

"It's me," she said, stopping directly in front of him, smiling.

"Sato Yui? The girl from the bar?"

"Of course," Stone said, not sure why he hadn't remembered her until she said her name. "Sato Yui, from the bar. How are you?"

"I'm burning up in this weather, seriously damp in a whole bunch of places, but otherwise very fine."

"And you cut your hair."

"Do you like it?"

"Absolutely."

"So, are you busy now?"

Was he? He wasn't sure. He tried to recall where he had been on his way to, but couldn't. He was aware of the heat pressing in on him from all sides, and of Sato Yui's eyes, which were like deep, dark pools of radiating light. This made no sense, he knew. Dark eyes filled with light, hot cold hearts, freezing to death in the middle of the worst heat wave on record. Anything seemed possible at this moment.

"You all right, Stone?"

"Just thinking about your eyes."

"I know. They are way too big for my face."

"I feel like I'm swimming in them. Does that sound crazy?"

"More like romantic as hell. Let's take a walk," she said, grabbing his arm and pushing him down the street.

Stone felt like a blind man being guided through the maze of some foreign city, maybe Tokyo, where everything was upside down and nothing made sense. Learn to appreciate the cultural differences. People from the other side of the world tend to behave unpredictably. They stand on their heads a lot and make fun of you for being upside down. No point trying to figure it out.

But that's what I do, Stone reminded himself. I figure things out.

Some things can't be figured, the voice of Sato Yui, apparently now inside his head, told him. Just go with the flow.

"Go with the flow," Stone repeated.

"Hey, that's what I was thinking," Sato Yui chirped.

They veered suddenly to the left, down a small alleyway littered with trash and debris, at the end of which was a door covered in rusty sheet metal. Sato Yui yanked it open with what Stone vaguely registered as impressive force and pulled him inside.

"Where are we?" he asked.

"Some kind of abandoned factory, I think. Creepy, huh? The kind of place a crime could happen in, don't you think?"

"Like a murder, you mean?"

"Yes! A murder. The body might never be found."

"Most never are."

"So, do you want to kiss me?" she asked, grabbing his head with both hands and pulling his face down to hers. Her hot lips were on his before he could formulate an answer, her tongue incising its way into his mouth.

"Why don't you unzip my shorts and touch me," she whispered. "To tell the truth, I'm not wearing any panties."

Stone, lacking the will to even consider resistance, did as he was told, pulling open the shorts and sliding his hand between her legs.

"Am I wet?" she asked, opening Stone's pants and pushing then down.

"Like a flood," he told her, beginning to rub the swollen flesh with his fingers.

"And you're stiff like a dead man," she laughed, stroking his cock with her small, powerful hand.

Stone closed his eyes and saw bright flashes of red light. He felt like he was being pulled out of his body through the top of his head. Sato Yui's grip on his erection was the only thing preventing him from total disembodiment; equal and opposite forces threatening to tear him in two. When he opened his eyes the dim basement was in the process of filling with a hot mist smelling of burning chemicals. Sato Yui, meanwhile, lighter than air, with the agility of a Chinese acrobat, was hanging from Stone's shoulders, her legs spread just above his erection. A deep, dangerous-sounding growl erupted from her throat as she lowered herself onto him. Stone gasped, struggling to breathe.

"Don't move," she whispered in his ear.

Even if I wanted to, he thought. He felt paralyzed, as if his life energy was being drained, siphoned off through the head of his penis.

"I love fucking in weird places," Sato Yui said. "Don't you?"

Standing up, with a girl hanging from his neck in some filthy, abandoned basement that had to be 100 degrees, at least. What was there not to love?

"Do you like my pussy?"

He tried to say yes, but all he could manage was a dribbling stammer. Sato Yui licked at his lips with her tongue, her breath in short, hot gusts against his face.

"I really want to come now," she said, digging what felt like very sharp fingernails into his shoulders. The sudden pain, as well as the warm, wet sensation of what was very likely blood running down his back, helped Stone focus his eyes. He was looking directly into hers, only the bottomless, black pools had been replaced by glowing, red warning lights, which burned their way directly into some very private part of his brain. "But my orgasm would mean your life, and I'm not quite ready to kill you."

Kill me, Stone thought, without fully understanding the meaning of the words.

"So, until next time, Stone," she laughed, sliding effortlessly off him, picking up her shorts and walking away.

"But…" he said, glancing down at his erection, which had taken on the appearance of some desperate, naked survivor in the midst of a natural disaster.

"Poor boy," she called back to him. "Why don't you just save it for Lisa? Or you could, you know, take care of it yourself."

Stone's eyes stayed glued on the small perfect oval of her bare behind until she disappeared into the mist.

Six

Lisa made it back to the Station in one piece, just barely. She felt like she had just run a marathon through Purgatory, or possibly on some airless planet much closer to the Sun than the Earth. Both her tee shirt and bra were soaking wet, uncomfortable in the extreme, with the added benefit that her nipples were now clearly visible. Ishikawa, on the other hand, though dressed for a brisk day in late October, hadn't even broken a sweat. Lisa had to wonder whether he was even human. Whether or not he was insane, she no longer wondered about. The extensive running he'd insisted on doing in one hundred plus degree heat, plus the close to orgasmic joy he displayed in the presence of a mutilated murder victim, had pretty much put that question to rest.

So the man enjoys running. That's hardly conclusive proof of mental impairment.

Okay, how about him pushing his nose into the fetid wounds of a corpse?

A dedicated cop who takes his work seriously.

Or possibly a lunatic on loan from the Japanese psycho ward.

And then there was his theory of the murders, briefly outlined to her on the ride back uptown. Maybe she had been a little light headed from all the physical exercise, but it definitely sounded crazy. Adding to her feeling of disorientation was the apparent disappearance of her partner. Stone had never made it to the Battery Park crime scene. His car, she had noticed, was still parked outside the station.

Ishikawa was already in her office, sipping on a bottle of water when she staggered in. A second bottle sat unopened on her desk.

"Don't tell me," she said. "You took the stairs."

"Elevators remind me too much of coffins," he told her.

"Isn't Japan like a country of elevators?"

"There is a small, but hard line group of us who refuse to ride in them."

"You're not involved in a cult, or anything like that, are you?"

"No," he smiled. "But I did take the liberty of purchasing a bottle of water for you."

"Thanks," she told him, unscrewing the cap and taking several substantial gulps. "Now I want you to do two more things for me."

"With pleasure, Detective."

"The first is close your eyes."

"Close my eyes?"

"Or you can just turn around."

"Is it a game?"

"No, I want to change my shirt. This one's rather wet."

Ishikawa jumped to his feet, turned and walked over to gaze out the small window in Lisa's office. "Your privacy is secured. And the second thing?"

Lisa pulled off her tee shirt and bra. In her locker she found a dry shirt, but no extra bra. She would be dry, but with no guarantee of nipple invisibility. Oh well.

"I would like to go over again what you were telling me in the car. Just to make sure I was hearing you correctly. And you can turn around again."

"Which part in particular?" Ishikawa asked, returning to his seat.

"For starters, that bit about our murderer being an ..."

"Akuma."

"Right. And an Akuma is ..."

"Think of it as a kind of demon."

"So not human."

"More accurately, both human and not human. But primarily not."

"You understand that it's not easy for me to accept this, from a rational point of view. I mean, as far as I know, most people do not believe in the existence of demons."

"Of course! I, myself, was such a person, a non-believer. I wasted much time and energy in order to disprove the possibility, but the conclusion was inevitable. Akuma. There is now no question in my mind."

Or, somewhere along the way you popped one screw too many and lost your mind.

"You must be thinking of me as a crazy Japanese."

"What? Now *that* is crazy."

"Consider the evidence so far, Detective. Does it make any sense rationally?"

"Admittedly, there are some gaps."

"People see what they want to see. It's never easy to accept the unacceptable."

"Okay, for the sake of argument, let' assume for the moment the whole demon thing is true, what do we do now?"

"We catch it."

"And how do we catch it?"

"Ah, that is the question I have been asking myself for many years."

"In other words, you don't know."

"No, but I do have a few promising theories. I also have some new software in my suitcase at the hotel that should be of great help."

"Software?"

"Technology is one of the two things we have exclusively on our side."

"What's the other thing?"

"A pure heart."

"Hmm."

"And now we must be off," Ishikawa announced, jumping to his feet and moving towards the door.

"To where, exactly?" Lisa asked.

"To your morgue. I must see the first two victims."

Stone came to, more than a little surprised to find himself lying in an alley, surrounded by garbage. His body felt like it had been in a train wreck, his brain more or less numb. His clothes, he realized, were wet, as if he'd been working out at the gym, which didn't seem likely. He was also aware of the intense heat and the absence of breathable air: Mid-day in a city on fire in the middle of a pile of garbage. All the years of hard work as a cop had obviously paid off. He was either hung over before noon – distressing enough, as he had no recollection of drinking – or simply losing his mind. The Stone magic had clearly crashed and burned. What was he without the magic? He thought of Lisa, of a kiss that should have happened, but didn't. How long ago had that been? And what about Ishikawa? Screw cultural differences, he thought, the guy was a weirdo, a first class freak, who was very likely already entertaining sexual fantasies about Lisa. Never underestimate the Asian's ability to be devious. He'd read that somewhere, back in the days when he still read. Not only was he losing his magic, he might also be losing his girl. Was Lisa his girl? Did he want her to be his girl? He had no idea what the hell he wanted.

Stone glanced down the alleyway to the street, which was currently filled with small, semi-transparent creatures, possibly made of overheated water vapor. Whatever they were, they all seemed to be watching him. Nevertheless, he had no choice but to pull himself up and get back to the real world, assuming such a thing still existed. His gun was still in its holster on his belt. If worse came to worst, he could always shoot his way out. All he had to do was get to the street. Not that going back to the station seemed like a good idea. He needed to take a shower and lie down. He would get to his car and go home. He could come up with plausible sounding excuses later.

Doctor Hammer was sitting on a stool, talking to the remains a young, blond woman stretched out on one of the dissecting tables when Lisa and Ishikawa entered the morgue.

"Detective Malone!" she said, smiling, unable to resist the temptation of glancing at the outline of Lisa's nipples through her shirt.

"Hope we're not interrupting anything," Lisa said.

"Not really. An apparent suicide, just brought in," she said, nodding towards the naked body."

"And you were questioning her?"

"More like commiserating. And you've brought a friend."

"This is Lieutenant Ishikawa, from Tokyo. He's, uh, assisting in our investigation of the recent murders."

"Really!" Hammer said. And then to Ishikawa, "*Konnichi wa. Hajimeimashite!*"

"*Domo,*" Ishikawa bowed. "*Nihon-go o hanashimasu ka?*"

"*Choto dake,*" Hammer said, returning the bow.

"I am very pleased with this turn of events," Ishikawa gushed.

"So I'm guessing you speak Japanese," Lisa said to Hammer.

"I sometimes listen to language tapes while I'm working. It relieves the tedium. How can I help you?"

"Lieutenant Ishikawa would like to examine the first two bodies."

"I suppose that can be arranged," Hammer said, motioning for them to follow her into the storage room. "So I've heard there's been a third."

"This morning at Battery Park. It should be here shortly."

"Something to look forward to. Was the victim a lawyer, by any chance?"

"Worked for an insurance company, I think"

"Oh well, but almost as good."

Hammer slid open the containers and removed the plastic coverings from the two bodies.

"Wonderful!" Ishikawa exclaimed, moving his face as close to the first body as possible, without actually submerging his head into the deep grayish wounds.

"He's sort of cute," she said to Lisa. "How's his mental health?"

"Not all the evidence is in on that yet," Lisa told her. "But it's not looking good."

"Quite beautiful," Ishikawa mused, running his hand lightly over one of the bodies. "A work of art in some sense, extreme, yes, gruesome, of course, but who are we to judge the direction and scope of the creative impulse."

"I see what you mean," Hammer said to Lisa. "So, Lieutenant Ishikawa, what's your connection to this case?

"Lisa answered before Ishikawa was able to. "We have reason to believe that the perpetrator may be Oriental, possibly female."

"Not female in the traditional sense," Ishikawa said without looking up. More a ..."

"Psycho-sexual Asian serial killer, with possible gender issues," Lisa quickly added.

"That's a mouthful," Hammer said, squinting at Lisa.

"No question," Ishikawa announced. "The wounds are consistent, the cutting indicative, the smell of sexual fury all too familiar."

"You can smell sex on a chilled corpse?" Hammer asked.

"I can smell Akuma."

"Akuma? I think I've heard that word before."

"I think he said a kuma," Lisa said. "Two words."

"If I remember correctly, a kuma is a bear."

"Yes. That's one theory we're currently working on," Lisa said, nudging Ishikawa towards the exit.

"Must we leave so soon?" Ishikawa asked.

"I think it's best," Lisa told him.

"A sexually enraged female bear is killing white collar professionals in New York City?" Hammer called after them.

"It's only a theory," Lisa shouted back, waving as she and Ishikawa disappeared through the swinging metal doors.

"This is all very exciting," Ishikawa said, stepping onto the elevator.

"I'm glad you think so," Lisa sighed.

"You should cheer up, Detective. I think we are getting close. I can ..."

"Smell it?"

"Yes!"

"Still, it might be a good idea not to tell everyone we meet about the whole demon thing."

"You may be right. Secrecy is, after all, the best policy."

"As opposed to honesty."

The elevator opened on the ground floor and Ishikawa bolted for the front door of the Station house.

"Where are you going now?" Lisa shouted.

"I must prepare for the hunt."

"But ..."

The elevator doors closed before she could finish the sentence. Just as well, as she had no idea what came after but. They opened again on Homicide and, of course, there stood the Captain, like some angry seismic event waiting to go off.

"Captain?" she said. "What a nice surprise!"

"My office, Malone," he either barked or growled. Lisa couldn't be sure which. "Now!"

She followed him in, closed the door and stood there waiting, feeling a bit like a high school girl just caught smoking in the bathroom.

"So, Detective Malone," he said, sliding into the chair behind his desk.

Lisa knew it was coming. She didn't exactly know what 'it' was, but she had to assume the worst. The Captain had figured everything out and was about to either fire her or have her arrested.

'Badge and gun on my desk, Malone.'

'At least give me a chance to explain, Sir.'

Anything you say at this point is only going to make things worse'.

"How about this weather then?" the Captain smiled.

"This weather?"

"Hottest summer in a Century, at least according to the imbecile who does the weather each night on Channel Eight."

"Yes, Sir. It, uh, has been hot."

"So we're in agreement about the weather."

"Absolutely, Captain. In fact, I ..."

"Let's see if there is anything else we can agree on, shall we? For instance, the obligation of all detectives to keep the head of their department informed on all ongoing cases in a regular, timely fashion. Does that sound at all reasonable to you?"

"Extremely reasonable, Sir."

"You know, I've been telling the same thing to your partner for the past ten years. Might as well be talking to some dead stiff down in the morgue. He'll never change and I'm tired of trying. The reason he still works in this Department is that, despite his insubordinate, fuck-you attitude towards authority, he gets results. You, on the other hand, Detective, are just starting out. You're young and still capable of learning, and one of the most important things you can learn is called following proper procedure. Am I making myself clear?

"As crystal, Captain."

"I'm glad to hear that. Now, Battery Park."

"Same M.O., same level of brutality as the first two victims. No obvious physical evidence at the scene, the victim's remains are probably already downstairs."

"So we definitely have a summer serial on our hands. Shit! Are you okay with this? You're sure you can handle these crime scenes?"

Once the dizziness and nausea subside, you mean?

"No problem, Sir."

"How did Lieutenant Ishikawa handle it?"

Pretty much like a deranged sex addict at a Las Vegas porno convention.

"Totally professional. He's also convinced that our murderer and his are one and the same."

"Progress of a sort, I suppose. Where is he now?"

"Uh, I think he went back to his hotel. He seemed a little tired."

"Probably the lingering affects of jet lag."

"That's just what I was thinking."

"And Stone?"

Your guess is as good as mine.

"He's, uh, following up on a possible lead in the case, uptown."

"This is all I ask," the Captain said, opening the small refrigerator and pulling out a bottle of apple juice. "Care for a cool beverage, Detective?"

"I'm fine, Sir."

"As long as I'm kept informed, I'm happy. Do I look happy to you, Malone?"

"You do, Captain."

"One more thing before you go, Detective, and please don't take this the wrong way. All things considered, I'm not sure it's a good idea for you not to be wearing underwear on the job."

"Sir?"

"Not that I either subscribe to or tolerate any sort of double standard in my precinct, but, frankly, the ease with which anyone can see your, uh, nipples is probably not conducive to the professional atmosphere I try to maintain around here."

"I think I can explain, Captain ..."

"No explanation required, Detective. Just consider it a friendly advisory aimed at correcting a minor oversight. Now get out of here. You've got an extremely disturbed felon to find."

At least one, Lisa thought, walking back towards her office. She couldn't decide which was worse, the fact that she had lied blatantly to the Captain, withholding what might turn out to be crucial information in the case, or that she had been reprimanded for having her nipples on public display. In the grand scheme of things, of course, her not wearing a bra was irrelevant. A crazed serial killer, of the demonic ilk, at least according to Ishikawa, was in the process of terrorizing the city. It was also hot enough to burn witches at the stake without lighting a fire. Her partner, renowned for his prowess in any number of areas, had disappeared without a word. She felt lost and in way over her head. And yet it was her nipples that everyone was worrying about. Go figure.

After trying to call Stone's cell phone several times, Lisa decided to forget everything and just go home. Stone would turn up eventually. He would offer up some nearly credible explanation for his erratic behavior, which she would accept in return for a kiss and the vague promise of a bliss-filled future, however short term. Meanwhile, death, madness and the worst heat wave of the modern era would all be there tomorrow, doing their thing. No one was going anywhere. The night would bake itself into an uncomfortable sleep, and in the morning she would put on a clean, dry bra and go to work.

Seven

Ishikawa switched off the air-conditioning and opened the window as far as it would go, allowing the overheated clamor from the street below to wash into his room. He had always found the ongoing chaos of a big city the perfect background noise, as emotionally soothing as it was mentally stimulating. Each city's sound was different, with its own unique vibration; and while Tokyo, his home, resonated closest to his heart, he had learned to appreciate each city's imprint upon him. Moscow, for example, focused its energy in the gut. It was a city in a constant state of indigestion. Paris, ostensibly a feast for the eyes, worked its real magic subconsciously, a city of romantic urges and uncontrollable dreams. New York, on the other end, traveled straight to the groin. It was a city of hard, erotic edges and cruel, sexual tension, the perfect environment for the Akuma. She would be stronger here, all her powers enhanced, but also more visible and therefore, at least in theory, more vulnerable. One could only hope.

Ishikawa took the sword from his suitcase, unsheathed it and placed it on the floor with the blade point facing east. He then removed his clothes, folding them carefully and placing them on the bed, then assuming the relaxed lotus position directly in front of the sword, letting his eyes relax on its shimmering, razor-sharp edge. He took several slow, deep breaths, allowing his thoughts to move freely, observing them without interference. It was an exercise he had practiced many times in the past, occasionally with some success. With a little luck, his mind would gradually become empty, his ego dissipated to a slim pinpoint of distant light, at which time the sensations of his adversary would come. He would become attuned to the Akuma's frequency, her violent sexual energy would enter him and he would know what he needed to know; again, in theory. There were no guarantees. It was possible that he would sense nothing and end up with little more than an excruciating headache, or sense too much and turn into a raving madman. This, he recalled, had been the fate of Ito, his only friend in the Top Secret Demon Hunting Unit. Cocky Ito, who had been a member of the Zen meditation club in high school, was certain that he could bring the demon out of hiding, see its present human disguise and divine its true intentions. Poor Ito couldn't have been more wrong. The ensuing disaster had not only robbed him of most of his mental faculties, but had also sent up a warning to the Akuma that it was perhaps the right time to take its gruesome show on the road. Never a big fan of overseas travel, Ishikawa had nonetheless been compelled to follow. Several years and many cities later had brought him here, to this point in the unfathomable time/space continuum. He knew the risks, but what other choice did he have? The trick was to remain totally focused, but at the same time absolutely non-resistant, like the proverbial twig floating in the stream, or, in deference to the Akuma, like the proverbial body floating in the river of blood. Either way, it was imperative that his own energy remained centered and secure high in his body, at the heart chakra, or higher. Anything lower, stomach, intestines, or, God forbid, genitals, could be disastrous.

He took the deepest breath he could manage and whispered, "Come to me, Akuma. Reveal yourself now."

It seemed to be working. The faint image of a female appeared before him. She floated in a fine mist, apparently struggling to keep from being recognized. You will not resist me, he thought. I will know your human form. Unfortunately, the woman who emerged from the mist was none other than his ex-wife Noriko, wearing the same bright red pantsuit she had been wearing the day she announced she was leaving the marriage. She did not appear happy to see him now. The divorce document had cited extreme emotional hardship and total abandonment, as well as pointing out that the husband in question suffered from an incurable mental illness.

According to the court, demon hunting was not a valid reason for neglecting one's wife, even if she happened to be somewhat of a demon herself. Were all women merely demons in disguise, he wondered? He couldn't really blame Noriko. Her naturally nosey nature had required answers, but he and the other members of his unit had taken an oath of secrecy. It had included the clause, 'Willing to accept death before revealing the truth of our mission.' Eliminating the Akuma from the face of the earth was their one and only priority. Family, friends, lovers, pets, all had to be sacrificed. Noriko never understood. Even after he had broken the oath, worn down by her constant badgering, and told her, she had not been appeased. But then, not believing in the existence of the Akuma, why would she be?

"Forgive me, Noriko," he said without actually speaking.

"How can I forgive you?" she asked. "You destroyed our marriage over an illusion, a sick obsession."

"But the Akuma is real, I tell you."

"Real?" she snapped. "I'll tell you what's real. How about you stealing the best years of my life, forcing to me to age prematurely? Just look at me! Do you have any idea how much money I've had to spend on skin care products, none of which work in the slightest?"

"I never meant to hurt you, Noriko."

"Go to Hell, Toshifumi!"

She had almost never used his given name.

He expected her to begin hurling curses at him and all his ancestors, or, more likely, break down with heart-wrenching sobs. Instead, Noriko began to cackle, a high-pitched hysterical laughter that was akin to sharpened bamboo sticks piercing his heart. He almost felt like weeping. Thanks to him, Noriko, his wife, had gone insane.

"Get a grip on yourself, Ishikawa," he whispered. "It is only the Akuma playing with your mind, taunting you with your own pathetic weakness."

Noriko continued to cackle. "You will die soon enough, Ishikawa," she shrieked. "Your death will be as gruesome as it is mundane. Few will attend your funeral and no one will mourn your sorry soul."

Taken aback by Noriko's mention of death, something she had always refused to speak about during their marriage, even at the occasional funerals they had attended together, Ishikawa struggled to remain calm.

He continued breathing deeply and steadily. Now was not the time to weaken. The main event was at hand, the grand entrance of the beast. He was sure she knew he was summoning her. She would not be able to resist the temptation to show herself to him. He felt a slight twitching in the muscles of his lower back, detected the faint aroma of burning sulfur, reminiscent of certain hot springs in Japan, the unbearable stench of which considered not only pleasant, but excellent for the health.

"Hello, Ishikawa San. I've been looking everywhere for you."

"And I you, abomination from Hell."

"Who, from where?"

Again, it was not the Akuma. This time it was Detective Malone. She was standing before him, smiling suggestively, her long, red hair moving on some undetectable breeze.

"You should not be here, Lisa," he told her. "It's not safe."

"But I really wanted to see you," she said, beginning to undo the buttons of her shirt.

Something was very wrong here, but he wasn't sure what to do about it.

"Don't you want to help me undress?" Lisa asked, dropping her shirt and unzipping her jeans. "When you had your mouth between my legs yesterday, I really liked it."

Such a thing never happened, Ishikawa assured himself.

He watched, helpless, as she removed her bra and slipped her panties off. She stroked her breasts, running her hands down over her taut belly into the lush, auburn hair covering her most private of areas.

"Detective Malone, you must stop this and get dressed immediately!"

"Sorry, no can do," she told him, licking one of her fingers and sliding it between her legs. "Mind if I play with myself while we chat?"

"I absolutely do mind," he insisted.

"Funny, it doesn't look that way to me."

Ishikawa glanced down and realized that the worst had happened. While watching Lisa, he had gotten an erection. His meditative energy was being sucked downward, leaving him light-headed and virtually helpless. He tried willing it into submission, at least softening it somewhat, but that only made it more defiant. As if mocking him, it actually grew in stature and began to sway back and forth like some sexually agitated pendulum. In the same instant the sword started vibrating, the blade point slowly rotating until it was pointed directly at his groin. Just outside the window something howled, a pungent cloud filled the room, wrapping itself around him, burning his skin and making it difficult to breathe. The Akuma had found him, infiltrated unseen, rendering him a sitting duck, as they say. This was an unfortunate turn of events, not to mention a total failure on his part. The years of training, the countless acts of purification, the avoidance of earthly pleasures, all aimed at making him a worthy adversary of the Akuma. It had been nothing more than an exercise in self-delusion. Noriko had been right. He was a hopeless failure, clearly no match for the beast. The Akuma, of course, had known this all along and she was no doubt laughing at him. The Akuma was laughing, as was Noriko and by now probably Detective Malone, as well. He had become a laughing stock, a pathetic object of female (both human and inhuman) ridicule. Not that it mattered much now. Ishikawa knew that sometime within the next few minutes he would most likely be dead.

Lisa made it back to her apartment without completely succumbing to heat exhaustion. The promise of cool air and an icy alcoholic drink had made it possible. Filling the bathtub with ice and diving in wasn't too extreme to consider. With any luck the resulting brain damage wouldn't be permanent, nothing more than the loss of a few I.Q. points and maybe some short term memory. Which would suit her just fine. No knowledge or memory of the case, no recollection of three mutilated corpses, definitely nothing to connect her to Ishikawa and his insane demon theory. And while she was at it, she also wouldn't mind forgetting about the feelings she was starting to have for her increasingly odd and unpredictable partner.

And the memory of the sex with said partner?

In that area, new memory can be made.

Sure, just keep making the same mistakes.

How can great sex ever be a mistake?

And I suppose it hasn't occurred to you that all the weird stuff started at more or less the same time you decided to start indulging in this 'great sex' with your partner.

Ever hear of coincidence?

Are you even listening to yourself?

Look, leave me alone! I'm hot, tired and hardly in the mood.

Okay, maybe the ice-bath-induced mental impairment wasn't such a good idea. No way she had that much ice, anyway. All she needed was a little down time, a bit of R&R in her own private space, away from the craziness for a few hours. Not to be. First obstacle to the plan, the door to her apartment was neither locked nor shut. Someone had broken into her place, someone might still be in her place, stealing her worthless jewelry, or rifling through her underwear drawer. Just what she needed, some strung out moron who just happened to break into a cop's apartment. What were the odds?

Lisa removed the Beretta from the holster on her hip, assumed the standard crouching tiger position taught at the police academy and eased her way through the front door. The light was dim, no sound discernible, aside from the hum of the air conditioner. Had she left the air conditioning on? She crept into the living room, scanned it quickly and moved into the adjoining kitchen, quietly opening the refrigerator, just to make sure the intruder hadn't snatched her cold beer. The beer was untouched and the temptation to open one too great to resist. She figured that if anyone came out of the bedroom carrying a pillowcase filled with her bras and panties, she could put one in his leg, phone it in and finish the beer before the backup arrived on the scene.

One gulp of the cold liquid and her body relaxed a bit. It was then that she heard it, definitely coming from the bedroom, the distinct sound of someone snoring. Placing the beer bottle on the counter, she moved quickly down the hallway to the bedroom door. It occurred to her that she had never shot anyone before, had never had the opportunity. Did this qualify as a legitimate reason to discharge her weapon? Some creep breaks into your place and decides to take a nap in your bed. If that didn't qualify for a bullet, what did?

So you're saying Detective that the sleeping man resisted arrest?

He turned abruptly in a way that I interpreted as a threatening gesture.

In other words, turning over in his sleep.

He was in my bed.
You've also stated that you believed the man was holding a weapon.
I thought he was, yes.
Which in fact turned out to be a pair of your panties.
The man was obviously a pervert.
So you shot him three times in the chest.
I'll admit that one bullet probably would have sufficed.

Enough, Lisa told herself. We're way past second-guessing our actions. She turned the doorknob and nudged the door open an inch or so. Deciding to go in hard, she took a step back, kicked the door open and ran into the room, her weapon flailing.

"All right, asshole," she shouted. "One move and your snoring days are over, permanently."

At the same moment the shadowy intruder in her bed raised its head and mumbled something incoherent. It sounded a bit like Chinese.

"Do you speak English?" she shouted, taking a careful step towards the bed.

"Why are you yelling?" the intruder asked her.

Wait a minute, she knew that voice, recognized the blurry shape of the intruder's head.

"Stone?" she asked.

"Lisa, is that you? What's going on here?"

Lisa holstered her weapon and walked over to the bed.

"That was going to be my next question," she said.

"But why are you here?"

"Aside from the fact that you are in my bed, you mean?"

"Your bed?"

"Whose bed did you think you were in?"

Stone rubbed his face, groaned and fell back on the pillow.

"What the hell happened to you?" Lisa asked, sitting down next to him and touching his arm. She felt confused. Clearly she should be annoyed that Stone had broken into her apartment, but she was also feeling a little turned on finally having him in her bed. Did it really matter how he got there? Okay, it mattered. She would have to get to the bottom of it, but was there any huge rush?

"So you have no idea how you got here?"

"No, not really. The last thing I remember is coming to in some alley."

"Were you attacked?"

"Feels like I was. Shit! Maybe I'm losing my memory, or even more distressing, my mind."

"That would be terrible," Lisa said sympathetically. "But let me ask you another question. Are you wearing any clothes under my sheets?"

Stone reached under the covers and did a quick inspection. "Actually, no."

"Interesting," Lisa said, kicking off her shoes and lying down next to her sexy, possibly brain-damaged partner.

Doctor Hammer had decided to remain in the lab after hours to finish up with victim number three, the late John Wilbur, assistant vice president for a large insurance company. John, or what was left of him, lay quietly on one of the stainless steel dissecting tables. His wounds reminded Hammer of photos she'd seen of shark attack victims. And while there was little doubt in her mind that Wilbur had fallen prey to the same killer of dead men numbers one and two, there were differences in this one's wounds. These were less precise, more randomly violent, as if the killer was reaching for new levels of insane fury. What would victim number four look like, she wondered? How much more injury could be inflicted upon a human body? She had to admit that she was slightly excited to find out, from a professional point of view only, needless to say.

"Well, John," she said, as she began to probe the first of several deep incisions in the victim's chest. "May I call you John? I'm not going to lie to you and say there's any chance you might recover from this. You're a mess, almost non-recognizable as a human being. On the brighter side, it's pretty much a given that you had a damn good life insurance policy, hopefully one with a double indemnity clause for unnatural death. That should at least soothe the widow's sorrow. What? Not married? What about next of kin? Perhaps some mentally challenged second cousin who you spent your entire life trying to avoid? I know what you're thinking, John. There is no justice in this life, neither is there any in death."

Further stimulating Hammer's curiosity was what the Japanese policeman Ishikawa had said about the killer's identity. A simple Internet search had confirmed that, according to legend, the Akuma was a type of Japanese female demon, extremely powerful and motivated exclusively by the need to commit sexual homicide; in other words, an inhuman sex-crazed monster with a penchant for mutilating and murdering her victims, almost always men. Not to be confused in any way with some of the more extreme radical feminist factions currently operating in the Tristate area.

"Death by supernatural intervention," Hammer mused, extracting what looked like a fragment of black claw from Wilbur's chest cavity. "Seems like our girl broke a nail while she was busy eviscerating you, John. She's getting sloppy. Hey, they always do, although, if we're willing to entertain the hypothesis that you were killed by a Japanese demon, there is no 'they'. This is a first, which, if you think about it, makes the whole experience sort of special for you. And now, if you don't mind, I'm going to examine your genital area."

John Wilbur's penis told pretty much the usual story, traces of semen, some other fluid not readily identifiable, almost certainly having engaged in sex just prior to death. The M.O. of a demon, sex equaled death, one inevitably evolved into the other. On some level it made perfect sense. It was only man-made convention that kept the two artificially separated. At least John got off just before he died. Some people cling to life so hard they never get off.

"And what have we here?" Hammer asked, extracting a long, black hair from John's inner thigh. "Definitely not yours. I won't even bother asking how it got there."

"How do you think it got there?" a woman's voice asked.

Doctor Hammer felt the flesh on the back of her neck bristle. She turned her head in the direction of the voice and noticed that the autopsy room was rapidly filling with a pungent chalky gray fog. This was, needless to say, highly unusual. Autopsy rooms were generally not susceptible to fog-like conditions; maybe in San Francisco, but not here. She tried to stand up, but a hand (whose hand, she couldn't help wondering?) placed firmly on her shoulder prevented her from moving.

"Leaving so soon, Doctor?"

"Who are you?" Hammer asked nervously.

"I think you already know," the voice whispered into her ear.

"I have no idea."

"That's disappointing. My work is lying right there in front of you."

Hammer glanced down at John Wilbur and shuddered. "What do you want?"

"I'm not exactly sure. Maybe I just enjoy listening to you talk to dead bodies. Why do you do that? Do you think they can hear you?"

Before Hammer could answer a second hand began to gently caress her neck, then move slowly down the front of her white lab coat.

"Or maybe, like you, I'm just a disturbed romantic, hopelessly attracted to the darker elements of experience."

Despite the blurring effect of the fog, Hammer was able to confirm that the hand busy unbuttoning her lab coat was human, most likely belonging to a female of diminutive stature, which, judging by the strength of the hand holding her in place, seemed illogical.

"I'm so fascinated by what you do," the voice continued. "Faced with meaningless brutality, you discover meaning, extracting small, but significant truths from the great lie of random death."

"I try," Hammer managed, the pain in her shoulder beginning to radiate to her neck and down her back.

"You're too modest, Doctor Hammer. Taking pride in one's accomplishments is perfectly natural. Being the best at what we do is all that matters. Don't you agree?"

Hammer, biting her lip to divert the pain, nodded agreement.

The roaming hand, meanwhile, had worked its way inside her blouse and was gently stroking her breasts. She heard the crisp tear of fabric and felt her bra slide away. The hand was cold against her skin, the fingers beginning to knead the flesh around her left nipple.

"I love your tits, Doctor. They're large, aren't they? Voluptuous. I bet men spend a lot of time thinking about your tits. Tell me, in the heat of passion has a lover ever become so excited that he or she made you bleed? From your nipples, I mean."

The sudden intense pressure of thumb and index finger on her nipple, the sharp nails cutting into the delicate flesh, made Hammer cry out.

"Do you like it, Beverly?"

"No," Hammer said, her voice trembling. "Please stop."

The small, powerful fingers shifted to the right nipple and began squeezing.

"Maybe you didn't understand the question. You like what I'm doing to your nipples, don't you?"

"Yes, I like it," Hammer said, fighting back tears.

"Of course you do, because you understand that without pain there can be no real pleasure. And as we both know, the secret lubricant of love is warm, fresh blood."

The hand abandoned her nipples and emerged from inside her blouse, the small delicate fingertips smeared red.

"Your blood, Beverly," the voice told her, the bloody fingers lightly touching Hammer's lips."

Hammer had the sudden urge to bite the hand, possibly take off a fingertip, but she resisted. She swallowed hard and began to sob.

"I'd love to stay and play, Doctor Hammer, but unfortunately I have an appointment to get to. But don't worry. I'm sure we'll meet again."

With that, the painful pressure on her shoulder subsided, the fog dissipated and Hammer was once again alone in the autopsy room, sitting next to the battered remains of John Wilbur.

Eight

It hadn't taken Lisa long to conclude that the most direct route through the recent confusion and professional missteps, not to mention the optimal solution to the present moment's lingering oddness, was sex. Okay, maybe it wouldn't exactly solve anything, but it would definitely improve her mood. Besides, she was a firm believer in trying to work with whatever circumstances were thrown at her; in this case, the inexplicable presence of her partner's naked body in her bed.

She eased her hand under the sheets and began to play with the coarse hair on Stone's chest, periodically grazing the nipples with her fingertips. He reacted to this by not reacting at all, unless one could call simulating a near catatonic state a reaction. A more direct approach was obviously called for. There was one component of Stone's anatomy that she knew would commiserate with her desire, so she abandoned the furry plateau and headed south, into the tropics, where life-affirming heat was pretty much a given. As her fingers glided over his muscled belly Stone began to breathe noisily through his nose, reminiscent of an old man with a chronic sinus condition. Lisa was not deterred. She knew that his penis would be alive and well, immune to whatever brain impairment might be afflicting its owner. But then predicting the future was never going to be a sure thing. Lisa knew this as well as anyone, but it did little to lessen her shock at discovering Stone's until now sure bet hard-on shrunken and, apparently, sound asleep.

"Stone," she asked, "Are you sure you're all right?"

"I guess so," he said. "Why?"

"Why? What about this?" she said, poking his penis with a finger.

"Ouch," he said. "And what about it?"

"Well, for one thing, it's not even remotely hard."

"What can I say? It sometimes behaves that way."

"Not in my experience, it doesn't."

"Look, Lisa, give me a break. I've been through a lot recently."

"I thought you had no memory of what you've been through recently."

"That's right. So ..?"

"So, if you have no memory of what you've been through, how could you know that you've been through a lot?"

"Is this some kind of interrogation?"

"Yeah, as opposed to foreplay."

"Jesus, what's with you?"

"Why are you being such a wimp?"

"Why are you being such a bitch?"

"Hold on there a minute, Mister mentally impaired, breaking and entering Detective guy. Did you just call me a bitch?"

"I may have. I can't really remember."

"How convenient for you."

"Come on, Lisa," Stone said, putting his arm around her shoulder and pulling her towards him. "Can't we just lie here together for awhile?"

It occurred to Lisa that she probably was being a bitch, a needy, selfish bitch, in fact. Her shrink, if she had been stupid and desperate enough to actually have a shrink, would no doubt tell her that she was projecting her anxiety and fear of relationship onto Stone. And despite the fact that the concept of projection was incomprehensible to her, she would be forced to accept it because her shrink had said so. He would go on to point out, with as much irony-soaked smugness as he could muster, that Lisa's apparent compulsion to turn Stone into a mere object of sexual satisfaction was nothing more than an attempt to deny the real feelings she was having for him. Forget about homicidal demons, love was the scary boogieman in the room.

"I'm sorry," she said, snuggling up to him.

She rubbed her face against his cheek, which felt a little like exfoliating with course sandpaper, but she didn't care. She adored his three-day growth of beard. She kissed his nose, ran her fingers through his wild hair. She tugged him closer, rubbing the back of his neck, caressing his shoulder. Which is when she discovered the scratches on his back.

"Oh my god," she said, probing the wounds with her fingers.

Stone flinched. "What the hell is that?"

"Let me see," Lisa told him, pushing him over onto his stomach to get a better look. There were six parallel incisions, purplish-black and still moist with blood, three of them running from the upper edge of each shoulder to just below the shoulder blade. "How did this happen?

"I have no idea," Stone said, straining to look over his shoulder at the wounds. "What does it look like?"

"Just lie still," she ordered, pushing his head down, grabbing some tissues from the box beside the bed and dabbing lightly at the wounds. "My best guess is that either you were recently flogged, or attacked by a large predatory bird, possibly a hawk."

"Doubtful."

"Or you've recently engaged in sadomasochistic sex with some psycho slut you met in a bar."

"Definitely not."

"How can you be sure, suffering as you are from temporary memory loss?"

"That I would remember."

"There is one way to be sure," Lisa said, pulling back the covers, shifting Stone's body and moving her face down to his crotch.

"Okay, what are you doing, Lisa?"

"I'm smelling your cock."

"That is so ridiculous."

"Exactly what a guilty, memory-impaired cheater would say."

"And?"

"Oddly enough, it smells faintly of rotten eggs."

"Maybe I had sex with a sadomasochistic chicken."

"You're a guy. Anything is possible."

"Oh please!"

"In any case, you should definitely take a shower, after which I'll put some anti-bacterial cream on these wounds."

"Good idea," Stone said, sliding out of bed and walking unsteadily towards the bathroom.

Ishikawa opened his eyes to the blare of car horns and a chorus of angry voices shouting from somewhere nearby. Were they yelling at him? Had he committed some cultural faux pas that had agitated a mob into action? It didn't seem likely. As far as he could tell, he was still in his hotel room. He was lying on the floor, a hot, wet wind smelling of human anxiety and day-old garbage flapping the curtains at the open window. Neon streaked shadows ran across the ceiling.

And, perhaps more importantly, he was still alive.

Attempting to sit up, he felt the pain. Touching the source, he found the wound, a thin cut running diagonally across his abdomen. There was blood on his fingers. The sword, lying next to him on the floor, also had a thin coating of blood along its edge. He had been cut with his own sword.

"So interesting!" Ishikawa exclaimed, struggling to his feet and grabbing his white boxers from the bed. Not only had the Akuma resisted its natural urge to kill him, it had demonstrated a sense of humor by marking him with his own weapon. Was that irony? He could never be certain, irony being such a murky concept, particularly for the Japanese. Maybe it had something to do with the fact the word irony in Japanese was *hiniku*, comprised of two Chinese characters that translate as skin and meat. Irony equaled skin-meat. Obvious, perhaps, to fuzzy university professors with no experience of the real world, but he had never quite gotten it. Then along comes a demon that provides a practical application of the idea. The skin is cut, but the meat beneath it is left untouched, saved, perhaps, for a more spectacular demonstration of the concept later on.

Clearly, the Akuma was evolving, becoming more complex, from a straightforward, homicidal sex fiend to a more sophisticated demon, a demon capable of applying the tricky concept of irony. This made Ishikawa smile, not only because it defied all the official rules of demonology, but also because a more complex Akuma, an Akuma that had incorporated wry humor into its deadly arsenal, would be more inclined to make mistakes and therefore, theoretically, easier to hunt and kill. Yes, it seemed to make sense.

Instead of putting on his boxer shorts, Ishikawa used them to wipe the blood from his stomach and threw them on the floor. He took his suitcase from the closet, removed the flash drive from its secret compartment and inserted it into the laptop on the desk. The files he had discreetly removed from Detective Malone's office were waiting in the inside pocket of his trench coat. The same Detective Malone who, a short time earlier, had removed her clothes and attempted to pleasure herself in front of him.

No, Ishikawa, he told himself. Do not go there. Indulging in sexual fantasies about beautiful Caucasian police detectives is not part of your present agenda. There is no room in your well-regulated and highly disciplined brain for such things. Banish such thoughts now! Besides, there is serious work to be done.

He had the information he needed and the technology to apply it. He had the experience and the correct state of mind. And now he also had irony. What more was required? The next move was his. From the room's small refrigerator, he took a mini-sized bottle of whisky, poured it into a glass and sat down in front of the computer.

Draining half the glass, he reached out a very determined finger and hit the return key.

The program, originally developed by his team and upgraded periodically over the past few years by Ishikawa himself, was designed to analyze the Akuma's attack patterns on any given spatial grid – in this case, New York City – and then extrapolate with a high degree of probability the approximate time and location of future attacks. For all its dark intelligence and creature-like cunning, the demon was not entirely free of constraint. Ishikawa believed these were instinctual, similar to animal migration patterns, or mating rituals, and also environmental, based upon both the physical and psychic attributes of the space in which the demon was operating. In a sense it was the city itself that determined the Akuma's hunting schedule.

The fact that the program had been less than entirely successful in the past Ishikawa ascribed to the incoherent natures of the cities in question, rather than to the technology. Most large cities were ill defined, physically illogical and for the most part unfathomable. New York, on the other hand, so skilled at suggesting out of control chaos, was, from a physical point of view, entirely rational, predictable, verging on mundane. As the saying went, it's easy to lose your mind in New York, but almost impossible to lose your way.

From the police reports of the fist two murders, Ishikawa entered the locations and approximate times the attacks took place. He knew the location of the third attack and, based upon his own inspection of the body, his best educated guess of the time. With these data points, plus the secret algorithm he himself had invented, the program would pinpoint the details of the next attack and display it on a highly accurate two-dimensional grid corresponding to the island of Manhattan.

Ishikawa poured the remainder of the whisky, smiled and waited.

Lisa hated ambivalence, didn't really believe in it. Do it or don't do it, but spare me the wishy-washy uncertainty, was her motto, or one of them, anyway. So why was she feeling ambivalent about joining Stone in the shower?

Well, let's see. He is acting on the strange side and there's a good chance he's been screwing around behind your back.

So, big deal! So he screwed some long finger-nailed bimbo in a moment of impulsive male stupidity. Guys do that.

But Stone is not just some guy. He's the guy that's gotten under your skin, making you go all mushy- soft and doe eyed.

That's just pure crap. Stone is nothing more than a means to an end, namely a sumptuous, time-arresting orgasm, or, even better, two.

You are so in denial.

And you are really starting to piss me off.

Lisa slipped out of her clothes and walked quietly into the bathroom. She opened the shower stall door and stepped into a thick cloud of steam. Only the blurry outline of Stone's body was visible through the warm mist. She stepped towards him, at the same time reaching out her hand and lightly touching his arm. Stone's reaction to this was completely unpredictable. He jumped, his body spinning rapidly around like some deranged dervish in a Turkish steam bath, until he was looking directly at her.

"Who are you?" he demanded, his eyes wide, dark and fearful.

"It's me," Lisa told him, gently rubbing his arm. "Are you all right?"

"Sorry," Stone said. "I think maybe I blacked out for a minute."

"You're starting to worry me," she said, slipping both arms around his waist and pulling him towards her.

"Yeah," he said, resting his face against her shoulder. "I'm starting to worry myself."

Poor baby Stone, she thought. He was like a frightened little boy with a boo-boo. A tinge of guilt flitted through her brain. Her own sexual desire had blinded her to his needs, although, at this point, she wasn't exactly sure what those were. Still, she knew he was hurting. He was more like a battered puppy or a lost child than a tough he-man cop. He was her soaking wet little puppy dog with a ... big, fat erection.

"Jesus!" Lisa said.

"A totally unreliable witness," Stone muttered.

"You're telling me," she said, torn between interrogating the intruder that was pressed firmly against her stomach and simply ignoring it.

It was probably just a physiological response to stress, something guys did when they were hurt, falling apart and temporarily unhinged. What had Hammer said about hanged men with hard-ons? The last thing on Stone's mind right now was sex, his erection more a call for help than a desire to engage in any sort of erotic behavior. What he required was her reassuring touch, but not there, anywhere but there.

But it's calling out to me.

Can't you ever think of anyone but yourself?

But...

Lisa suddenly felt herself being pushed backwards towards the opposite wall of the shower. She hit with a wet thump, her head banging painfully against the tiles.

"What the hell are you doing?" she cried.

By way of reply, Stone offered a guttural growl reminiscent of sounds made by agitated apes squabbling over food.

Gorilla in the mist, Lisa thought to herself, just as Stone's body landed hard against hers. With one hand he grabbed her hair, the other slipped under her right thigh, lifting her body and spreading her legs apart, pinning her to the wall. He entered her with the force of a missile launch, forcing the air from her lungs in a wet gasp.

He fucked her hard and fast, like a machine, like a maniac, a beast, hurting her, making her scream and come repeatedly.

"You fucking bastard," she screamed. "If I survive this, I swear I'll kill you."

"Kill me," Stone repeated.

"No, I won't kill you. I'll just cut your balls off."

"Do it!" Stone howled, ejaculating into her with the intensity of an out of control fire hose.

"Son of a bitch," Lisa said, shivering through one final orgasm.

Stone groaned like a man who had just been punched hard in the gut, then collapsed on the shower floor, pulling Lisa down on top of him. She pushed herself away from him, but was unable to stand up. She just sat there, her back pressed against the tiles watching the water from the shower splatter against his body.

Nine

"**I** did what?" Stone asked, his voice trembling.

He was sitting on Lisa's bed, a bath white towel wrapped around his waist. After the water had turned cold, Lisa had forced herself to get up and drag Stone out of the shower. It was either that, or let him drown. Somehow she had managed to get him back to her bed.

"Not to put too fine a point on it," she told him, brushing her hair in the bathroom mirror. "But you sexually assaulted me."

"Get out of here," he said. "I'm not the kind of person who would do something like that."

"You're a guy, right?"

"I swear to you, Lisa. I have no memory of us having sex in the shower."

"Maybe you recall banging my head against the wall? No? Okay, how about coming inside me?"

"I'm really sorry, but the last thing I remember is ..."

"Yeah, I know, waking up in an alley."

"I was going to say standing in the shower, alone."

Lisa walked into the bedroom wearing a pair of pale green pajamas. She generally didn't wear pajamas. They reminded her of growing up in her father's house, where sleeping in the nude was considered a sign of sexual perversity and quite possibly the influence of Satan himself. Girls, apparently, were especially susceptible to evil impulses. But after her shower encounter with Stone, she was feeling vulnerable. She also couldn't entirely rule out the possibility that her partner was possessed by the Devil.

"I see two possibilities," she told him. "Either you're lying, or you're seriously fucked up."

"Well, I'm not lying," he said, dropping back onto the bed.

Lisa went and sat down next to him. She was no longer feeling angry about what had happened. Stone was obviously going through something and, in fact, all things considered, the sex had been way up there on the satisfaction scale. Anytime a girl loses count of the number of orgasms she's having, the experience can't be viewed as all bad. Besides, if there was anyone to blame it was Stone's cock, which obviously had a mind of its own and a zero concept of polite behavior in stressful situations.

"Look," she said. "Maybe we should just go to the hospital emergency room and have you checked out."

"Just what I need, official confirmation that I'm losing it. The Captain is already thinking I'm not up to this case."

The case, Lisa thought to herself. It all came suddenly shrieking back; three mutilated bodies, Ishikawa, a Japanese demon prowling the city streets. She had intended to fill Stone in on the whole demon slant, but now had to wonder if the news might not push him totally over the edge. He may have been a brain damaged sex offender, but he was also firmly grounded in the school of cop realism - hard facts, tangible evidence and plausible solutions. Throwing a demon into the works at this point was not going to be helpful.

"How about we just get some sleep and see how things feel in the morning?" Lisa suggested.

"Sounds good," he said. "But how about a drink first?"

"I think we can handle that."

Lisa put ice in two glasses, added scotch, the ideal nightcap, no water, of course, and carried them back into the bedroom. As she handed one glass to Stone, his cell phone started to ring.

"Don't answer it," she told him.

"It could be important," he said.

"Not if you don't answer it."

It was Hogan; sounding like he'd recently washed down half a bottle of sleeping pills with a pint of bourbon and was calling to ask when he could expect the coma to kick in.

"Stone," he drawled. "Glad I caught you."

"Hey, Hogan. Are you all right?"

"Not sure about that, but I thought this might interest you. Had an anonymous call about an hour ago, some woman reporting strange activity on the top floor of an uptown tenement."

"What kind of strange activity?"

"Something about a glowing red fog and some kind of weird howling."

"Our red-eyed Chinese mystery lady."

"It crossed my mind, what's left of it, that is. Anyway, call it sick curiosity, or straight up brain-aching insomnia, but I'm going to head over there and check it out. Thought you might want to join me."

"Yeah, sure. Give me the location."

"115th and First, northeast corner."

"Right next door to our second dead guy."

"The perp sometimes actually does revisit the scene."

"Okay, I'll get there as soon as I can, and listen, Hogan, wait for me."

"Don't worry. I'm too fucking old to be playing the hero."

"I don't think you should go," Lisa said, watching Stone get dressed."

"It's sort of my job," he told her.

"Except that you're not well."

"I'm actually feeling much better."

"Really? What did I just say?"

"You told me that I'm not well. See? I remembered."

"Which proves nothing."

"As I'm sure this lead will prove to be, but, you know, we are looking for a seriously deranged motherfucker who will only keep killing until we stop him."

"If it is a him," Lisa offered

"What else could it be?" Stone asked.

How about a Japanese she-demon?

Lisa shrugged. "At least let me go with you."

"No, it's better that you get some rest. After all, you were recently assaulted, sexually."

"Not funny."

"Sorry. And don't worry. I'm sure Hogan and I can handle this, whatever it is. I'll fill you in tomorrow."

"Fine," Lisa sighed, watching him leave.

"And I'll have someone stop by to fix your front door first thing in the morning."

Lisa fixed herself another drink, and then walked aimlessly around the apartment. She felt too agitated to sleep, which, all things considered, wasn't unreasonable. Things just kept getting crazier and, contrary to popular belief, the home was no haven from it. She decided to get into bed and watch a little late night TV. First, the pajamas had to go. If by some miracle she managed to fall asleep wearing them, she was certain she would wake up back in Merlin, Ohio, her father shouting at her from the bottom of the stairs to get her lazy butt up out of bed.

An unbidden flashback of her father standing in her room reminding her that slugabeds never got anywhere in life, as she cowered under the covers totally nude. It was just more comfortable sleeping naked and it made it easier for her to touch herself, something she was pursuing at the time with what might be described as a near-obsessive fervor.

"Are you going to get up, young lady?"

"As soon as you leave, I will."

"I'm not budging until you are out of that bed."

"Have it your way," she had said, pulling the covers back and standing up.

The chords in her father's neck had audibly creaked, his jaw dropped and his eyes clouded over. It was the last time he came into her room in the morning, although he never lost an opportunity to espouse the virtues of bedtime clothing. Young women of virtue did not sleep in the altogether. It hadn't taken Lisa long after that to realize that she was most likely not a young woman of virtue.

She slipped naked under the covers and hit the remote. As usual, there were lots of channels but nothing on. She pressed a number randomly and landed on a movie station showing an old black and white Japanese sci-fi film. There were lots of people in gray uniforms running around and shouting, then shots of women and children running along the road screaming. The voice-overs in English reminded her of conversations she had had with Ishikawa, minus the hysteria. In any case, something was obviously very wrong. She didn't understand what it was until the giant, prehistoric-looking bird appeared and began to destroy Tokyo. A group of scientists dressed like deep-sea divers was summoned by the military and ordered to dispose of the giant bird, but Lisa dozed off before they could figure out how to accomplish this.

She dreamed that she was sitting on a chair in an unfamiliar room. She was, needless to say, naked. There was a television in the corner, its screen filled with white, humming static. From an adjoining room she could hear voices. She was certain one of them was Stone's. Apparently she was waiting for him. Suddenly the door of this other room opened and a small Japanese woman wearing a black and gold kimono entered. Lisa wanted to look at her face, but felt that she wasn't supposed to. The woman began to walk slowly around the room, coming to a stop just behind Lisa. She felt the woman's hands on her shoulders, rubbing her gently for a moment before slowly moving her hands down to Lisa's breasts. She lightly touched the nipples with her fingertips, making Lisa shudder.

"Stone will be out soon," the woman whispered. "He and I were just fucking. His cock is so big, don't you think?"

Lisa wanted to speak, but she realized that her mouth was full of blood. She glanced down and noticed that the blood was dripping from her lips onto her breasts and stomach, thin red rivulets running into her pubic hair.

At that moment another door opened and Lisa's father walked in. He was wearing an old-looking army uniform, possibly World War II vintage.

"Daddy?" Lisa tried to say, but with all the blood in her mouth it sounded like the watery moan of some ocean creature.

"How many times have I told you, young lady," her father said sternly. "I will tolerate neither nudity nor lesbian perversity under my roof!"

Lisa tried to say that the woman toying with her nipples was not a lesbian, but rather a demon, quite likely from Hell.

Daddy ignored her, leering instead at the kimono-clad fiend. "So, why don't you introduce me to your Oriental friend?"

Lisa jerked awake and sat up on bed. She felt as if all the air had been sucked from her lungs. On the TV the giant bird and another smaller bird, possibly the big bird's offspring, were flying off into the sunset. As she glanced at the clock on the bedside table, her cell phone started ringing. She grabbed it and pressed the connect key.

"Stone?" she asked expectantly.

"In a manner of speaking," a familiar voice informed her. "I am Ishikawa."

"Ishikawa?" Lisa said, slightly confused.

"I hope you are not sleeping at this moment."

I don't know, am I? Lisa wondered. "Unless you're calling me in a dream, or I'm talking on the phone in my sleep, I must be awake."

"That makes sense," Ishikawa confirmed.

"May I ask *why* you are calling me?"

"Certainly, you may," Ishikawa said.

Silence. Lisa waited, listening to the click of digital seconds passing.

"Okay," she finally said. "Why are you calling me?"

"I have a significant lead on the Akuma," he said excitedly.

"No," Lisa moaned, sinking down into the bed. "Not the Akuma."

"Oh yes. The entire case could be resolved tonight, but we must act swiftly."

"We?"

"After all we've been through together, I thought you might want to be a participant in the mission."

Had she and Ishikawa been through a lot together?

"And the mission is ..?"

"I believe I know where the Akuma will strike next. I intend to be there to prevent this attack and, with the help of various god-like entities that I scarcely believe in, defeat the beast once and for all."

"Sounds ambitious," Lisa yawned. "And do you know when?"

"To the best of my calculations, in exactly eighty seven minutes."

"Eighty seven minutes?"

"Well, a bit closer to eighty six now."

"Are you sure about this?"

"Sure? No. But there is a seventy eight percent probability that I am correct."

"All right," Lisa said, guessing that getting any sleep was probably no longer an option . "Where shall we meet?"

"I will be outside your apartment in ten minutes."

"Wait a minute, you know where I live?"

Ten

The first thing Doctor Hammer did was to cautiously check the labs, autopsy room and morgue to make sure that whoever had been there was now gone. Confirming that she was alone, she locked the main entrance door and walked to her small office at the rear of the M.E. complex. Once safely inside, she took the bottle of Seconal from her desk draw, shook out one of the beige pills and popped it into her mouth. In the interest of warding off the headache she could feel building at the back of her skull, she decided to take an oxycontin as well. She then poured a half glass of whiskey from the bottle she kept in her office for 'medical emergencies' and washed them down. Any other doctor would have of course advised against this reckless mixing of drugs and alcohol, but Hammer didn't care. It was, after all, her body and she could irreparably damage it in any way she saw fit. Possibly all her years working with dead bodies had jaded her to the 'live healthy, live happy' message.

Checking her pulse, she found her heart rate alarmingly elevated. "You have to calm down," she told herself.

Easier said than done, at least until the drugs kicked in. She went through a list of possible explanations for what had just happened; 1) she'd imagined the whole thing, 2) she'd had some sort of paranormal experience, 3) too much time alone in the lab, staring at mutilated remains, had caused her to hallucinate, 4) she had fallen asleep during the autopsy and dreamed it. They were all plausible, if slightly unconvincing, assumptions, except for the dull ache in her right shoulder and the throbbing pain in both her nipples.

She entered the bathroom adjacent to her office and removed her white lab coat. The front of her blouse was stained with blood. As she pulled the blouse off, the severed bra fell away. Her large breasts, less firm than they had once been, were easy enough to tilt upwards, allowing her to perform an inspection. The nipples themselves, apart from being more swollen than usual, no doubt from the pincer-like pressure applied by the petite-fingered intruder, were undamaged. Each areola, however, had sustained a narrow, razor-thin incision upon which tiny clumps of coagulated blood continued to cling. She washed the wounds and dabbed them dry with a towel, briefly wondering if there would be visible scars. In certain cultures, the marking of a woman's nipples, either with fingernails or teeth, was considered highly erotic. And she had to admit that while the event in autopsy had been violent and terrifying, there had also been an element of sexual stimulation to it. The practiced sexual predator had a knack of blending seemingly irreconcilable concepts; the purest terror was always wrapped in paradox.

A sudden wave of warm, comfortable light-headedness forced Hammer to sit down. She reached for her glass and drained the remaining whiskey, considering its route from mouth to stomach to intestine to blood vessels and eventually to brain, a complicated journey made simple by the miracle of anatomical design. The muscles in her neck and back were now so relaxed that walking would be a challenge. Her excited heart was by this time barely beating. She glanced down at her swollen nipples and wished that someone, anyone, really, with the exception of the late John Wilbur, was licking them. The anti-infectious properties of saliva were, after all, well documented.

Not that there weren't much more important things to be thinking about.

"For example?" Hammer asked out loud, her voice sounding like a drunken coed at an all-night sorority bash.

All right, let's see. After a careful consideration of all the evidence, it was apparent that her late night visitor had almost certainly been the Akuma; hence the Akuma was real, not only real, but almost certainly responsible for the ongoing murder spree. It also meant that the supernatural was real, and that the crazy Japanese cop

THE CUTEST LITTLE DEMON IN TOWN

Ishikawa had been right. And while none of this was acceptable to a medical scientist, of whom Hammer did an excellent impersonation, she had long ago come to terms with the unavoidable truth that the scientific method, rationality and objective fact were but a thin veneer stretched across the irrational chaos of life; the antiseptic band-aid struggling unsuccessfully to contain the festering wound.

"Oh my god, Lisa!" Hammer blurted out, her eyelids suddenly feeling like hundred pound weights were hanging from them.

Lisa was lovely, wasn't she? And she had lovely nipples. They had been tantalizingly visible through her shirt this morning. Stop! That's not what I'm talking about. Lisa could be in terrible danger. I have to call her immediately and warn her. The phone on her desk was accessible, but she had no idea what Lisa's cell number was. She needed her own cell, but that was nowhere to be seen. It was probably lying on a table out in the lab. She stood up and stepped erratically towards the door. She made it only as far as the couch she kept in the office for the occasional quick nap, upon which she collapsed with a lighter than air sigh.

Traffic had miraculously thinned and the heat had subsided a bit. Driving with the windows down it almost felt comfortable, like one could take a breath without fear of the lungs bursting into flame. Or maybe it was just that he felt clear-headed again, on the job, with a purpose. And while he seemed to have lost an entire day, with only bits and pieces of memory left over from it, he knew who he was at this moment. He was David Stone, New York City Detective, and he was damn good at what he did. Granted, life in general was more difficult to navigate, but wasn't that true for everyone? Everybody lost their mind occasionally, screwed things up and assaulted their girlfriend in the shower. Okay, maybe not everybody. The point was that he was back, past the trouble, totally in focus. Lisa would forgive him, he would catch the bad guy and life would make sense again, at least for a little while.

He took First Avenue all the way uptown. Once you passed 96th Street, the landscape took on a more menacing feel, a bit like being in the midst of an undeclared war with no clear sense of who the enemy was, or what your optimal exit strategy might be. When in doubt, open fire. It didn't matter that you were shooting at shadows or that the world had quietly ended while your back was turned. You pushed on, did what you could to make things a little better than they were, or at least not any worse.

Hogan's car was parked on the southwest corner of 116th and First. It was empty. Stone got out and looked around, then tried calling Hogan's cell phone. No answer. The building in question, on the northeast corner, was a crumbling six-story brownstone, abandoned, another sad reminder of urban blight and the breakdown of the middle class dream. Stone stared at it for awhile, looking for what he wasn't sure. Maybe he was hoping to catch sight of Hogan waving from one of the windows, letting him know that all was well, that the serial killer with blood red contacts and carrying a portable fog-making machine had surrendered without a struggle. Case closed.

Stone checked his weapon and was about to cross the street when he saw the flash of red light. It was there for an instant and then gone. Top floor. Stone sprinted to the building's front door, which was open, then up the stairs. By the time he reached the top floor, he was breathing hard, a reminder that being in good shape was pretty much an illusion and that quitting cigarettes had probably been a waste of time. There were two apartments on the floor. The light had come from the front apartment facing the street. Stone slowly edged the door open and slipped inside. There were four small rooms, all of them showing signs of fire and water damage. The smell was a combination of damp smoke and mold, mixed with the lingering aroma of human despair. In a low voice he called Hogan's name, but there was no reply.

The rear apartment had a totally different smell, as bad, if not worse, a bit like the aftermath of a high school chemistry experiment gone berserk, the kind that required the evacuation of the entire school. It reminded him of something, but he couldn't quite place it. The first three rooms were empty. In the last room he found Hogan, sitting on the floor, leaning awkwardly against the wall. Even in the dim light, it was clear that Hogan was not in good shape. His face was cut up, shirt torn partially off and at least one nasty looking wound across his chest. But his eyes were open and he was breathing.

"Jesus, Hogan," Stone said, squatting down and examining the chest wound. He pulled out his phone and punched in the police emergency number. "This is Stone, Homicide South, badge number 873966. I've got an officer down, corner of 116 and first. We need a wagon here a.s.a.p."

"Guess I should have waited for you, huh?" Hogan said.

"Damn right you should have waited," Stone said, applying pressure with his hand to what felt like a pretty deep laceration in Hogan's chest. "What the hell happened?"

"Not really sure," Hogan wheezed. "One minute I was on the street waiting for you, the next I was on my way up the stairs, running up the stairs, and you know I don't run. It was like I didn't have a choice. No idea where I was going, but for some reason I had to come into this apartment. That's when all hell broke loose."

Several violent coughs forced him to stop talking.

"Try to take it easy," Stone said. "The ambulance is on the way."

"Couldn't see very well," Hogan continued. "It was like trying to fight a fucking ghost."

"So you didn't get a look at who did this."

"I saw something," Hogan managed, just before a renewed coughing fit.

"Maybe you shouldn't talk now," Stone told him. "We can go over all this later."

"Listen, Stone, I don't think I'm going to be doing much talking later."

"Of course you are," Stone laughed. "You look like shit, as usual, but your wounds aren't that bad, not for a tough old bastard like you. You'll be back at your desk by next week, smoking two packs a day and reminiscing about the good old days with anyone dumb enough to listen to you."

"These aren't the wounds that have me worried," Hogan said, gesturing with his head towards his lap.

Only then did Stone notice that the front of Hogan's trousers were soaked in blood, a large pool of it collecting under his legs, slowly spreading across the greasy linoleum-covered floor.

"Oh shit!" Stone said.

"Yeah," Hogan wheezed. "I'm pretty sure the motherfucker sliced off my dick."

Stone pulled off his tee shirt, folded it up and pressed it down hard on Hogan's groin. "We need to apply pressure," he shouted.

"Too late, my friend," Hogan said calmly.

"Fuck that attitude," Stone said, the blood already starting to soak through the shirt. "The wagon is coming. I can hear the siren."

"Listen to me, Stone," Hogan whispered, grabbing hold of Stone's arm and pulling him closer. "It wasn't no man."

Stone registered the confusing double negative, but saw no point in mentioning it. "So you're saying it was a woman who did this? The Chinese woman?"

Hogan slowly nodded. "Not human."

And then Detective Chet Hogan took a deep breath, released it with a whistle reminiscent of air escaping a punctured tire and died.

Pressed for time, Lisa pulled on a pair of black jeans and a black tee shirt, grabbed her gun, shield and car keys and was out the broken front door. Half way down the stairs from her fourth floor walk-up, she realized she had neglected to put on any underwear. It reminded her of the old days, all the nights she had snuck out of parent's house to meet boys, most of whom she never really liked very much, to go dancing, to a party, or just out for a romantic walk in the nearby woods. Whatever the venue had been, the inevitable outcome was always sex. The absence of underwear had always been an extreme turn on to these boys. As far as they were concerned, girls always wore underwear. Any girl who didn't was either some kind of radical with wild ideas and a mysterious agenda, or a slut with few if any inhibitions. Lisa had preferred to think of herself as a radical slut, sexually promiscuous, but at the same time principled and not totally apolitical.

Ishikawa was waiting for her on the sidewalk just outside her building. No surprise that he looked like a man dressed for a wedding, rather than a late night demon hunt. The early morning air had shifted from hot to just very warm and humid. Still, Lisa was certain that, with the possible exception of a few of the deranged homeless, he was the only man in Manhattan wearing a trench coat.

He greeted her warmly, smiling and shaking her hand. "I am so pleased that you have submitted to my request."

None of her late night boy dates had ever used a line like that. Theirs were more like, "I have a hard on the size of a baseball bat, so how about it, bitch?" Needless to say, they never actually did.

Not really knowing how to respond the Ishikawa, Lisa said, "You look nice tonight. Sort of formal."

"Well, Detective, this could be a very important night."

"Like a wedding night?"

Ishikawa made a slight hissing sound. "Much more important than that."

"So, my car's just down the street. Where are we heading?"

He pulled a piece of paper from his coat pocket and looked at it under the streetlight. "West 17th, very near the river."

"That's the meat market," Lisa said, starting the car's engine.

"Meat market?" Ishikawa asked. "Meat is sold there?"

"You could say that. Actually there are still a few meat processing companies in the area, but more significantly it's a place where gay men get together, you know, mingle, seek out companionship."

"Homosexuals?" Ishikawa exclaimed. "Very interesting!"

"If you're gay, I suppose. You're not ..?"

"Not gay," he said solemnly. "Not anything, really."

Okay, Lisa, time once again to change the subject.

"Uh, so how exactly do we know where we're going?"

Ishikawa proceeded to outline his software program and its results, which sounded borderline ridiculous. He also described what he called his interactive experience with the demon earlier in the evening, which Lisa thought had paranoid/schizophrenic delusion written all over it. Still, she wanted to at least appear supportive.

"So," she said. "Do we know what this demon looks like?"

"Unfortunately, that piece of the puzzle I was not able to ascertain, but I believe we are looking for a being resembling a young Japanese female."

"Well," Lisa said, taking a left on 17th Street. "That should narrow the search. I mean, there can't be more than, what, twenty thousand young Japanese females in town at this very moment."

The sarcasm was completely lost on the demon-obsessed Ishikawa.

"Unless, of course, we are lucky enough to confront the demon in its actual form," he continued. "Then there will be no possibility of mistaken identity."

"Yeah, let's hope for that."

"Yes, except in that case, we will both almost certainly die."

"Good to know," Lisa said, parking the car a couple of blocks from the river. "I'm so glad I agreed to come with you tonight."

At two in the morning, 17th Street and Tenth Avenue felt like the crossroads of bad dreams. No matter which direction you took you knew there weren't going to be any positive outcomes. Lisa and her Japanese escort moved west on foot, through the viscous aftermath of garbage, sweat, the sticky residue of acid rain and other, even more terrifying, substances that coated the street. The Market was relatively quiet, possibly due to the lack of breathable air. Only one bar on the corner of West End Avenue was showing signs of life, outside of which a few shirtless men stood drinking beer. They stopped talking as Lisa and Ishikawa walked by, staring, probably wondering why the red head in black and the Asian guy in a tuxedo were strolling around this neighborhood in the middle of the night. Lisa was beginning to wonder the same thing.

"Now what?" she asked, scanning the surrounding area for any sign of a demon. As if she knew what a demon sign would look like.

Ishikawa checked his watch. "Ten minutes. I think we need to move further west."

"There is not much more west," she told him. "Unless you feel like a swim?"

"Those buildings over there," he said, slipping through a hole in the chain link fence erected to prevent sensible, law-abiding people from vanishing off the face of the earth.

The buildings in question were the remnants of abandoned warehouses and decaying piers, full of gaping, nearly impossible to see at night, holes leading directly to the murky river below. Structural danger aside, the buildings were also the preferred meeting place for certain hard core elements of the gay community, tough serious-minded men who took a dim view of hetcrosexual voyeurs, an even dimmer one of cops.

"I'm not sure this is such a good idea," Lisa said.

"The history of progress is built on bad ideas," Ishikawa replied, squatting down along side a wooden pier mooring.

That almost sounded like it could be true, Lisa thought to herself. She squatted next to him. They were no more than five meters from the silently flowing black river. Lisa figured that if the demon didn't find and kill them the fumes from the river would.

"Do we have a plan?" she asked, opening the safety strap on her holster.

"A plan?" Ishikawa asked, staring directly into her eyes.

It was a little like looking into the eyes of some unknown species of fish in an aquarium.

"I mean, assuming our demon shows, are we thinking capture?"

"The demon will strenuously resist being captured," he said.

"So we kill it," Lisa said, removing the Beretta and cocking a shell into the chamber.

"Yes," Ishikawa said, but your gun will be of no use, I'm afraid."

"Right. Bullets don't kill demons. How silly of me."

"No need to feel silly. This is, after all, your first time."

"Are you suggesting I'm a virgin?" Lisa asked, hoping a bit of less than serious banter would lighten the increasingly grim atmosphere.

Ishikawa did not take the bait. He remained intent, stoic, impervious to distraction.

" So what does?" Lisa enquired.

Again, it was like a slow motion confrontation in a fish bowl. Words were nothing more than air bubbles on the surface of the glass.

"What does kill a demon?" she clarified.

"There is only one way to kill the demon," Ishikawa intoned, as if he were reciting directly from the anti-demon handbook. He reached behind his back and in one smooth, rapid motion pulled out a very beautiful, very sharp-looking sword. "We must cut off her head, preferably while she is engaged in the sexual act with her intended victim."

Eleven

S ato Yui stood naked in front of the mirror in her new apartment on the Lower East Side. As much as she disliked people, she had to admit that, as far as human females went, she was an extremely pretty one. Her eyes, her lips, her hair, all pretty. Even her hands were pretty.

"And don't forget your breasts," she reminded herself, lightly stroking the two perfectly shaped mounds. She took the nipples between her pretty fingers and gently squeezed, trying to imitate the sound real girls made when you squeezed their nipples, a kind of breathless fluttering through moist lips. She loved her lips when they fluttered. She moved her hands slowly down to her waist, across her belly to her hips. Her flesh was so firm and warm. One hand glided off into the patch of black hair nestled just above her sex. With one finger she touched the moist opening between her legs. She shuddered, taking quick little breaths, just as the young Japanese woman whose apartment she now occupied had done.

Poor girl. It had been her fist sexual experience with another woman and, as fate would have it, her last. She glanced over to where the girl's naked body lay on the bed. She had said her name was Sachie Miura, from Nagoya. Now she was simply dead girl from nowhere with throat slit. These things sometimes happened. Young Asian women leave home and come to New York looking for adventure, something to help them forget the predictable boredom of their lives in Japan. They made valiant efforts trying to fit into an alien culture. Some of them actually succeeded. Some inevitably ended up occupying body bags in Doctor Hammer's laboratory of the talking dead.

At least the Miura female had found a little adventure before joining the grim gray line of her hard to even remember ancestors. Sato Yui had befriended her in a nearby coffee shop. She told the

Miura female that she had just arrived in town and didn't know anyone. She needed a place to stay for a few days while she looked for a place of her own. The Miura female, so trusting, so desperate for companionship, hadn't hesitated to offer.

"You can stay with me," she had squealed, her eyes all bubbly and damp. "For as long as you need."

A friend in need is a friend indeed. How could the Miura female have known that Sato Yui was less a friend than a cruel, inhuman monster with a predilection for spilling blood. After a few beers in the apartment, Sato Yui had kissed the Miura female. The Miura female had pretended to resist, crying, "No, no, we shouldn't," between each succulent kiss. By the time Sato Yui had removed the Miura female's clothes, stroking her body, sucking the tender flesh of her nipples, her feigned protests had turned to whimpers of pleasure.

"Tell me what you want?" Sato Yui had demanded.

"No, I can't," the Miura female had pleaded. "Please don't make me."

"Tell me!" Sato Yui insisted, applying easy, but not entirely pain-free, pressure to the Miura female's throat.

"I want ... I want ..."

"Say it!"

"I want you to ... to use your mouth on my ... my sex."

Don't let anyone tell you that the Miura female did not have her special moment of forbidden pleasure. With Sato Yui's mouth between her legs she had slithered like an eel out of water, clawing at the bed sheets with hands that were not quite as pretty as Sato Yui's, her bird-like orgasms coming one after another in rapid succession. She cried for more, at the same time begging Sato Yui to stop. She gurgled things in a Japanese dialect that Sato Yui was not familiar with. Sato Yui had killed her during the end of a quivering climax, the Miura female's final orgasm of her brief, mostly uneventful life. It rarely got more poetic than that. With one quick flash of claw across the throat, the sexual act was perfectly punctuated by the quiet simplicity of death. Without a doubt, the Miura female had died happy.

In return, Sato Yui inherited an apartment. She was tired of having to rest in amorphous form in drafty abandoned buildings between hunting sessions. The whole pure demon energy state was becoming tiresome. She much preferred her girl body and was finding it more comfortable and easier to remain in for longer periods of time. As an experienced world traveler, she could say with assurance that she had never been in a more compatible city. Her powers were at their peak, he senses acute. She was a pretty little killing machine with a sexy body and her own apartment. Who knows, maybe she would even get a part time job. Exotic dancer sounded appealing. She could dance in the evenings, kill after work and still have plenty of time for shopping during the day. Even a perfect, extra-dimensional demonic entity could improve herself here. America really was the land of opportunity.

It was already past ten by the time Lisa got to the station. After squatting in stale river dampness for several hours with Ishikawa, she had barely had time to shower and change her clothes before leaving for work. Hours wasted, as far as she was concerned. No demons anywhere in sight. A couple of homeless guys had crawled by, one strung out lunatic with a skull and crossbones tattoo on his forehead who made threatening gestures, demanding that she and Ishikawa help him return to his home planet, but was ultimately dissuaded from violence by the sight of Ishikawa's sword. Did it make any sense that a cop in formal wear was carrying a Japanese sword? Even in New York City, it pushed the boundaries. In the grand, increasingly absurd scheme of things, on the other hand, it was almost normal.

Ishikawa had acted a little hurt when Lisa suggested that his computer tracking technology might have a flaw. Apparently the fact that it had not worked was no proof that it did not work. This was perhaps an example of Asian logic. Things often worked best when they did not work at all. According to Ishikawa, the problem was not in the software, but with the Akuma.

"How so?" Lisa had asked, much too exhausted to care about the answer.

"The Akuma was there," he told her, as they drove back to his hotel. "But she knew we were there, too, waiting for her."

"So the Akuma is no dummy," Lisa had said with a yawn.

"On the contrary, she is very smart. Much more troubling is the possibility that she has developed the ability to read minds."

"Terrific! So now we're facing a supernatural serial killer with psychic powers. That should make it much easier to defeat."

"More likely impossible," Ishikawa sighed, determined, it seemed, to ignore sarcasm at all costs. "I may be forced to admit failure."

"Wouldn't it be easier to admit a programming error?"

"I must think," he had said, slipping from the car and walking dejectedly into the hotel lobby.

As Lisa stepped out of the elevator into Homicide, Officer Mendez, a small, attractive woman with enormous breasts, gave her the bad news. Detective Hogan had been killed. Panic rippled through Lisa's body.

"What about Stone?" she asked, her voice shaky.

Stone was fine, Mendez told her, although nobody knew where he was. According to officers at the scene, Stone had taken the death of his old friend hard. She went on to say, her voice shifting to a barely audible whisper, that the Captain was in an especially foul mood, on the warpath and out for blood. Lisa thanked her for the heads up, thinking she should disappear into her office as soon as possible. But Officer Mendez, in her new role as information overseer, was not quite finished. Doctor Hammer had apparently left an urgent message. She needed to see Detective Malone as soon as possible. It sounded very urgent, Mendez reaffirmed. She wasn't sure, but it might even be a life and death situation.

Again Lisa thanked her. Officer Mendez assured her it was not a problem. She was more than happy to be able to help. She lived to serve, would do anything Lisa required. Lisa suddenly had the feeling that even a kiss would not be beyond the call of duty. It made sense. If anyone in the Department were a lesbian, it would probably have to be Mendez. In the rarified air of lesbian seduction, the gravitational pull of her breasts alone was enough to guarantee her a position of prominence. Lisa almost felt like kissing her first, just to relieve the building tension, but decided against it.

"I'll keep your offer in mind," Lisa smiled, pulling away and walking rapidly to her office.

As soon as she was safely out of sight she tried Stone's cell phone. No answer. Based on recent behavior, Hogan's death had probably sent him running to the nearest bar. He was lying somewhere drunk, experiencing the peculiar pleasure of brain cell death on a massive scale. Or maybe he was in the arms of his favorite whore with the razor blades glued to her fingernails. There were plenty of valid reasons why girls should never start caring about guys.

She was about to try Hammer when the shouting started, the unmistakable boom of the Captain, clearly on the blood-seeking warpath.

"Am I the only one is this Department with the capacity to think?" he bellowed. "Am I completely surrounded by morons? Where the hell is everyone? Where are the forensic reports I asked for two hours ago? Where in God's name is Stone?"

The Captain was on the move and there was little doubt of his direction. Lisa sat down at her desk and held her breath. Her office door opened explosively, the Captain entering like an angry force of nature.

"Malone," he bellowed. "What the hell is going on around here?"

"Sorry Sir," she said. "I just got in and don't really know."

"Just got in? Did you wake up this morning thinking perhaps that you were a socialite on a pleasure cruise, that time was as irrelevant as the price of milk?"

Did that mean that the price of milk was somehow relevant? Lisa wondered. Was everything secretly relevant in ways she would never be able to comprehend? She felt confused.

"Actually, Sir, I was on a stake out all night."

"What stake out? I didn't authorize any stake out."

"It was sort of spur of the moment, with Ishikawa."

"And?"

"It didn't pan out."

"Why am I not surprised? And where the hell is your partner? *You probably don't want to know.*

"I'm sure he'll be here soon."

"Soon? I've been hearing about soon for ten years. I'll tell you what's going to happen soon. You're all going to find yourselves demoted to traffic duty in one of the outer boroughs. We've got cops being killed, cops missing, reports missing."

"Is there something I can do, Captain?"

"Yes there is, Malone. Get your butt down to the morgue. As if we didn't have enough problems, Doctor Hammer has apparently flipped out and locked herself in the lab. You go down there and talk to her. Figure out what's bothering her and fix it. Now!"

"I'm on it, Captain," Lisa said, jumping up from her desk and running for the elevator.

"And you tell that woman she's treading a very thin line."

"I will, Sir."

When Lisa reached the morgue she found the outer door locked. She pressed the bell on the wall next to the door and waited. A moment later, Doctor Hammer appeared, recognized Lisa through the small glass panel in the door and let her inside.

"Lisa," Hammer said, taking the Detective's arm and guiding her into the rear laboratory. "I'm so glad you're here."

"Are you okay?" Lisa asked.

"Yes, I'm fine."

"The Captain said you had flipped out."

"How ridiculous. I haven't flipped out."

"Really?"

"Well, all right, perhaps I did flip out a little earlier, but I'm completely non-flipped out now. The flip has been reversed."

"You do seem a little agitated."

"This is not agitation," Hammer insisted. "This, my dear, is science, pure and simple. Well, maybe not so simple."

"So why was the door locked and is that blood on your lab coat?"

"So many questions," Hammer smiled, checking a large boxy-looking machine busy humming and vibrating on one of the counters. "Did you take an inquisitive pill this morning?"

"Things have been just a little strange recently," Lisa told her. "An answer or two wouldn't be the worst thing."

"You're telling me," Hammer said, sitting down on one of the metal stools in the lab and motioning for Lisa to come closer. "Anyway, I locked the door because I'm in the middle of a very important experiment and did not want to be disturbed."

"And on your coat?"

"Yes, it is blood, but that's not important now. I have something to show you."

Hammer stood up and began unbuttoning her lab coat.

"Doctor Hammer?" Lisa said, slightly alarmed. "What are you doing?"

"What does it look like I'm doing?" Hammer asked, undoing the final button and dropping the coat to the floor. "I'm showing you my nipples."

Oh my god, Lisa thought. Was there some kind of weird lesbian virus thing rampaging through the Department? "Why would you do that?" she asked nervously.

"Because," Hammer said, unhooking her bra with the same stylish ease she applied to opening the chest cavity of a dead body, "I feel that it's a vital component of the point I am trying to make."

No one was ever going to accuse Beverly Hammer of normalcy. A case could even be made that she took no small amount of pride in her ability to demonstrate the abnormal in all its quirky permutations. She had an offbeat sense of humor and she certainly took pleasure in her ability to shock, but this was different, not to mention a little scary.

"Well?" Hammer warbled, reminding Lisa of giant birds decimating Japan's major cities.

"Well what?" Lisa said, feeling as if she might start to cry.

"Exactly what kind of detective are you?" Hammer demanded, scooping her hand beneath one breast and thrusting it at Lisa.

Lisa instinctively took a quick step back, while at the same time noticing the odd looking marks on Hammer's nipple.

"What is that?" she asked.

"Exactly!" Hammer shouted. "Look closer."

Reluctantly, Lisa leaned forward until the wide pinkish areola of the nipple occupied most of her field of vision. It was like exploring the landscape of some pinkish alien planet, at the center of which rose an impressive volcanic peak. Running diagonally through the pink terrain was a long, black and bluish looking wound.

"How did this happen?" Lisa asked, tempted to touch the area with her finger.

"I had a visitor last night," Hammer said, scooping the other breast into view, which had a nearly identical wound.

"Who was it?"

"That is the question I wrestled with for most of the night. After extensive thought, as well as the consumption of a variety of controlled substances, I was able to eliminate every possibility but one."

Hammer paused here, her eyes as wide open as Lisa had ever seen them. Lisa waited, afraid to even take a breath. Time, for all she knew, may have actually stopped.

Finally, Hammer whispered the answer. "Akuma."

"Oh no," Lisa moaned. "Have you been talking to Ishikawa? Was he here?"

"Trust me, my late night interloper was not Ishikawa."

"Well, did you see it?"

"Not exactly. I believe it was invisible, although I did see its hands."

"It has hands?"

"What kind of a murderer would it be without hands?"

"And it did that to your nipples?"

"That is correct."

"Still," Lisa sighed, "I really wish it could be something else. Anything, really, besides an invisible demon."

"Of course you do," Hammer said, placing one arm around Lisa's shoulder, which inadvertently pressed her breasts against Lisa's chest. "We all do, sweetie."

"The Captain will never buy it. Neither will Stone, for that matter."

"Well," Hammer said, dashing over to the machine on the counter, switching it off and opening its small door. "They may have no choice."

She extracted something from inside the machine and dropped it in Lisa's hand. It resembled a small piece of jagged black rock.

"What am I looking at?" she asked.

"I removed it from John Wilbur's chest," Hammer said, re-hooking her bra and picking up her lab coat and slipping it on. "I think it's a small section of a claw. It's miraculously tough, but also pliable. Its tensile strength is virtually off the charts."

"Which means?"

"I took the liberty of doing a carbon 14 dating scan on it."

"You can do that here?"

"Lisa, I can do almost anything here. How do you think I use all the budgetary funds the city continues to pour into forensics?"

"You buy a carbon dating machine."

"More accurately, a portable mass spectrometer. The point is that one can never have too much technology, and I believe this result proves it admirably."

"I'm sure it does," Lisa said, "but ..."

"Guess how old this piece of claw is?" Hammer asked gleefully.

"I have no idea."

"Hence the significance of the word guess."

"Uh, twenty-five years old."

"A bit older."

"A hundred?"

"It's ten thousand years old, give or take a century."

"So you're saying that our serial killer is ten thousand years old."

"Yes."

"And this ten thousand year old whatever it is was in this lab last night."

"Again, yes, although judging by hand size and skin color, it is also a petite Asian female approximately twenty years of age."

"How is any of this possible?" Lisa asked.

"It isn't," Hammer smiled. "That's the terrifying beauty of it."

Lisa sat down and dropped her head into her hands.

"Another interesting detail," Hammer continued. "I removed a strand of black hair that was wrapped around Mister Wilbur's scrotum."

"Let me guess," Lisa said. "From the head of a petite Asian female, approximately twenty years old."

"Right," Hammer said. "Most likely Japanese."

"So what do we do now?"

"Quitting our jobs and relocating to Los Angeles wouldn't be the craziest idea."

Twelve

Stone stayed at the crime scene until the coroner arrived to take away Hogan's body. The forensics boys were already hard at work; Stone knew they wouldn't come up with anything. Slight deviation in M.O. aside, it was the same killer. Hogan hadn't been killed outright so that he could be found alive, upping the impact of the crime on whoever found him and also sending a message. This is what happens when you get too close, you end up with your genitals cut off and then you die in a big puddle of your own blood in some uptown hovel. The question was who was sending the message.

Stone mulled over Hogan's last words as he drove back downtown. "It wasn't no man. Chinese. Not human." Hogan had always had a thing about the Chinese. He didn't trust them, believed that the Chinese mafia was in the process of quietly taking over the country. He had spent a lot of time and energy on the Chinatown gangs, without much success. The possibility that a Chinese woman could be involved in the current serial case had probably perked his interest. It was one more chance for him to finally get the inhuman Chinese bastards. Not that Hogan was a racist. For an old timer with a basically misanthropic view of the human race in general, he was fairly tolerant. He just had this thing about the Chinese.

Midtown Homicide was in a state of agitated mourning when Stone got there. A few of the guys from Hogan's unit were standing around, jittery, trying to figure out what came next. Stone walked over and they all exchanged sympathies. One of them, Detective Mancini, who had been with Hogan for quite awhile, threw his arms around Stone and hugged him.

"Tough night, huh?" he said.

"Yeah," Stone agreed.

"Hogan able to tell you anything?"

"Not really," Stone lied. "He was pretty far gone by the time I got there."

"God damn shame," Mancini spat. "Hogan was a hell of a cop, taught me everything I know."

Nothing to brag about Stone thought, nodding total agreement.

"Well don't worry about it," Mancini continued. "We're going to get the bastard who did this."

"Damn straight," one of the other Detectives added.

"We're thinking it was a set up," Mancini said. "Payback from that uptown gang we've been putting pressure on for the past month or so."

"Sounds promising," Stone told them, thinking dead end.

"What was the name of that gang banger you and Hogan had in here for questioning?"

"Sanchez," Stone said. "Jesus Sanchez."

"Yeah, we'll start with that motherfucker."

"We'll crucify the son of a bitch," someone shouted.

"Just let me know if I can help."

"Thanks, Stone. We will."

"Listen, Mancini," Stone said, taking the Detective aside. "Was Hogan still paying attention to the Chinatown gangs?"

"His pet obsession, you mean? The man had a bug up his ass when it came to the Chinese. Wouldn't even have lunch in a Chinese restaurant."

"So his files would still be active?"

"Far as I know."

"Mind if I take a look at them while I'm here?"

"No problem. Just help yourself."

Stone sat down at Hogan's desk with a stack of files that Hogan had whimsically labeled "The Chinese Conspiracy." True to his old school roots, the handwriting was barely legible. Undeterred, Stone dug in and began going through them.

After exiting the supernatural world of the medical examiner's office, and managing to get past the evil ogre inhabiting the Captain's body without being seen, Lisa sat down at her computer and initiated a Web search on the word Akuma. Surprisingly, there were more than five hundred entries. Most of it dealt with the various myths, legends and folklore of the demon, many with imaginative illustrations of what the demon might look like, ranging from sexy girls with sharp fangs and long claws to creatures resembling dinosaurs. All of it was more or less useless, until she happened upon a long, intelligent-seeming article written by a Professor Kenji Ishikawa.

"Coincidence?" Lisa wondered out loud.

Professor Ishikawa outlined the history of the demon, running from the dawn of time to the present. He discussed where demons come from – an extra-dimensional realm of pure chaos – how they are periodically launched into the familiar four-dimensional human world – due to occasional rifts in the space/time fabric creating portals of entry – and why – attracted to increasing levels of human violence and/or insanity. In Japanese culture, the Akuma was both feared and respected, as it was often viewed as a kind of avenging angel, a deranged patron saint for women suffering abuse at the hands of men. Thus the Akuma was always female in nature, its victims almost always male. It was a sexually motivated predator, brutal, vicious, completely lacking in compassion. Its power was virtually limitless, trying to fight against it virtually futile. The demon's only weakness, apparently, was an inability to remain in the four-dimensional realm indefinitely.

"I feel better already," Lisa said to her computer screen.

She glanced up and saw Stone in the outer office, talking to Mendez. Her first impulse was run to him, throw her arms around him and kiss him, but she resisted. He looked directly at her then, finished his conversation with the busty chatterbox officer and walked towards her office.

"Hi," he said, closing the office door, coming over to Lisa and kissing her softly on the lips.

Wow!

His hair was wild and he was about a half hour away from a full-blown beard, but his eyes were bright and he looked a lot less confused than the last time she'd seen him.

"I'm so glad to see you," she said. "I was worried. Are you all right?"

Stone nodded. "Yeah, I'm good."

"Sorry about Hogan."

"Yeah," he repeated. "But, you know, these things happen."

Do they, Lisa wondered? Okay, she knew they did, knew cops occasionally died in the line of duty, but Stone's blasé attitude was a little disconcerting. Possibly he was in denial about the death of his old friend.

"The important thing," he continued, "is that something positive comes out of it."

"And has it? Lisa asked.

"I believe it has," he said. "I'm finally beginning to understand what's been going on with these killings."

"Really?"

"Our mysterious Chinese woman with the red eyes."

"You know what ... I mean ... who she is?"

"Not yet, but I believe she's part of a Chinese assassination team set up and funded by one of the Chinatown gangs. She and her accomplices killed Hogan and the other three victims."

"But what's the motive?"

"Revenge," Stone announced, sounding as if the case was solved and all that was left to do was tidy up the details.

"But how are the four murders connected?"

"That's where things get intricate. It took some digging into Hogan's files, but I've already got possible connections with the first two victims."

"The IRS guy and the stockbroker?"

"Right! The insurance guy is a tougher sell, but I know it's there. I'm telling you Lisa, I feel like I'm back on my game, working the magic again."

"That's great," she smiled. "But I think we need to talk. I ..."

Stone cut her off by placing a finger to her lips. "If it's about what happened in the shower last night, trust me when I tell you that I'm genuinely sorry. Chalk it up to temporary madness and forgive me."

"But ..."

"No buts. We'll talk tonight, I promise. Hopefully we can also do some other things that don't involve talking. Right now I have to brief the Captain, then dig up some of my old Chinatown informants. These are Hogan's notes on the Chinese gangs," he told her, dropping a thick manila envelop in her hands. "If you don't mind taking a look, I could use your insight."

She watched him leave on his newfound burst of magical Stone energy, not sure if things had just gotten better or worse. When she glanced back down at the computer an especially scary-looking representation of the Akuma was staring directly at her.

After a fitful night's sleep, including several terrifying nightmares, Ishikawa had showered, finished two glasses of whiskey and now, wearing only a bath towel, was occupied with writing farewell notes to relatives and friends in Japan. Based on recent developments, he felt the notes were necessary. The only thing a demon hunter had on his side was the assurance that the Akuma's behavior was prescribed, that there were patterns of behavior, however gruesome, outside of which the demon could not function. He was no longer sure that this theory applied. His sense was that the Akuma was adapting, perhaps using the collective psychic energy of the city to mutate into some new version of itself. And while he could appreciate the demon's effort, even feel a certain grudging respect for it, he no longer believed that this shift in demon behavior was in any way beneficial to him. On the contrary, he was now faced with the very real possibility of failure; not only professional failure, but also death. After years of living out of a suitcase in cities all over the world, New York would very likely be his final resting place. This was assuming that the demon would not pursue him into whatever afterlife awaited him.

For better or worse, he wasn't sure, but after writing one note to his irresponsible younger brother Kento and another to the only remaining living partner from his original team, Yuji Ito, who was currently confined to a mental hospital in Yokohama, there was no one else to write to. He had no friends to mourn his death under mysterious circumstances in the Big Apple. There was Noriko, of course, but news of his demise would most likely prompt her to buy a new dress, go to the beauty parlor and then out to celebrate.

"Sadly, Ishikawa," he said out loud, pouring himself another whiskey, "this is your fate."

The sudden knock on the door felt like a pounding inside his brain. Whoever it was obviously had no problem ignoring the 'Do Not Disturb' sign hanging from the doorknob. So typical of Americans to assume written notices did not apply to them.

"There is no one currently here," he shouted.

"I know you're in there, Ishikawa," a woman's voice shouted back.

It sounded like Lisa, but how could he continue to trust his own senses? For all he knew, it was the Akuma standing on the other side of the door impersonating Lisa.

"Are you a demon?" he asked.

"Only when I have my period. It's me, Detective Malone."

"Lisa?"

"Yes. And I have just braved a raging fireball and an army of overheated zombies to get here. So please let me in."

"Really?" Ishikawa said, opening the door.

"No, not really," she said, walking inside and closing the door behind her. "But it is hot enough outside to suspect that the end of the world is upon us."

"I, too, have my suspicions," he agreed.

"Wow!" Lisa said noticing Ishikawa's virtual nakedness, as well as the nasty cut across his stomach.

"What is wow?" he asked.

"Nothing. I guess I'm just used to seeing you dressed somewhat more formally."

"Oh," he cried, grabbing the towel and tugging it higher. "Please forgive me."

"That's okay," Lisa said, bending to get a closer look at the stomach wound. "And what is that?"

"A minor accident. Nothing to worry about."

"You accidentally sliced open your stomach?"

"I was cleaning my sword, my mind wandered, I paid the price."

"I see."

"By the way, why are you here?"

"Well, you seemed sort of depressed last night after the big demon bust."

"The demon's bust?" Ishikawa asked, confused.

"Never mind. The point is, are you all right?"

No big surprise that Ishikawa would be unable to answer this question with the ease and promptness that more normal people simply took for granted. Maybe it had to do with the fundamental conflict between literal-mindedness and the obsession with the supernatural; it left Ishikawa in a kind of social no man's land in which the simplest things potentially became the source of monumental confusion.

As he pondered his reply, Lisa had time to give his body the once over. She liked what she saw. His upper body was not so much muscular as taut, with a polished leanness reminiscent of long distance runners (brief flashback to the foot race across Battery Park). The skin was a golden brownish color. The nipples, larger than Stone's, were black. She wondered how Ishikawa's skin would taste, if licking his nipples would make him moan. Most guys were pretty silent when it came to having their nipples licked, as if moaning somehow undermined their masculine tough guy status. Maybe Japanese guys were different; maybe nipple licking had a different connotation in Japanese culture. What lay beneath the white bath towel she could only surmise, but it would have been a lie to say she wasn't somewhat interested.

Ishikawa, meanwhile, was very aware of Lisa's eyes on him, and if time had not suddenly stopped he would have said something, or, even better, excused himself to the bathroom and gotten dressed. Lisa's eyes, a beautiful aqua green color, suggested curiosity, as if she were examining some sort of exotic species. Undoubtedly, she found him strange, possibly insane, but there was also a subtle mystery expressed, perhaps even a hint of something erotic in those lovely eyes. Now he *was* being insane. How long had it been since he was dressed in nothing but a towel in a hotel room with a woman? Was it possible that he had never been in a towel in a hotel room with a woman? There had been that prostitute in Budapest, but everything she said had been in Hungarian. For all he knew, she had been telling him what an ugly little Oriental rodent he was as she smiled, stroking his member with her unnaturally long, eastern European fingers. The problem with being trapped inside a moment of time is that everything tends to take on a significance it does not necessarily deserve.

Lisa decided that breaking the silence was a better outcome than dying as a result of it.

"I'm just going to go ahead and assume that you are okay."

"I think that's for the best," he said with a sigh of relief. "Now, may I offer you a drink?"

"Let's see, I'm on duty, it's eleven in the morning. So why not?"

Drinks in hand, they both sat, Lisa on the bed, Ishikawa in the chair behind the desk. Rather than risk sinking again into silence, Lisa outlined the details of Hogan's murder, based on Stone's preliminary report. The M.O. had changed slightly – that Hogan had still been alive when Stone found him and that, unlike the previous victims whose lower bodies had been left virtually untouched, Hogan's genitalia had been cut off – but the consensus was that it was the work of the same killer. She also recounted Doctor Hammer's story of her run in with the Akuma in the lab, including the wounds to her nipples and the recovered piece of claw, carbon dated to the early Stone Age.

The only question, based on Ishikawa's impassive expression throughout her dissertation, was whether he had heard anything she'd said. She really didn't want to have to repeat it.

"So what do you think?" she asked hopefully.

"If all of this is true," he said, "things are even worse than I imagined."

So you were paying attention.

"How much worse?"

"The Akuma is changing its behavior patterns, speculating, learning how to play."

"If you want to call the removal of a man's penis playful."

"The severed sex organ is a warning. The Akuma does not give warnings. The visit to Doctor Hammer's lab and the cutting of her nipples were the Akuma's attempt at fun."

"And demons don't have fun."

"Not in my experience."

"I was doing a little research on Japanese demons. I came across an interesting article by a Professor Kenji Ishikawa. Same last name," she said, pointing at Ishikawa. "Is that a common family name in Japan?"

"It is fairly common," Ishikawa said, averting his eyes away from hers. "But Kenji Ishikawa was my father."

"So the whole demon hunting thing runs in the family."

"My father did not hunt the demon. He made love to it."

"Is that even possible? No! Please don't tell me your mother was an Akuma."

"I was not speaking literally," Ishikawa said tersely.

What? You choose this moment to start peppering the conversation with metaphor?

"So by love, you mean ..?"

"My father was a traditionalist, an idealist who believed there was a legitimate place for the Akuma in human society. He saw them as a manifestation of some higher purpose, one part of a natural whole that could not be excised without serious consequences. His conviction on this matter caused a rift between us. He never fully understood the beast. And now, as it turns out, neither have I. Do you think that qualifies as irony?"

Lisa shrugged. "It certainly could."

"I'd like to think so."

"What happened to your father?"

"He was killed."

"By a demon?"

"No. He tripped, fell onto the train tracks at Osaka Station and was killed by an Express Bullet Train."

"Do you suspect that the demon pushed him?"

"Why would it? My father was its best friend on Earth. He dreamed of ameliorating the beast, possibly transforming it into a symbol for the neophyte women's liberation movement in Japan."

"Is there a women's liberation movement in Japan?" Lisa asked.

"For the most part underground," Ishikawa said. "But its existence has been tentatively documented."

"So what, a few women get together to complain about their husbands?"

"More than that. Some of them have reportedly threatened to refuse sex for an entire week."

"Crazy radicals," Lisa said, reaching into the back pocket of her jeans for her ringing cell phone. "Malone. Yeah, go ahead. What? Really? Where? You've got to be kidding. Never mind. No problem. As it turns out, I'm nearby."

Lisa disconnected and stared directly at Ishikawa.

"More bad news?" he asked.

"Seems like our friend has struck again."

"Do we have a mutual friend?"

"Let me rephrase. There's been another murder."

Ishikawa jumped up from his chair, almost losing his towel. "Where?"

"Here, in this hotel, two floors down, room 413."

Thirteen

Doctor Hammer sat in a corner of the Captain's office watching him pace back and forth from wall to wall, approximately fourteen feet by her estimate, occasionally shaking his head and muttering to himself. She had been the captive audience to this performance for ten minutes and thirty-seven seconds, according to her watch. Even by the Captain's standards of punishing underlings with bouts of anger-inspired silence, this was a long time. She assumed he was either searching for just the right words to convey what he had on his mind, or having some sort of mental breakdown. Walking Psychosis Syndrome came to mind, although she couldn't rule out some form of fugue. Classic fugue sufferers, of course, generally just walked away, often never to be seen again. The Captain's version was more or less circular, meaning that no matter how far he walked, he would always end up in exactly the same place. Mental illness quite often equaled this level of futility.

"Excuse me, Captain," she finally said. "I'm just wondering if there is anything you want to say to me, or if you only invited me in to watch you do this."

This provoked a noticeable increase in muttering volume, but a decrease in walking speed. The episode was winding down. Hammer waited patiently for the second act. The Captain stopped, rasped like a bear with a large trout lodged in its throat and returned to his desk.

"Doctor Hammer," he said, pulling a bottle of Diet Coke from his mini-fridge and twisting off the cap. "What planet are we living on?"

"I'm sorry?"

"All right, let's try another. What century are we living in?"

"If this is some kind of test, Captain, it's far too easy."

"You're right. Instead, why don't we discuss your most recent forensic report?"

"Certainly. Any part of it in particular?"

"Gee, I don't know. How about the part stating that some piece of claw you pulled out of a dead guy's chest is older than the pyramids?"

"Much older, actually."

"Or that the claw in question does not correlate with any currently known species groups. Wait a minute, I've heard that before."

"The saliva," Hammer reminded him.

"And now the claw."

"Yes."

"Doctor Hammer. Do you expect me to accept any of this as scientifically verified fact?"

"As it was verified scientifically, Captain, yes I do."

The Captain sighed, rubbing his face with his hands.

"Let me explain to you, Doctor, exactly what it is we do around here. Not that I should have to, but you, apparently, have suffered some sort of rational lapse. So, just to review, our task here is to solve crime. We pursue evidence methodically, objectively and, lest we forget, rationally. We build a case until it is flawless and then allow the law to run its proper course. You, as the Medical Examiner, are expected to supplement that evidence through the application of an established scientific method, objective, rational, irrefutable; in other words, no crazy bullshit, no extremist insane theories. Now do you think that anything in your report reflects the criteria I've just outlined?"

"Science doesn't lie," Hammer said with conviction.

"Perhaps not, but scientists often do."

"Are you suggesting, Captain, that I ..?"

"You have been acting strangely, Doctor. I think even you would have to agree."

"There is no objective criterion for measuring strangeness."

"You locked yourself in the god damn lab for five hours."

"I've already explained that."

"Not to my satisfaction."

"Solving this case may require an expanding of perception on the part of certain individuals."

"As if I had any idea what that meant."

"I believe the killer was in the lab last night."

"In the lab? How is that possible?"

"I also believe that the killer may not be human."

The Captain's eyes narrowed and his jaw jutted forward accusingly. "Did you say not human?"

"Something supernatural."

"Stop!" Burke shouted. "Stop right there. I'm going to pretend you didn't say that. I also have half a mind to put you on administrative leave, effective immediately. Do you think I can take supernatural to the Chief, to the Commissioner, or, God forbid, to the media? Do you have any idea what supernatural will do to my credibility, to the reputation of this Department? No, it won't do, Doctor!"

"I think you should take a look at my nipples," Hammer suggested, beginning to unbutton her lab coat."

"Have you lost your mind completely?" the Captain bellowed. "Did you suppose that you could lure me over to your side with the promise of sexual favors?"

"Captain, believe me, I wasn't ..."

"Enough! Take this report, return to your lab and begin re doing your tests."

"Perhaps we should remove your brain and attempt to carbon date it," Hammer hissed, grabbing the reports and leaving the office.

"Fine," Burke yelled after her. "Maybe you should do your nipples while you're at it."

This parting blast from the Captain got the attention of everyone in the outer office. All work ceased, silence descended. The Captain glowered, daring anyone to make a comment, but there were no takers. The word nipples was erased from everyone's memory and work resumed.

It had to be the new world's record for responding to a crime scene. Step on an elevator, press a button and ten seconds later you're there. This, of course, did nothing to lessen the impact of actually arriving at the crime scene, not to mention the sheer creepiness of it happening in Ishikawa's hotel. Coincidence was pretty much not an option. No one appreciated this more than Ishikawa himself. The quasi-ghoulish zeal he had demonstrated at Battery Park, while not totally absent, had clearly been tempered by self-doubt in the face of a demon with the sheer audacity to commit murder in the demon hunter's hotel. Instead of running at full speed into the room, he held back, allowing Lisa to go first. If they hadn't been walking into a blood-drenched horror show, she might have been able to appreciate his gentlemanly attitude.

The crime itself did little in the way of inspiring confidence. Instead of just one badly mangled guy, there was a badly mangled guy and a less mangled, but equally dead, woman. The guy was lying on the bed; the woman was sitting in a chair, her hands tied behind her back. Aside from the slash across her throat, some nasty scratches on her breasts, and the fact that she was naked, she might have been waiting for a bus, or about to have her hair done. She was pretty, wholesome-looking, early thirties, with brown hair and a perfect little nose. She liked to laugh, but was modest in her behavior and her desires. The man, on the other hand, had not come through the experience quite so intact. The thought, 'man attacked by presumed extinct saber toothed tiger,' ran through Lisa's head. The upper half of his body seemed to have had most of the skin flayed off. The incisions, running diagonally from shoulders to waist, effectively left

THE CUTEST LITTLE DEMON IN TOWN

the torso in four separate sections. The head, completely severed from the body, reclined on a blood-soaked pillow, its eyes still open.

There were two crime scene technicians in the room, one of them, Lisa noticed, busy vomiting in the bathroom. The other was going about his job, but he looked pale, like someone who had just encountered his first authentic ghost.

"Are you okay?" Lisa asked him.

He shrugged the question off. "I've been doing this for five years, never seen anything like this. I mean it's almost so horrible that it's not, like it can't be real, so it's probably not as bad as it looks."

Lisa nodded, thinking that, from a mental health point of view, denial sometimes made good sense. "So what can you tell me?"

"Whoever did it knows how to be tidy. No prints, no fibers, no fluids, except for the guy's. Most of the blood is his, too. Not really sure how the wounds were made."

"Super sharp claws," Lisa muttered.

"Sorry?"

"Nothing. How about the woman?"

"Compared with him," he said, indicating the dead body on the bed, "she was relatively untouched. Aside from the significant trauma to the throat, I mean. No sign of sexual activity, anyway."

"So the perp tied her up then made her watch as she did the guy."

"What do you mean she?

"Uh, just trying to be politically correct. You know, in the brave new world we pretend to inhabit, he and she are pretty much interchangeable."

"Yeah, tell me about it."

"Any I.D.?"

"Out of state driver's licenses, Mister Stanley Rosencrantz and his wife Helen. Tourists, probably. Not exactly your fun-filled vacation in the Big Apple."

"Even Jersey would have been better than this," Lisa said, following correct murder scene procedure by making an insipid, completely inappropriate joke, thereby conveying a certain insensitive toughness.

"Actually, I'm from Jersey," the tech guy said with a hurt expression.

Oh well, you win some and you lose some.

"Don't feel bad," she told him. "I'm from Ohio."

Tech guy managed a feeble smile. "Listen, we're just about finished, so as soon as my assistant is done puking, we're out of here. You'll stay until the wagon arrives for the bodies?"

"No problem," Lisa told him.

Ishikawa, she noticed, had moved in for a closer look at the body on the bed. She went over and stood next to him. This close, Mister Rosencrantz really did defy all the odds on just how horrific things could get. Granted, life was mostly pain and disappointment, but hardly anyone deserved being carved into pieces, especially while on vacation, with his wife looking on, no less. Lisa wondered why she was handling it so well and not cuing up for her turn at the toilet. Oh my God, she thought. Am I starting to get used to this? Have I become jaded and desensitized, or, even worse, immune?

"What do you think?" she asked. "Another change in M.O., two victims instead of the usual one. Maybe it's not our girl."

"Our girl?"

"Sorry," Lisa whispered. "Your demon."

Ishikawa shut his eyes down to tiny slits and pursed his lips. The message was pretty clear; either dream on, or you've got to be kidding.

"Okay," Lisa said. "So what's the story on the woman?"

"Her story? I don't ..."

"Why is she here?"

"It's as if the Akuma wanted a witness to the act."

"The ultimate captive audience. Forced to watch the show, then killed as an encore."

"I'm afraid the Akuma is becoming socialized," Ishikawa sighed.

"Parties, Internet dating, not averse to threesomes," Lisa mused. "From simple psychopath to complicated sociopath."

"I'm not sure you appreciate the seriousness of the situation, Detective Malone," Ishikawa said rather sternly.

"If you had only said young lady instead of Detective Malone, it would have been a decent impersonation of my old man."

He threw her the confused fish in an underwater pressure chamber look again. "I don't understand."

"Look, I appreciate the seriousness of this," Lisa said, shifting her gaze from one dead Rosencrantz to the other. "The question is what are you going to do about it?"

"I'm thinking an immediate return to Japan is not out of the question."

"You're just going to give up, is that it?"

"I must accept the fact that I am no longer a match for the Akuma."

Lisa laughed. "Have you ever been a match for it? Have you ever even gotten close?"

"Well, I ..."

"The answer is no. Not even close. And why is that? It's because the demon has always been too perfect. Now that's changing. It's changing, from perfect, extra-dimensional demon to less than perfect New York demon chick. She's feeling bored. She wants to play. Specifically, she wants to play with you. That's your opening. Do you see it?"

"If by wants to play with me you mean wants to kill me in some horrible fashion then yes, I do."

"Play with, kill, whatever. The point is, the demon is changing, you have to change with her."

"Are you suggesting that I must somehow transform?"

"Yes, I am."

"You realize I am Japanese. In my culture change is seldom sought, even less regarded favorably. We are what we are and we make the most of it."

Was this what Asian fatalism sounded like?

"You're in America now, my friend," Lisa told him. "Change is an option, at least in theory."

"The desire for change at all costs is nothing more than an easy fix in a world of increasing chaos."

"Maybe so," Lisa said, thinking how odd it was to be having this conversation while standing next to a mutilated dead body. What would Rosencrantz have to say on the subject? Let's wait until your body is sliced into several pieces, he would say. Then we'll talk about change. Perhaps Hammer would be able to get a more substantial response out of him. "The bottom line is this. Do you want to be remembered as the typical Japanese who failed, or as the demon hunter who at least tried?"

"Can't I be both?"

"No. It's definitely an either/or situation."

"In that case, I'll need some time to consider my options."

Stone had arranged to meet Harry Fang at the Lame Duck Restaurant on Mott Street, a slimy pit of potentially poisonous food and mostly bad vibe, but relatively easy to find in the demented maze of Chinatown. Harry, a small time felon and mean little prick, had reluctantly decided to cooperate with law enforcement as an alternative to serious jail time. Not the ideal information source to be sure, but Harry's complete lack of loyalty and his willingness to roll over on his cronies made him an asset. How Harry had continued to stay breathing for all these years was something Stone could never quite figure out. Harry believed it was because of his auspicious relationship with the gods; Stone preferred to see it as the simple luck of a mean-spirited idiot.

Chinatown was like something out of a bad dream. The extreme heat had apparently caused all the kitchens to detonate, the odors of Kung Po, Moo Shu and spicy Pao pork mixing with the already rampant air pollution into a tasty toxic cloud that hovered a few feet off the ground. Tourists and locals alike, overcome by the fumes, staggered along the streets in a slow motion shuffle, their skin and eyes burning, desperately seeking the perfect place to have lunch. Stone joined the throng, trying to keep his breathing as shallow as possible, one hand on his holster, just in case anyone tried to take a bite out of him.

From the street the Lame Duck resembled an ornate relic from a long lost era, a funeral parlor for ravenous ancestors trapped in long term limbo. Inside, in dim, smoky light, mourners met in secret to plot the next big event in a long history of sadness and cultural misunderstandings. There was something about Chinatown that turned a man philosophical, no choice but to go with it. It was either that, or just start shooting people at random.

Stone pushed his way through the front door and waited for his eyes to adjust to the light. Harry Fang was hunkered down in a booth in the back, a baseball cap pulled low over his forehead. Stone slid into the booth and smiled. Harry seemed nervous, his small dark eyes darting, a thin line of spit hanging from his lower lip.

"Hey Harry," Stone said. "Long time no see. Good of you to agree to meet me."

"Yeah, like I had a choice," Harry dribbled.

"Sorry to see you're still suffering from that loose saliva thing."

"Only when I talk to cops.

A slinky Chinese beauty with lethal eyes interrupted them, inquiring if they cared for tea. Stone ordered two bottles of beer and, just to be polite, asked for a menu.

"Hungry, Harry?" Stone asked.

Harry Fang sneered, pulling a cigarette from his pocket and lighting it. "So what is this, Stone, a social visit?"

"As much as I enjoy your company, Harry, no, it isn't"

"You know what happens to me if anyone figures out I'm talking to a cop, right?"

"I also know what happens to you if I suddenly come across that missing evidence. What was it, human trafficking or weapons smuggling? I can't remember. Either way, it's ten to fifteen upstate."

"So you got me by the balls, as usual."

"Do you even have balls, Harry?"

"Fuck you, Stone and tell me what you want."

The waitress reappeared with the beers. She smiled at Stone as she set them on the table. "If you don't see what you want on the menu," she whispered, "just ask."

"Get lost," Harry growled with a wave of an arm.

She stared at him as if she were considering ripping his little head off, said something nasty-sounding in Chinese and walked away.

"I see you still have a way with the ladies," Stone said. "I guess that's something you never lose."

"Yeah, Stone, you're hilarious. Now how about getting to the fucking point."

"Sure, Harry. The thing is, I need information."

"Ever hear of the Internet?" Harry asked, blowing a thick plume of smoke at Stone's face.

Stone smiled, casually reaching across the table and grabbing Harry's wrist, applying just enough pressure to make him wince.

"Okay, okay," Harry cried. "I get it. You need information."

Stone took a hit from his beer bottle and released Harry's arm. "My sources tell me there's a new group of kids in town, almost certainly operating with gang approval."

"What kind of group you talking about?"

"Hit team, professional, highly lethal. A female running the show."

"What? You got to be kidding me."

"Do I look like I'm kidding?"

"So what's their deal?"

"I'm guessing it's some sort of twisted, out of control revenge."

"The Chinese people have a legitimate claim to such things," Harry wheezed.

"Tell that to the world's fastest growing economy and a billion and a half smiling faces."

"We're not all smiling."

"Only because smiling makes the uncontrollable drooling worse."

Harry sneered at the insult. "Anyway, the gangs don't operate that way. Or if they did, it would have to be for something pretty fucking big."

"That's what I'm thinking, something big. What I need to know is what it is and who I'm dealing with."

"Sounds to me like you're chasing after ghosts."

"Come on, Harry. No new players on the scene? No scary-looking female strangers on the street?"

"Plenty of scary-looking chicks around, but none of them running assassination gigs."

"Now how would you know that for sure, Harry?"

"I don't know for sure, but ..."

"All I'm asking is that you check around with some of your punk contacts in the gangs. You know, you've been hearing crazy rumors and do they know anything about it."

"I could get killed asking questions like that, Stone."

"Yeah, and you could get killed crossing the street. Look, do this for me and you're off the hook. The evidence hits the shredder. But no bullshit. These assholes killed a friend of mine the other night."

143

"Right, no bullshit."

"Oh and Harry, I'm in a bit of a hurry on this one."

After the wagon had picked up the Rosencrantz', Ishikawa wandered back to his room to sulk and Lisa headed back downtown to the station. Not surprisingly, traffic was heavy and lethargic, long lines of metal containers in an environmental death grip. Even with the air conditioning running full blast she was perspiring, feeling damp and sticky, and not al all in a good way. Most people found unbearable heat non-conducive to sex, but she wasn't one of them. The hotter it got, the more she wanted it. On the other hand, the cold had pretty much the same affect, which suggested that the weather had absolutely no influence on her sexual urges. Murder obviously didn't either. Cop leaves scene of gruesome double murder and immediately starts thinking about sex. Perhaps, Detective, you should consider speaking with one of our department psychologists.

Her mind drifted to Stone, the current man in her life, who seemed less in her life today than he had been a few days ago. It was almost as if the murders they were investigating were pushing them apart, forcing them onto separate, mutually exclusive paths; for him it was the sensible cop path, real life killers in real time crime, for her the loopy path of unreal monsters and a mentally unbalanced Japanese detective. So why was she so sure that Stone was traveling into a dead end, while she was getting closer to the truth?

Traffic came to a complete stop at 23rd and Fifth. On the corner, a man who looked more qualified to be washing windshields for spare change than making a prime time speech, was exhorting a small, unenthusiastic crowd on the end of the world. Lisa lowered her window to listen in.

"We will all burn," he shouted. "Murder, madness and mayhem will descend upon us. The devils who kill for pleasure are among us, their evil is limitless."

Lisa wondered why the deranged always seemed able to sum up the state of things so succinctly.

Without warning, the man broke through his audience and ran directly for Lisa's car. His face was in the window before she had time to react.

"I know you," he yelled through rotting teeth.

"Really?" Lisa replied, slowly removing her gun from its holster. "Who Am I?"

"It doesn't matter now," he told her. "The demon is coming and it will rip the eyes from you head and then drink from the bloody sockets."

"Guess what?" Lisa said, pointing her gun at the man's forehead. "She's already here."

"The man jumped back and glared. "Blasphemer!" he screamed, as traffic began to move again and Lisa moved with it.

Fourteen

It was close to two o'clock when Lisa got back to the station. The place seemed unnaturally quiet, more like a funeral parlor than a big city precinct. Police stations were supposed to be hubs of controlled frenzy, people racing against the clock shouting out memorable one-liners, cops and criminals locked in the unrelenting dance of good versus evil. This was more like walking into a wax museum. Sergeant Murkowski was at the front desk looking either extremely bored or recently deceased, but he perked up a bit when he saw Lisa. Along with the majority of males in the Division, and several of the females, he believed that flirting with and/or fantasizing about Lisa was more or less a requirement of the job; Malone, the rookie Detective with the body of a goddess and the attitude of a smart, sarcastic hooker. Talk about work-related perks. Lisa played along because it made things more interesting, and because, as far as she could tell, there was nothing wrong with being popular.

"Hey, beautiful," he smiled. "Hot out there?"

"End of the world hot," she told him.

"At this point, I'm not even sure I'd care," Murkowski oozed, "except that I wouldn't be able to see you anymore."

"Unless you and I are the only survivors," Lisa told him with a wink. "Think about it."

"Oh, don't worry, I will."

"So what's going on around here, Sergeant?"

"A heat induced crime wave is my best guess. Eight murders in the past twenty-four hours, and that's not including your two new ones. Basically, we've got bodies lined up in every possible direction. It's like an assembly line of death out there."

"Nice image," Lisa told him. "Did you come up with that yourself?"

"Yeah, well, you know how it is. I've got time on my hands here, the mind tends to wander."

"Any word from Stone?"

"Yeah, he called in. He's in Chinatown, digging around, should be back later this afternoon."

Lisa recalled the story of the last Detective who had gone digging around in Chinatown. His body was found two weeks later in a landfill on Staten Island.

"The Captain?"

"At the Commissioner's office, probably getting his rear end spanked."

"Well, he probably deserves it."

"I'll tell him you said so."

"Thanks."

"Not much life in Homicide at the moment," Murkowski said. "In fact, you may be the only one up there."

"That's okay," Lisa told him, heading for the elevator. "I can use some alone time."

""I respectively have to disagree, Detective. A woman like you should never be alone. That's why I'm thinking about you and me, tonight, exploring the possibilities of carnal love. Considering how fucked up things are, what do we have to lose?"

Lisa smiled. As far as middle-aged lechers went, Murkowski was definitely one of the nicer ones. "Well, let's see," she told him. "For you, probably your life. For me, the slim remains of my self-respect."

"One of the things I love about you," Murkowski laughed. "You've always got the right answer."

"Almost always, anyway," Lisa said, walking to the elevator.

True to the Sergeant's word, Homicide was like a graveyard. Lisa went to the bathroom and washed her face, then poured a cup of coffee, no doubt well past its prime, and carried it to her office. She sat at her desk and let her mind wander, watching as it jumped around from one thing to another – Stone, Ishikawa, sex, the dead couple in the hotel, the weather, Officer Mendez' boobs (*seriously*?), the future, destiny, the possibility of free will, whether or not she'd get laid tonight. The list, apparently, was endless. What did it take, she wondered, to be able to focus on just one thing? Possibly only geniuses could do it, or maybe murderers could, too. At the very least, cutting someone into pieces would require a certain single-mindedness of purpose.

Lisa was about to begin writing her report on the hotel killings when she noticed a woman walking around in the outer office. She was young, petite, wearing next to nothing and unmistakably Asian.

"Excuse me," Lisa said, leaving her office and walking towards the woman. "Can I help you?"

"Oh hi," the woman said. "Sorry to bother you. I was just looking for Detective Stone."

Lisa was struck by the young woman's face. Not beautiful, exactly, but perfect in a way that was hard to describe, particularly the eyes. They were the largest Asian eyes she had ever seen, dark oval-shaped orbs that seemed to sparkle and could easily swallow a man whole, or a woman for that matter.

"Are you all right?" the woman asked.

"Sorry," Lisa said. "I was just noticing your eyes."

"I know," she laughed. "They're so big they make me look like some kind of freak."

"Not at all," Lisa told her. "They give you the appearance of a girl who can have just about anything she wants."

"I like the sound of that."

The two women stood there for a moment gazing into each other's eyes. It was like a contest of who would blink first. Lisa's eyes were no slouches when it came to exerting their will over others, but up against the mesmerizing black disks of the tiny Oriental girl, she was clearly feeling overmatched.

"You have beautiful eyes," the young woman told her. "Like two emeralds."

"Thanks," Lisa said, noticing that the vision in her emeralds had gone slightly blurry and she was feeling a little dizzy.

"In Japan people say that you can look into a person's eyes and see their soul. The funny thing is that the same Japanese people go to great lengths to avoid making eye contact. I guess it's a kind of irony."

Lisa laughed, but not wholeheartedly. Whoever this cute, little Asian girl was, Lisa was pretty sure she didn't like her. She certainly didn't trust her. "So, how do you know Stone?"

"Oh, he and I are friends. Well, sort of. We only met last week."

"I'm Stone's partner," Lisa said, wondering why Stone wouldn't have mentioned meeting the hot little Asian chick with the hypnotic eyes. Unless of course he had a good reason for not mentioning her, say, for example, that he was secretly screwing her on the side.

Jealousy, Lisa? Not very becoming and hardly your style.

Not jealous, only curious.

We'll see.

So you're Lisa!" the woman exclaimed, jumping and clapping her hands together. "I'm so happy to meet you. Stone has told me so much about you."

"Really?"

"Are you kidding? He talks about you all the time."

"As long as you don't believe anything he says," Lisa told her, wondering if there was any way she could arrest the giant-eyed home wrecker and have her locked up for a few days. Indecent exposure was one possibility. The girl was about a centimeter of sheer, cut-off tee-shirt away from having her breasts exposed.

"You know, I'm so rude," the woman said. "I haven't even introduced myself. I'm Sato Yui, from the island of Japan. I'm in New York researching a book on crime."

"So you're a writer," Lisa said, glancing at Sato Yui's hands. Extra-long fingernails would have gone a long way to explain the scratches on Stone's back, but there were only regular looking nails on small, slim fingers.

"It's my dream," Sato Yui said.

"I wish you success," Lisa said, secretly wishing that Sato Yui's tourist visa expired tomorrow. She would even be willing to drive her to the airport, just to make sure she got on the plane.

"You're so sweet," Sato Yui smiled. "Stone is letting me interview him for my book. Maybe I could interview you, too."

"I don't know," Lisa said. "I haven't been a Detective very long and ..."

"That's perfect!" Sato Yui squealed. "It will be like a fresh perspective on the New York cop scene."

"I am pretty busy right now."

"With the murders, right? Stone told me about them."

"Did he?"

"How about this? I'll give you the phone number at my apartment. If you decide you can, just give me a call."

Lisa handed her a pen and a pad of paper. Sato Yui jotted down her number and handed it back.

"Anyway," Sato Yui said. "I should be going."

"I'll tell Stone you were here," Lisa told her.

"That's okay, I'm sure I'll be running into him."

Lisa stood there and watched her leave, finding it difficult not to stare at her really cute backside barely contained in an even tiniest pair of shorts. She wasn't sure what to make of her conversation with the Japanese girl, or why she was suddenly feeling uneasy, but she hoped that there would be a fingerprint left behind on the pen or note pad. In any case, she was clearly looking forward to interrogating her partner about his secret relationship with Sato Yui from the island of Japan.

THE CUTEST LITTLE DEMON IN TOWN

After getting very little from Harry Fang – although the Chinese waitress did give him her phone number and a promise of the best sex he was ever likely to have – Stone spent the next several hours looking for Li Yuan, a part-time prostitute for the Chinese elite and a fairly successful drug dealer in her own right. He had met Li during his undercover narcotics days in Chinatown. This was before the Divisional Chief had been discreetly informed that large amounts of gang money were being funneled into the pockets of city officials, possibly including the mayor, and that the sensible course of action was to back off. After that, it was either kiss the crusty old backsides of the gang bosses, or ask for reassignment.

Just before the chop suey hit the fan, Stone had set up a deal with Li for five kilos of heroin. At the time he didn't know that Li, a classic Asian beauty with an independent mind and a fearless streak in the face of death, was operating behind the backs of the gangs. Stone's plan to get to the gangs through Li turned into both of them having death proclamations placed on their heads. Only the fact that he was a cop (killing one would have been bad publicity) and that she was the favorite call girl of several gang bosses had saved their lives. Somewhere in the middle of it, he and Li Yuan had become lovers, the threat of their own imminent demise turning out to be the ultimate sexual turn on. The sex was so hot that it had no choice but to burn itself out fast. It had smoldered for a while, reluctant to die, but in the end there were no regrets. He had moved on to Homicide, she had disappeared back into the vaporous Chinese nightlife of sex, drugs and forsaken dreams.

It had been ten years since he'd seen her. He wasn't sure if she would throw her arms around him and kiss him, or try to put a bullet in his head. Either way, Li would probably know who was ordering the gruesome high profile hits and who was carrying them out. And she would tell him, just as a way of saying fuck you to the sacred code of silence that seemed to be a prerequisite of gangs everywhere. Only problem was that he couldn't find her. No one knew for sure what had happened to Li Yuan. Someone told him that she had returned to Shanghai with a wealthy husband, another that she had had plastic surgery and was living somewhere in Florida, still another that she had been killed by an angry boss who blamed her for his inability to achieve an erection. He asked everyone he talked with to have her get in touch with him and left Chinatown.

Halfway back to the station his phone started ringing.

"Hi, Stone, are you still in Chinatown?"

"No, I just left. Who is this?"

"It's me, silly. Sato Yui."

The Japanese girl from the bar, he reminded himself. "How did you know I was in Chinatown?"

"Oh, Lisa told me."

"Lisa?"

"Your partner. She's really pretty, you know?"

"When were you talking to Lisa?"

"That doesn't really matter, does it? What does matter is that I need to see you now."

"Now?"

"Stone, there is no time like the present."

"I suppose that's true, but I'm pretty beat, on my way back to the station."

"But Stone, think about it, you need to see me, too, don't you?"

He had no idea why, but he was fairly sure that he did. "Yes," he told her. "Now that you mention it, I really do need to see you."

"So come to my place. It's on your way."

"Okay, give me the address."

Sato Yui rattled off an address on the lower east side. He knew the area well enough, the upscale side of down and out, a volatile mix of local freaks and tourists, the place to have a late brunch, score some crack, or simply vanish from the face of the Earth. Once the fascination of shopping for eccentric junk and watching the parade of weirdoes faded, there was always the attraction of sudden and anonymous death.

"See you soon," Sato Yui sang into the receiver just before hanging up.

Lisa finished her report on the mutilated Mister Rosencrantz and his merely murdered wife, picked up the pen and note pad and went down to the forensics lab. She found Hammer in autopsy with no less than four mangled bodies on stainless steel tables. Mrs. Rosencrantz' body, still looking quite lovely despite having been dead now for several hours, waited patiently in the corner.

"Lisa," she said. "I'm glad you're here. There's a number seven scalpel on the table over there. Could you get it for me?"

"I wouldn't know a number seven scalpel even if someone was stabbing me with it," she said, walking to the table in question.

"Then just bring everything that looks like it might be a scalpel."

Lisa scooped up several scalpel-like implements and brought them over. "Mind if I ask what you're doing?"

"Just redoing several tests on the serial murder victims, as per the Captain's orders."

"Why would the Captain want you to do that?"

"Good question," Hammer said, making a new incision into the grayish flesh of someone's chest. "Apparently he has an aversion to scientific fact, preferring instead a falsification of evidence."

"I don't understand."

"The time frame on the claw made him snap."

"Not surprising, I suppose. Did you tell him about your experience the other night?"

"I even tried to show him my nipples. From his reaction, I might have been trying to force feed him the ebola virus."

"His loss," Lisa said, scrutinizing the body Hammer was carving into. "Is this Wilbur?"

"No, this is Goth. Wilbur's over there."

"Wouldn't it be easier to just re-do the reports?"

"Of course it would, but I'm just too agitated to even think about paper work."

"What about the new guy, Rosencrantz?"

"Same deal as the others, although I'll have to invent some realistic sounding explanation for an upper body severed into four neat pieces. Maybe something terrorist-related. You know, there's apparently nothing a radical Muslim extremist won't do to get into heaven."

Lisa sat herself down on a stool and sighed.

"Is all of this starting to get to you?" Hammer asked, her expression oddly soft and understanding.

"It's just that I'm not sure what's really going on. Stone is acting strange, Ishikawa is acting even stranger and I'm in the middle somewhere beginning to seriously entertain the idea that a demon is running around the city cutting people into pieces. Is it true, or is Ishikawa's craziness starting to rub off on me? I have no clue."

"What does your female intuition tell you?"

"That I probably should have gone into the entertainment field. You know, cash in on my good looks and extremely underdeveloped sense of morality."

"If it's any consolation," Hammer told her, digging deeper into the dead body of Goth, "you do entertain me."

"Likewise," Lisa smiled.

"Now that we've settled that issue," Hammer said, "let's get back to Stone. What's up with him?"

"Let's see," Lisa said. "Memory loss, sudden changes in personality, odd, erratic behavior and, most recently, his conviction that a Chinese execution squad is responsible for the first three victims, plus Hogan, Rosencrantz and his pretty wife."

"Talk about the male imperative to remain rational at all costs, even as it provokes a mental breakdown. And Ishikawa?"

"Also freaking out, but in a much more passive way. He's convinced that the demon is altering its etched in stone behavior patterns and he's feeling inadequate to deal with it."

"You haven't been fooling around with him, have you?"

"With Ishikawa? Of course not."

"You're not even a little curious?"

"I did see him this morning in nothing but a bath towel."

"And?"

"And nothing. I think I may be entering an anti-male phase."

"A brief period of lesbian experimentation might actually do you some good."

"Oh please."

"If it makes you feel any better, I, too ..."

"If you're about to admit to being a lesbian, I'm not sure I want to hear that right now."

"I was going to say that I, too, believe there is a demon on the loose. I don't know what it means, or even if it's possible, but the evidence does support the hypothesis that something weird and quite possibly supernatural is going on."

"Great! So you, Ishikawa and I will end up in some ex-cop psycho ward together. We'll be drugged into oblivion and forced into group therapy sessions with alien abductees and born again Satan worshippers"

"It almost sounds like fun."

"Anyway," Lisa said, getting up and showing Hammer the pen and note pad. "I'd like you to check if you can get a fingerprint off these."

"Put them over there," Hammer said. "I'll do it when I finish with this. Did the print come from the Rosencrantz crime scene?"

"Not exactly," Lisa said, proceeding to tell Hammer about her peculiar run in with Sato Yui. Hammer stopped in mid-dissection and listened intently.

"So this was a young Japanese girl," Hammer said when Lisa had finished her story.

"Yeah."

"With weird eyes."

"As I said, yes."

"And you have no idea how she got up to Homicide."

"I don't know. She must have got past Murkowski. The man was on the verge of slipping into a coma when I came in."

"Lisa, are you listening to yourself? Why aren't little bells going off?"

"I don't know. Little bells almost never go off."

"Consider, will you?"

"You don't think ..."

"Didn't Ishikawa say that she would appear as a young Japanese woman? Wasn't it a young Asian female who visited me in the lab the other night?"

"But she gave me her phone number. Tracking her down won't be a problem."

"Which only suggests that, as far as she's concerned, you pose no threat."

"And Stone is ..."

"Probably screwing a demon."

"I was going to say that he's in serious danger."

"It's quite possible that his memory loss and the she demon are connected."

"She's clouding his mind."

"She may be clouding ours as well."

"Which means what?" Lisa asked.

"It means," said Hammer, her expression beaming, "that until further notice, no one among us can be trusted."

"Don't you think that's a little extreme?" Lisa asked.

"Probably," Hammer agreed. "All right, we'll agree that you and I can be trusted. Everyone else, however, we remain suspicious of until proven otherwise."

Fifteen

Stone knew what he was doing as he walked up the stairs in Sato Yui's building, but he wasn't quite sure why. He needed to see her. That much was clear. She needed him and he needed her. Need took precedence over all other considerations. It didn't matter whether or not he wanted to see her. He was pretty sure that he didn't, not right now, anyway. He had other things to do, a murderer to find, a partner to make love to, a Captain to placate. All of it would have to wait.

Sato Yui answered the door wearing only a pair of skimpy panties. "Stone!" she squealed. "What a nice surprise."

"Sorry," he said. "I just had the feeling that I needed to see you."

"That's okay. I'm happy you're here. You must think I'm some kind of little slut walking around nearly naked."

"I don't mind it," he told her, his eyes focusing in on the small perfect mounds of her breasts, the hardened points of her nipples.

"It's just so hot in here."

"It's hot out there, too."

"You should take off your clothes," she suggested. "Believe me, you'll feel better."

Stone stood there impassively as Sato Yui pulled off his tee shirt, unbuckled his jeans and tugged them down around his ankles. "Nice," she said, on her knees in front of him. "From what I've seen, you are a physically superior human male."

The comment registered as vaguely odd to Stone, but he was in no position to question it. Sato Yui pulled his jeans over his feet and then slid his boxers down and off, her fingers lightly grazing his balls in the process.

"Let me look at you," she said, standing up and making a slow tour around his body. "Oh my God, how did you get these scratches on your back?"

"I'm not really sure," he told her.

"They're beautiful," she said, tracing the lines of the wounds with her fingers. "So violent and sexy."

"Do you think so?" he asked, shivering as her lips began kissing the wounds.

"It's amazing," she said, moving her hands slowly down his back until they were resting on his muscled behind. "I'm feeling so much like a real girl today."

"As opposed to ..?"

"Let's kiss," Sato Yui whispered, grabbing Stone's hand and pulling him towards the bedroom.

She pushed him down on the bed and crawled over him like some hungry cat toying with its prey before the inevitable kill. Her small mouth came down slowly on his, sucked briefly on the lower lip then quickly pulled away. She smiled, her tongue provocatively flicking the edges of her lips.

"Are we done kissing?" he asked.

"For now," she told him. "You have other tasks to perform."

"Such as?"

"First you can suck on my nipples," she told him, sliding upwards until her breasts were directly above his face. "But not too hard. Suck on them as if this was our first date."

Isn't this our first date? Stone wondered. The movement of a swollen nipple the color of charcoal to his mouth precluded an answer. He closed his eyes and gently licked the nipple cone, allowing it to slip between his lips. He felt as if he were floating down into some pool of pure light, so pure that it was incapable of being reflected. The pool, he realized, was bottomless, that it was possible to fall into it forever. At the same time, he knew somehow that the pool was only an illusion, that it was Sato Yui he was being absorbed into. Images began flashing across his brain, unfamiliar people and places, the face of a beautiful woman in the grip of ecstasy, shifting imperceptibly into horrible agony. Somewhere in the distance he could hear Sato Yui's rhythmic moaning.

"Now the other one," she said hoarsely, pulling the nipple from his mouth and replacing it with the other. Sex seemed nice. She could feel herself becoming aroused, the warm and wet thing happening between her legs and no sign of a shift in physical form. She remained a complete human female enjoying the pleasurable sensations of having her nipples sucked. She was also aware of Stone's erection poking against the fabric of her panties just about where her anus was. I have an anus, she thought, seeing it as just one more piece of evidence of her being a girl. She tried to imagine that big thing of his going in there and it made her shiver with nervous pleasure. What would it feel like? Would it make her want to kill, or become all weepy and desperate like some silly anal virgin? She considered putting his thing in her mouth, sucking and moaning, as girls are prone to do in these circumstances, but decided to be selfish, as girls are even more prone to be in most circumstances.

Stone opened his eyes as the nipple was retracted from between his lips. "I really want to fuck you now," he told her.

"Sure you do," she told him, "but not a good idea."

"How could it not be?" he wanted to know.

"I'm having too much fun being a girl," she said, which made absolutely no sense to him. "Besides, you're working for me today."

"All right," he said reluctantly.

"I want you to give me an orgasm with your mouth," she announced, slipping her arms around him and flipping him around until he was on top.

"How did you do that?" he asked.

"Guess I'm stronger than I look. Now pull off my panties and get busy."

No sooner had his mouth touched the soft warm flesh of her sex than she had her first orgasm. From there her exuberance seemed to expand exponentially. Several explosively wet orgasms followed in short order. Despite his best efforts to hold her down, his hands gripping both her buttocks with all his strength, Sato Yui managed to thrash about like some crazed predator caught in a steel jaw trap. When she finally finished, her head falling back on the bed with the weight of death attached to it, Stone could barely move. His mouth felt like he'd spent several hours in the chair of some sadistic dentist.

"How was that?" he summoned the strength to ask.

"Super!" Sato Yui cried. "I'd like to try it again."

"Really?" he asked nervously.

"But enough fun for today. Besides, I have an appointment to get ready for. Too bad about your big disappointed thing."

Stone waved away the apology. "That's okay," he said, glancing down at his erection, which he barely recognized. It was like some alien entity awaiting instructions to launch its attack on planet Earth. "I should probably be going, anyway."

"So until next time," she said, jumping off the bed. "There is one other thing I'd like you to do before you go."

"What is it?"

"It's over there in the closet."

Stone walked over and opened the closet door. "Jesus Christ!" he gasped, staring directly into the obviously dead eyes of a naked young woman with her throat slit open. "Who the hell is this?"

"That is the Miura female," Sato Yui said.

"The what?"

"My roommate, or former roommate, I should say."

"What the hell happened to her?"

"I'm not sure. I think she became seriously depressed and decided to kill herself."

"By slitting her own throat?"

"I know. It's creepy, isn't it? Anyway, I'd like you to dispose of the body."

"Wait a minute," he said, the image of himself being locked up in a cell for several years racing through his head. "I can't do that. This has to be reported, investigated, the cause of death legally determined."

"I don't think that's a very good idea, Stone," Sato Yui said. "Do you think that's a good idea?"

"Now that you mention it, probably not."

"Probably not?"

"Definitely not."

"So the best solution is for you to put your pants on, wrap the Miura female in something and take her somewhere."

"Take her where?"

"The trunk of your car for starters. After that, it's up to you."

"Right. The trunk of my unmarked police car is the perfect place to store a dead body."

"That's what I was thinking."

Stone got dressed, rolled the dead girl's body into a blanket, wrapped masking tape around it and carried it to the front door, not totally impervious to the absurdity of hauling a dead body from building to car, in the early evening, in one of the busiest neighborhoods in the city. But if that's what Sato Yui wanted …

"Thanks a lot," she said, standing at the front door, still naked, as he hoisted the body over his shoulder and stepped out onto the landing. "You are a savior."

"Not to mention the accomplice to a crime," he said.

"That too," she smiled. "See you soon."

Lisa returned to her office and called the police switchboard, asking to have Sato Yui's phone number checked for an address. As she hung up the phone it immediately started ringing. It was Sergeant Murkowski at the front desk.

"I've got a guy down here," Murkowski droned. "Asian ancestry, I'm guessing, claiming he knows you. Looks like a bum from where I'm sitting."

"This you call me on, but the cute little Asian chick with the Devil eyes you let up here without even checking."

"No idea what you're referring to, Detective."

"Never mind. Did you get the gentleman's name?"

"What is it?" she heard Murkowski ask the man. "Says his name is Ishikawa."

"He's okay. Let him up."

The man who stepped off the elevator bore very little resemblance to the Ishikawa she knew. His perfectly pressed suit and respectable tie had been replaced with a dirty pair of jeans and a faded orange tee shirt with "Bite me, please!" written across the front. He was also wearing a yellow baseball cap and a pair of black wrap-around sunglasses. Only the familiar dark gray trench coat gave him away.

"My God!" Lisa said. "What happened to you?"

"I took your advice," he told her.

"I advised you to start dressing like a homeless person?"

"No, you advised me to embrace change. It was not easy for me to admit, but I finally concluded that you were perhaps right."

"That's great, but I'm not sure changing your fashion sense covers the change we were talking about."

"Of course, I realize that. This is merely one element of the change which I am currently undergoing."

"Care to elaborate?"

"Very much so."

Sensing a familiar pause defying all known time limits, Lisa forged ahead.

"In that case, please do," she told him.

"I believe that the problem involves the hemispheres of the brain, specifically, my brain."

At last, his obviously severe brain problems come to light.

"I have been relying much too heavily on the rationally motivated left hemisphere, while completely ignoring the right. I assumed that a combination of thought and technology, a left-brain phenomenon, would provide me with the advantage I required. Now I realize that the key lies elsewhere, specifically in the right."

"In the right," Lisa repeated.

"Intuition," he said, his voice trembling slightly. I must intuit my adversary, disregard common sense and feel my way forward."

"Interesting, " she said, more to be polite than anything else. "The instinctual approach to solving crime."

"Exactly! The Akuma is above all else an instinctual creature. This is her primary motivation. I must connect with her on that level, see as she sees, become the beast, as it were."

"So, based on this, your new plan is ..?"

Before Ishikawa could answer, Lisa's phone rang. She wrote something on a small pad. "Yes!" she said. And then to Ishikawa, "Sorry, please continue."

"Are you sure?"

"Absolutely."

"Where was I?"

"Your revised plan."

"Right! I intend to roam the city randomly, thoughtlessly, as it were, moving solely on impulse. I will enter the flow of humanity and drift with the ease of the sleepwalker. Questioning nothing, I will lose myself in all of life's irrelevant details; succumb to the most facile survival strategies. Using this method, I am convinced that eventually the Akuma's path and mine must intersect."

"It sounds promising," Lisa told him, wondering if she had any sort of moral, or possibly legal, responsibility to have Ishikawa committed for a thorough psychological work up. "But you may not have to go to that much trouble."

"It's no trouble," he told her. "But why not?"

"Because," Lisa said, a big smile on her face, "I have the demon's address."

Lisa and Ishikawa had just gotten to the elevator when the doors opened and, hardly a surprise, there stood Captain Burke. A momentary face off occurred while the Captain scrutinized the oddly dressed man at Lisa's side. There was, he was forced to remind himself, no accounting for taste. Pathetic sloppiness for some was for others an open declaration of self-worth, or possibly a misplaced sense of rebellion against authority. In a democracy, all personal statements were encouraged, no matter how annoying or grotesque. Far be it from him, a mere police Captain, to throw these people into a jail cell until they either smartened up, or agreed to hire a personal style consultant. The Captain shook his head and shifted his attention back to Lisa.

"Where are you off to, Malone?"

"Uh, I just got a hot tip. On my way to check it out."

"In Chinatown?" he asked.

"Yes, Sir," Lisa lied.

"I assume you're coordinating with Stone."

"Just got off the phone with him, Captain."

"That's good," he said, shifting his gaze back to Ishikawa. "Do I know you, sir?"

"It's Lieutenant Ishikawa," Lisa laughed.

"Hello, Captain," Ishikawa said, removing his sunglasses.

"Sorry, Lieutenant," the Captain said. "I didn't recognize you. You're, uh, dressing a bit differently."

"He's been undercover," Lisa offered. "In Chinatown."

"Excellent!" the Captain said, smiling relief. "Just keep me informed, Malone."

"You lied to the Captain about me," Ishikawa said, as they walked to Lisa's car.

"Yes, I did."

"Are we going to Chinatown?"

"No, that was also a lie."

"But we are coordinating with Detective Stone."

"Not exactly."

"He is still your partner, isn't he?"

"Yes, but it's possible that Detective Stone has gone temporarily over to the dark side."

"The dark side? I ..."

Lisa, borrowing a gesture from the Captain's play book, threw up a hand as a stop sign. "I'll explain everything, or at least I'll try to explain everything, in the car."

With traffic crawling along like an ant army on barbiturates, there was plenty of time for Lisa to relate to Ishikawa her run in with the Japanese girl calling herself Sato Yui. She also outlined Stone's recent odd behavior and her suspicion that the demon, a.k.a. Sato Yui, might be exerting some influence over him. How else to explain his memory loss, the scratches on his back and his sudden obsession with secret Chinese hit squads on a murder/mutilation spree? Besides, a woman can always tell when there's another woman in the picture, even if the other woman turns out to be a supernatural non-human entity.

After Lisa finished, she waited for Ishikawa to respond, but he remained silent. Was it possible that he had dozed off while she was speaking? With his cap pulled down, it was impossible to tell.

"Are you awake?" she finally asked.

"I believe so," he told her. "Although with each passing day it becomes more difficult to know for sure."

"Life is a dream," Lisa said, gazing up through the windshield at a thick orange/yellow haze in the process of wrapping itself in an obscure strangle hold around the city.

"Only in a dream would the Akuma have its own apartment," Ishikawa offered.

"In Alphabet City, no less."

"Alphabet City. Is it a real place?"

"You can judge for yourself."

"Is our plan to knock on this Sato Yui's door and ask her if she is the Akuma?"

"No, our plan is to park outside her building and wait."

"I'm relieved. Direct confrontation could prove to be very hazardous to our health."

"Sooner or later confrontation is inevitable, don't you think?" Lisa asked.

Ishikawa sighed, slowly nodding his head. "Inevitable."

"I thought that's what you wanted."

"Very often the closer we get to the object of our desire, the less we desire it."

"Boy, that's no lie."

"And if your assumptions are correct, we may have an additional problem."

"And that is ..?"

"Detective Stone. If he has had intimate contact with the Akuma, he could very well be in some sort of trance state. This could render him extremely unstable, and he will follow her instructions without question."

"So you've seen this before."

"No. Never. But again, with each minute that passes, I understand the Akuma less."

"You're the demon expert who knows absolutely nothing about demons."

"And it has only taken me ten years of hard work to accomplish this."

Sixteen

S ato Yui, dressed in a black, silk miniskirt and a white, sleeveless, see-through blouse, minus underwear, of course, strolled along the streets of Soho in a state bordering on rapture. The bombardment of physical sensations upon her near-perfect human body was like a drug, making her feel both sexy and famished. The variety of aromas drifting on the hot moist air made her senses reel and her mouth water. Clearly, she needed to kill something soon, but was not quite ready to abandon the tense excitement of anticipation. She was learning to appreciate the experience of mingling with humans, sensing their thoughts and desires, their lurking fears and anxieties. Humans were so complex, their heads filled with continuous noise as they struggled to behave in a civilized way. Somehow they managed to keep their primitive animal natures contained, although the price they inevitably paid was excruciating boredom. Sato Yui's work was to liberate the animal, relieve its boredom through unimaginably exciting sex and then suck the life energy from it.

She entered a small art gallery and made her way through the crowd, feeling the eyes of men and women upon her. How could they resist? She was art in motion, creativity in its purest form, a combination of beauty, eroticism and the threat of annihilation. Could they sense the danger? Did they understand on some level that the irresistible creature before their eyes was less the perky Asian tourist in the killer outfit, more the insatiable hunter who killed without even a glimmer of remorse?

She stopped in front of a large painting about which a small group of people was in an apparent frenzy. She overheard phrases such as, "existential anguish," "fundamental chaos of the universe," "primordial sexual urges" and "the essential schizophrenic nature of reality." Why was it, she wondered, that the less humans had to say, the more effort they put into saying it? If they knew what chaos really looked like they would be too afraid to even utter the word.

"Do you like the art?" a voice just behind her right ear asked.

Sato Yui turned her head and looked directly into the big blue eyes of a very attractive young woman with choppy brown hair, pale white skin and a nicely put together body wrapped in something clingy and black. Now this was interesting. Here she was out hunting for a male victim, some guy with a nice body and a functional sex organ, and her first taker turns out to be a female. Was she giving off some lesbian vibe? If so, she had no choice but to blame the Miura female. There had been the woman at that imbecile Ishikawa's hotel, but nothing sexual had happened with her. Well, almost nothing sexual. That had been mostly for fun, even if the woman hadn't been able to see it that way. Humans so desperately lacking in imagination weren't easy to understand. Death was inevitable; exciting death by supernatural cause was rare. If, by some sudden miracle of destiny, it were happening to you, why wouldn't you put a little more effort into appreciating it?

"Like it?" Sato Yui exclaimed to the blue eyes. "I love it!"

"Me, too," the woman said, subtly shifting her body closer to Sato Yui. "It's so powerful and wild, don't you think?"

"Like a monster off its medication."

The young woman laughed. "I've known a few of them."

"So have I," Sato Yui told her, thinking to herself that there were monsters and then there were monsters.

"I'm Maya, by the way."

"I'm Sato Yui, from Japan."

"Wow! Are you here on vacation?"

"It's more like a hunting trip."

Maya looked confused. "A hunting trip?"

"You know," Sato Yui laughed. "Hunting for thrills, adventure, new experiences."

Maya nodded knowingly. "This may sound crazy, but would you like to go somewhere, maybe for a drink or something?"

Even more crazy, Sato Yui was actually considering it. "Are you here with a guy, by any chance?"

"Relax," Maya said. "I'm alone."

"Oh, that's too bad," Sato Yui said.

"You mean you're interested in a three-way?" Maya asked, her eyes lighting up.

"New experiences," Sato Yui reminded her.

"Listen, I have a boyfriend. I guess you could say we're bi-sexual. We could go to his place. I'm sure he'd be pleased."

"How is he in bed?"

"Like a crazed beast, but don't worry. You'll be completely safe."

Sato Yui had no doubts concerning her own safety. The safety of the lovely bi-sexual Maya and her unsuspecting boyfriend, on the other hand, was an entirely different matter. "If you say so," she said, following Maya out of the gallery.

"My boyfriend lives in a kind of seedy part of town," Maya said, leading Sato Yui away from the crowds on the street, down a narrow, abandoned alley. "I hope you don't mind."

"Aren't you afraid to walk around here alone at night?" Sato Yui asked.

"I'm used to it," Maya said. "Besides, I always carry my pepper spray."

They walked further into a maze of darkened street flanked by bulky brick buildings, most of which appeared empty.

"This is one of the old warehouse districts," Maya said, stopping and guiding Sato Yui into a small alleyway between two buildings.

"Is this where your boyfriend lives?" Sato Yui asked.

"No," said Maya. "I just wanted to ..."

"Kiss me?"

"Is it okay?"

"Actually, I was hoping you would."

Maya pressed herself against Sato Yui and began kissing her, the fingers of one hand tracing the outline of Sato Yui's nipples through her shirt. To her surprise, Sato Yui found herself liking it. She slipped her arms around Maya and placed her hands on Maya's firm backside. She felt Maya's tongue slip inside her mouth, and she was able to resist the urge to bite it off and swallow it. Instead, she opened her mouth wider, allowing Maya to leisurely explore the inside of her mouth. Maya moaned softly and Sato Yui did her best to copy the sound. Maya ended the kiss and gazed into Sato Yui's eyes.

"You have wonderfully delicious lips," she said. "And I can't wait to lick and suck on your nipples."

A sexy thing to say, Sato Yui thought to herself. Not only did she think it, she felt it. The words of a human female had made her feel sexy. She guessed this wasn't the first time Maya had dragged some unsuspecting Asian girl down an alleyway, tempting her with kisses and the promise of suckled nipples. Maybe it was all about exploring the possibilities of human sex, wherever they lead, or maybe Maya and her boyfriend were into other things, too, like murdering the girls Maya brought home for their sexual pleasure. Either way, Sato Yui was very interested to find out what came next.

Maya pulled Sato Yui back onto the street and they resumed walking. They were holding hands and giggling, like a couple of teenagers on the verge of slipping beyond the conventional rules of heterosexuality at all costs. Not exactly the Akuma's thing, but Sato Yui was enjoying the sensation while it lasted. The three dark figures suddenly appearing directly in front of them seemed to have materialized out of the air; large, hulking forms that might have been some other species of demon, except for the unmistakable smell of human male.

"Well, well, well," one of them said. "What have we here?"

"Looks like a couple of whores who got lost," another one said.

"Nah," the third added. "They're just girls out looking for a big dick."

"Hey," the first one said. "In that case, they are in luck, cause I got a huge dick right here in my pants."

"So where you bitches going?" the middleman in the insipid chorus wanted to know.

"It's okay," Maya whispered to Sato Yui. "Just stay behind me."

"What's that, bitch?" one of the men asked, as the three formed a semi-circle around the two girls.

"I said fuck you and get the fuck out of our way," Maya snarled, pulling the pepper spray from her bag.

"Fucking cunt," the guy said, his fist coming around like a fast moving shadow, catching Maya on the side of her face, which sent her flying into the brick wall of the nearest building. "No reason to go acting all belligerent. All we want to do is fuck you."

"Yeah," added the guy on the left, snapping open a blade "And maybe cut you a little."

"Hey," guy on the right said. "Tonight's our lucky night. We got ourselves an Oriental cunt here. You know what they say about that Asian pussy."

"So why is she smiling?" middle guy wanted to know. "Why you smiling, bitch?"

Sato Yui was actually enjoying the performance of the three thugs. Their energy smelled of stupidity and unfocused rage. Typical human males stripped of their civilized masks, going primitive in an effort to affirm their pathetic manhood. There was almost something appealing about them, but, of course, they had to die. Their misfortune to have bumped into Sato Yui when she was right in the middle of feeling like a sexy human female with Maya. She unbuttoned her blouse and slipped it off, then unzipped the skirt, slid it slowly down her legs and carefully stepped out of it. The thugs weren't quite sure what to make of this. In their experience, potential rape victims were generally not so cooperative. Sato Yui's pre-rape striptease was totally new and therefore disconcerting.

"Wait a minute," one of them said. "Is she supposed to do that?"

"She's not even wearing underwear," another one said. "Tearing off the panties is the best part."

"Relax," the third and obviously more philosophical of the trio said. "Just because this has never happened before don't make it bad. What we're dealing with here is cultural variety. Asian chicks clearly react to rape differently. I'm inclined not to question it and just try to enjoy the experience."

The other two had to admit that this probably made sense.

"Cultural variety," the guy in the middle snarled, taking a menacing step towards the naked Sato Yui, only to be stopped in his tracks by the sudden, violent shaking of the Asian girl's body, followed by a weird reddish-tinted fog that had appeared out of nowhere and felt like it was burning the eyes right out of his head. "What the fuck?" he spluttered, as the sharp point of a claw entering just below his chin silenced him in mid-question. Before the other two men could react, Sato Yui shifted the claw upwards, essentially slicing the front of the man's head open. Two nearly perfect halves of his face fell away in opposite directions, settling on either shoulder. The man's body collapsed, its blood pulsing out in long streams that made a slight sizzling sound as it hit the humid air. His two friends stared down at the mess at their feet, each trying to comprehend what had just happened. Conflicting impulses rattled around in their stunned brains; basic human stuff, fight or flight, ruthless revenge for the death of their friend, or a more sensible cutting of their losses. What they saw when they looked up rendered all of it beside the point. The cute little Asian bitch had turned into a large, greenish gray monstrosity, with claws and fangs and two scary, blood-red eyes, the glow from which was turning the whole street into a red-filtered nightmare.

"Fucking inhuman cunt," one of them hissed, but it came off sounding more like a plea for mercy than a threat.

"Sato Yui's claws flashed, catching the guy who had just spoken behind the head. In one brutally fast motion, she pulled him forward, sunk her teeth into his throat and tore away most of it. The last thug standing emitted a high-pitched wail and tried to take a step backwards. Only when he was unable to move did he glance down and notice that the crazy Asian monster bitch had stabbed him in the stomach. He barely felt it as the blade of her claw began to churn his guts, turning his insides to pulp. He was still staring into those red eyes as Sato Yui cut off his head, which made a whooshing noise as it sailed across the street.

Sato Yui licked the blood from her claws and growled, but not in a satisfied way. This was not the evening of lust and bloodshed she had planned. Not to mention that the interesting female sexual moment with Maya was probably lost forever; Maya, whom she was actually starting to like. She turned to where the girl had fallen. Maya was sitting with her back pressed against the building. Her face was contorted and wet with tears, her eyes were wide open, too filled with fear to be able to blink, her lips twitching uncontrollably. There was absolutely nothing sexy about any of this. Terrified humans were, at best, boring. Regrettably, the natural progression of the present situation led inexorably to the death of the female Maya. Sato Yui moved to the terrified girl and kneeled down next to her. The smell of human trauma mingled with other female odors, some bitter, some sweet. One neat slice across the throat and it would all vaporize, a spicy afterglow of life and death floating away on an invisible gush of wasted energy.

Sato Yui, pushing herself back into human form, decided against it. She wasn't exactly sure why. Was she actually feeling something for the human female? She shrugged, lightly stroked Maya's cheek, then picked up her clothes and walked away.

Stone came to uncomfortably contorted on the front seat of his car with a throbbing headache and, once again, no clear-cut recollection of anything that might explain it.

"Shit!" he said, sitting up and looking around. Judging by the view through the front windshield of downtown Manhattan on the other side of the river, he concluded that he was somewhere along the Brooklyn waterfront. The light suggested early morning. Another chunk of dead time to contend with, which, with an obviously impaired memory, didn't seem likely. It was the last thing he needed right now, as close as he was to unraveling the ongoing Chinese murder conspiracy and thereby reinforcing his top cop status in the Department. Or was it more accurate to say that he wasn't even remotely close to unraveling anything, and that the top cop award was almost never handed out to obvious mental cases? Better not to even think about that.

Maybe Lisa had been right about him needing to go to the hospital. That would at least give the doctors an opportunity to stand around speculating why a healthy thirty five year old man was losing his mind. They would study his brain, run every test imaginable and come up with various possibilities, none of them particularly reassuring. His career would be threatened. He'd be assigned a desk job until the mystery of Stone's brain was resolved. Unless it was never resolved, in which case he'd be offered early retirement on a crappy pension and the insincere gratitude of his fellow officers. In hushed voices they would all concur that the Stone magic had all along been nothing more than a fluke. They all knew it would never last.

Stone groaned, started the engine and pointed the car at the nearest bridge back into town.

Lisa got to the office early. Having been up most of the night with Ishikawa staking out Sato Yui's apartment, there hadn't been much point in trying to sleep. She needed to do several things, including avoiding the Captain, checking with Hammer on the hotel homicides and figuring out what to do about Stone. She placed Stone last on the list because the likelihood of her actually figuring that one out was remote, bordering on impossible. If her suspicions were correct, he had become a serious impediment to solving the case. He might even be in league with the demon murderer, but this would be difficult to prove, particularly to the Captain, who would no doubt react to her accusation by suspending her, or possibly having her committed for psychological observation and, if need be, electro-shock therapy at some undisclosed location; hence the importance of avoiding the Captain, at least for the time being. Her personal relationship with Stone was also up in the air. She just wasn't sure how she felt about sleeping with a guy who might be having sex on the side with a demon. Her belief in non-exclusivity and the freedom of sexual choice did not extend quite that far. Call her shallow and inauthentic, if you like.

And what else, Lisa?

Else? There is nothing else.

So nothing happened last night.

Last night? It got dark; there was no visible moon; it remained hot enough to fry chicken on the hood of a car...

Blah, blah, blah.

All right, fine. Ishikawa. There, I said it. Happy now?

Just helping you keep it honest.

God, how I hate you!

After several unsuccessful hours of waiting for Sato Yui to make an appearance, she and Ishikawa had given up and driven back to his hotel. He had invited her up for a drink. She had agreed. It had only taken three whisky and sodas to push Ishikawa completely out of character. He became what could only be construed as an emotional wreck, opening up about his life in Japan, his failed marriage and the years of sacrifice that demon hunting had demanded of him. At one point, his eyes actually began to tear up. Lisa had started out feeling slightly bored, trying to come up with a polite excuse to leave, but his story had eventually touched her. Possibly it was all the whisky. It had occurred to her that, beyond the probable insanity, the behavioral quirks and the obsession with quirky monsters impersonating hot little Asian females, Ishikawa was also a human man, presumably with real-life human needs.

"How long has it been since you've been with a woman?" she had asked.

There was a look of puzzlement on his face. "I am with a woman now."

Okay, too nuanced. "I mean how long since you've had sex?"

"Oh!" he had said, fidgeting uncomfortably. "It's a delicate question."

"I'm sorry. I shouldn't have ..."

"Five years and seven months, give or take," he blurted out. "And you, if I may ask?"

"Uh, three days, give or take."

"Of course!" he had said, his voice damp with disappointment. "You are a beautiful healthy young woman, who ..."

For reasons still not completely clear, Lisa had cut him off with a kiss, at first just a peck on the lips, but quickly evolving into something deeper and more passionate. The specific time line was difficult to reconstruct, but it wasn't too long after the kiss that Lisa was standing naked in Ishikawa's hotel room. He got out of his clothes with the speed of a high school boy on the brink of finally losing his virginity. The two of them had stood there naked, bathed in the glow of neon from the flashing sign on the building across the street.

"Considering our professional responsibilities," he had said, "do you think it's appropriate?"

"Probably not," she had answered. "But then your demon could appear at any moment and slice us up into human sushi."

"So really there are no rules."

"I couldn't have said it any better," she said, taking his hand and guiding him to the bed. She sat on the edge, positioning him so that he was standing directly in front of her. In truth, there was a part of his anatomy that she wanted a better look at. It (uncircumcised, to answer a previous question) lacked the stubborn mass of Stone's, but was certainly nothing to joke about standing around the water cooler at the office. It had a tapered smoothness about it that made it both attractive and friendly. It may have been the user-friendliest penis that Lisa had ever seen, a penis that would do what it's told and not assume that its mere existence rendered it worthy of female worship. It had responded instantly to her touch, swelling and lengthening in a way that reminded her of Ishikawa's sword emerging from its sheath. She tugged it gently towards her and let it slip into her mouth.

"I hope you don't mind," she mumbled.

Ishikawa's response was a mixture of Japanese folk song and the gleeful warble of prehistoric cave men discovering for the first time the ability to make fire. Within minutes, he began to moan, legs trembling, lips pursed, head thrown back in surrender. Talk about fast, Lisa had thought as he came, but then, notwithstanding the occasional self-stimulation in the shower, five and a half years was a long time between ejaculations. She had expected it to have a flavor that somehow defined it as Japanese, maybe the taste of green tea or seaweed, but it hadn't. She had been forced to conclude that sperm was merely sperm, probably the same no matter where it came from.

The subsequent fucking was also a surprise. Unlike the Korean guy Lisa had dated briefly in college, who had treated her nipples like elevator buttons and seemed to believe that effective love making required the transfer of vast quantities of saliva from his mouth to hers, Ishikawa was light, precise and relatively saliva free. He moved inside her as if he knew what he was doing, even if he was a bit tentative from the long lay off. Lisa had tried to imagine herself as a geisha, or a concubine (did the Japanese have concubines?) and that Ishikawa was some tough samurai, who rarely spoke and spent most of his time slicing up his adversaries; but who, after a long hard day of terrorizing helpless villagers, knew how to come home and satisfy his woman. Midway through this fantasy, she had had her first orgasm. Two more had followed. Shortly afterwards Ishikawa had managed a second ejaculation and then collapsed like the victim of a sudden stroke, his face flushed, his breath coming in short rasps.

"Are you all right?" she had asked.

"At this moment I am in heaven," he wheezed.

"Do Japanese people even believe in heaven?"

"Not officially, but we are practical enough not to rule anything out. Do we need to talk about what just happened?"

"No."

"Perhaps later."

"How about never?"

"That sounds much better."

Lisa slipped out of her reverie and saw Stone standing in the doorway.

"Jesus," she said. "I didn't notice you there."

"I guess not," he said, walking into her office. "You were off somewhere in fantasyland. Thinking about what, I wonder?"

Lisa smiled nervously. "Never mind that. Where the hell have you been?"

"In Chinatown."

"For two days?"

"That's what this kind of investigation requires."

"Any results from *this investigation*?"

"You know the Chinese mindset. Time is not a relevant concept. But I have a sense that things are slowly coming together."

"Oh really!" Lisa said, making no effort to disguise her sarcastic tone.

"Hey, are you okay?" he asked, reaching for Lisa's hand. "You seem strange."

"I'm fine," she said, sliding her hand from underneath his. "But we have to talk."

"You can talk in the car." This came from the Captain, who had no less mysteriously taken Stone's place in the doorway. "Triple homicide in Noho, or whatever goddam Ho it is this week. Could be the work of our serial. I want both of you on the scene now."

Seventeen

"Don't you just love it?" Stone said as he and Lisa drove to the latest crime scene.

"Murder, you mean?" Lisa asked, the hot glare through the windshield beginning to give her a headache.

"No, I mean our job, hunting down the bad guys, making a real difference in the lives of people, leaving the world a slightly better place than we found it."

"Yeah, sure," she told him. " So what are you hiding from me?"

"What? I'm not hiding anything from you."

"Okay, so why are you lying to me about not hiding something?"

"I have no idea what you're talking about."

"Tell me about Sato Yui."

"Who?"

"Cute, petite, Japanese, adorable butt, very scary eyes. Does any of this ring a bell?"

"The girl from the bar," Stone said, as if he were suddenly recalling some vaguely significant event from early childhood.

"Oh, you met in a bar? Why am I not surprised?"

"One time. She came up to me and asked something about doing an interview, but I never heard from her after that."

"Really! She seems to know you quite well."

"I don't see how that's possible. Anyway, why are you asking me about her?"

"Because I have reason to believe that she may be involved in these murders."

"Involved how?"

"As in she's the doer."

"You think Sato Yui is our serial killer," Stone laughed.

"Yes, I do. Ishikawa and I ..."

"Ishikawa? Is he still in town?"

"Yes, but you probably wouldn't recognize him."

"This is crazy, Lisa. Ishikawa is certainly crazy. You may be catching whatever it is he has. The Chinese gangs are responsible for these crimes."

"And you're sure about that."

"Ever hear of the Stone magic?"

More like the Stone delusion.

"Two days a go a couple of out of town tourists were murdered, same M.O., same excessive level of blood curdling carnage. What possible link could they have had with the Chinese gangs?"

"I don't know, but that's why we investigate. The connection is there, I'm sure. We just have to find it. Where were they killed?"

"In Ishikawa's hotel. How's that for a coincidence?"

"Have you considered the possibility that Ishikawa might be responsible?"

"So he's working with your Chinese murder squad."

"For all we know. Asians do tend to stick together."

"Now who sounds crazy?" *Not to mention slightly racist.*

"No crazier than suspecting a sweet, not to mention tiny, Japanese girl of being able to tear bodies apart."

"So, she's sweet? You've obviously tasted her then."

"I was referring to her disposition. She's a tiny girl of sweet disposition who is clearly incapable of committing these crimes."

"Unless she's not really a girl."

Stone turned into a narrow alley and stopped the car. The crime scene lay before them. It had been cordoned off with squad cars on either end of the alley and an ambulance parked farther down the street.

"I know I'll regret asking this," he said, "but if she's not really a girl, what is she?"

"A sexually motivated predatory Japanese demon," Lisa told him.

Stone stared at her for a moment, shook his head and got out of the car. Lisa sat there watching him walk away. Aside from his obviously cute rear end, there was nothing she particularly liked about him at this moment. She opened her door and followed him into what could have been a movie set for one of those low-grade blood and gore flicks that always go immediately to Amazon Prime. Blood being the operative word; it was everywhere in awe-inspiring quantity. The smell of blood and reheated dead flesh permeated the air, bodies and parts of bodies were strewn about on the street, the uniforms on cite mulling around in a kind of slow-motion stupor, all of which played nicely into the *night of the living dead* movie theme.

"So what have we got?" Stone asked the Sergeant on scene.

Do you have to ask? Lisa thought to herself. Just take a look around.

"Three males, twenty to twenty five years old, possible gang bangers, all killed in an excessively brutal fashion."

"That's for sure," Lisa said, bending to get a better look at a man whose face was hanging in two pieces around his bloody collar. "Any idea how this was accomplished?" she asked one of the crime scene tech guys.

"My best guess is that a powerful electric saw was placed underneath his chin and..." He made an upward cutting motion with his hands.

"The decap's head was found twenty feet from the body," the Sergeant informed them.

"Suggesting that whoever cut off his head then picked it up and shot putted it across the street?" Stone said.

"Maybe the perp's in training for the Olympics," the Sergeant offered with a half-hearted laugh.

"And the third one?" Stone asked.

"Throat torn out," the tech guy answered. "Possibly by a large dog."

"So let's see if I get this," Lisa said. "Our killer was out walking his dog, carrying an electric saw, he runs into these three large guys and he and his dog proceed to murder and mutilate them. Is that what you're telling us?"

Think of it as one possible scenario," tech guy sneered. "Except for the severed head. The cut was too clean for a saw, more like a large knife or possibly a sword."

"Maybe our guy is one of those, you know, Japanese samurai," one of the officers said, which got a collective chuckle from the group.

Not funny, Lisa thought, thinking about the one person she knew who actually carried a sword.

"All right," Stone said to the Sergeant. "Once forensics is finished you can get the morgue boys in here to clean up this mess."

"Excuse me, Detectives," a young officer walking briskly up the alley called out. "It looks like we might have a witness, a young woman."

"Where is she?" Lisa asked.

"We found her on the next street over, covered in blood, but it doesn't appear to be hers. The EMT's are with her now."

"Did she say anything?" Stone asked.

"She's pretty incoherent, most likely in shock, but she kept mumbling something about red eyes, whatever that means?"

"Red eyes," Stone repeated, looking pleased.

Oh right, Lisa thought. The Chinese hit squad run by a homicidal female with glowing red eyes.

"They're just about to take her to the hospital," the officer told them.

"I'll ride with her," Lisa said.

Stone nodded his agreement. "I'll meet you back at the station," he told her.

"How's she doing?" Lisa asked the EMT as she hopped into the back of the ambulance.

"She's got a bump on the back of her head and a bruise on her cheek, but other than that no physical injuries."

"Can I talk with her now?"

"You can try," he said, handing Lisa a small black leather bag. "This was lying next to her in the alley."

Lisa poked around in the bag and pulled out a wallet with a driver's license in it. Maya Jensen, twenty-five years old, address in Scarsdale. The girl on the license had a very pretty face, with lively eyes and sensuous lips. Except for the streaks of dirt and dried blood and the fact that the lively eyes were now glossed over, dull looking, it was the same face lying on the gurney. Lisa pulled over a small stool and sat down next to her.

"Hi Maya," she said as soothingly as possible. "I'm Lisa. How are you feeling?"

Maya blinked her eyes several times and tilted her head in the direction of the voice. Her lips began to tremble. Lisa took hold of her hand. "Don't worry," she told her. "You're safe now."

"So much blood," Maya whimpered.

"Did you see who did it?" Lisa asked.

"She killed them," Maya whispered, choking back tears.

"She?"

"But it wasn't her."

"So she was someone else."

Maya nodded. "A ... monster."

Lisa leaned closer to the girl and lowered her voice. "Did the monster have a name?"

Maya's mouth moved, the sound uttered on a breathless sigh. "Sato Yui."

In the hour or so he had been hanging around on the street outside Sato Yui's building, Ishikawa had fended off offers for a quick, no questions asked blowjob, primo weed and authentic snuff videos. A cheery-faced Japanese couple with cameras slung around their necks had stopped long enough to remind him about Japanese pride and then stuff a five-dollar bill into his trench coat pocket. "Drugs aren't the answer," the man had whispered in his ear. "Now go buy yourself a hot rice ball."

In a more rational state of mind he might have returned the money and attempted to explain to the man the actual nature of his mission, but this was neither the time for rationality nor explanations. The success of his task and therefore of his life, however vague and lacking in anything that might be construed as a viable future, depended now on the suspension of all thought. His goal at this point was to remain as irrational as possible, to lurk about mindlessly, non-resistant to the ebb and flow of bizarre life around him, attuned to the instinctual pulse of events. He was convinced that he would recognize Sato Yui when he saw her. She would be unmistakable, the demon hidden inside the little girl's body. He would then follow her, absorb her behavior patterns and begin to formulate an unthinkable, and quite likely futile, plan.

The Japanese woman who appeared from the building next to the one Lisa had pointed out was taller and less pretty than he had expected, but he knew right away that it was Sato Yui. Lisa had probably been mistaken about the address. She moved up the street quickly, occasionally glancing around nervously, as if fearful of her surroundings. As if the Akuma had anything to fear. "Brilliant," he said out loud, making sure to keep a safe distance. The guise of timid helplessness was a masterstroke. Who would suspect that the fragile Japanese female on her own in the big scary city was actually a powerful monster that murdered with the whimsy which other girls applied to choosing a shade of lipstick?

It occurred to him that this was the very first time in all his years of hunting that he had actually seen his adversary. It was a special moment, the precise instant when the balance of power shifted, presumably in his favor. A wave of confidence swept over him, putting to rest most, if not all, the nagging self-doubt and uncertainty. How foolish he had been to consider giving up. Adaptation had been the hidden key to success all along; only he had been too focused on so-called correct procedure to see it. Thank God for Lisa. She had opened his eyes to the truth that there was more than one way to catch an Akuma. In fact, she had done much more than that, also giving him the opportunity to feel like a man again. Lisa, naked, in his arms had resurrected him, awakening his nearly dead emotional core. Everything as a result had changed, the world looked different, felt different. Happiness was once again more than just an abstract, mostly unattainable, concept. Even the Akuma, now walking a mere half-block in front of him, was no longer merely the unspeakable abomination, the essence of pure evil that had to be destroyed at all costs. It/she had become something more complex and it was no longer possible to assign it/her an absolute status. It was becoming clear to him that evil was never pure and that the visualization of evil required the ability to also love. Love, after all, did conquer all.

Ishikawa was right on the verge of calling this irony, thereby claiming an understanding once and for all of the elusive concept, when the young woman suddenly veered right, disappearing into a small shop. He approached cautiously, surprised to discover that the shop was a bookstore specializing in Japanese literature in translation. This was puzzling, even for a man now firmly secured in the irrational. Yes, even in English, the fiction of Abe, Ishigaki and Murakami would be a distinct pleasure, but, as far as he knew, the Akuma was not in the habit of reading fiction, or anything, for that matter. The Akuma had no hobbies and only one extremely lethal habit. Unless, of course, this was just another reminder of how little he actually knew about his opponent. It was possible that the

Akuma was a voracious reader, that she devoured words with the same intensity that she tore apart human flesh and bone, perhaps finding within the covers of the Japanese masters her own brand of perverse inspiration.

Moving in for a closer look, he strained to be able to see through the shop's front window, but the glare from the sun's reflection turned everything inside the shop into distorted shadows. Risking exposure, he stepped forward and pressed his face to the glass. As he did, the door opened and Sato Yui stepped out carrying a small plastic bag. She stopped for an instant and stared at him, then quickly walked on up the street. He allowed her to put some distance between them before recommencing the pursuit. He expected her to look back to see if he was following, but she didn't. She walked rapidly, to the point of almost running, all the way to First Avenue where she turned sharply left. Ishikawa, worried that he would lose her, began to run, his sword bouncing painfully against his back. As he reached the corner and turned, she was waiting for him.

"Why are you following me?" she asked angrily, her voice much louder than one would have expected a Japanese woman willing to use in public.

"Excuse me?" he said, out of breath. "I'm not ..."

"Spare me the stupid excuses," she snapped. "My parents hired you to spy on me, didn't they?"

"Your parents?"

"For a private detective, your style is pathetic. I spotted you the second I left my building."

"I think you may be mistaking me for someone else," he tried to tell her.

"Enough!" she shouted, punctuating the warning by raising her leg in a lightening-fast, karate-style kick, the point of her shoe catching Ishikawa squarely in the testicles. "Just tell my father, 'Nice try, but fuck off!'"

As he buckled, collapsing in agony on the street, he was vaguely aware of her walking briskly away.

No telling exactly how long he lay there, semi-conscious, waiting for the pain to subside. When he opened his eyes he was looking directly into the pretty face of a young Japanese woman with the largest black eyes he had ever seen.

"Hi Ishikawa," she said. "I think you've been looking for me."

Eighteen

"So this, Malone," the Captain shouted, shaking the piece of paper as if it were flypaper that he couldn't get off his hand, "is your idea of a witness statement."

Lisa was sitting in a chair against the wall, feeling like a high school student who had been sent to the Principle's office for the umpteenth time this week. Stone was sitting next to her, looking, as far as she could tell out of the corner of her eye, on the smug side; as if to say, hey, rookie detective, what else can you expect? They screw up and then they get flayed alive for it. That's life in the big leagues.

She resisted the urge to kick him hard in the shin. "I was very careful to take down the statement word for word, sir,"

"And did you bother to read it over before handing it to me?" the Captain wanted to know.

"Having heard it as I was writing it, I didn't see the need to read it again. But if the grammar is in any way offensive ..."

The Captain cut her off. "Let me refresh your memory, Detective." He slipped on his glasses and began reading.

"I and a young Asian woman, Japanese, I think she said she was, had just left an art gallery in Soho and were walking to my apartment when the three men approached us. There intent was obviously to rape us, and probably worse. I attempted to defend us with the pepper spray in my purse, but I was punched in the face and knocked to the ground. As I lay there, terrified, the Japanese girl, who called herself Sato Yui, suddenly turned into something inhuman, horrible, a monster! She then proceeded to very quickly kill all three of the men."

Lisa raised her hand. "Captain, if I could just ..."

The Captain used his much larger hand to demand silence. He continued reading.

Question from Detective on duty, Lisa Malone. "Could you possibly describe what this so-called monster looked like?" Witness response. "It was big, a dark grayish color, I think, sort of lumpy; large, sharp-looking teeth, long black claws. Detective Malone asks if there was anything else? Witness replies: "Only the eyes. They were like spotlights filled with boiling blood, the light from them turned everything red." Interview terminated due to witness beginning to weep uncontrollably.

"Now," the Captain growled. "Is there anyone else in this room who agrees with me that this statement is complete bullshit, bald-faced lying bordering on a contempt charge?"

"Why would she lie?" Lisa asked.

"I don't know," the Captain said. "Why do people take drugs, or need to see shrinks?"

"Her tox screen was clean," Lisa reminded him.

"So maybe she's a psycho."

"And maybe she isn't."

"Look," the Captain said, clasping his hands together as if about to burst into evangelical prayer. "We have a serial killer, or killers, on a city-wide rampage, bodies are piling up in the morgue, our medical examiner is having some sort of nervous breakdown, my ulcer is threatening to blow a hole in my stomach and neither of you have given me squat. The Commissioner is so far up my ass over this that I'm actually looking forward to my next proctologic exam. What I don't want to hear about are monsters, sex-crazed apparitions attacking nipples, prehistoric fingernails, or DNA from unknown species sub-groups. What I do want is something substantial. I want hard evidence. I want a killer in handcuffs. And I want it now! Stone?"

"The Chinese gangs are responsible for these crimes, Captain," Stone responded. "And I'm very close to proving it."

"Oh please," Lisa said under her breath.

Stone threw her a look. "I've got a solid connection between the Chinese and the first two victims, only a matter of time before I link this death squad to the others. Hogan was convinced the Chinese were behind all this and I'm convinced, too."

"If I remember correctly, " the Captain said, "Hogan also believed that the Chinese were responsible for the attack on Pearl Harbor."

"Okay," Stone said. "He got that one wrong, but his instincts as a cop were never too far off. Besides, it's the only scenario that makes any sense."

"It makes no sense," Lisa said.

"More sense than the testimony of a traumatized witness, or the ramblings of an unhinged Japanese cop, who, for all we know, isn't a cop at all."

"Enough," the Captain boomed with an explosion of air that seemed to make the room shake. "Clearly, there is some disagreement between the two of you on this, and maybe after it's all over we'll think about reassignment, but for right now I want you working together, as a team, with a single goal. Go after this Chinese hit squad and bring them down. Am I understood?"

"Absolutely," Stone answered.

"Malone?"

"There's no I in team," Lisa said, feeling immediately contemptible for it.

"That's the spirit I'm looking for, Detective," the Captain smiled.

Lisa again raised her hand.

"Yes, Malone," the Captain sighed.

"Excuse me, Sir," Lisa said, "but don't you think it would be worthwhile to bring in this Sato Yui for questioning? If she was in the alley last night during the attack, it makes sense to hear her version of what happened."

"I suppose it couldn't hurt," the Captain agreed. "Assuming we can find her."

"I'm sure Detective Stone can find her easily. After all, she and he are friends."

"What? You know this woman, Stone?"

"Only in a very casual way," Stone insisted. "We're definitely not what you would call friends. Far from it."

"Still," Lisa said. "Talk about you're coincidences."

Stone glared at her, while the Captain rubbed his chin and eyed Stone.

"Well," the Captain said. "Let's find out where she lives."

"Oh, we already know where she lives," Lisa told him. "Don't we, Detective Stone?"

"All right then," the Captain said. "Send someone in a black and white to pick her up."

"Actually, Sir," Lisa said, "It might be better if we sent a tactical unit."

"In full body armor, you mean?"

"It would be prudent."

"Thanks for the advice, Malone," the Captain said, without a trace of sincerity. "But contrary to what you may have seen on TV crime shows, we do not send S.W.A.T to pick up potential witnesses."

"Then let Stone and I bring her in."

"I want you two full-time on the Chinese gangs. No excuses. Send Mendez. She always seems to be walking around here with nothing to do."

"That was a low blow," Stone said, as he and Lisa left the Captain's office.

"No lower than this whole Chinese fantasy of yours," she shot back.

"Which only proves how much you still have to learn about investigating the crime of murder."

"Oh really? On our way to the triple homicide this morning, I told you I thought Sato Yui was our serial killer. Two hours later, a witness gives us her name as the perp. How do you explain that?"

"I don't."

"What a surprise."

"For all I know, Lisa, you may have let the name slip during the interview."

"Give me a little credit, will you?"

Hey, we all make mistakes."

"Yeah," Lisa said, walking towards her office. "Tell me about it."

Stone ran after her. "Wait a minute," he said, taking hold of her arm. "We have a professional difference of opinion here, it's not personal. I mean, what about us?"

"Until further notice, there is no us," she told him.

"Why? Because I refuse to accept your theory that a young Japanese woman is a murdering monster?"

"No, not entirely."

"So then tell me why."

"Because," Lisa said, grabbing the door of her office and pushing it closed. "I'm pretty sure that you're sleeping with that monster."

"This can't really be happening," Ishikawa said, sitting in a retro coffee shop with a 60's theme somewhere on the lower East side, staring directly into the disarmingly pretty face of a girl calling herself Sato Yui. "Are we actually here?"

Sato Yui smiled and sipped her coffee.

"And you drink coffee? Is that even possible?"

"Relax, Ishikawa," she told him. "Things change. Either we change with them, or we cease to exist. I can drink coffee, shed tears and even have orgasms. Do you know why?"

"No, why?"

"Because I'm a girl."

195

"But in fact you're not a girl," he reminded her. "You're an Akuma from a trans-dimensional space/time which defies human understanding."

"And you're the ultimate Japanese windbag. Do you even listen to yourself? You are so trapped inside your limiting definitions that you can't appreciate the miracle right before your eyes."

"I'll admit I have no expertise in miracles, but I know ..."

"You know nothing," Sato Yui hissed, without losing her cheerful smile. "You're like some reanimated corpse fixated on an obsolete fantasy. You've spent all these years trying to find me and kill me, without any success at all. Have you ever asked yourself why you are such a failure?"

Ishikawa hung his head. "Admittedly, it is not the sort of question I'm comfortable asking."

"Because in your single-minded obsession with me, you lost sight of what it means to be you. The moment you gave up your manhood, turning into an automaton, a salary man with a sword that hunts supernatural entities, your failure was assured."

"It's an interesting theory," he said, cautiously sipping his coffee. "But how is it that you know so much?"

"I read a lot."

"Really?"

"No! The only reason I know more than you is because I'm not a total moron."

"Oh," Ishikawa said, suddenly feeling, for reasons that could never be explained, let alone justified, a certain attraction, possibly even bordering on something sexual, to this girl, who was not a girl, but actually a demon in the usurped body of a girl. "And yet, I have found you now."

"More accurately," Sato Yui corrected him, "I found you. But that doesn't change the significance of our story."

"Our story?"

"Do you want to hear it?"

"Perhaps even more than I wanted my father to tell me just once that he loved me."

"Your father was even more of an asshole than you."

"Knowing that already doesn't make it any less painful to hear."

"Sorry," Sato Yui said as if she really meant it.

Janis Joplin's, 'Piece Of My Heart,' began playing on the coffee shop's sound system.

"I love this song," she said, closing her eyes and swaying to the music. "I miss the 60's, don't you?"

Ishikawa thought about it and wasn't sure if he did or not. "Can we get back to the story?"

"You're so uptight."

"Uptight?"

"Stiff. A real starched shirt. You need to learn how to live in the moment."

"An interesting observation coming from a non-living entity."

"Fine, have it your way. The story. Insipid demon fanatic hunts demon for years. Loses family and friends. Becomes an outcast. Never even gets close to killing demon. Then demon and pathetic human hunter arrive in New York City. Everything changes. Demon begins to feel at home, learns how to manifest in human form more or less permanently. She starts to enjoy her life as an attractive, young female killer. Hunter humanoid, until now clueless, also begins to change. He suddenly feels again. He has a human heart, after all. He may even be falling in love. As a result, he is able to meet the long sort after object of his desire. In a coffee shop, no less."

"I am not falling in love," Ishikawa corrected her.

"Pathetic in love loser is also in denial."

"She means nothing to me."

"She? Do you by any chance mean Lisa Malone?"

Ishikawa shook his head violently.

"Don't want to talk about it?" Sato Yui teased.

"Is there an end to the story?" he asked.

"Of course there is. But do you really want to get there so fast?"

"I need to know."

"I guess I owe you that much," Sato Yui said. "The end, as it turns out, is full of irony."

"I was hoping it would be."

"Your inability to catch me has prevented me from killing you. As an unfeeling, one-dimensional robot, you were both doomed to fail and, in a way even I can't fully explain, protected from a well-deserved and utterly gruesome death. Now that you have returned to the ranks of the emotionally living, thanks, no doubt, to the lovely Detective Malone, you can, in theory, kill me, or, much more likely, you will die trying. Interesting, wouldn't you say?"

He had to admit that it was, not only interesting but also most likely true. His own salvation ensured his death. It was irony, clear and uncomplicated, at last! "So you're going to kill me," Ishikawa asked, wondering if he should risk reaching for his sword, but immediately realizing the futility of it. Even though the situation he found himself in was unique, the chances of successfully decapitating a demon sitting across the table from him in a 60's theme coffee shop had to be virtually non-existent.

"Do I really have a choice?" Sato Yui asked.

"I suppose not."

"Whether or not I'll also have to kill Lisa is another matter."

Ishikawa bristled, making a half-hearted effort to rise from his chair. "If you so much as touch her, I'll …"

"You do love her," Sato Yui said, looking happier than an Akuma was supposed to be able to look.

"My life is falling apart," Ishikawa sighed, dropping back into his seat.

"All life is falling apart," she said. "That's what makes it so interesting. Everything breaks down eventually."

"Even you?"

"Yes, even me, but on a time scale beyond your puny human brain's ability to comprehend."

"You won't be able to stay in human form indefinitely."

"We'll see about that."

"Even an Akuma cannot defy nature."

"Watch me."

"When will you kill me?"

"That would be telling."

"Just one more thing. My sense is that you are indeed the Akuma, but how can I be absolutely certain?"

"Listen to your heart," she told him.

"My heart is filled with black dust," he sighed.

"I'm actually starting to like you," Sato Yui said. She threw him a seductive look and placed her hand on his leg. Her large eyes watched him intently as she began to stroke his thigh, her fingers moving closer to his still slightly tender testicles. To his surprise, he felt what could have easily been the initial stirrings of an erection. And then he was aware of the razor-sharpness of the claws, cold as icy steel, scratching against the fabric of his dirty jeans.

"Will this do?" she asked. "Or should I open an artery?"

Nineteen

"You look like a wreck," Doctor Hammer said to Lisa, who had just walked into the autopsy room and dropped onto one of the extremely uncomfortable stools. "Have you been getting any sleep?"

"If you're asking me when I'll be waking up from this unending nightmare, I don't know."

Hammer was working on the bodies from the previous night's triple homicide. She had them lined on stainless steel tables and was jumping around from one to the other, like some hyperactive assembly line worker on forced overtime.

"Is that standard autopsy procedure?" Lisa asked her.

"I'm streamlining," Hammer answered. "Since the Captain has abandoned all interest in reality, I figure my results won't matter much. I may even go accidental death on these three, although act of God is not out of the question."

Lisa groaned and stared down at the floor.

"Still banging your head against the concrete wall of male authority?" Hammer asked, probing the neck area of the guy with the missing head.

"We've got a witness to this party," Lisa said, indicating the three dead bodies. "She names Sato Yui as the killer. She also apparently witnessed Sato Yui turn into a demonic entity. The Captain dismissed her as a drugged-out psycho, while insinuating my own gross incompetence as a police officer."

"And Stone didn't rush to your rescue?"

"Please! Don't even utter that name in my presence. I feel like killing him."

"Poor baby," Hammer said, dropping her scalpel, walking to Lisa and putting her arms around her. "I did warn you about becoming emotionally involved with your partner."

"First of all, you didn't so much warn me as coax me into it. Second, I'm not emotionally involved."

"That's okay," Hammer cooed, kissing Lisa lightly on the forehead. "You can tell Mommy all about it."

"I really wish you wouldn't do that."

"Kissing you, or using the Mommy reference?"

"No, I meant hugging me with your gloves on. I don't want to get home and discover blood and muck all over my clothes."

"Oh, sorry," Hammer said, pulling off the gloves and throwing them on the headless guy's body.

"What should I do?" Lisa moaned.

"First thing," Hammer said, beginning to rub Lisa's shoulders, "try to relax."

Lisa had to admit that the tension she was feeling began to dissolve as the doctor's adept fingers worked on the knots in her muscles. She would have preferred some strong, anonymous guy's hands on her, someone who wouldn't speak unless spoken to, agenda-free and relatively sane, but she was smart enough to know that such ideal situations were few and far between. She breathed deeply, trying to forget everything she had ever known, at least for the moment. Doctor Hammer, reading the exhalation of breath as a signal of submission, moved her hand down Lisa's back. She pushed Lisa gently forward, working the spine, kneading the muscles of her lower back.

"I hope you know that I'm on your side," Hammer whispered in her ear.

"I do," Lisa sighed.

"And that I would do anything for you."

Lisa nodded, feeling grateful to have at least one friend, even if she was on the crazy side. Hadn't she read somewhere that the insane were actually extremely loyal in friendship? They might forget your name, or try to suffocate you in your sleep, but their loyalty was virtually canine in quality. This was a comforting thought for Lisa, at least until Hammer's hands slipped around to the front of her body and began rubbing her belly. From there, they drifted under her tee shirt and upwards, until they were placed firmly on Lisa's bra-covered breasts. At the same time, Hammer began to place light little kisses on Lisa's neck.

"Uh, what are you doing?" Lisa asked, her body tensing.

"I'm not sure," Hammer told her. "Does it really matter?"

"You're feeling me up and kissing my neck," Lisa said. "It almost has to matter, doesn't it?"

"I suppose so," Hammer said, as she began to caress Lisa's nipples through the fabric of her bra.

"So Stop!" Lisa insisted.

"Sorry!" Hammer said, releasing Lisa's breasts and walking back to the headless corpse. "I guess it's just all the recent stress, the feeling that I may be losing it, while at the same time not even knowing anymore what 'it' is."

"I understand," Lisa said, pretty sure that she didn't.

"Do you?" Hammer asked, her voice trembling. "Can anyone ever understand what another human being is going through?"

"No," Lisa admitted, moving to Hammer and placing a hand on her shoulder. "But pretending to understand counts for something, right?"

Hammer laughed, an odd, straight-from-the-asylum cackle that made Lisa nervous. "You're probably thinking that I'm the monster.

Monster? No. Weird, sexually conflicted, middle aged doctor to the dead? Maybe.

"Not at all," Lisa said soothingly.

"I hardly have any friends," Hammer told her, pulling on a clean pair of surgical gloves. "There's no one, really, that I can talk to."

"We're friends," Lisa told her. "You can always talk to me."

"Thanks! I appreciate that. But there's more."

"There is?"

"I'm afraid so. Again, it could simply be all the ongoing pressure of the current situation, but I think I'm falling in love with you."

"In love with ..?"

"Wait!" Hammer said, turning and placing a latex finger to Lisa's lips. "There's even more. Maybe it's because I feel that time is running out, that we all could be dead at any moment. I don't know, but I want to confess everything to you."

Really? Everything? Are you sure?

"I don't think that's necessary," Lisa said.

"But it is," Hammer insisted, her blue eyes open so wide that Lisa expected something to pop.

"All right," Lisa agreed. "If it's that important to you."

"I had a sexual relationship with Stone."

"What?"

"It was a long time ago and it didn't last long, but I thought you should know. I also performed oral sex on the Captain, but only once. He was younger then and much less of an asshole, and I was in a particularly dark place in my life."

"I've been having sex with Stone for the past month," Lisa blurted out.

"I knew that already," Hammer smiled.

"You did? How? Did he tell you?"

"He didn't have to."

"Okay then, I slept with Ishikawa."

"No way!"

It was at that moment that Lisa's cell phone decided to ring. She pulled it out of her jeans pocket and jabbed the receive button. "Malone."

"Hi, it's me. Ishikawa."

"Of course it is."

"Were you expecting my call?"

"No, but your name came up recently in conversation. Are you all right?"

"I think so."

"Where are you?"

"I'm in the alphabet town. I just met the Akuma."

"You did? You actually saw her? Are you hurt?"

"No need to worry. We only had coffee together."

"Coffee?"

"And conversation. I have learned much."

"And let me guess, nothing at all."

"As usual, you read my mind. I want to see you."

"Why?"

"You know why."

"Oh God!"

"Yes, if in fact there is one."

"Okay, listen, let me call you back."

"Ishikawa," she said to Hammer as she terminated the call. "He's just run into the demon."

"And?"

"They had coffee, apparently. And a chat."

"Things just keep getting stranger and stranger," Hammer said.

"Shouldn't there be a limit on strangeness?" Lisa asked.

Hammer threw up her arms in surrender. "It's anyone's guess. Now tell me about sex with the crazy Japanese."

Officer Mendez double parked the squad car in front of Sato Yui's building and took the stairs up to the fourth floor apartment. She knocked, firmly, but not over-aggressively, and waited.

"Who is it?" a female voice asked from behind the door.

"Police Department, Miss," Mendez replied in the calm, clear voice in which she had been carefully trained to speak. Speak with authority, but never with either a tone of disdain or anger. Convey a sense of subtle urgency, but never instill fear. The officer who speaks correctly is least likely to have to draw her weapon. Mendez glanced at the .38 holstered on her ample hip. "We'd like to ask you a few questions."

The door swung open and there stood a small, stunningly attractive Asian female with large black eyes, wearing a short pink bathrobe, her wet hair standing up in silky black spikes. Officer Mendez' breath evaporated in her chest, forcing her to take several quick gulps of air.

"Hi, I'm Sato Yui," the woman in pink announced. "How can I be of help?"

"This is purely a formality, Miss Yui, or is it Miss Sato? In any case, we, and by we I refer to the New York City Police Department, are investigating a crime that occurred two nights ago in the Soho art and upscale leisure district. Based on our preliminary investigation we have reason to believe that you may be able to contribute valuable information to this ongoing case."

Perfectly phrased, Mendez told herself.

"Wow!" Sato Yui said. "It sounds interesting, but I'm not so sure what it all means."

"Not to worry about that, Miss. The civilian population rarely does. If you wouldn't mind, we'd like you to come down to the station, just to answer a few questions in what we like to call a more controlled environment."

"Am I being arrested?"

"Nothing like that," Mendez said, slipping into the voice of total reassurance she had learned at the Academy. "This is purely voluntary on your part."

"Well, okay then," Sato Yui smiled. "Is it all right if I get dressed first?"

"Absolutely," Mendez told her, stepping inside and closing the door. "Take all the time you need."

The apartment was small, but neat. It was well lit and, aside from the subtle aroma of female, most likely Oriental, odor free. In a word, it was comfy, the sort of place one could imagine oneself being invited over to, by a potential witness, for example. Please come over once you get off duty and we can be more comfortable, have a chat, maybe a little wine. Yes, I'd like that. Good, so it's a date.

Sato Yui walked into an adjacent room, probably the bedroom. Mendez heard what sounded like drawers being opened and closed. It was understandable. What one wore, even if one was only going to the local police station for polite interrogation, mattered. Mendez wondered what the Japanese woman would be wearing when she emerged from the bedroom; something simple, yet stylish was her guess, nothing overstated or evocative. She was not at all prepared for Sato Yui dashing out of the bedroom naked.

"Sorry," the deliciously nude young woman cried. "I'm just trying to find a clean pair of panties."

Don't overreact, Officer Mendez reminded herself. Keep it strictly professional, detached, but also remain observant. Follow proper procedure. She trained her eye on the naked girl's body, imagining it as a piece of evidence, the acute observation of which would be critical should she be called to testify in open court. She began making a list: skin smooth, a perfect shade of golden yellow; breasts small, but pert, nipples stiff and pouting, the color of wet mud; waist slim to the point of non-existent; buttocks small and firm; pubic area glossed with black silk. Overall impression: Wow! Obviously, the wow part would be omitted during actual testimony.

"I know how annoying the hunt for clean underwear can be," Mendez managed to say.

Sato Yui dragged what appeared to be a laundry basket from under the kitchen table and (Oh God, no, please don't do that!) bent over to rummage through it, revealing a partial, but no less mesmerizing, glimpse of the Asian girl's sexual area, her private parts, otherwise known as her vagina, or, to put it in cruder terms, her cunt. *Cunt, cunt, cunt. Oh God!* Cease observation immediately, Mendez demanded of herself, her heart fluttering in her chest, pulse thumping rapidly.

"Found them," Sato Yui announced, pulling a tiny black thong from the basket. "I usually don't even both to wear them, but since we're going to a police station."

"Yes," Mendez said, feeling a little faint. "Panties can often mean the difference between, uh, guilt and innocence."

"What?"

"I mean, I ..."

"Are you all right, officer?" Sato Yui asked, walking naked, thong in hand, to the swooning Mendez.

"It's just the heat," Mendez told her.

"You'd probably feel better if you took off that uniform."

"I'm sorry?"

"I was just agreeing with you," Sato Yui said, peering directly into Mendez' eyes. "This heat is a bitch. Oops! I probably shouldn't use bad language in front of a police officer. Would you like to sit down, or maybe have a glass of water?"

Mendez waved away the offer. "I'll be fine. As soon as you're ready, we should be going."

"Okay," Sato Yui said, floating towards the bedroom. "I'll be dressed in a minute, possibly less."

Twenty

L isa made it back to her office, her head swirling, shut the door and fell into the chair behind her desk. The last thing she wanted to do was to try and figure anything out, but the information was there, raging away in her brain, demanding answers. Was this what detectives routinely had to put up with? She doubted it. No way a serial-killing demon on the loose was routine. Still, maybe her father had been right all along. She wasn't cut out to be a cop. Cops saw too much horror, aged fast, lost their hair even faster and ended up either insane and alone, or having to make ethical compromises that definitely jeopardized the possibility of getting into heaven. She felt reasonably safe on the hair loss issue and had never been particularly enamored of the whole going to heaven concept. Desolate loneliness and/or some form of mental illness, on the other hand, could not be ruled out and were therefore a concern.

Or was the real problem that she, completely sane and thinking clearly, was surrounded by the insane? It wasn't too much of a stretch to make the case. Stone, her partner and erstwhile lover, was in the grip of a Chinese conspiracy and death delusion and quite likely having sex with the demon responsible for all the carnage. Doctor Hammer, notwithstanding her support on the demon theory, had turned the morgue into a kind of macabre fast food shop, had had sex with Stone and who knew how many others and, lest we forget, had just tried to feel her up. Ishikawa, who, through an act of possible stupidity on her part, was now Ishikawa thinking less about the demon threat and more about having sex again with the red-headed detective. Not to mention that his focus had apparently shifted from killing the demon to chatting her up in coffee shops, while dressing like a deranged bum. The Captain, in theory the ultimate voice of authority and reasonableness, was so in denial that ...

The intercom buzzed. Who else would it be? "Yes, Captain?"

"I'd like to see in my office, Malone."

"Really? Why?"

"Thanks for asking, Detective, but wrong response. Get your butt in here now!"

Lisa entered the Captain's office and sat down, anticipating another tongue lashing on her silly girl fantasies about monsters, which, dare she even mention it, were totally supported by the evidence. Why even bother?

"Before you say anything, Captain, let me just tell you that I've come to my senses and no longer put any stock in the deadly demon scenario suggested earlier. As we all know, the evidence, no matter how compelling, can sometimes be wrong. Admittedly rare, but it happens."

"That's good," the Captain said, choosing to ignore what might have been perceived as a cynical criticism of his authority. "I'm relieved to hear it."

"My new motto in this case is, 'Get The Chinese!' No doubt they deserve it."

"Yes, well, with some sense of discrimination."

"Right. Obviously, not all the Chinese are bad. I mean there must be a few good ones."

"Are you feeling all right, Malone?" the Captain asked, reaching into his mini-fridge for a soda.

"Never better, Sir."

"I actually called you in here on a separate matter. Early this morning the body of a young Asian female was pulled out of the East River, nude, throat slit open, wrapped in a blanket."

"Do we suspect the Chinese, Captain?"

"Forget the Chinese for the moment, Malone."

"If you say so, Sir."

"The blanket around the body was wrapped in water resistant packing tape. The downtown crime lab was able to get a print off this tape.

"That should greatly facilitate apprehending the perpetrator," Lisa smiled.

"Yes, that's correct, Detective. The only problem is that the print in question belongs to your partner."

"Stone's print? That's not possible, Captain."

Or was it? If her suspicions were correct, Stone was no more than a helpless puppet at this point, strings pulled courtesy of Yui Sato. Unless, of course, the body in the blanket turned out to be Sato Yui, in which case, big relief, case closed.

"I'm not jumping to any conclusions on this," the Captain said. "But obviously I need to talk to Stone. He's not answering on either police band or his cell. If he contacts you, get him in here. The sooner we clear this up, the better."

"I'll do my best," Lisa said. "Will there be anything else, Sir?"

Lisa waited, either for more bad news, or permission to leave, preferably the later, but the Captain apparently had other things on his mind. He had pushed himself halfway out of his chair and was staring intently through the glass partition of his office. His eyes were different, stretched open and glossed-over, like some realistic-looking giant stuffed panda. It made him even scarier than usual.

"Who is that?" he asked, a discernible quaver of excitement in his voice.

Lisa turned and looked through the office window. Standing in the outer office with Officer Mendez was Sato Yui. She was dressed entirely in pink, pink halter-top, pink mini skirt and pink rubber shoes. Pretty in pink. Pretty pink poison. Her hair, sexy and urgent, appeared to have been recently hit by lightening. Only the black sunglasses she had on made the overall image bearable.

"That's Sato Yui," Lisa sighed.

"Interesting," the Captain chuckled. "So that little girl out there is your monster."

"If I were still subscribing to the monster scenario, yes, she is. Fortunately, I've seen the light on that score."

"Interesting," the Captain repeated.

And deadly, but don't let that little detail stop you from going out there and making a complete fool of yourself.

"Shall I interview her, Sir?" Lisa inquired.

"No, no," the Captain said, slicking back his hair (unnecessary due to near-total baldness) and straightening his tie. "I think I'll handle this interview personally."

Of course you will, Lisa thought, imagining the consequences of this. The Captain would fawn all over the little Japanese monster, offering her soft drinks, the promise of immunity, possibly the ceremonial keys to the city. He'd need the Mayor's approval on this, but it shouldn't be a problem. Sato Yui would squeal and squeak, feign innocence and excruciating modesty, all the while wrapping the Captain around her deadly little finger. Before anyone had a chance to react, the Captain would be working as a tag team partner with Stone, killing on Sato Yui's instructions and blaming everything on the Chinese.

"Captain," she said. "I really think that I ..."

Burke threw up a giant panda paw, demanding silence. "I want you to observe my questioning of the witness, Malone. Watch, listen and learn."

"Permission to shoot the witness if she begins to hypnotize you, Sir," Lisa couldn't resist blurting out.

The Captain ignored the question. "Afterwards, we'll begin to consider your transfer to a less stressful area of the Department. Possibly bookkeeping."

"Or bee-keeping?" Lisa said. Which made no sense at all, she knew, but it hardly mattered. She might just as well have said Official Department Prostitute, for all the effect it would have had on the Captain's imbecilic smile.

He, suddenly deaf to everything but Sato Yui's insidious low-level hum, the mating call of the inhuman homicidal maniac, was already looming over the pink-clad Asian, gushing, extending his hand, traces of saliva appearing at the corners of his mouth. He was easily twice her size and at least two hundred pounds heavier, a classic example of size not really mattering. He escorted Sato Yui to one of the interview rooms, one giant hand barely touching one of her tiny shoulders. Please accept our apologies for this inconvenience. Just a few routine questions and you'll be on your way. No doubt you have better things to do. Would you care for something to drink, or maybe a sandwich? No? Are you sure? Detective Malone can run out to the ethnic food store, no problem. Rice crackers and green tea? Seaweed snacks?

Lisa followed, taking up a position in front of the interview room's one-way mirror. She could listen to the interview without being observed, although she was certain that Sato Yui knew she was there. That was the problem, or at least one of them. Sato Yui seemed to know everything in advance. She had supernatural powers and no intention of using them for the benefit of mankind. She most likely knew where all of the players in her little soap opera of death were at each moment and what they were thinking. She was cute enough to eat and definitely needed to die. Oh, right, killing her was as close to impossible as finding happiness in love. A position in bookkeeping wasn't actually sounding that bad.

"So, Ms. Sato," the Captain said, sliding into a chair across the table from Sato Yui. "I hope you understand that this is simply a procedural matter. A crime was committed, your name was mentioned by a possible witness and we are more or less required to follow up."

"No problem," Sato Yui said, bouncing up and down in her chair. "To tell the truth, I'm very interested in crime."

"Are you?"

"I'm writing a book on it. American crime. It's so unbelievable to people in Japan."

"The price of freedom, I suppose," the Captain said.

"Yeah, I love America."

"I'm glad to hear it. We may have our problems, but this is still the greatest country on Earth. Of course, Japan is also great."

"Japan sucks."

"Well all right, if you say so."

"So what do you want to know?"

"Uh, well, about the other night. Based on our information, you and another woman, one Maya Jensen, were walking just east of the Soho art district when you were attacked by three men."

"Oh, right. It was so scary and horrible."

"I'm sure it was. I know this is difficult for you, but just take your time."

"You have nice eyes, Captain. Has anyone ever told you that?"

"Well, uh ..."

"So full of wisdom and other things."

"I have been around awhile."

"Don't be silly," Sato Yui giggled. "You are so young-looking, it scares the heck out me."

"Really," the Captain said, his lips making a weird bubbling sound. "Compared to you, I'm ancient. Like the ancient mariner, you know?"

Lisa fought off the urge to gag.

"Not so sure," Sato Yui pouted. "I don't know very much, but I am a girl."

"No question about that," the Captain told her. "Girl all the way."

"You're sweet," Sato Yui said, pulling off her sunglasses.

"Oh no," Lisa said out loud. "Don't do that."

Wham! Too late.

"So where was I?" the Captain asked, staring directly into Sato Yui's eyes.

"About the three guys," she reminded him.

"Right. Well, the thing is, they all turned up dead. Slaughtered might be a better way of, uh, putting it, no need to be overly explicit, but we, uh, were just wondering if you ..."

"I saw the whole thing," Sato Yui cried. "I still have nightmares about it."

"Poor thing," the Captain said soothingly, reaching across the table and stroking the monster's hand. "We have professional counselors standing by, or, if it would help, dinner tonight?"

"You want to eat me?"

"Eat with you, is more what I ..."

"The other girl tried to fight back, but I hid. I was so scared for my life."

"What a load of crap," Lisa said.

"Of course," the Captain almost whispered. "Perfectly natural, but ..."

"And then these other people came. They were angry, seemed real crazy, like humans on drugs, or something. They attacked the three men, shouting and screaming things as they...you know?"

"Did you happen to catch what they were saying?"

"No, sorry, I don't speak Chinese."

"You're saying they were speaking Chinese?"

"I'm sure of it, one woman and four guys. I think they knew martial arts. I'm just thankful they didn't kill me, too."

"Just perfect," Lisa said, looking towards heaven, where all she saw was a darkened void of expanding nothingness.

Sato Yui dropped her head and began to weep.

"So totally fucking fake," Lisa shouted.

Sato Yui looked up, glanced at the window, smiled briefly, and then recommenced weeping.

"No need for that," the Captain reassured her. "It's over now."

"But what if they find out I talked to you and come after me?" Sato Yui asked through her tears.

"Not to worry. It's our job to protect you. And until we catch these Chinese fiends, we're prepared to offer you police protection. We'll have an officer with you at all times."

"Will you protect me?" Sato Yui whined.

"Me, personally?" the Captain said. "As much as I'd like to, I have a Department to run. I could, of course, stop by from time to time to, you know ..."

"How about Detective Stone?"

"Stone is, uh, heading up the task force on this case, therefore quite busy."

"Task force?" Lisa said.

" But there's Detective Malone."

Sato Yui smiled. The Captain watched Sato Yui, feeling that his head might explode at any minute. Lisa threw up her hands, shook her head and walked back to her office. She slammed the door, sat down and waited. Waiting on the beast, but which one? A moment later, the door opened and the Captain walked in.

"And that, Malone, is how it's done, he announced.

"Impressive, Sir," she told him. "Although I'm slightly confused why you didn't go all the way and offer to adopt her."

"Insubordination, Malone. It's not a pretty word in my book."

"I'm sorry, Captain, but I don't care. Take my badge if you want to, but I am not babysitting that evil bitch."

"That so-called evil bitch is a vulnerable, traumatized girl who needs our help."

"Like an pit bull needs help chewing off the head of a toddler"

"Let me make this clear, Detective. Sato Yui is no monster."

"I wonder if you'll still feel that way once she starts slicing open your torso. Or will the fact that you're having sex with her as she cuts into you make it all worthwhile?"

"You're pushing me, Malone, and I'm seriously considering the option of psychological counseling."

"Personally, sir, I think it would really help you at this point to talk to a professional."

"I meant for you!" the Captain shouted. "Look, I get it that, however irrational, you have issues with this woman."

"Germans who hated Hitler were also considered irrational."

"All I'm asking is that you give her a ride home. I'll assign Mendez to the protection detail."

"Then Mendez will end up dead."

"No one is going to end up dead, Malone."

"We all end up dead, Captain."

"Just give her a fucking ride home!"

"Fine!"

"Good!"

The slamming of the door as the Captain walked away continued to echo throughout the Department for what seemed like several minutes.

Twenty-one

I shikawa wandered around the East Village feeling more alive than he had felt in a very long time. Life. It burst out in every direction he looked, bubbling, overflowing, enchanting. People busy expressing themselves. It hardly mattered that their efforts were mostly trivial. He was suddenly surrounded by men, women and those who fell somewhere in between doing their very best to exude some sense of meaning, to give purpose to their lives, the more outrageous the better. On some level they already understood that life was meaningless, that there was no hope in trying to figure things out. Things were as they were and always would be, but it was the bizarre, often grotesque attempt to pretend otherwise that made the crucial difference. Everyone was doomed; giving expression to that innate sense of doom made life worth living. An additional pleasure was the discovery that irony apparently pervaded the entire Universe.

Where had he been all these years? he wondered. When had he forgotten that occasionally having feelings was not totally irrelevant? Partly to blame, of course, was his Japanese upbringing. The key to success in Japan resided in the ability to repress emotion, to avoid any behavior that might single one out as different, and therefore a potential source of social discord. Japanese society functioned best in the absence of an emotional response. One could, of course, always get drunk and vent his hidden rage at this social insult against nature; but in the morning, with a headache and a deep wound of guilt in his heart, he was expected to assume life as normal. The so-called toughness of the Japanese spirit, he realized, was nothing more than a mask of fear.

It made perfect sense, therefore, that he had devoted himself to the life of the analytical hunter, seeking out the dark emotional core of life in order to excise it, to make the world's predictable sameness safe again. The Akuma, he realized, could be viewed as the ultimate result of emotional stagnation, the primordial urge to reassert the possibility of the ambiguous; good and evil, the out of control heart, sex, death, love, chaos. The very things his own culture feared so much made the Akuma necessary. Was it possible that his father had been right all along? Needless to say, the Akuma was still his mortal enemy, but it was now possible for him to also feel a kind of kinship with her. He was finally able to understand the seemingly stoic samurai who, as he decapitates his unfaithful wife, could utter the words, 'I still love you,' and mean it. Her indiscretion had made the final act inevitable, but he could not remain immune to his own inner feelings. Sometimes we are forced to kill the things we love, but never with a carefree heart. He also knew that the upcoming confrontation would not address any essential imbalance in the scheme of things, nor would it be a victory for any particular philosophical position. When it happened, it would be nothing more than a mild ripple on the cosmic wind, a settling of non-existent scores. Only the emotional experience of it would continue to reverberate.

He was suddenly aware of a young girl standing directly in front of him. Either impoverished, or dressed in the height of style, he couldn't be sure. She was thin, wide-eyes, her face smeared with what appeared to be dirt. She had full, moist lips and the fragile limbs of a ballerina. She seemed a girl on the verge of dancing, or perhaps crumbling into a lifeless pile of bones. Aside from the heavy black eyeliner and the metal stud through her lower lip, she could have stepped right out of a Dickens's novel.

"Excuse me," she said. "Do you have any drugs?"

"I'm sorry," he told her. "But no."

"In that case, do you want to buy some?"

"Drugs? No. I'm too busy to bother with drugs."

"If you used drugs, you probably wouldn't be so busy."

"Drugs are illegal."

"So is your fashion sense."

"Drugs will kill you."

"Life will kill you."

"What is it that you want?" Ishikawa asked, reaching into his pocket and pulling a clump of wrinkled bills.

"Soliciting a minor for sex? That's definitely illegal."

"Sex? I don't want sex."

"Are you sure? Twenty dollars will get you a very decent blowjob. See this?" she said, tapping the stud in her lips. "Trust me, you'll be amazed."

"I'm sorry," Ishikawa said, beginning to feel nervous. "I have a girlfriend."

"Seriously? You?"

"Well, all right, not exactly a girlfriend, but I have a sense that things are moving in that direction."

"In other words, you've got the hots for some girl who doesn't even know you exist."

"For your information, we have already made love."

"Made love?" she laughed.

"Ishikawa nodded, more vigorously than he intended.

"Let me guess. Since then she's avoiding you like the herpes virus."

"Are you some sort of expert on love, or something?"

"I know how dumb all guys are."

"Is that so."

"It's like an incurable disease. All guys have it. You're a guy, ergo ..."

"Anyway," Ishikawa said, sensing that if he didn't get away from this person soon, he never would. "I'm very busy and should be going."

"Busy with what?"

"If you must know, I'm hunting."

"Hunting? In the East Village? Hunting what?"

"Demons. Do you know anything about demons?"

"Oh God, yes."

The loud blast of a car horn made Ishikawa jump. He turned involuntarily to locate the source. When he turned back, the girl was gone. If it even was a girl, he said to himself, walking quickly down the street.

After stopping at his apartment for a quick shower and a change of clothes, Stone headed back to Chinatown. Where else? He didn't seem to have a choice. The case was in Chinatown, as were the answers. The challenge was finding them. Not a problem, because that's what he was good at. Okay, he could be honest and admit that this case was more of a challenge than any case he had ever worked on. There was some fuzziness about it, as if the case itself has created a fog inside his head. A Chinese fog, perhaps. Made sense. Maybe something the Chinese were putting into the water. Still, he was convinced that he was on the right track. He had only his infallible gut to go on and his gut was screaming Chinese.

He parked on a side street smelling of decaying animal flesh (type unknown) and stepped out into a wall of instantly debilitating heat. Was it possible that Chinatown was hotter than everywhere else in the city? It wasn't beyond the realm of possibility that the gangs were tampering with both the water and the air, which, if true, would require adding bio-terrorist charges to the numerous homicides. Homeland security would probably have to be brought in. Why the gangs would be doing such a thing was another question, but then this slipped easily into the realm of inscrutable Asian intent. With the Chinese, anything was possible. It could be some thousand year old grudge just now coming to fruition on the streets of New York, or the revenge of still furious dead ancestors troubled by perceived ethnic slurs muttered by some white guy during the Boxer Rebellion. Time meant nothing to these people and nothing was ever forgotten.

Stone pushed his way through the thick humid air. The usual crowds in the street were hard to get an accurate reading on. People were out of focus and slightly distorted, as if their heads were slowly dissolving, turning into bubbling lumps of flesh; hapless tourists with false smiles unknowingly on the verge of significant brain damage. Welcome to Chinatown. Sorry if the experience turned you into a quasi-human vegetable. We aim to please, but cannot be held responsible for the diminished immune system of the corrupted Caucasian. Eventually he was once again standing in front of the Lame Duck. Was he supposed to be meeting Harry Fang? It seemed reasonable. Harry knew a lot more than he had said. He hated cops but feared prison more. He would tell Stone what he wanted to know simply because the alternative was not an option. Stone opened the door and stepped into darkness, cool as a tomb, smelling of graveyard incense and cat urine. No sign of Harry. No sign of anything. The place was virtually deserted. Even the guy standing behind the bar looked mummified. He took a booth in the back and waited. He closed his eyes for a moment and rubbed his face. When he opened them the waitress with the fierce eyes was standing next to his table.

"I've been expecting you," she said.

"Really?"

"No," she laughed, throwing a copy of the menu in front of him. "But I have been expecting something. Guess you're it."

"Pretty quiet in here," he said, trying not to look directly into her eyes. He focused on her nose, which was small and slightly pointy. Not your typical Chinese nose. He was tempted to ask if she was one hundred percent Chinese, but couldn't rule out her taking it as an insult, pulling a knife from under her apron and trying to stab him.

"So are you going to order something, or just stare at the menu?"

"What's good?"

"Honestly? Nothing."

"I'll just have a beer."

She threw him a familiar hiss and walked silently away. Watching her go, Stone found himself thinking about Lisa. 'There is no us,' she had said, just before slamming her office door. What was that about? Okay, maybe the case had gotten to her, but was that any reason to turn on him? Talk about inscrutable. Compared to the mind of a woman the Chinese version was an open book, illustrated, with easy to follow instructions. He blamed Ishikawa, who had fed her the inhuman monster bullshit and was obviously influencing her in any number of unhealthy ways. But still, Japanese girls turning into demons and murdering people was seriously over the top, unless, of course, it wasn't about the monster itself, but what the monster represented in Lisa's mind. Maybe she was having feelings about their relationship that were just too hard to handle. Her own conflicted feelings had created the monster, it resided in the relationship and he, by default, became the monster's messenger. It made sense. Women had the capacity to be strange in ways men would never be able to comprehend.

The waitress returned with two bottles of beer, placed them on the table and took a seat across from Stone.

"I took the liberty of letting you buy me a drink," she said.

"Is it okay for you to sit here with me?"

"As you're the only customer," she said, pouring the beers, "it's probably all right."

"Great!" he said, raising his glass. "Cheers!"

"So what's your story?" she asked, the glimmer of a smile on her very red lips.

"I'm just here looking for a friend," he told her.

"I'll be your friend."

"Actually I had someone in mind."

"Not that asshole, Harry Fang, I hope."

"Yeah. You know where he is?"

"Hopefully lying dead somewhere."

"I take it you don't care much for Harry."

She hissed out of the corner of her mouth, took a gulp of beer and began running one of her small delicate feet up Stone's leg. "I've got a room upstairs we can use. Show you a real nice time. Only fifty bucks."

"I'm a cop," he told her.

"So what? Lots of cops come in here looking for a hot fuck."

"Lots?"

"The nicer ones even pay."

"Got any names?"

She closed an imaginary zipper across her lips, easing her toes to within a centimeter of Stone's crotch. "So, what do you want?"

"Information," he told her.

"Hey, I'll tell you lots of stuff you don't know. We can talk while we fuck."

"I don't think you've got the kind of information I'm looking for."

"Trust me. Once I'm fucking you, you won't care at all about that."

"I'm sure it would be terrific," he told her, finishing off his beer. "But I really have to get going."

"Why go? It's so hot out there, smells bad, plenty of bad guys who wanna kill you. You stay with me, you never gonna be sorry."

"What's your name, anyway?" Stone asked.

"Zang Fu," she told him.

"Is that a real name?"

"Real enough for casual sex."

Stone observed Zang, a classic Asian beauty with the eyes of a woman who would slit a guy's throat in his sleep for snoring too loud. She could seduce customers into ordering the most expensive dish on the menu, then scare them into eating fast and clearing out for the next hungry tourist. He considered the possibility that it was a waitress he was looking for. What better cover for a Chinese contract killer than a waitress in a Chinese restaurant with no customers? His gut was trying to tell him something, but he wasn't sure what it was. Maybe having sex with Zang Fu would make things clearer.

"Can I ask you a personal question?" he asked her.

"You want to know if my pussy is super tight?"

"I'm certain it is, but no."

"Do I swallow? Absolutely!"

"Happy to hear it, but I'm more interested in whether you've ever killed anyone."

"I've broken many hearts, stolen a few souls, turned more men than I can count into helpless dogs."

"Not exactly what I'm looking for."

"So just tell me what you want," Zang Fu pleaded, her toes twitching rhythmically against Stone's crotch.

"I'm after a cold, calculating psychopath," he told her. "A Chinese monster with a deadly agenda."

"I can be that," Zang Fu said, her eyes suggesting imminent death. "But it will cost a little extra."

• • • •

"THIS IS SO MUCH FUN," Sato Yui cried. "I mean, you and me in the same car, going for a ride. Who could have ever guessed?

Lisa pulled the car out into traffic, which was moving like some large, slow beast on the verge of disappearing back into the evolutionary slipstream. Great, she thought. Trapped in an eternal gridlock with a clever little demon in the passenger's seat, a demon that could carve her up into bite-sized pieces in the time it took the next traffic signal to change from red to green.

"It's so cool," Sato Yui continued. "Now we have a chance to really get to know each other. Who knows, maybe we have things in common? What are your hobbies? Aside from sex, I mean"

"Look," Lisa said. "Give it a rest. We both know what's going on here and you're not fooling anyone with your bubbly, wide-eyed Japanese twit in the big city routine."

"If you say so," Sato Yui sighed, putting her legs up on the dashboard and reaching for her sunglasses.

"And leave the glasses on," Lisa told her.

"Gee, what a grump. What is it, trouble in your love life."

"What would you know about either love or life?"

"Now you sound like Ishikawa," Sato Yui said, spreading her legs so that the air-conditioning could cool off her hottest girl parts. "Ever meet a guy with a bigger pole up his butt? Do you think he's secretly gay?"

Ishikawa's ultimate sexual orientation was admittedly unknown, but that was beside the point. What mattered more was the fully loaded, matte finish .9 millimeter Beretta on her hip. One quick shot to the little beast's head. It probably wouldn't kill her, but it might give her a headache and shut her up for awhile. She glanced over at Sato Yui, who had her head thrown back, a smile on her face, her skirt riding up around her hips, vividly displaying the tiny black thong she had on and a good portion of her bare backside. Demons, she had to admit, knew how to pick bodies to inhabit.

"Do you find me attractive?" Sato Yui asked.

"Trying to read my mind again?"

"You think I can read minds?" Sato Yui squealed. "That would make me pretty much invincible."

" Pretty much annoying is more like it."

"I'm a girl who just wants to have fun."

"So killing is fun?"

"You have no idea."

"So what's holding you back? Why don't you just kill me now?"

"You're driving me home, for one thing. And, oddly enough, I like you. And if it comes to the point that I have to kill you, I really want it to be special."

"Okay, here's another idea. Why not just go back to wherever it is you came from? Demon land, or whatever you call it?

"Boring, boring, so boring."

"But that's who, or should I say what, you are. There's no changing that, right?"

"At one point, you were an angry teenage slut who screwed guys just to get back at your father. People can change."

"People, yes. Homicidal demons, I doubt it."

"As if you know anything about what demons can or cannot do."

"I don't want to know. I just want you to go away."

"Sorry, I'm staying."

"Fine. Then just be a silly little girl who has silly sex and does silly things. Stop the killing."

"I think I saw that written on the side of a bus the other day. 'Stop the killing.'"

"You find murder funny?"

"In fact, there is a humorous side to it, but humans generally don't get it."

"Especially your victims, I'm guessing."

"I have to say that this morally indignant cop thing you're doing is not very appealing. Besides, you don't even care about that."

"Really? So what do I care about?"

"All you really care about is whether or not I'm fucking Stone."

"I could care less about that," Lisa said, squeezing the steering wheel, imagining it was Sato Yui's pretty little neck. "So, are you?"

Sato Yui giggled. "Technically, no. As a practice, I kill the men I fuck. But I am working on resisting that urge. Otherwise, how will I ever find a steady boyfriend?"

Lisa gritted her teeth and jerked the car into the next lane, cutting off a car in the process. The man in the car hit his horn and screamed something about fucking bitches that shouldn't be allowed to drive. She was tempted to stop, get out and shoot the prick.

"You feel helpless, don't you?" Sato Yui said, shifting her body so that she was facing Lisa. "Part of you wants to kill me, another part wants to have sex with me."

"That's ridiculous," Lisa said.

"Which part?"

"Can I ask you something?"

"Anything."

"Why are you here. I mean, what's the real reason? Why here, why now?"

"The easy answer is that here is where I've always been meant to be. Or it could be the heat, which I find very stimulating, or this town, which I totally love. But the more I think about it, I realize that the real reason I'm here is you."

Lisa pulled the car over in front of Sato Yui's apartment. "You're here because of me?"

"Thanks for the lift," Sato Yui said, hopping out of the car. "I'll see you again soon, Lisa Malone."

Twenty-two

B y the time Lisa got back to her apartment it was already dark, or as dark as it ever got in the city of too many bright lights mixed up with the psychic spill-off of eight million angry insomniacs. Maybe if everyone just went to sleep for a while, the lights would go down and madness levels would begin to recede. Did Sato Yui sleep? Did she eat, pee, and watch TV? It was one thing to have a supernatural killer on the loose, quite another when you have to give the killer demon a ride home and she's cute and friendly and scary and wearing a tiny black thong under her pink miniskirt. Nothing made any sense.

She felt like screaming, but it was too hot and she was way too tired. Instead, she fixed herself a large glass of vodka with ice and disconnected the phone. Cop or no cop, she really had no interest in hearing from anyone she knew. The murders would pile up regardless. The insanity would carry on, the morons would continue to get elected to public office and the planet would slowly slip into an irreversible death spiral. What was the point in caring?

She switched on the TV for the latest weather news. The heat wave, she was informed, would continue more or less indefinitely, water supplies were running low, pollution levels were at their highest recorded levels and random violence seemed to be increasing exponentially.

"Even if you're feeling hot, desperate and at the end of your rope," the smiling weather guy cautioned, "don't take it out on the people around you. They're hot, too. And numerous studies have proven that killing them will not have any appreciable affect on the overall temperature. In fact, the strenuous act of murder, particularly in high humidity, is a primary cause of dehydration. So, while killing someone may appear the only recourse in this weather situation, doing so is only going to make you feel hotter. I guess that's irony, folks."

"Oh fuck you," Lisa shouted at the TV, thinking that the pleasure of shooting the weatherman would probably be worth the potential temperature increase.

She pulled off her clothes and stepped into the shower, turning the water temperature knob to hot. She remembered hearing somewhere that taking hot showers helped keep your body cool. It was one of those scientific facts that defied logic, but was guaranteed to work. Conserve water by avoiding unnecessary showers, the weather guy had made a point of mentioning. Okay, but first define unnecessary. She stood there a long time hoping the global storm in her head would run its course and then leave her in peace. Avoid excessive thinking, as an overheated brain equals an overheated body, which may be a contributing factor in random acts of violence. What she really wanted not to think about was the last time she had been in the shower with Stone, so, of course, that was the one thing she couldn't stop thinking about. Contained within that particular experience were all the reasons she no longer cared about him, possibly hated him and also wished that he was here with her now. Poor conflicted Lisa. Her partner practically rapes her, allows and evil demon to take control of his mind and still she misses him. She wondered what the Department shrink would have to say about it. Something about rape as the ultimate metaphor for the desire to both kill and have sex with the father. The multiple orgasms experienced during the rape, on the other hand, symbolized her willingness to die rather than confronting her own confused and paradoxical feelings vis-à-vis that father.

Still, Lisa thought as she washed her body, a couple of really good orgasms were the perfect antidote to many if not all of life's little paradoxes. She was tempted to prove the point, but resisted, sensing that erotic self-stimulation was exactly what Sato Yui would want her to do. Spend thirty minutes in the car with the adorable little monster and what choice would a healthy young woman have but to go home and masturbate. Sorry to disappoint you, demon. This girl isn't falling so easily under your spell.

Sure, sure, but let's get back to Stone, the shrink suggests.

What about him? Like any guy with dreamy eyes and a superb penis, he was destined to be a big disappointment in the murky realm of love. Not to mention that falling in love in the first place made about as much sense as playing Russian roulette with and old-fashioned .38; maybe fun for awhile, but ultimately destined to leave a gaping hole in your head, or heart, depending on how good your aim is.

So, the shrink says with a knowing nod and an annoying smirk, to offset these lingering fears of emotional commitment, you go and have sex with the Japanese Lieutenant, whom you already know is seriously unstable, in the grip of some dangerous trans-cultural fantasy that you can never hope to grasp.

"Can't a girl have sex simply because she feels like it?" Lisa asks, exiting the shower and grabbing a towel. "Spur of the moment, sex for sex sake, go with the impulse. Why bother second guessing the erotic urge?"

It's a pretty fiction, the shrink responds. Life without rules, however, is untenable and mostly chaotic.

"Maybe life is supposed to be that way," says Lisa, slipping on the silk kimono she wore when feeling sexy mattered more than actually being sexy. Or was it that looking sexy occasionally took precedence over feeling sexy?

Who are you looking sexy for? Doctor psychoanalyst wants to know.

"My father, obviously."

Hmmm.

THE CUTEST LITTLE DEMON IN TOWN

Lisa made a mental note to never, under any circumstances, agree to spend any time with anyone in the mental health field and fixed herself another drink. She had just popped a frozen pizza into the microwave when there was a knock at the door. She walked over and looked through the peephole. It was Doctor Hammer's face, presumably with body attached, appearing as large as the full moon in autumn and way more melancholy. The impulse to ignore the knock was strong, but Lisa's upbringing kicked in, as it often did in moments of ethical dilemma. When the doorbell rings, we always answer it. No explanation ever given for this social imperative, except that it was both the American way and the Christian thing to do. And what if the person on the other side of the door is a disturbed expert on death with extremely vague sexual affiliations? We grit our teeth, ask for God's help and answer it anyway. Technically, Lisa reasoned, no doorbell ever rang. A random knock is certainly not the same as a ringing bell, right? No answer.

Lisa sighed, opening the door a crack "Doctor Hammer?"

"Oh Lisa," Hammer said, pushing open the door and forcing her way into the apartment. "Thank God you're here. I hope I'm not interrupting."

"Well, I ..."

"I just could not stay in my apartment another minute," Hammer declared. "Sleep was totally out of the question. I've even become immune to sedatives, apparently. Do you know what it's like to be unnerved to the point of wanting to jump out your skin? Sometimes the only thing you can do is talk it out with a friend."

Lucky me.

"What are friends for?" Lisa asked less than enthusiastically. "Care for a drink?"

"Perfect," Hammer said, tossing her bag on a chair, walking into the living room and dropping onto Lisa's sofa.

"Vodka okay?"

"You read my mind." Hammer took a cigarette out of her bag and lit it. "Hope you don't mind if I smoke."

"I didn't know you did," Lisa said, searching around for something to serve as an ashtray.

"I don't, or I didn't. I guess it's just this whole demon business. I mean, the unbelievable strangeness of it aside, I can't shake the feeling that she's, you know, out there somewhere, stalking me. Somehow smoking just seems to fit this paranoid scenario."

Lisa brought in the drinks and a small dish for Hammer's ash and sat down in the chair opposite the sofa."

"You look lovely in that robe, by the way," Hammer said, sipping her drink, her eyes caressing Lisa's body.

"Thanks," Lisa smiled, suddenly aware that she was naked underneath the kimono. "Anyway, I don't think you have to worry about Sato Yui."

"No? That night in the lab she told me she'd be seeing me again soon. If that wasn't a threat, I don't know what is."

"I wouldn't read too much into it," Lisa told her, wondering how long Hammer was planning on staying. "Just something a girl says."

"A girl?"

"I feel silly calling her the demon all the time."

"Is she starting to get to you, too?" Hammer asked, expelling a large plume of smoke from her mouth that had nowhere to go.

"Of course not," Lisa coughed. "Actually, we had her into the station today for questioning."

"It's about time," Hammer said, stubbing out her cigarette and lighting another. "What happened?"

"Aside from the Captain slobbering all over her, nothing much."

"At least tell me that you locked her up afterwards."

"Not exactly. Afterwards, I gave her a ride home."

"Oh my God," Hammer cried, her eyes filling with tears. "So in other words, she's still out there, sucking the marrow from the darkness, conjuring her next attack on the good people of this planet."

"I guess that's one way of putting it," Lisa said.

Hammer grabbed her bag, rifling through it until she found the white handkerchief, then dabbing at her eyes. "This is all very upsetting," she sobbed.

Lisa didn't care much for this new weepy vulnerable version of Hammer, much preferred the sardonic, hard-edged slightly crazed version, but she moved over next to her and placed her hand lightly on the weeping woman's shoulder. "It's really okay."

"No," Hammer sniffled. "It's not. Everything is falling apart and now I'm going to lose you."

"You're not going to lose me." Lisa tried to sound reassuring.

"Oh please!" Hammer said. "It's only a matter of time before she sucks you into her psychotic supernatural web. You'll be under her spell, doing her bidding and I'll be left alone with no one but the crazy Japanese cop to sort out this mess."

"Trust me," Lisa said. "That's not going to happen."

"Promise me," Hammer said, resting her head on Lisa's shoulder and wrapping her arm around Lisa's waist."

Lisa's promise was interrupted by the sensation of her kimono sash being undone. Hammer's lips were on her neck, her fingers slipping inside the silk, skirting the edge of Lisa's left breast. Answering the door had clearly been a big mistake. She wasn't sure whether to jump up, feigning outrage and disgust, or let the doctor go ahead and get it out of her system. In stressful situations people are much more likely to behave abnormally. Allowing them to indulge their abnormal fantasies is often the best way to diffuse the incident. She was almost certain she had read that somewhere.

Lisa's robe, meanwhile, was now completely open, Hammer's eager hands massaging her breasts.

"Such lovely nipples," Hammer murmured, moving her face to the left one and inhaling it into her mouth with the sound of something being sucked through a portal into the vacuum of space.

Lisa's eyes closed and an involuntary, but nevertheless audible, moan left her lips. Why was it, she wondered, that pleasure always took precedence over all other considerations? Hammer's infomercial on sex, death, love and pain came rushing back to her. The stranger it gets, the more we get off on it. For an instant, the thought of what it would be like to be making love with Sato Yui appeared in her head. Something about the little demon's backside that was hard to shake, the adorable ass of an ungodly fiend. "No, no, no," Lisa said out loud, trying to will the image away.

"No," Hammer cooed, "is often just another way of saying yes."

"You have been talking with Ishikawa, haven't you?"

"Forget about him now."

"Uh, Doctor Hammer, I really don't think ..."

"Isn't it about time you started calling me Beverly?" Hammer said, switching over to Lisa's right nipple.

The sudden knock on the door was both a relief and a new source of anxiety. Lisa turned her head towards the sound, Hammer, as if suddenly stricken with paralysis, stopped what she was doing in mid-suckle. They both waited for the next knock.

"Who do you think it is?" Hammer asked, as the knocking recommenced.

"The way the evening is going," Lisa said, gently pulling herself away from Hammer's embrace, "it's probably my parents. The first time in their lives to venture out of Ohio and they choose to come to the City of Supernatural Sin and surprise me."

"Well don't answer it," Hammer whispered, attempting to prevent Lisa from moving away.

"I've already tried that once this evening," Lisa told her, slipping her breast from Hammer's grasp and tiptoeing to the door for a look through the peephole. "Apparently I have a compulsion when it comes to answering doors."

It was Ishikawa, smiling, hopping from one foot to the other, his baseball cap sliding back on his head, making him look like some mentally challenged Asian guy who has completely come to terms with his disability, so pleased with his handicap, in fact, that he was going door to door to discuss it with total strangers.

Lisa glanced back at Hammer. "It's Ishikawa."

"The Japanese cop?"

"How many Ishikawa's are there?"

"Millions, I would guess."

"Well we only know the one."

"I don't think he should see me," Hammer said, jumping up and grabbing her bag.

"Why not?" Lisa asked.

"He'll know we were having sex."

"Okay, first of all, we were not having sex."

"Fine. Whatever you want to call it."

"I don't want to call it anything."

Another knock. "Lisa, are you in there?"

"I'll hide in the bedroom," Hammer said, walking quietly down the hallway.

Lisa threw up her hands, noticed that her robe was still open and tied it. She waited until Hammer was safely concealed, a little concerned that she would later find the doctor naked under the sheets, and opened the door.

She tried to fake surprise. "Ishikawa? What are you doing here?"

"Sorry," he said, stepping inside and rapidly glancing around. "I had to see you. Is this a bad time?"

"I was just about to go to bed," Lisa said, hoping that Hammer hadn't heard her say it.

"Forgive me," Ishikawa said, his eyes now anxiously focused on the tantalizing outline of Lisa's body beneath the sheer silk. "May I tell you that you are so beautiful in that kimono? It reminds me vividly of my former life as a Japanese."

" Suggesting that you are not a Japanese now?"

"Of course, I am still Japanese, but these new feelings I'm having force me to question all basic assumptions."

Oh God, not feelings, not about me.

"Nothing wrong with feelings, I guess."

"Many of these feelings concern you," Ishikawa said, his dark eyes softening.

Shit!

"Really?"

"And the Akuma."

"What sort of feelings? For the Akuma, I mean."

"They are unclear, but, for better or worse, I think I begin to understand how my father must have felt. In his own unfortunate way, he knew that complexity always forces upon us certain compromises. I see now that his approach to the Akuma was not entirely without merit."

"I think it's a good thing that you are resolving these issues with your dead father."

"So you have had a similar experience?"

"Not really, but then my father is a real jerk, not to mention still living."

"It's all happening so fast," Ishikawa said, his eyes blinking rapidly.

"I feel the same way," Lisa told him.

"Do you really?"

"Well, maybe."

"The Akuma intends to kill me," he said.

"She told you that?"

"She may have, but, more importantly, I feel it to be true."

"Again," Lisa said, feeling distracted, "feelings are good, but they can also be misleading."

"I think I'm in love with you."

"Which only proves my point about misleading feelings," she quickly added.

"I'm such a fool," Ishikawa cried, turning away and wiping his eyes.

Great! Another weeper. Exactly what I needed tonight.

"If this is about the other night ..."

"The night you returned my soul to me."

Lisa shuddered. Trying to navigate a less than hopeless path for her own soul was challenging enough. The last thing she needed was having responsibility for someone else's. It certainly wasn't part of her job description. As she attempted to formulate a response that would be clarifying – vis-à-vis the whole ethically murky concept of the one night stand - and at the same time not overly damaging to Ishikawa's emotional revival, there came yet another knock on the front door. Not since she had inadvertently made it known that she would be amenable to having sex with the entire high school football team had she been this popular. Not that she had ever followed through. As it turned out, one muscular moron was pretty much like another. It was then she had learned that the road to sexual satisfaction was far more complex than she had assumed. Ironically, her father had been totally supportive of her dating the school jocks. As he saw it, playing sports was right up there with fighting in wars and serving Jesus. Imagine Jesus giving up a promising football career to enlist in the army in order to kill for his country and you begin to get the idea. 'Nothing more wholesome and down to earth than an athlete,' her father was fond of saying. No need to mention that, in later life, several members of the team were arrested for spousal abuse, two turned into pedophiles and one became a modestly well-known Ohio serial killer. So much for sex and organized sports.

Ishikawa shattered the reverie. "Aren't you going to answer the door?" he asked.

"Why should I?" she said. "What are the chances that it's going to be anything but bad news?"

"Still, when someone knocks an answer is expected."

"Have you been talking to my parents?"

"I'm sorry?"

"Go ahead, tell me that Japanese people would never even consider not answering the door?"

"It would be viewed as a radical departure from convention, as well as raising suspicions that would be difficult, if not impossible, to assuage."

"Assuage?" Lisa said, walking to the door to once again look through the peephole. "We may have to re-think your progress on the turning into an actual human being front."

She half-expected it to be Sato Yui, there to finish off in one neat package the three people on Earth who had any faith in her existence. Most people put all of their energy into getting some kind of existential feedback from those around them. Not so with demons, apparently. The last thing a demon wanted to be reminded of was that she was a demon. But instead of Sato Yui standing in the hallway, it was Stone, looking tired and beat up, but no less attractive in his usual primitive, bestial sort of way.

Are you forgetting that the man may be a minion of the monster?
I realize that, but as far as I know, he has no interest in sports.
Murder can be a sport.
So can shutting up and leaving me alone.
She is so in denial.
I couldn't agree more, Doctor.
"Please be quiet!" Lisa demanded.

"I'm sorry," Ishikawa said. "I was only going to ask who ..."

"No, not you," Lisa told him. "It's Stone."

"Stone?" Ishikawa exclaimed in a whisper, as if he were hearing the word for the first time in his life. "He might be here as an emissary of the Akuma. He could kill the both of us without giving it a second thought."

"Trust me," Lisa said. "That's not going to happen. Although, it is possible that he might feel like killing you."

"Really?"

"Sorry, but he's not a big fan."

"Of sports?"

"Of Ishikawa."

"What should I do?"

"Hide somewhere."

"In the bedroom?"

"No, definitely not the bedroom. Use the bathroom, door at the end of the hall."

"I really don't feel the need to use the bathroom."

"As a hiding place," Lisa hissed.

"By the way," Ishikawa asked as he headed down the hallway. "Has someone been smoking in here?"

"Just go!"

Twenty-three

"I was about to give up," Stone said as Lisa opened the door. "What took you so long?"

"I was, uh, meditating."

"You were meditating?" Stone laughed.

"Why is that amusing?"

"It's not. I just didn't know you did that sort of thing."

"Well I do. Any objections?"

"No. Does it work?"

"It must. I'm no longer feeling like killing you for being such an asshole."

"I'd call that a positive development," Stone said, slipping his arms around Lisa's waist and pulling her towards him.

"No longer feeling like killing you," Lisa said, putting her hands on Stone's chest and gently pushing him away, "is not the same as wanting to cuddle with you."

"Look, Lisa, I know things have been strange recently."

"Putting it mildly."

"Okay, very strange, but I don't get why it should affect us personally."

"But it is personal," Lisa said, walking into the kitchen, picking up the vodka bottle and waving it at Stone, who nodded. "It's all about the personal. Who we are now and who we will be afterwards. There's no way to keep things separate."

"It's just a case, Lisa," he said, taking the offered drink. "Keeping things separate is what we do. Otherwise, we can't function. And once this is resolved and the bad guys are behind bars, we'll be exactly who we were. Do you remember who we were before the killings started?"

"I'm not so sure it wasn't the killings that got us started."

"I get it, the whole death as sexual turn-on scenario. Sounds like you've been talking too much with our whacky Medical Examiner."

Lisa glanced towards the bedroom, wondering if the doctor had her ear pressed to the door. "At least Doctor Hammer isn't blind to what's really going on."

"And you think I am?"

"Yes," Lisa admitted, but I'm sure it's only temporary. Like snow blindness."

Stone put down his drink and began to pace around the living room. "I have no choice but to blame Ishikawa for all this, him and his crazy demon ideas. I knew the guy was bad news from the moment he walked into my office. Somehow he convinced you and Hammer to join his insane demons club."

"Yeah, well, if the evidence is compelling and you've got an eye witness, joining the club starts making sense."

"Oh come on, Lisa," Stone said, his dreamy eyes turning – oh my god! – slightly demonic. "There is no way that demons are ever going to make sense. Not in the real world, anyway."

"So now you're an expert on reality?" Lisa asked, trying without much success to make her eyes as scary-looking as his.

"I know that when the world feels like its becoming unhinged and the madness levels rise to the point that you want to start shooting all the weirdoes on sight, that's the time to stay focused and objective. And when I break this case, which I will do very soon, you'll see that I was right all along."

"I hope so," Lisa said. "Oh, by the way, the Captain is very anxious to talk to you. Something about the body of a young Asian woman pulled out of the river."

"Did he say why he wants to talk to me about it?"

"Uh, let's see ... oh, right! The body was wrapped in a blanket that had been secured with that waterproof duck tape, you know the kind, and your fingerprints were all over the tape."

"My fingerprints?"

"Apparently."

"It's not possible."

"Which is what I told the Captain."

Stone pushed his fingers through his hair and recommenced pacing. Lisa watched him as he moved around her small living room. He was a gorgeous man with so much potential, the near-perfect lover (no longer reasonable asking for absolute perfection) and, until a week or so ago, a damn good cop. Until the little Japanese monster in the sexy underwear came along and sucked him into her private black hole of evil. Could she really blame him for falling so easily under the demon's spell? As much as she might have wanted to, she doubted there was any man alive, with the possible exception of Ishikawa, who would be able to resist the allure of the tiny girl beast. Even Lisa had felt it, the nearly irresistible sexual attraction. Was it really his fault? Well, yes and no. No, because it had never been his choice and, let's face facts, he was a man and men tended to go for hot little Asian girls, demon or not. They had brains wired to seed the entire female population and they tended not to discriminate along racial, ethnic lines. Japanese women were particularly irresistible, as they artfully combined young girl innocence with the savvy style of a high priced hooker. Sato Yui was a lethal threat precisely because she could seduce the pants off a dead man. She was seduction personified. Even Lisa wasn't totally immune. One look into Sato Yui's eyes had convinced her that this perky little demon could take over the world, if she put her mind to it. On the other hand, yes, it was Stone's fault, because for all his talents, toughness and good looks, he was weak-willed. And there was no excuse for that, at least according to her father.

"Of course!" Stone blurted out in mid-pace. "It has to be a set-up."

"Don't tell me," Lisa said. "The secret Chinese death squad."

"Who else? They know I'm getting close, don't want the publicity that would result from killing a cop, so they come up with a diversion to get me out of the picture."

"How did they get your prints?"

"These people are extremely clever, Lisa. They've had several thousand years of practice being smart and sneaky."

Lisa was pretty sure that the dead body in the river had been Sato Yui's doing, but trying to make that case to Stone seemed futile at this point. Better to let him pursue his Chinese phantoms. It would keep him out of the way while she and Ishikawa attempted to deal with the actual killer. Not that she had any particular faith in their ability to accomplish this task. She would probably die in the process, sliced apart and bled out, while Stone ended up living with some Chinese cocktail waitress, smoking opium and having wild, Shanghai-style sex all day long. Such were the fickle ways of fate.

Not even to mention what Ishikawa was doing in her bathroom all this time, even worse, Hammer in her bedroom. She glanced down the hallway, listening for any telltale signs from her hidden guests, but all was quiet, perhaps too quiet. When she looked back at Stone he was talking excitedly on his cell phone. She hadn't heard it ring. Was he faking a call to get out of having to finish the conversation? Would he suddenly end the call and say something like, 'I'd love to stay and finish this conversation, but I really have to go.'

"So I'll see you at eleven," Stone said, pressing disconnect. Then to Lisa, "See, what did I tell you?"

Lisa's expression conveyed that she had no idea what he might have told her.

"That was Zang Fu," he said, as if with the mention of the name, if it even was a name, all now was clear, the truth had been revealed and the war was finally over.

"Another of your Asian gal pals?" Lisa asked.

"More along the lines of a recently acquired contact within the Chinese community."

Nice euphemism, Lisa thought, imagining what the recently acquired contact probably looked like: Tall, slim, with small pesky breasts and sinister hips, lips that pouted for penis regardless of what she was talking about, cold ancient eyes carved from two lumps of coal and the ass of a thirteen-year-old gymnast.

"And what did Zang Fu have to say?" she asked.

"She's located Harry Fang. He has information vital to the case and has agreed to talk."

"So basically you're going back to Chinatown tonight to meet Zang and Fang."

"That's the plan," Stone said, finishing off his drink and digging around in his pocket for the car keys.

"I know you think this is important," Lisa said, walking over to where Stone was standing. "But I really think you should go see the Captain first."

Stone shook his head. "The Captain can wait. Last thing I need right now is the long-winded Q & A over some dead girl in the river. Besides, this could be the opening I've been looking for."

"Still, I don't think you should go."

"Because ..?"

"I don't know. Call it a bad feeling."

Stone reached for her and pulled her towards him. "It's sweet that you're worried about me. But this is about the job and my reputation. It's something I just have to do."

"But ..."

Stone cut her off with a kiss, his yummy lips back in action against hers. Her urge to resist quickly faded, her mouth opening to his tongue, her legs turning rubbery. He slid his hands down onto her backside and lifted her slightly off the ground. Sex, she realized, was probably the one guaranteed way to keep him away from Chinatown tonight. I can make that sacrifice, she thought, moving her hand to the outline of his cock inside his jeans, at the same time moaning softly into his kiss. There was only one problem, well, two of them actually, Hammer and Ishikawa. The thought of them with their ears pressed to doors while she had sex with Stone on her living room couch was not especially appealing. Maybe she wasn't as sexually liberated as she claimed to be. Or, more likely, the fact that both Hammer and Ishikawa also wanted to have sex with her just made the whole thing too weird and murky. No sense getting either of them more worked up than they already were.

As she considered the implications, Stone ended the kiss and eased her back to a standing position. "We'll continue this as soon as I get back," he said.

"I don't know if I can wait," she blurted out.

"Me either," he smiled, moving towards the door.

"We could go to your place."

"Give me an hour, two at the outside," he told her. "By the way, have you been smoking?"

"Uh, you know, the occasional one, just to take the edge off."

"Better be careful. It's very easy to get hooked. Trust me, I know."

Sure, Lisa thought. Allow your mind to be co-opted by a demon, leave your fingerprints on some dead girl in the river and then go hang out in the middle of the night with some Chinese slut and her dog-faced pimp. Clearly you are someone who should be giving advice on the dangers of smoking.

"You're right," she told him. "I obviously have to quit."

She shut the door behind him, feeling somewhere between a delayed orgasm and a sudden cerebral aneurism. Now all she had to do was deal with the two lunatics hiding in her bedroom and bath. For the first time in her life she actually felt like smoking a cigarette.

Sato Yui stood in front of the mirror having a minor life crisis. The urge to go out and hunt was strong, but it lacked the usual clarity she was accustomed to. The single-minded determination of her demon brain seemed to have been overridden by a kind of general female fuzziness. The finely honed point of the kill instinct was blunted by other random, distracting thoughts, first among them an apparent inability to decide what to wear. She had already tried on three outfits, each time feeling vaguely dissatisfied, ending up naked in front of the mirror again. Even her hair was behaving in a slightly annoying way. Making matters worse was the small blemish she had discovered on her chin earlier. What was that about? Perfect supernatural entities did not get pimples. They did not have bad hair days, or if they did, they didn't care about it. Was Sato Yui starting to care? Was she actually turning into the silly girl that Lisa had accused of being? Were the pleasures of living the life of a girl worth the required sacrifices?

Fortunately, supernatural entities were not compelled to engage in this sort of tedious self-analysis. Focusing her mind, she pushed herself out of Sato Yui's form, allowing her true Akuma identity to emerge. It was more difficult than usual, a little painful, in fact, but she managed it. She studied her so-called actual self in the mirror, the wrinkled, grayish green skin covered in lumps and protrusions, the large blood stained eyes, hair like soggy black seaweed, uneventful breasts with long sagging nipples, arms like tentacles adorned with five razor-sharp claws, where her sex should have been a grizzled mat of dark gray fur, like something that grew on the side of ancient rocks and smelled like the inside of a crypt, her powerful, animal-like legs with the bony, hoof-like feet of a deformed giantess. Overall, it was not a pretty picture. The beast was repulsive, even unto itself. For the first time in its lengthy existence the cold-hearted, unemotional killer, presently known as Sato Yui, felt like crying.

Pulling herself back into human form, which felt almost good enough to qualify as a mini-orgasm, Sato Yui slipped on her tight black jeans, a slinky sheer white sleeveless top and her red plastic sandals. She smiled at herself in the mirror. This was who she really was, not that grotesque monster claiming to be her. She was Sato Yui, young, vital and brimming with nasty impulses. She would find a guy, fuck him and then kill him, but would refrain from eating any of his body parts. Instead, she was thinking that afterwards she would go somewhere and experiment with Indian food, or maybe Thai.

Outside, she saw the young policewoman with the large breasts sitting in her police car. Officer Mendez, so close to full-blown lesbianism that the slightest cute girl breeze could push her irrevocably over the edge, sent by the large, dim-witted police Captain to ensure her protection. The same police Captain who was probably at this very minute thinking about what it would be like to have sex with Sato Yui. The irony of it all screamed out and was almost as tasty as human blood.

"Officer Mendez, right?" Sato Yui said, bouncing up to the squad car window.

Mendez blushed. "It's nice of you to remember my name."

"Are you here to protect me?"

"Just following the Captain's orders. He wants to make sure that you are in no danger."

"That's so sweet," Sato Yui cooed. "But it must be boring just sitting out here in your car."

"All part of the job," Mendez said, her eyes inadvertently focused on the Asian girl's breasts, spectacularly visible beneath her shirt.

"Well okay," Sato Yui said. "I guess I'll see you later."

"Uh, are you going somewhere?" Mendez asked.

"That was the plan. Why?"

"It's just that protecting you will be more difficult if I don't know where you are."

"That makes sense, but I wouldn't worry."

"Can I at least ask where you're going?"

Sato Yui thought about this for a moment. "All right, if you must know. I'm on my way to find a guy in some bar and then kill him while we're having sex."

For an instant, Mendez' face froze in nervous disbelief, but then her expression softened and she began to laugh. "You almost had me there for a minute."

"So you got my joke?" Sato Yui asked. "I'm still a novice when it comes to American sense of humor."

"No, I got it," Mendez chuckled. "On the dark side, but definitely funny."

"Oh good!" Sato Yui sighed. "But to tell the truth, I wasn't joking."

"You weren't ... joking?"

"Got you again!" Sato Yui squealed, hopping up and down outside the squad car. "Say, why don't you come with me?"

"I don't know," Mendez said, chewing her lower lip.

"You're supposed to protect me, right?"

"That's true, but ..."

"Oh come on," Sato Yui cried. "I really want to have fun and feel safe at the same time."

"But I'm wearing my uniform," Mendez said.

"Hello? Haven't you noticed what people wear in this neighborhood?" Sato Yui asked. "People will just think that you're some good-looking dyke into fetishes with serious control issues."

"All right," Mendez said, getting out of the squad car. "But just for the record, I'd prefer it if you didn't call me a dyke. I like to think of myself as a woman with all her options open."

"Me too!" Sato Yui said with a seductive wink, grabbing Mendez' hand and pulling her down the street. "Let's go find some interesting options."

Captain Burke paced around the small living room in his house in Queens, occasionally glancing at the clock on the wall, which only confirmed that time, in it's insidious way, continued to pass at a snail's pace. He was unable to sleep, couldn't bring himself to watch TV and didn't feel much like eating. Instead, he was smoking unfiltered Camels and drinking gin straight up. He was probably the last man on Earth who smoked unfiltered Camels, but he didn't care. He was agitated and therefore compelled to pace. Pacing and smoking just seemed to go together, and there was something about the inhalation of toxic chemicals in a flavor-rich, no-nonsense cigarette that helped him focus. The sources of his agitation were numerous and not easy to definitively pin down, but as he paced he went through the possibilities in his head.

Oddly enough, it was one year ago to the day that his wife of twenty-two years had walked out on him. Two suitcases, all the bankbooks and the keys to the car were all she left with. He could still hear the sound of the front door as it slammed behind her. The usual reasons had been given, a neat litany of marital problems, all of them his fault. Insensitive, emotionally detached, consumed with the job, incapable of caring and apparent impotency. Sure, he could have done more, said something to stop her, but most of the accusations were true and the numbness of too many years hadn't exactly been conducive to communication. Oh right, that was another one to add to the list, an inability to communicate. Hey, a cop's wife lives a cop's life. This little slogan carried the ring of truth for cops, but no so much for their spouses. Which probably explained the unusually high divorce rate in the Department.

Mention of the Department forced him to reach for the gin bottle. He poured as he paced. Cops had to sometimes sacrifice their personal lives for the job. That was the standard logic. In the fuzzy realm of rationalizations, it made sense, but only as long as the job made sense. If, on the other hand, the Department you're running is falling part, on the verge of slipping into anarchy, it's harder to make the case that a middle aged man pacing around in the middle of night in an empty house drinking gin right out of the bottle is anything but pathetic. Not only did he have a serial killer in a heat wave on his hands, he had to cope with a schizophrenic medical examiner, Malone, a novice with potential, but who apparently believed in monsters, and Stone, the best detective on the squad, who was currently implicated in a murder.

And then there were the disconcerting, oddly erotic feelings he was having about the young Japanese woman he had interviewed earlier in the day. Not at all like him to indulge in fantasies vis-à-vis potential witnesses. Not like him to fantasize about anything. Frank Burke might have been accused of being many things, but a dreamer wasn't one of them. You didn't get to be a Captain with your head in the clouds, or, more to the point, up some sexy young girl's skirt. And yet here he was thinking about giving Sato Yui a call, maybe asking her out for a bite. Even as a tentative idea in his head it sounded ridiculous. Gorgeous, sexy Asian teen, middle-aged cop with thinning hair and a volatile ulcer, the equation just didn't add up. At the same time, it was hard to ignore the fact that there had been some little spark between them in the interview room, something in her eyes that had said, 'call me sometime, age is not an issue.' Nothing ventured, nothing gained. He could always call her on the pretext of making sure she was safe, no hostile-looking Chinese lurking about, no death threats shot through the window on burning chopsticks. He'd be happy to come by, just to check the locks on the windows. Maybe on the way he could stop at the all night Japanese food store for some take out sushi rolls. Who knew, a little female companionship might be just what he needed to ward off the bug that was nibbling away at the edges of his brain; a girl who could take your mind off things for a while, the pleasurable illusion of not being who you are, for a couple of hours, anyway. Burke took a final hit from the gin bottle and was about to reach for the phone when it began to ring.

Twenty-four

L isa finished her drink then walked down the hall to check on Hammer. As she feared, the woman was sound asleep in her bed. Even worse, the doctor's clothes were lying in a pile on the floor. Hammer was naked under Lisa's sheets, her pale face pressed into Lisa's pillow. She had just begun to snore as Lisa shut the door and moved on to the bathroom. Terrified of what she might find Ishikawa up to, she knocked before opening the door. He was sitting on the toilet, fortunately with his pants up and the cover down, his eyes closed, legs wrapped in a painful-looking lotus posture. The lunatic was meditating on the toilet, proving perhaps that meditation was possible anywhere, or that, with the right encouragement, there was nothing the mentally ill couldn't accomplish.

Before she could say anything, Ishikawa opened his eyes and looked at her.

"Am I interrupting?" she asked.

"Not at all," he said, slowly unwrapping his legs. "I have occupied my time acquiring insight."

"Into the case?"

"Not exactly," he said, standing up and stretching. "One of the drawbacks of meditation, in my experience, has always been the lurking fear that one will have to, you know, 'go' while one is meditating. I have discovered that meditating on the toilet virtually eliminates this fear."

"As far as insights go, that is a real mind opener," Lisa told him. "But I think it's time we were going."

"Where are we going?" Ishikawa asked, following her back into the living room.

" This is incredibly rude, I know, but I actually meant that you should be going."

"Oh," he said, looking as if his best buddy had just stolen his very first girlfriend.

"It's just that I'm really tired and I'm sure that tomorrow will be another day of false leads, confusion and a general sense of hopelessness. I need to sleep."

"Of course, I understand. But I was hoping we could talk about us."

"I thought we agreed we wouldn't talk about us."

"I think we agreed not to talk about 'it.' That was before there was an us to talk about."

"I'm not so clear on how 'it' became us."

"I believe it happened about the same time that I turned into a human being again. That's when it hit me."

Don't ask! Don't ask!

"And by *it* you mean ..?"

"That I am crazy in love with you."

Told you!

Lisa forced a smile. "I'm flattered, really I am, but it's just that right now, with everything that's going on, I don't think ..."

"Say no more," Ishikawa said. "My selfishness is inexcusable."

"I'm not saying that having similar feelings would be impossible for me, only that, at the moment, there are more important things to think about."

"You mean Stone."

"Stone," Lisa sighed.

"Are you in love with him?" Ishikawa asked.

Was she? She seriously doubted it. For one thing, Lisa Malone didn't fall in love. And even if, against her better judgment, she had been moving in that direction, it had come to a screeching halt the moment Sato Yui appeared on the scene. It was just too hard to have deep feelings for a man who kept a secret demon lover on the side. She still cared about Stone, certainly desired his body, but love?

No way! Falling in love was a fairytale, something cooked up by obsessive/compulsive males in order to keep insecure girls wistful, weepy and helpless. Did she really believe that? Did it make any sense not to?

Ishikawa, meanwhile, was waiting for an answer. How to respond to a question for which all the answers only raised more questions? A yes would quell his ardor, while at the same time inflicting damage on the man's recently awakened status as a human being with a functional heart; a no would give him hope, however false, that a possible future existed in which he and she could somehow evolve into a couple. The simple answer was that she didn't believe in love, or at least couldn't afford it, and that the 'happy ever after' life was nothing more than a silly illusion, the pursuit of which even more a waste of time than chasing demons all over the face of the Earth. How much of this Ishikawa would be able to grasp was another matter. The simplest thoughts in one's head often turned out incredibly complex when spoken out loud.

When in doubt, fall back on the cushion of feminine vagueness and vulnerability.

"I'm so confused right now," Lisa said, burying her face in her hands. "Perhaps later we can ..."

Ishikawa instantly melted. "Can you ever forgive me?" he pleaded, lightly touching Lisa's arm.

"No," she sobbed. "You shouldn't blame yourself."

"Who else can I blame? I have behaved despicably, like some utterly selfish beast. I should go."

"Perhaps it's for the best."

"Will I see you tomorrow?" Ishikawa asked with a look of fish-eyed longing.

"I'd like that."

Lisa shut the door behind Ishikawa, wondering if she had been mean to him. Probably, she had. She actually liked the weird Japanese cop, couldn't rule out a casual fling with him somewhere down the road, assuming that actually being down the road at some point wasn't just wishful thinking, but at the moment there were more pressing issues to contend with. First on the list was getting Hammer out of her bed and on her way. The only problem was how to accomplish this without ending up in the bed with the desperate but pushy Doctor. The woman seemed to have a knack for always getting her way. Just a few kisses before I go. No, not like that. Take your clothes off and get under the sheets. If it helps, simply think of it as being a good friend. And really, what's the harm?

Lisa was halfway down the hall when her ringing cell phone rescued her. Even an annoying call in the middle of the night was preferable to what she was facing in the bedroom. Or at least so she thought as she raced to answer it. The Captain's somber voice was less than reassuring.

"Sorry to call so late, Malone, but I thought you should know."

"Know what?"

"Stone's been shot."

"Oh my God!" Lisa said, bracing herself against the wall to keep from falling down. "Is he ..?"

"Unknown," the Captain intoned. "I'm on my way to the site now. Maybe you should meet me there."

"I'll be there as soon as I can."

"Southeast corner of Chiang Kai-Shek Memorial Park. Do you know it?"

"I'll find it," Lisa told him.

Sato Yui dragged Officer Mendez into an East Village bar called, appropriately enough, 'Two Steps From Hell.' At one in the morning it was crawling with an interesting cross-section of the human element: punks, Goths, guys in suits, women in leather, boy toys, small time felons, a few high school girls pretending to be vampires and a smattering of tourists trying to live for a moment on the wild side. They found an empty table and ordered Black Russians.

"I can't really believe I'm here," Mendez shouted to Sato Yui, over the ear-splitting music coming out of the sound system.

Sato Yui smiled, scanning the room for a perspective male partner who might be in the mood for the best orgasm of his life, followed, of course, by a prolonged and excruciating death. "See anything you like?" she asked Mendez.

"What do you mean?" Mendez asked, focusing on a pale-skinned blonde wearing a black leather jacket and an extremely short white skirt. The girl, sitting at the bar, aware of Mendez' eyes on her, turned, spread her legs and subtly hiked up her skirt. It didn't take a detective to realize she wasn't wearing any underpants.

"Not her," Sato Yui said, finishing her drink and waving for the waitress. "I'm thinking that male is on the menu for this evening."

"Are you talking about a three-way?" Mendez cried, her voice high-pitched and squeaky.

"If it helps you to think of it that way, then yeah."

"I really don't see how that's possible."

"Why not?" Sato Yui asked, finishing off her second Black Russian, while continuing to scour the room for potential victims.

"For one thing, I'm on duty. I shouldn't even be drinking. If the Captain finds out I was involved in some kind of kinky sex thing on the job, I'll be lucky to find work as a security guard at Walmart. I might even end up in jail."

Sato Yui leaned over and gave Mendez a light kiss, no more than an evocative tasting of lips, but the effect was more or less immediate. Mendez' eyes drifted slightly out of focus, her jaw softened and an unmistakable moan escaped from her large, sensuously-shaped mouth. "You need to learn how to relax," Sato Yui told her. "Besides, as long as you're with me, you are following orders. It hardly matters what we're doing."

"I guess that makes sense," Mendez muttered, her gaze shifting slowly back to the blonde at the bar.

Sato Yui, meanwhile, was focused on the smiling guy crossing the room on a direct route for their table. He was tall, young and reasonably good looking, trying his best to look casual and off beat in a well-tailored, expensive-looking suit that screamed out conventional asshole by day, iconoclastic pretender by night; in other words, a more or less perfect candidate for what she had in mind.

"Sorry to just barge on over here," he said, flashing a set of perfect white teeth. "But I couldn't help noticing you two. I mean you're like the equation that brings extreme opposites into complete harmony. I feel like the universe is being explained to me, right here, right now."

Terrific, Mendez though, eyeing the man suspiciously. Another phony intellectual twit with an out of control hard on and, even worse, a message to convey.

"If you like what you see," Sato Yui said, sounding like some baby bird about to be fed, "join us."

"Just one thing I have to know," the guy said, sliding into a seat and looking at Mendez. "Are you a real cop?"

"If she was a real cop," Sato Yui answered, "would she dress like one in a place like this?"

"That's a good point," the guy said. "But that gun looks pretty real. Is it?"

"Hang around long enough and you may find out," Mendez sneered.

"Okay," the man laughed. "I begin to get your scene. I can dig it."

"Good!" Sato Yui said, waving her empty glass at the waitress. "Why don't we all dig it together?"

"Fine by me," he said. "And perhaps I can offer you ladies a synthetic pleasure enhancement in tablet form that I just happen to have here in my pocket. He extracted a small vile, popped the lid and shook out three small white pills. "It's the latest version of Ecstasy," he told them. "Guaranteed to keep you happy and horny all night long."

"Okay, that's it," Mendez said, her hand moving to the .38 on her hip."

Sato Yui froze her with a glance. "What my friend means is that we would love to try your happy and horny enhancement."

"You won't regret it," he said, sliding two pills across the table, while popping another into his mouth.

Sato Yui washed hers down with her fresh Black Russian. "Now take your medicine," she told Mendez. Mendez did her best to resist, but in the end she really had no choice. Her control of the situation had been rescinded the moment she stepped out of her squad car. Sato Yui's perky little breasts had seen to that. "Come with us," they had called out to her. She cursed herself for being so weak-willed. She was nothing more than a wishy-washy slut who didn't deserve to be wearing the N.Y.P.D badge. With a sigh of surrender, she picked up the little white pill and put it in her mouth.

Lisa broke as many traffic laws as she possibly could, but it still took her twenty minutes to reach the crime scene. All she could think about was that Stone had been shot and she should have been with him. They were called partners for a reason. If she had been there the outcome might have been different; one dead bad guy instead of one dead Stone lying in a soggy pool of his own blood. Wait a minute, what was she thinking? She didn't know that Stone was dead. No one had told her that he was. Did she somehow sense it? Was this what the sensation of death felt like, why it felt like her insides were being ripped apart and that the entire city was about to vaporize in a huge toxic cloud?

The park, named after some Chinese guy who had apparently failed to prevent Communism from spreading like a cancer throughout China, appeared to be under siege. There were cop cars everywhere, police barricades blocking off all the entrances and enough people on scene to mount a small invasion. Uniform, forensics, somber-looking guys in suits, the occasional press straggler, all of them agitated, sweating profusely, moving around in some highly choreographed, yet seemingly chaotic, dance.

She found the Captain standing in the midst of the frenzy, talking to a tall Chinese guy wearing sunglasses. As she approached, the Chinese man offered an inconspicuous bow and disappeared into the shadows.

"Where is he?" she demanded.

"Take it easy, Malone," the Captain said, reaching out his hands and placing them firmly on her shoulders. "He's already on route to the hospital."

"Lisa sighed relief. "So he's not dead."

The Captain sucked in air and glanced for an instant upwards at a night sky that should have been there, but wasn't. "I won't lie to you, Malone. He took one in the chest and another in the head, small caliber, based on the shell casings we found. He's hanging on, probably because he's a tough bastard, but it's anyone's guess at this point."

"Lisa's body trembled and she really felt like screaming. "I should have been with him."

"No you shouldn't have," the Captain told her. "If you had been, chances are you'd be on your way to the hospital too, or the morgue."

"But we're partners," she said, trying to push back the tears that were bubbling up inside her eyes.

"That's right," the Captain said. "And that means that now you put all your energy into finding the asshole or assholes who did this."

"Oh, I already know who did this."

"You do?"

"Stone told me who he was going to meet tonight, Li Zang and Harry Fang, two of his so-called reliable Chinese contacts. So now all I have to do is track them down and shoot both of them in the face."

"Wrong, Malone," the Captain said, in what came across as a kind of sympathetic growl. "First of all, we don't go around killing suspects. Second, you're too close to this one; it's way too personal for you, and that's a one-way ticket to screwing up big time. Tomorrow morning we'll have a top priority briefing on this and I'll assign a team to investigate. The point is that we follow procedure. Without it, we're no better than the scum we try to put behind bars."

"Not good enough, Sir."

"Well it will have to be. The last thing I need is you out looking for revenge and getting yourself killed in the process. As of right now you're on desk duty until further notice. I know this seems harsh, but you'll just have to trust me that it's for the best. Anyway, we can always look on the bright side."

She would really have loved to see one, but couldn't. "Is there a bright side, Captain?"

"Only that this attack seems to confirms Stone's suspicion about the connection between the serial killings and the Chinese gangs. I'm guessing that once we pick up this Zang and Fang duo we'll be a hell of a lot closer to solving the entire case."

Lisa nodded, more out of exasperation than anything else, then started to walk away.

"Where are you going, Malone?" the Captain called after her.

"To the hospital," she told him. "By the way, who was that Chinese guy you were talking to?"

"Chinese guy? What Chinese guy?"

Twenty-five

L isa straggled back into her apartment a little past five in the morning, feeling dirty, corrupted, permeated with the smell of antiseptic and a billion or so insidious germs. What was it about being in hospitals that made people feel like killing someone, or, as an alternative, simply giving up and dying? A few hours in the waiting room and she had developed so many symptoms she'd been tempted to have herself admitted; headache, nausea, blurry vision, inner-cranial sound, possibly in the form of voices and a throbbing in her chest that just didn't feel normal. The occasional nurse had drifted by, smiling broadly, but who was kidding whom? It wasn't as if anyone sat in hospital waiting rooms because it was fun. Bad news was built into the situation. The place reeked of bad luck and tragedy on a cosmic scale. Maybe she just wasn't the kind of person who could wait for anything for very long and remain in a good mood. She had twice jumped up, flashed her badge at the nurse's station demanding answers, but had received only unconvincing expressions of understanding and the bland assurance that everything that could be done was. She had been on the verge of threatening one of these phony-smile nurses with her gun, when a bleary-eyed doctor dressed in bloodstained green had appeared with the news. Stone had survived the surgery; he was stable, but critical, currently in intensive care recovery. Both bullets had been successfully removed. The chest wound would cause no serious complications. The wound to the head, on the other hand, was more problematic. It was just too soon to say if, or to what extent, there would be any brain damage. The best thing Lisa could do at this point, she was informed, was to go home and get some rest.

"Rest?" she had barked. "Do you seriously think I can rest? That's my lover in there."

"You're ..?"

"Partner. That's my partner in there, and his bloody, brain-damaged head is, in some weird way, my fault."

"I see," the doctor said, reaching out a hand, which Lisa jumped away from. "It's not at all uncommon for a police officer's partner to experience a certain amount of guilt in these situations."

"Oh please! Spare me the psycho-soothing-sounding crap, okay? Look, if I could just see him, maybe get into bed with him for awhile …"

"On second thought, it might be best if we simply have you checked into the hospital for the night. You could be in shock."

"Yeah," Lisa said. "I don't think that's a good idea."

"Trust me, I'm a doctor."

"Trust you?" Lisa snapped. "I'd sooner put my faith in the advice of a strung out crack addict."

"Or I could just call security."

"You do realize that I have a gun," Lisa told him, slapping her holster a few times for emphasis.

"So do our security guards," the doctor reminded her.

Lisa toyed with the idea of a late night shootout in the hospital. She was almost in the mood for it. A couple of bored, underpaid night watchmen, what kind of real resistance could they mount? Sure, they'd go through the motions, not wanting to appear completely incompetent in front of the doctor and nurses, but in the end they'd be either dead or wounded, and then she'd be faced with the whole rigmarole of trying to come up with a reasonable explanation for entering into a gun fight with hospital personnel, rather than simply following the doctor's advice and taking a sedative. Besides, truth be told, she was exhausted.

"All right," she told the doctor. "I'll go. But I'll be expecting an update on my partner's status first thing in the morning."

The doctor promised he would. "And by the way," he added. "If you have anything at all narcotic in your medicine chest, I would take it as soon as I got home."

It wasn't until she stumbled into her bedroom that she remembered the sleeping Hammer, curled up like some large albino cat in her bed. Not exactly what you want to crawl under the sheets with under the best of circumstances, but it was too late and she was too tired to do otherwise. She pulled off her clothes, regretting that she wasn't wearing any underwear, and slipped under the covers. Hammer immediately unfurled, slowly turned and draped an arm around Lisa. It gave her an odd feeling, but it was also comforting. Comforting was what she needed right now, a Mommy figure to hold her tight and chase all the scary things away. It hardly mattered that Hammer was perhaps the most ill equipped female on the planet to play Mommy. In a crisis of this magnitude even a polymorphic perverse middle-aged scientist with a penchant for dead bodies and drug abuse would suffice.

"Where have you been?" Hammer muttered, her sleep breath rolling over Lisa in a sticky cloud.

"Crime scene," Lisa told her.

"Oh no!" Hammer snorted. "Not another mutilation, I hope."

"Just a gun shot victim," Lisa sighed.

"On the mundane side, but a relief, I suppose."

"Yeah," Lisa said, closing her eyes, giving into the sensation of being dragged down into a bottomless hole. "Big relief."

Officer Mendez woke up in a musty smelling bed in a room she did not recognize. She had a throbbing headache, her tongue felt as if it had been injected with sawdust and she was naked. She eased herself up on one elbow and tried to get her bearings. The room was small, hot and dusty, the kind of place you would choose to crash in only if your mind was so blown apart by alcohol or drugs that making choices was no longer a credible option. Something resembling her uniform lay in a pile on the floor. She eased her head back down on the pillow and shut her eyes. Images of the previous night began to filter back; she, Sato Yui and the ecstasy man stumbling down some street on the edge of the Alphabet City, laughing, touching each other, drinking vodka right from the bottle, eventually ending up in some fleabag hotel on Avenue D. They had checked into a room, this room, with the fading yellow wallpaper and the water stain splotches across the ceiling, and proceeded to get naked. Beyond that, the details were fuzzy. She knew there had been sex, lots of sex, in all kinds of variations, and other things, things her mind refused to recall, but which worried her nonetheless. No difficulty remembering that Sato Yui had run the show, treating her and whatever-his-name-was like a pair of puppets in some erotic sideshow. Tom, that was his name, Tom the puppet boy with the very pointy penis. Oh God, had he actually put it in her anus at some point? That would explain the discomfort she was feeling in that area. She shuddered at the thought of unprotected anal sex with an anonymous drug user. Why would she do such a thing? Oh right, she did it because she had been told to. Sato Yui, the petite boss of bosses with the tits of an angel, had insisted and Sato Yui seemed to have a way of getting what she wanted.

Mendez brought her hands up to her face and gently rubbed the hurting areas around her eyes, which only seemed to antagonize the pain. She allowed her arms to drop, the left one over the edge of the bed, where it dangled lifelessly, the right onto the mattress, where it landed in something wet and sticky. Forcing herself to turn her head and open her eyes, she saw the blood stains on the sheet, leading directly to the back of a man, no doubt pointy Tom's, which was covered in nasty-looking, dark-red cuts. The sudden realization that she might be lying in bed with a dead body was like a chilling wake up call in the hotel of the doomed. Her only hope at this point, however slim, was that, if Tom was dead, she hadn't been the one who killed him. Not that this would matter much at her trial. Accessory to murder didn't really sound all that much better than murder. As she struggled to come up with options, of which there seemed to be none, Tom's body shifted and he began to snore.

Thank God! Tom was alive. The possibility of ten to fifteen behind bars was no longer staring her in the face, the end of a promising career in law enforcement still was. The only sensible thing to do was leaving the scene before the wounded Tom woke up. The sooner she got out of there, the sooner she could start pretending the whole thing had never happened. Easier said than done. Moving her body turned the pain in her head from merely terrible to beyond enduring, but she managed to slip out from under the covers and stand up. For an instant, she felt okay; better than she expected to feel, until the nausea came like a sudden tidal wave forcing her to stagger into the small bathroom and vomit. If there was one sure way to make a bad headache worse, it had to be throwing up. The more you did it, the more everything hurt. Once the gag reflex had run its course, she pulled herself up in front of the dirty little sink and splashed water on her face. This actually helped, allowing her to focus her eyes again, except that the face staring back at her in the mirror was unrecognizable, the scary, almost inhuman face of a drugged-out, hung-over former cop. And that wasn't even the worst of it. Glancing down, she noticed the long, reddish scratches running across her breasts and belly. She felt the urge to cry, but knew that would only antagonize the pain in her head. Besides, there was no time now to lament the possibly permanent disfigurement of her two best features.

Walking as quietly as possible back into the room, she slowly dressed. Tom moaned in his sleep a few times, but showed no sign of waking up. The only problem was that her holster, lying under an ugly-looking orange vinyl chair, was empty, her weapon nowhere to be found. A cop could expect to lose many things during her career, her friends, her spouse, her mind and possibly her life. The one thing a cop never lost was her service revolver. Short of shooting an innocent bystander, it was the worst thing a cop could do, more appalling even than taking illegal drugs and having casual sex while on duty. As she eased her way down the hotel stairs to the street, she was forced to accept the fact that, possibly as soon as tomorrow, she would be looking for a new line of employment. The one small hope that still lingered was that no one had stolen her patrol car.

After leaving Lisa's apartment, Ishikawa had started walking. He walked because doing anything else felt pointless. Movement, somehow, was crucial. In general, the Japanese people were not comfortable with staying still. A person in motion had a future, however pointless it might be. Stopping to take a breath, look at the scenery, or, God forbid, think things over was just begging for trouble. One moved forward to avoid the ignominy of falling back into failure. The possibility of moving forward into failure had never been covered during orientation, but it was no longer a concern. Failure, as it turned out, had been written into the original script. It was one of those little details that had been glossed over, covered up with an aura of illogical exuberance. Demon hunters, in fact, are never successful. In the long history of demon hunting, the good guys had never won. The suppression of this tidbit of truth had been as necessary as it was ultimately fatal. How interesting, he thought (he was almost tempted to call it ironic) that it had required finally coming into actual contact with the demon for the truth to be revealed.

Still, at the very least, he had rediscovered the ability to feel. No small accomplishment for an otherwise abject failure. It hardly mattered that, as a result, he was now painfully in love with a woman who did not return his feelings, unable to sleep or think clearly and, for the first time in many years, perspiring profusely. Emotional distress was nothing more than a proof of life. He was a living emotional wreck on the bypass of absolute uncertainty, and in some odd way he didn't particularly mind it.

Not that his ultimate destination had ever been in doubt. Within thirty minutes of apparently mindless walking, he was standing outside Sato Yui's apartment. He had come to doubt whether he could bring himself to kill the Akuma – despite the fact that his entire adult life had been nothing more than an elaborate rehearsal for just that – but he could still stalk her. Or was it just that he was feeling the need to be close to her. In some darkly tragic way, the person he was had always been determined by the beast. He had been blind to it for so many years, but now it made perfect sense. It had only required New York City, its inherent madness and highly charged chaotic energy, to reveal the truth. Were the changes he was experiencing nothing more than a reflection of the same changes the Akuma was going through? Were their existences so intertwined? More to the point, could he even survive without her?

Ishikawa shook his head violently in an effort to end the interior inquisition. His brain, rattled by heat and sleeplessness, was in no shape to come up with definitive answers. Instead, he had crossed the street, found a secluded spot in a shadowy niche between two buildings and proceeded to wait. He knew somehow that he wouldn't have to wait long. This, too, proved to be incorrect. Two hours later – which had felt more like two hundred years – he was still in his niche, nervously exhausted and seriously considering giving up. And then he saw her, walking down the street with two people, one of them wearing what looked like a police officer's uniform. Sato Yui led the way, bouncing along and giggling, like some perfect little animated creature, occasionally spinning around to say something to the others, who had to struggle to keep up, their insistent laughter echoing off the surrounding buildings before being sucked upwards into the thick, humid clouds overhead.

Ishikawa followed at a safe distance, through the catacombs of the Lower Eastside, until the trio entered the four-story tenement with the hotel sign hanging precariously above the entrance. He knew, of course, what was about to happen. After a brief period of perfunctory foreplay the Akuma would make its dramatic appearance and death would quickly follow. Two unwitting humans seduced and abandoned, trapped within an unforgiving trajectory of sexual frenzy and murder. The same hopeless scenario had occurred a countless number of times in the past and would continue on into the future. Still, it occurred to him that he had never been this close. The opportunity he had sought for so many years was at last upon him. All that was required was for him to follow through, take the initiative, and fulfill his function. He saw himself entering the hotel, moving stealthily up the stairs and bursting into the room with sword flashing. In the grip of its bloodlust the Akuma would be temporarily distracted. With one expertly executed snap of the blade the drama could finally end.

So why was he unable to move? He stood there staring at the hotel, the seconds clicking off in his head, his legs trembling. Moving a hand slowly behind his head, he took hold of the sword's leather handle, his perfectly crafted sword, forged by a master craftsman in the mountains east of Osaka.

"For what purpose do you require this sword?" the white-haired Master had asked.

Ishikawa had hesitated, reluctant to expose himself to the usual ridicule whenever demons were mentioned. Pressed by the old man's probing eyes, he had finally blurted it out. "This sword will be used to dispatch an Akuma back to the realm of Hell from which it came."

The old man had smiled, nodding his understanding. "In that case, you will need the very best sword that I can create. It must be as pure as the first snowfall on sacred Mount Fuji, yet as hard as a young man's cock poised for the first time before the quivering loins of a beautiful virgin."

"A beautiful image, Master."

"Indeed!"

"I humbly thank you," Ishikawa had said, bowing deeply.

"Anything for a good cause," the Master had laughed. "As long as you understand that it's going to cost extra."

It was a sword fit for the noblest of samurai, but Ishikawa was unable to extract it from its leather sheath. It wouldn't budge. He lacked the necessary strength to even hold the sword, let alone cut off the head of the all-powerful demon. What was a man who was both helpless and without hope? He had in his possession perhaps the most perfect weapon on Earth, and yet he was impotent. His head hung, he had walked slowly away.

Finding Ishikawa sitting on the steps outside her apartment did absolutely nothing to improve Sato Yui's mood. She was angry, mostly with herself, which was new and therefore somewhat interesting, but not particularly fun. Her status as a first class demon was in serious jeopardy. Sure, she wanted to be a real girl, but being nothing but a girl was not something she had bargained for. Particularly after she had arranged the latest killing situation with such style. Did the effort put into preparation count for nothing anymore? Mendez, the lesbian cop, and the human male with the boring name and annoying smile had literally begged for death, but she couldn't bring herself to do it. She had barely been able to hurt them, nothing more than a few half-hearted scratches with tentative claws that would have made even an average, run of the mill Akuma shamefully blush. Maybe she could blame the whole fiasco on Stone. The sudden image of him being shot in the head by the Chinese female had upset her. She had actually felt it as the bullet entered his brain, the dull, squishing sensation of massive tissue damage, which had instantaneously resulted in the breaking of the connection between them she had put so much effort into creating. Stone, or what was left of him, was no longer under her control. Dealing with the Chinese bitch responsible was something she really looked forward to, but it would have to wait. All she wanted now was to be alone, away from people. Humans sickened her, none more so than Ishikawa.

"Please don't tell you that you've been waiting for me," she said to the pathetic, so-called demon hunter.

"Not really," Ishikawa told her. "I just couldn't think of anywhere else to be."

"Try thinking harder and then go away."

"I followed you tonight, watched you go into that hotel with those two people. I knew you were going to kill them, but there was nothing I could do."

"Sounds like the latest version of the story of your ridiculous life," Sato Yui said impatiently. "The well-intentioned loser who just can't get it up."

"I could have saved those people, possibly even destroyed you, but I was incapable of action."

"Yeah, well, maybe it's something going around, like a virus."

"The purpose of my existence has abandoned me. There is nothing left for me to do."

"Except hanging around annoying me?"

"I am surrendering, admitting defeat, ready for you to kill me. I only ask that it be quick and as painless as possible."

It was tempting. No one had ever actually asked to be killed before. Her victims had always acted as if their impending deaths were the greatest injustice ever inflicted upon the human race. Not that they ever had that much time to formally protest. And it wasn't as if Ishikawa didn't deserve it. She would of course disregard the quick and painless request, opting instead for a lengthy and horribly painful demise. She imagined the final act in Ishikawa's execution, the decapitating cut delivered with enough force to send his head flying upwards at incredible speed. It would be the first human head to leave Earth's gravity, becoming a kind of orbital warning to all future demon hunters. Japanese children would learn about it in school. A new national holiday might even be created in Japan to commemorate it. A nice image, but ...

"As much as I'd like to," she told him, "I'm not really in the mood. And I have more important things to deal with right now."

"In that case, Ishikawa sighed, his face dropping into his hands, "I'm lost."

"You're not lost," Sato Yui said, aware of the absurdity of an Akuma offering advice to a human, particularly the human whose sole ambition was her own destruction. "You're just one-dimensional, fixated and stupid. You need to get past all this and move on with your life, for lack of a better term. Go back to Japan, get your pension and open a dry cleaning shop, or something."

"I see what you're saying," he said, slowly rising to his feet. "It's over between us, isn't it?"

"Nothing lasts forever, Ishikawa," she called after him, wondering if just killing him now might spare him a lot of heartache later on.

Twenty-six

The Captain was just wrapping up his presentation on Stone's shooting and the growing city-wide Chinese menace when Lisa got to the office. Waking up hadn't been the problem, sleep having become pretty much an arbitrary variable in her life, so much as Hammer, who had taken Lisa's naked presence next to her in bed as a tacit acceptance of their budding relationship. Hovering over her like some sexually aroused bird of prey, the Doctor had delivered a barrage of frantic kisses to her eyes, nose, lips and breasts before Lisa's will to resist had kicked in. Fortunately, she'd had the Stone-has-been-shot-in-the-head card to play, which had drained the erotic exuberance from Hammer's body faster than the suction machine in the morgue drained blood from a corpse.

"Oh God no," Hammer had cried, falling away from Lisa to her own side of the bed. After a few moments of quiet hysteria, she had slipped out of bed and walked into the bathroom. Lisa had taken the opportunity to dress quickly, albeit in the same clothes she had worn the day before, and leave the apartment.

"To recap," the Captain said, jabbing his finger at the photo stuck to the white board in the middle of the briefing room. "We're looking for this man, Harry Fang, small time drug dealer, petty thief, part-time pimp, and a female, also Chinese, goes by the name of Li Zang, although that could certainly be an alias. We know very little about her, but suspect she's probably a prostitute posing as a waitress, or vice-versa. Either way, locate one, we'll most likely find the other. I want you to get out there and do just that. And remember, this is Chinatown we're dealing with. We don't want to ruffle feathers unnecessarily, so keep it low keyed, people. Be subtle, which means do not shoot anyone unless it is absolutely necessary."

After the various teams had left the briefing room, the Captain turned to Lisa, wiggling a finger to indicate his desire for her to follow him into his office. "Get any sleep, Malone?" he asked, once he was securely ensconced behind his desk.

"Not much, Sir," she told him.

"These are difficult times for us all," he mused. "Nothing brings this into focus with greater clarity than an officer down. The Commissioner wants results on the Stone shooting and he wants them sooner rather than later. At the same time, he's insisting on a kid glove policy vis-à-vis the entire Chinese problem."

"I'm not sure I understand," Lisa said.

The Captain smiled at Lisa's naiveté. There are a lot if important people in the Chinese community, Malone. Chinese businesses, many of which are actually legitimate, not only contribute to the city's economic vitality, but they are a substantial source of tax revenue. Not to suggest that the reputable leaders of Chinatown don't want this serial-killing death squad apprehended, but, at the same time, we need to keep in mind just how important image is to these people. Which is why the Commissioner feels – with the Mayor's approval, by the way – that while we should pursue this band of murderers with the utmost zeal, we should also show a certain restraint vis-à-vis how far up the food chain culpability travels."

Lisa had very little idea what the Captain was talking about, but she was painfully aware that he had just used the term vis-à-vis twice. Her mind was distracted by Stone, not to mention the annoying detail that there was, in fact, no Chinese death squad, but, in the interest of conversational politeness, felt she had to say something. "So, in other words, the Chinese gang bosses are allowed to continue feeding on human flesh, as long as they avoid the affluent white meat."

"A colorful metaphor, Detective," the Captain said, reaching for his can of diet Coke. "And, sadly enough, more or less accurate."

"Sounds like dirty politics to me, Sir."

"You're right about that, I'm afraid, but it's the nature of the beast. It's all about who benefits and how many have to suffer as a result. It's rarely about fairness or justice. As long as the casualty rate is kept reasonably low and preferably ethnic, the politicians don't lose any sleep."

"I'm sorry that I'm not quite that cynical yet, Captain."

"No need to apologize. Just give it time. Stay a cop long enough and you'll be drinking your cynicism straight from the bottle, most likely with gin chasers, alone, in a house you've lived in for twenty-five years without ever feeling at home."

"Not a pretty picture, Sir."

"Putting it mildly, Malone, but it's better to know what's coming and be ready for it, than to have it sneak up on you in the dead of night when it's way to late to do anything about it."

"So you're telling me to be prepared."

"Precisely, and also to think carefully before committing to home ownership in the suburbs."

"Thank you, Captain," Lisa said. "I'll try to remember that. In the meantime, and sorry to change the subject, but I really feel that I should be out looking for Zang and Fang."

"And I believe we've already had this discussion, Malone. Stone is out of the picture, for how long we don't know. I want you to take over the case. Go over his files on the Chinese murder team, find me some evidence that links these bastards to our serial killings."

"But Captain ..."

The Captain held up his trademark hand of silence. "No further discussion. Now get out of here. I've got a missing officer to deal with."

"Who's missing?" Lisa asked.

"Mendez," the Captain said with obvious annoyance. "I had her keeping an eye on that witness, the young Japanese woman who was in here yesterday. Can't recall her name."

"Sato Yui," Lisa said, having to bite her tongue to keep herself from shouting *I told you so.*

"Right. Anyway, her patrol car was found this morning parked in front of the witness's apartment, no sign of Mendez. Hopefully, she'll turn up."

The real question is in how many pieces will she turn up?

"Yeah," Lisa said, getting up to leave. I hope so, too."

Lisa scooped up all the files she found lying on Stone's desk and carried them back to her office. She wouldn't have minded so much searching through them for new leads, except she already knew there was nothing to find. This made the work not only tedious, but a complete waste of time. It didn't take her long to begin noticing Stone's delusional touch. In the Clifford Goth file, for example, he had underlined in red marker the entry that Goth had once suffered food poisoning in a Chinese restaurant and had threatened to sue. In the margin, Stone had scribbled, "Motive for Goth's mutilation?" In the John Burnett file, Stone had found it 'significant' that Burnett had once dated an exotic dancer of Chinese ancestry. The double homicide couple from Ishikawa's hotel had apparently joined a tour group visiting the Great Wall in April 2000. Several people on the tour, possibly including the dead couple, had later been heard to complain that the Great Wall wasn't all that great. Poor brain-impaired Stone, she thought. Using these criteria there was probably no one in the entire New York Metropolitan area not connected somehow to the Chinese, and therefore potential targets for the insidious death squad. What made the whole thing even sadder is that, even while under the spell of Sato Yui, the real killer, Stone had actually been trying to come up with something. As a result of his efforts, he had become a suspect in the death of a young Asian female, identity yet unknown, and was now staring at the possibility of living out his life as a vegetable. The ridiculous irony of the situation did nothing at all to lessen the sadness.

THE CUTEST LITTLE DEMON IN TOWN

Lisa closed the files, shut her eyes and sighed. She felt that somehow she should have been able to prevent all this, but whatever had been required – more courage, force of will, emotional commitment, sex appeal? – she had been unable to produce. Maybe if she had allowed herself to love Stone and not been so terrified to tell him about it, he would have been able to resist the demon. Her father would have wasted no time labeling this a failure on her part, as well as using it as an opportunity to remind her once again that she just didn't have what it took to be a cop. Maybe the bastard had been right all along. After all, how many housewives in Ohio were being haunted by demons? On the other hand, how many weren't?

Lisa glanced up onto the outer office and saw an extremely disheveled version of Officer Mendez standing in the middle of the floor staring at her. As their eyes met, Mendez burst into tears and ran straight for Lisa's office. She crashed through the door, shut it behind her and collapsed into the chair opposite Lisa's desk.

"Jesus, Mendez," Lisa said. "You're alive."

"Just barely," Mendez sobbed.

"What the hell happened?"

"I wish I knew for sure. I was supposed to be keeping an eye on Sato Yui. One minute I was, the next I was … doing terrible things."

Lisa poured a glass of water and handed it to her, along with a box of tissues. Mendez pulled a wad of tissues from the box and violently blew her nose.

"Don't cry," Lisa told her, gently patting her shoulder. "As bad as it was, it could have been a lot worse."

"I don't see how," Mendez sniffled. "Bad enough that I voluntarily submitted to anal intercourse, but I lost my gun and my squad car. The Captain is going to crucify me."

"Not necessarily," Lisa said, trying desperately not to conjure up an image of Mendez having anal intercourse. Some things you just didn't need to see. We can fix this."

"Have you been listening to me, Malone? I drank and took drugs and had random sex on duty."

"Forget all that," Lisa said. "None of it ever happened."

"It didn't?" Mendez asked, her face twisted in tear-stained confusion.

"No. This is what really happened. You were sitting in your car, following orders, when two people accosted you at gunpoint and forced you out of the car."

"Who were they?"

"You don't know because they were both wearing ski masks. But they were definitely speaking Chinese."

"Chinese?"

"That's the new key word. Chinese. Two Chinese people kidnapped you. They took you somewhere in Chinatown, roughed you up a bit, maybe even one of them forced you to have anal intercourse, as disgusting as that is to even consider. These people were monsters, animals and, most importantly, fluent in Chinese. Somehow, you managed to escape."

"How did I escape?"

"Just be vague about that. After all, you're probably in shock."

"I actually think I might be."

"All the better," Lisa told her. "Just stick to that story and your job is secure. You might even get a promotion out of it. Now get out of here and go see the Captain."

The real question was, Lisa thought to herself, as she watched Mendez walk slowly towards the Captain's office, why the officer with the formidable bust was still breathing? People who played with Sato Yui generally ended up dead, and not in a particularly nice way. Mendez had spent the night with the demon and lived to tell about it. What did it mean? On the other hand, why even bother asking? Meaning was the lost commodity in all this, the missing factor in the summer of scorching madness. Once you accepted the premise that an ancient Japanese Akuma, in the guise of an adorable, oversexed teenager, was rampaging through the city on a vicious murder spree, with apparent impunity, no less, the prospect of reasonable explanations for anything pretty much went out the window.

After Mendez had slipped inside the Captain's office, Lisa turned her head and glanced out the window. The view, under the best of circumstances never anything to write postcards home about, was now completely obscured by thick, agitated gray clouds, which seemed to be pressing their weight against the glass, intent upon getting inside. You knew things were out of control when even the clouds turned pathological. It occurred to her that there might be some connection between the weather and Sato Yui's presence in town. The demon had admitted being attracted by the extreme heat, but perhaps she was the cause of the ongoing atmospheric chaos. How long, she wondered, before the 'Demon Factor' would become a routine component of the weather forecaster's lexicon?

"We have a sweeping high pressure system from the north, which could certainly bring some much needed relief, except for the mysterious demon factor, which, as we've learned from experience, can easily turn this mass of cool air into a metaphorical blood bath of boiling misery."

She closed her eyes and immediately began falling through a roiling funnel of thick clouds that smelled of ammonia and made her nose and throat burn. When she opened her eyes she was standing in Stone's hospital room. As she stood there watching him, his eyes opened and he looked directly at her. He tried to speak, but the only sound he could manage was a gurgling grunt that left drool hanging from his lips. She wanted to go to him, to tell him that it was going to be okay, but was unable to move. She also knew that what she was witnessing might be nothing more than the involuntary muscle and nerve reactions of a man in an irreversible vegetative state. The doctors had warned her about getting her hopes up. He might seem to wake up, might even appear to recognize you, but all you're seeing is the uncontrollable echo effect of a mind more or less in a state of mush. Mush? Was that an acknowledged medical term? There may also be certain physiological responses to phantom stimuli. As she had no idea what that meant, she asked if perhaps an example could be given. Well, perhaps you've noticed that as we've been standing here chatting the patient has gotten an erection. Lisa shifted her glance from Stone's blubbering lips to his groin. It was true. The unmistakable tenting effect under the white sheet left little room for doubt. Don't be alarmed, the doctor advised. It's actually not uncommon. Way less uncommon than you think, Lisa thought. Even with a more or less normal human brain, the man had an almost constant hard on. She guessed this was nothing more than a sad symbol of Stone's consistency and determination to always be ready for anything. If she touched it, would he feel anything? Oh My God, Lisa, that is so inappropriate. Tell me, doctor, could a man in such a vegetative state have sex?

In a purely physical sense, I suppose he could, but what would be the point?

Lisa was debating whether or not to throw all caution to the wind and demonstrate the point in question when she became aware of another presence in the room. It was Sato Yui, wearing a pale blue patient's gown; her black hair slicked back, her eyes the size of shiny black saucers. She floated across the room, stopping on the other side of Stone's bed.

"Hi, Stone," she said, totally ignoring Lisa. Stone stared up at the ceiling, gulping and gurgling. "Don't bother trying to speak," she told him. "To tell the truth, I didn't drop by to chat." With that, she untied her gown and let it drop to the floor. No surprise that she was naked underneath. The demon's aversion to underwear was by this time well documented. She took hold of the bed sheet and flicked it back, exposing Stone's engorged penis. "I did promise you a fuck," Sato Yui said, hopping onto the bed and positioning her perfectly compact body over his erection. "And I always keep my promises. Well, all right, that's not exactly true, which I suppose makes this even more special."

Lisa felt her blood begin to boil. Bad enough that the pint-sized demon slut assumed she could just stroll into a hospital room and have sex with her brain-damaged partner, but she also expected Lisa to just stand by quietly and watch? The presumptuous little bitch. Lisa reached behind her head with her right hand and felt the leather handle of Ishikawa's sword. What was it doing there? Ishikawa had given it to her, claiming that he had forfeited the right to ever use it again. Take it, he had said, as a token of my undying affection. If anyone can kill the Akuma, it is you. She slid the sword from its sheath, grasping the handle with both hands. As she cocked her arms with a supple twist of her body, she noticed the shimmer of light playing along the blade. It reminded her of happier days at the sea, the sun glistening on the water, she in her string bikini, confident that her barely concealed body could easily conquer any male on the beach. How she had gotten from there to here she wasn't quite sure. Sato Yui, meanwhile, had already begun the slow rise and fall of her body on Stone's mindless member, quiet growls rumbling in her throat. Lisa took a deep breath, imagining all her power focused in her shoulders and arms and took a swing, the blade whistling through air on a direct route to Sato Yui's lovely little neck. It traveled to within perhaps a centimeter of the target when it abruptly stopped, the momentum of the blade reversing, sending painful shock waves into Lisa's hands and arms, forcing her to drop the sword. Sato Yui turned her head at the sound of steel crashing to the floor and smiled. "Oh hi, Lisa," she giggled. "I didn't notice you standing there."

"Malone!"

Lisa eyes snapped open and slowly focused on the monstrous form standing in the doorway of her office. As the fog cleared, she understood that it was the Captain and that he was shouting her name.

"Sorry, Captain," she said. "Did you call me?"

"I've been calling you for the past ten minutes," he told her.

"Again, sorry. I was ..."

"Never mind that now. We've got a fresh crime scene in the Alphabet and I want you over there."

"A crime scene, Sir?" Lisa said, rubbing her eyes and trying to stand up.

"Double homicide," the Captain barked. "Could be Zang and Fang."

"Could be?" Lisa asked.

"Well, once we gather up all the body parts and forensics does the puzzle work, I'm hoping we'll get positive identification. Take Mendez with you."

"Mendez? Isn't she ..?

"A brave young officer is what she is, Malone. Definitely on the fast track to getting her Detective's shield. A commendation from the Mayor isn't out of the question. I only wish I had a few more like her around here."

You mean repressed lesbians who allow themselves to be seduced by demons and then let some random guy screw them in the ass?

"I couldn't agree more, Captain. Mendez is ... sorry, words fail me."

"You can think about it in the car and let me know later," the Captain told her. "Now get your butt moving. I'll be expecting a full report by this afternoon."

Twenty-seven

I t hadn't been a problem for Sato Yui to locate the two Chinese creeps who had taken it upon themselves to put a bullet in Stone's brain, thereby depriving her of a faithful human servant, who also happened to be very good in bed. The scent of his blood on them was like a beacon. It hardly mattered that they had meticulously scrubbed themselves afterwards, or that they had visited a local shrine and burned incense, praying to their impotent gods for protection. She could have followed them across time if she'd had to. The nicest thing about it was that they were hiding in an apartment not ten minutes walking time from her place. She almost had to like them for making it so convenient.

As she got closer, she could hear them talking. Fortunately, Chinese was one of the many languages she had mastered over the years. Not easy, by any means, but with so many Chinese swarming all over the planet, it had seemed necessary. The female, Zang, was apparently in love with the male, Fang. This was difficult for Sato Yui to understand, and not only because love was such a vapid, illusory concept that humans wasted great amounts of time and energy lamenting over. Her sense of Fang was that he was a low-life loser, a pathetic, ignorant bastard, even by human standards. The willingness of the Zang female to ignore these obvious inadequacies in the male Fang suggested either a serious mental problem, or some other deeply hidden agenda. The Zang female, it seemed, was quite adept at both blatant lying and subtly masking her real intentions. She claimed to have shot Stone to protect Fang, but even Fang the moron couldn't quite believe this. Questioning the lie, on the other hand, wasn't really an option, as it risked uncovering far more uncomfortable information, information that his already tentative self-esteem wouldn't have been able to bear. Not that any of this mattered. In the same sense that love was blind, death was the great revealer. Zang and Fang would die in a bloody puddle of their own tedious lies.

When Sato Yui knocked on the apartment door, all sound from within ceased. She knocked again and waited. There was the sound of footsteps trying to move silently to the door, then more silence and finally, a female voice. "Who is it?"

"Hello there. I'm Sato Yui, representing the Asian/American Anti-Defamation League. Are you by any chance of Asian ancestry? And if so, have you been the victim of any racially motivated discrimination within the past six months?"

"Fuck off, Bitch," the voice snarled.

"You'd be amazed how often I get that very same response."

"If you don't leave now, I'm going to shoot you through the door."

"Have I a caught you at a bad time? Are you in the middle of making dinner?"

Another pause ensued, with the sound of muffled voices. Fang in the background urging Zang to just open the fucking door. Zang resisted, saying it looked like some tiny Japanese bitch, and she was more inclined to just shoot her in the face than open the fucking door. Fang reminded her that, even through doors, bullets fired from guns make noise, suggesting that opening the door and pistol-whipping the bitch made much more sense.

Fine!" Zang said, again placing her eye against the peephole. "Have it your fucking way. Oh My God!"

"What is it?" Fang wanted to know.

"The bitch is getting undressed in the hallway," Zang reported. "And she's not wearing any underwear."

"Definitely, let her in," Fang told her, conjuring images of all the things he and Zang could do with a Japanese sex slave at their disposal.

"I don't know," Zang told him. "The hallway is filling up with some kind of weird fog."

"That's just your breath clouding the peephole," Fang said. "Open the fucking door."

Zang threw Fang a lethal glance and opened the lock. With the turning of the doorknob, Sato Yui pushed herself into Akuma form. It wasn't easy and it hurt like hell, which only increased her desire to inflict deadly torment on the two Chinese. Zang flung open the door with every intention of making the undersized Japanese sorry she had ever been born. This evaporated at more or less the same instant she realized that the naked Japanese girl had disappeared, replaced by a large, angry-looking monster. The expression on her face rapidly shifted from anger to disbelief to absolute terror. The shriek she might have emitted at that moment was cut short by the Akuma's claw, which entered the Chinese woman just below the breastbone, emerging with a popping sound from the middle of her back. Zang's eyes blinked rapidly several times, a thin trickle of blood running over her lips and down her chin. Harry Fang, assuming the scene before him couldn't really be happening, was slow to react. Before he had time to close his mouth and stand up, Sato Yui had lifted the Zang female, carried her across the room and dumped her in Fang's lap. Zang, still conscious, watched as the claw was withdrawn from her body with a wet sucking sound, at which point she began flapping around on top of Fang like a not quite dead tuna fish on dry land. She also managed to tap into the adrenaline reserve required to make screaming possible. She screamed, more or less directly into Fang's ear. Fang cursed, struggled unsuccessfully to get up and then he, too, began screaming. A slashing claw across Zang's throat silenced her almost immediately. Fang continued wailing as Sato Yui sliced Zang's upper body into several precise sections, although the sheer volume of blood washing over him seemed to have an almost calming effect. He became quiet, experiencing a moment of clarity in which he reflected upon his immediate situation. It was obvious that something very strange was happening and that his chances of surviving it were not looking at all good. He could faintly hear the voices of his ancestors hurling threats and angry lamentations at him from beyond the grave. Many of them had scores to settle, of which even death, apparently, had not allowed them to let go. He realized that the afterlife would be no picnic, more or less a replay of his miserable existence, except that the agonies of the afterlife would probably be eternal. Which is when the screaming recommenced. Harry Fang wasn't sure of the source, but he couldn't rule out the possibility that they were his screams, and that they would be the last earthly sounds he ever heard.

"I don't know how I can ever thank you enough, Detective," Mendez gushed as Lisa eased the car into the traffic flow. "You really saved my ass."

Let's just leave your ass out of this.

"So what should I be expecting?"

Judging by your recent behavior, some form of STD would be my guess.

"About the crime scene, I mean."

Based on what the Captain had said, Lisa was expecting the worst, another blood-drenched nightmare courtesy of the city's resident demon. What she couldn't figure is why Sato Yui would kill Fang and Zang. If in fact it was Fang and Zang. Was it possible she was getting even for Stone, her suddenly brain dead puppet? And if so, how could Lisa go all law-enforcement-judgmental about it? How could she blame Sato Yui for doing exactly what she had wanted to do, minus the horrific mutilation, of course?

"Ever been to a slaughterhouse?" Lisa asked.

Mendez shook her head. "You think the crime scene will be as bad as that?"

Lisa smiled. "Imagine a lesbian bar, no cover, reasonably priced drinks and all the women present are gorgeous, scantily clad slave girls whom you can sample free of charge."

Mendez squinted at Lisa and sunk back in her seat. "All right, I'm imagining it."

That would be the equivalent of a slaughterhouse compared to what you're about to see."

Mendez went quiet, which was fine with Lisa. No point in trying to sugar coat reality. Lisa had learned this the hard way, through the grim experience of investigating murders so brutal that they had forced her to question most, if not all, of her basic assumptions. Her partner lay vegetating in a hospital bed, the mental stability of her two allies in the battle against the demon was questionable, at best, and her sex life had degenerated to the point that she might as well have been living in a convent. If Mendez had ambitions of joining the Detective ranks, she would have to be prepared for the worst. So it was good that she was taking the time to absorb the implications of what awaited them in the Alphabet.

"Can I ask you something?" Mendez said.

"You want to know how I handle it, how I manage to do the job without screaming my head off?"

"Actually, I was going to ask if that bar you mentioned is a real place."

"Okay," Lisa said. "Forget the damn bar. Forget your stupid gay girl fantasies for a minute. This is very serious business."

"Sorry!" Mendez told her. "It's just that I assumed you were ..."

"Me?"

"So you're not ...?"

"Not even a little bit."

"Are you sure? I mean it's so hard to be sure about anything these days."

True enough, Lisa had to admit. When was the last time she had felt sure about anything? She was fairly sure that Stone could satisfy her as a lover, but that had gone to hell pretty quickly. Certainty no longer existed. It was as obsolete a concept as believing that God answered your prayers.

Well maybe if you actually took the time to pray, young lady!

Mom, please! Now is not the time.

"The point I'm trying to make," Lisa continued, "is that we are faced with a situation with which the human mind can have a very difficult time coping."

"Are we still talking about sexual diversity?" Mendez asked.

Lisa sighed, jammed her foot on the accelerator and then immediately had to brake hard. Who were all these morons who insisted upon driving around in traffic that no longer moved? The prospect of getting anywhere by car had become about as likely as winning the Jumbo Lottery. Why even bother? "We're talking about your friend, Sato Yui."

"Trust me, Malone. That girl is no friend of mine."

"Yeah, well, that girl is no girl."

"Are you saying she's actually a guy? Now I am freaked out."

The thought of slipping the Beretta from her holster and performing a mercy killing on Mendez flitted through Lisa's head, but it would have been difficult to explain and the paperwork alone would have made her regret it. Better to just ignore the annoyance. Maybe it was the lack of sleep that had her on edge. Mendez was only trying to find a less than intolerable place for herself in the world, and you couldn't really condemn a person for that. Give the young officer a chance to grow, let her see what a real crime scene looked like, the blood, the body parts, the smell of unnatural death and afterwards the inability to ever get any of it out of your head. Besides, they had miraculously arrived at the scene, a tenement on Avenue D & 5th, in the very heart of the dead zone, on the absolute edge of nowhere. A couple of squad cars were parked out front, plus the wagon from the morgue. Even from outside, the building had unfortunate history written all over it. Nothing good had ever happened here.

She and Mendez took the stairs to the fourth floor, with each step the temperature rose and the odor of impending trouble increased. Mendez handled it okay until they stepped into the apartment. Blood was the color of the day and ripped apart bodies were the primary motif. No question about the decorator. Mendez, paralyzed in the doorway, started gasping for air. Lisa caught her just as she was about to collapse. She guided her to the small bathroom, positioned her in front of a toilet that looked like he hadn't been cleaned in a couple of years and shut the door. The sound of puking began almost immediately.

"Ever see anything like this, Detective?" one of the forensic technicians asked. Lisa had never seen him on scene before.

"Unfortunately, I have," she told him. "You new?"

"Transferred down from the Bronx South two weeks ago. Thought I was escaping the really ugly shit."

"Yeah," she said, easing her way around clumps of mangled flesh. "Seems like there's no escape from that. What can you tell me?"

"Pretty sure we're dealing with two individuals, one male, one female, almost definitely of Asian decent. Whatever killed them is speculation at this point. The lab should be able to be more definitive."

Lisa already knew what killed them. "Any I.D.?" she asked.

"Nothing so far."

"According to the file on the guy we're looking for, he has a serpent tattoo on his right buttock. See anything like that?"

"Hey, Charlie," the tech guy called to his partner. "You come across the male's ass?"

"Yeah," Charlie said. "I think it's over here in the corner."

"Take a look. Anything on it?"

"In addition to the blood, you mean?"

"Yeah."

"Looks like a snake, or something."

"Say hello to Harry Fang," Lisa told them.

"What kind of guy tattoos a snake on his behind?" tech guy wanted to know.

Lisa was thinking anally retentive, drug dealing imbecile, but merely shrugged.

"Oh, and we found this," tech guy said, holding up a plastic evidence bag containing a handgun. "Looks like a .32 caliber."

"That fits," Lisa told him. "Stone was shot with a .32."

At that moment, a ghostlike Mendez staggered out of the bathroom, took one look around the room and ran back to the toilet.

"Rookie?" the tech guy asked, nodding at the bathroom door.

"And a lesbian," Lisa said, almost stepping on what was very likely a female's head. "Li Zang, I presume," she said to the bruised, blood-spattered face.

"Excuse me, Detective," a uniform standing in the doorway said. "No witnesses we can locate, but the old lady three doors down says she heard what sounded like screaming."

"Makes sense," Lisa said.

"Says she thought it was someone's TV."

"It's always someone's TV, isn't it?" Lisa said.

"Want me to get a formal statement?"

"How old is she?"

"I don't know, about a hundred."

"Don't bother," Lisa told him, walking to the bathroom door and knocking. Mendez opened the door and more or less fell into Lisa's arms. "I think we've seen enough here," Lisa whispered to her. "What do you think?" Mendez, who looked like she might not be finished throwing up, slowly nodded. Lisa guided her to the door and down the stairs.

Captain Burke was sitting at his desk, three crushed cola cans stacked up in front of him, when Lisa walked into his office. There was also a thin cloud of smoke hovering a foot or so beneath the ceiling, which, based on the smell, was the result of a lighted cigarette. A good detective wastes no time reading the scene. Stone had taught her that. The Captain had been drinking cola and smoking, which probably explained the big smile on his face. He was high on nicotine and processed sugar.

"So, Malone, what news from the crime scene."

"Another serial-sized mess," she told him. "Same gruesome M.O. and a fairly positive I.D. on Harry Fang. Not that there was much left of him, but then asses don't generally lie."

"I'll take your word on that," he said, reaching into the refrigerator for another cola. "What about the woman?"

"No way to be sure the dead female is Li Zang without DNA confirmation, but we'll go on the assumption that it is."

"Of course it's her," the Captain said. "Who else could it be?"

"Well, Sir, assuming that there are an approximately eight hundred million or so Chinese females currently alive on the planet ..."

The Captain cut her off with an energetic jab at the air with his cola-free hand. "I'm not sure you're grasping the relevant point here, Malone. The case is solved and you're the one who solved it."

It would have been the first case she had actually solved, which, let's face it, is every detective's dream, but, as much as she would have liked to, she couldn't quite see it. "I'm sorry, Sir, but how so?"

"It's fairly obvious, Detective. Zang and Fang, for reasons we may never completely understand, have been engaged in a serial murder spree, some sort of drug-inspired, culturally-deluded insanity, most probably. It took the Chinese community a while to react, as hopelessly trapped in the past as they are, but eventually, very likely prompted by Stone's shooting, they caught on to the fact that a pair of murderous lunatics on the loose was bound to have an adverse effect on business, not to mention their reputations. So they took action."

Lisa smelled the familiar aroma of obfuscation, the kind of low level white wash sycophantic functionaries cooked up to protect those above them, as well as insulate their own fat butts. "But Captain, the alleged serial killers were killed in the exact same way that they allegedly killed. Does that make any sense?"

"From where I'm sitting, Malone, it makes perfect sense. Call it poetic justice and be thankful that this summer nightmare is finally over."

"And if more shredded bodies turn up?" Lisa asked.

"Copycats are always a possibility," the Captain smiled. "But I'm fairly certain we have seen the last of mutilated corpses, at least for the time being. Settled?"

"I'm still wondering why the killers would change their M.O. so drastically when they tried to kill Stone?"

"These people were homicidal maniacs, Malone, not total idiots. Of course you change your M.O. when you want to take out a cop. Create the illusion of an arbitrary shooter with no connection to the other murders. Someone randomly shoots a cop in Chinatown. No huge surprise. Police attention is nicely diverted. It's what I would do."

Give it time, Sir. The way things are going you could easily turn into our next serial killing sensation.

"So I guess Stone was right," Lisa said with about as much conviction as the day she's been coerced by her parents and a sexually deviant priest into accepting Jesus Christ as her personal savior. Self-esteem had really taken a hit that day. She half-expected the

Captain to lean over and pat her behind, reminding her that Jesus especially loves little girls with nice firm bottoms.

"Leave it to Stone," the Captain coughed, picking up an empty cola can and crushing it. "A total pain in the rear end, but the guy you could always count on for results. A damn shame that this time it cost him ninety percent of his mental faculties."

"It may not be as bad as we thought," Lisa told him. "Apparently Stone opened his eyes this morning and made a prolonged blubbering sound."

"Blubbering, huh?"

"Prolonged blubbering, Sir."

"Well, all we can do is hope," the Captain sighed, taking a prolonged gulp from his cola. Miracles do happen. Admittedly, not often and certainly not to me, but if anyone can fight their way back from brain death, it has to be Stone. By the way, how did Mendez handle herself at the crime scene?"

"I'd have to say, Captain, that she gave all she had to give."

"Good to know. That young woman has heart."

"And plenty of guts."

"Any sign of Mendez' service revolver?"

Lisa shook her head. "But we did find a .32 semi-automatic, which is consistent with the weapon used on Stone."

"Something is lost, something else is found," the Captain said. "How the universe works, I guess. Good job, Malone. I won't forget the effort you put into solving this one."

Unsure what, if any, effort she had put into the case, a case which in reality remained unsolved, Lisa was at a loss for words. "Shall I check with Doctor Hammer on the Asian body parts, Sir?"

"Not necessary," the Captain told her. "Doctor Hammer has agreed to take a brief leave of absence. It was either that, or a mandatory check-in to psyche rehab."

Lisa returned to her office under a storm cloud of emotions, none of them particularly uplifting. At the same time, it would not have been inaccurate to describe her as numb. It wasn't so much that she resented the Captain for being a weak-willed pussy, for caving in to the vested interests that preferred the comfortable lie over the potentially painful truth, but some small part of her still held out for the noble gesture, the commitment to integrity and justice, however superficial. Not that it really mattered. Not that she really cared. She knew how the world worked, how expediency and self-interest greased the wheels, how the end always justified the means. That the end in this case equaled the death of the brain, the loss of the lover and the denial of the demon was just how things went. Winners and losers, causalities mounting exponentially, a city full of the walking wounded, gasping for breath, staring uncomprehendingly as the roads buckle and the planet shudders and the faces of people only vaguely recognizable begin to melt. It was better pretending not to notice. Go home, have a few drinks, take a shower and do not, under any circumstances, answer the door. Just one brief stop she had to make first.

Twenty-eight

It was twilight by the time she reached the lower east side. The usual tourist throng of thrill-seekers shuffled along the streets, blanched by the heat, warped by an atmosphere lacking sufficient oxygen. Did any of them have even the slightest sense that a monster resided nearby? Would it make any difference if they did? It was, after all, the monsters they were here to see, any grotesque deviation from the norm would suffice. Never mind that this monster would slice them up into little pieces as soon as look at them, running the gutter red with their blood. The threat of danger, of the potential for horrid, unthinkable death, was one of the perks of a summer holiday in New York. Just make sure there's plenty of film in the camera.

It occurred to Lisa as she climbed the stairs that dropping in on the demon unannounced might be the dumbest thing she had ever done. Even as emotionally unraveled as she was feeling, as in need of some kind of closure, self-preservation still mattered. She had no desire to end her life in a fourth floor walkup at the hands of an adorable Japanese serial killer. She also had no choice. A conversation with the little fiend was required. Not that she expected it to change anything, but for her own peace of mind, her ability to move beyond the nightmare, it seemed necessary. Taking a single deep breath she raised her arm and knocked.

"Who is it?" the voice of a little girl asked from inside the door.

Who is it? You're a supernatural demon. Don't you know who it is?

"It's me," Lisa said. "Detective Malone."

"If you're here to arrest me, now is really not a good time."

"I'm not hear to arrest you," Lisa told her. What would be the point? "I just want to talk."

The door opened slowly, revealing a small young woman with a bright red nose and erratic hair wearing a rumpled white bathrobe. Had a demon ever appeared so frail and helpless? Lisa's paucity of knowledge vis-à-vis demons notwithstanding, she tended to doubt it.

"You look terrible," Lisa said, more cheerfully than she'd intended. "What happened?"

"I think I caught a cold," Sato Yui sniffled.

"Can your kind even catch colds?"

"My kind?"

"Sorry. I'm just never exactly sure what to call you."

Sato Yui rolled her eyes and then sneezed. "Until this morning, my answer would have been no."

"It's really a shame," Lisa smiled.

"What do you want, Lisa?" Sato Yui sighed, flopping down on the couch in the small living room.

"I'm not really sure," Lisa told her, easing into a chair opposite the couch. "I guess I'm wondering what happens next."

"Why ask me?"

"Well, this is sort of your show, isn't it?"

Sato Yui threw her head back and groaned.

"You killed Zang and Fang."

"That was inevitable," Sato Yui said, reaching for the tissue box on the table next to the couch.

"I'm glad," Lisa said. "You saved me the trouble of killing them."

"Anything for the man you love."

"Stone is my partner," Lisa snapped. "Love has nothing to do with it."

Sato Yui offered a congested laugh. "Good luck pushing him in his wheelchair to the next big crime scene."

"Hey, he could recover."

"If believing that helps you, why not?"

"So what are you saying, he won't?"

"What I'm saying is that I have my own problems," Sato Yui coughed. "I'm an ageless Akuma from a super dimensional reality imbued with near limitless powers who has a human head cold. Dealing with the Chinese twins nearly killed me. I can no longer assume my Akuma identity without excruciating pain. I've apparently crossed some invisible line, allowed myself to be deceived by this crazy town into thinking that anything is possible. Turns out it isn't. Basically, I'm fucked and not in a very good mood about it."

"But you're still a very attractive young woman with her whole, uh, life ahead of her."

"Oh, please! Don't patronize me."

"Sorry," Lisa said. "But I can't help seeing this as a positive development. At least you won't be killing anyone else anytime soon."

"I could still kill you," Sato Yui wheezed.

"I'm sure you could," Lisa said. "But you should realize that that kind of exertion is only going to make your cold worse."

"I don't doubt it," Sato Yui said, blowing her nose.

"Can I ask you something? Has all of this been worth it?"

Do you believe in destiny?" Sato Yui asked.

"I'm not sure," Lisa told her. "Maybe."

"Everything that's happened was destined to happen long before either of us existed."

"Wow! So I guess we have no choice but to be who or what we are."

"Now all you have to do is figure out who or what that is."

"Right," Lisa said, standing up. "Anyway, I should probably be going."

"Are you sure? We could, you know, do stuff."

"Stuff?"

"Fuck, I mean."

"Don't you kill everyone you have sex with?"

"That's the old me you're referring to. The new me seems to have different priorities."

Lisa observed Sato Yui's swollen, red nose, her bleary eyes. "As tempting as the offer is, I am in a bit of a hurry. Besides, with a cold like that the last thing you should be doing is exerting yourself."

"You're probably right."

"Of course I am."

"Anyway, I'm happy you came by," Sato Yui said, getting up from the couch to walk Lisa to the door.

"Any idea what you'll do now?" Lisa asked.

"I'm thinking a change of scenery is in order. Maybe L.A."

"I hear it's nice there, and I'm sure you'll definitely blend right in."

"There's also a very good chance that an Akuma will be dispatched to hunt me down and eliminate me."

"Sort of like a supernatural Ishikawa."

"Only much less incompetent."

"As crazy as it sounds," Lisa said, "I actually think I'll miss you."

"Me too," Sato Yui coughed. "I always assumed that you and I would be lovers, whether or not it resulted in your death."

"Maybe once you're settled, I could visit you in Los Angeles."

"I'd really like that."

"You know," Lisa said, stopping just in front of the door. "I'm almost tempted to ask you to do it, turn into the demon, I mean, just so that I'd know what one looks like."

"I would," Sato Yui told her, "but I don't have the energy for it. Besides, the demon is generally not very nice."

"Oh well," Lisa sighed. "I guess this is goodbye then."

She had only intended to offer her hand in farewell, but somehow couldn't resist leaning towards the demon girl and planting a gentle kiss on her lips. Despite her runny nose, Sato Yui responded, opening her mouth and allowing Lisa's tongue to slip inside. Lisa's left hand, seemingly with a mind of its own, moved inside Sato Yui's robe, beginning to caress her breasts. At the same time, the demon was busy with the button and zipper on Lisa's jeans, one petite hand eventually slipping inside Lisa's panties and down between her legs. Lisa moaned deeply as two of Sato Yui's fingers slipped inside her. As strange as the situation was, her orgasm was more or less inevitable. It exploded with the silent intensity of a volcano on one of Jupiter's moons. After it subsided, the two of them stood there together for what felt like forever, Lisa's body softly shuddering. Eventually they separated, Lisa gazing into the demon girl's eyes, which for a brief instant glowed a deep and intense red. And then, without a word, Sato Yui stepped back inside the apartment and closed the door. Lisa remained where she was, leaning against the wall until her legs felt capable of walking again. As she eventually descended the stairs she felt a calm settle upon her, a sense of being both refreshed and renewed. And all it had taken was being fingered to orgasm by an extra-dimensional demonic entity. Who would have guessed it? Even if she had picked up the monster's head cold in the process, it somehow felt worth it.

Outside, the flow of humanity had eased off, traffic was sparse and moving freely and it actually felt cooler. Even the sky had cleared, the thick gray cloud cover having been replaced with a deep blue canopy of flickering stars and the bright, sharp edges of a crescent moon.

Lisa made the drive back to her place in record time, without either perspiring through her clothes or experiencing even minimal road rage. A parking space was conveniently available directly in front of her building. Things were clearly looking up, as if some darkly agitated ripple in the flow of time had suddenly self-corrected. The world felt back on track, the madness of the past few weeks diminished to manageable proportions. Not that there weren't any surprises still lurking, the occasional blurry patch, the mildly unsettling eruption upon the smooth surface of things. In this instance, it took the form of a sleeping Ishikawa, dressed again in his suit and tie, crouching against the wall outside her door. Next to him was a large black suitcase.

"Ishikawa?" she said, tapping him lightly on the shoulder.

His eyes snapped open. "Oh Lisa," he said. "I'm so sorry."

"Is everything all right?" she asked. "What are you doing here?"

"I just stopped by to say *sayonara*," he told her, getting to his feet. "Since you were not here, I decided to wait."

"Are you going somewhere?"

"Back to Japan."

"Really?"

"My work here is done. Or should I say that the work I came here to do remains undone, but as I am incapable of doing it, there is little point in staying."

"Don't be too hard on yourself," Lisa said. "You did your best."

"You are very kind to say so," Ishikawa said, looking as if he might start weeping.

Change the subject, Lisa!

"So, when is your flight?"

"It's not until tomorrow morning, but I have already checked out of the hotel. I'll just sleep in the airport's waiting room tonight."

"That's ridiculous," Lisa told him. "You'll stay here tonight and tomorrow morning I'll drive you to the airport."

"Are you sure that won't create an uncomfortable situation?" Ishikawa asked. "I mean, considering ..."

"I'm sure," Lisa said, opening the door and urging him inside. "Sleeping on my couch has got to be better than sitting up all night in the airport."

"I don't know what to say."

"It's the least I can do."

Ishikawa carried his suitcase into Lisa's living room, opened it and began rummaging inside. "By the way, there is something I want you to have," he said, removing his sword and offering it to Lisa.

"You're giving me your sword?" Lisa cried. "No, I couldn't, I mean won't you need it?"

"Why would a retired demon hunter require a sword?" he asked. "Besides, tradition demands that the sword be passed on from those who have hunted to those who are just beginning to hunt."

"But I'm no hunter," Lisa told him, really hoping that this was true.

"Trust me," Ishikawa said. "I know. You are a born demon hunter and you will have many opportunities in your career to demonstrate your skill in this area."

Lisa took the sword from Ishikawa. "I'm honored," she said, comforted by the fact that Ishikawa's knowledge into demons and demon hunting had been almost consistently wrong. The odds had to be in her favor. She would store the weapon in her bottom dresser drawer and never meet another homicidal demon in her life. With the possible exception of a short trip out to the west coast to visit Sato Yui.

You mean the Sato Yui with whom you recently had hallway sex?

Which we will definitely not be mentioning to Ishikawa. Or to anyone. Ever!

"Uh, how about a nightcap before bed?" Lisa enquired.

Ishikawa sipped his scotch in silence, occasionally stealing glances at Lisa, who was busy transforming the couch into a bed. "That should do," she said, with a final fluffing of the pillow.

"A more or less ideal sleeping place," he told her.

"Well, I'm exhausted. I think I'll just ..."

"Of course! After all you've been through, you need your rest."

"Help yourself to anything you can find."

"Thank you. I think I'll just watch some American TV for awhile."

"Hey, eighty-eight channels, both satellite and cable. Good luck finding something worth watching."

Lisa undressed, took a quick shower and fell into bed. It was possible that she had never felt so tired; her body ached, her brain screamed out for long-term unconsciousness. So many things had happened over the past few weeks and now it was all ending. Things always ended, she reminded herself. Rarely in a way that made much sense, but one couldn't have everything. Some new, unknown phase in her life was about to begin and sleeping through the transition seemed absolutely necessary. She would wake up tomorrow, or possibly the next day, to a new world, a cooler world, hopefully, with fresh insight and a renewed determination. The only problem was that no matter how hard she concentrated on falling asleep, the silly noise in her head just wouldn't quiet down. She thought about Stone, what might have been between them, and how, at some point, she would have to come to terms with a new partner. From there she began debating the pros and cons of calling someone in the L.A.P.D., giving them a heads up on the hot little demon that could be heading their way, but eventually realized that no one in their right mind would take such a call seriously.

Her brain raced on like this for twenty or thirty more minutes, by which time she was much too tired to sleep and, not to put too fine a point on it, beginning to feel horny.

What a surprise! The nympho Detective is thinking about sex again.

You know, I'm really becoming tired of you. Would am occasional smidgen of support be too much to ask for?

Hey, don't blame me. I'm only here because you need me here. What does that suggest to you?

That I'm secretly suffering from schizophrenia?

Ah, if it were only that simple.

Lisa groaned, gave the mental finger to the infuriating voice in her head and slipped out of bed. She put on her bathrobe and tiptoed down the hall. Ishikawa was sitting on the couch in his underwear, absorbed in a TV infomercial on some sort of miracle anti-wrinkle night cream. She cleared her throat to get his attention. When he looked up at her, she used one of the Captain's patented hand gestures to convey that he should follow her back down the hallway to her bedroom, preferably without speaking. Ishikawa, grinning like a man who has just discovered a big bucket of gold buried in his backyard, wasted little time complying.

THE CUTEST LITTLE DEMON IN TOWN

Seven

Don't miss out!

Visit the website below and you can sign up to receive emails whenever William Leigh publishes a new book. There's no charge and no obligation.

https://books2read.com/r/B-A-UOCEB-SSJZC

BOOKS 2 READ

Connecting independent readers to independent writers.

Also by William Leigh

Cannibals Don't Inhale
The Cutest Little Demon in Town